The Wings That
Fly Us Home

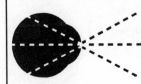

This Large Print Book carries the
Seal of Approval of N.A.V.H.

THE WINGS THAT FLY US HOME

DAYNA DUNBAR

WHEELER PUBLISHING
An imprint of Thomson Gale, a part of The Thomson Corporation

Detroit • New York • San Francisco • New Haven, Conn. • Waterville, Maine • London

THOMSON
GALE

ALL RIGHTS RESERVED

The Wings That Fly Us Home is a work of fiction. Names, characters, places, and incidents are the products of the author's imagination or are used fictitiously. Any resemblance to actual events, locales, or persons, living or dead, is entirely coincidental.

Wheeler Publishing Large Print Softcover.

The text of this Large Print edition is unabridged.

Other aspects of the book may vary from the original edition.

Set in 16 pt. Plantin.

LIBRARY OF CONGRESS CATALOGING-IN-PUBLICATION DATA

Dunbar, Dayna.
   The wings that fly us home / by Dayna Dunbar.
     p. cm.
   ISBN-13: 978-1-59722-426-0 (pbk. : alk. paper)
   ISBN-10: 1-59722-426-X (pbk. : alk. paper)
     1. Women — Fiction. 2. Oklahoma — Fiction. 3. Psychics — Fiction. 4.
Indians of North America — Fiction. 5. Large type books. I. Title.
   PS3604.U518W56 2007
   813'.6—dc22   2006035180

Published in 2007 by arrangement with The Ballantine Publishing Group, a division of Random House, Inc.

Printed in the United States of America on permanent paper
10 9 8 7 6 5 4 3 2 1

For my father,
Fred Warren Dunbar,
with all my love

ACKNOWLEDGMENTS

My deepest gratitude goes out to Brenda Adelman for her constant support and faith in me; to my family — especially my mother, Linda, who inspires at every turn, my sister, Debi, who is my biggest cheerleader, and my brothers Darron and Dustin; and to my hometown of Yukon, Oklahoma, for providing the blueprint for Okay and its inhabitants. I also want to thank Dr. Teresa Pijoan, tribal storyteller and professor of Native American studies, for providing me with the Indian prayers, blessings, words, and places in this book, and for making sure that the Native American portions of this book are accurate. I could not have written this story without her. Thanks also to my agent, Bob Tabian, who continues to understand and encourage my work, and to all the wonderful folks at Ballantine, including my editor, Johanna Bowman, whose care, talent, and input make writing such a joy.

CHAPTER ONE

Aletta watched the double-winged airplane with the open cockpit fly across a pale blue sky, its propeller buzzing like blades on a fan. Everything else faded away, and Aletta stared mesmerized even as the high-pitched hum of its engine turned into a series of sputters and groans. Suddenly, the small yellow plane tumbled end over end until it smashed into the earth, pieces of it flying everywhere, seeming as fragile as the shell of an egg dropped on the floor.

Aletta started so violently that Clester Henry yanked his hands from in front of her eyes. "My Lord, Lettie, I didn't mean to scare ya," he said.

The vision of the smoldering plane crash faded away and the gymnasium returned, with its smells of popcorn and sweat and the noise of squeaking sneakers and clapping fans. Aletta checked to make sure Gyp, her toddler, was still playing at her feet, then turned around and saw Clester, a guy she'd known since high school, his narrowed hazel eyes looking at her with concern from under his John Deere cap.

"Are you all right?" he asked. "You jumped like a wildcat."

Aletta forced herself to speak. "I didn't see you when I came in."

Clester had sneaked up behind her and placed his hands over her eyes. "Guess who?" he'd whispered, but she hadn't heard him because the moment he touched her, the little plane buzzed in her ears and the horror of it going down played out in front of her eyes. Her psychic gift had sprung to life when he touched her, just as it did when she touched someone. Usually, she could control how much she saw, but when she wasn't expecting the visions, they came on through like a runaway train.

"My littl'un's right out there," Clester said, pointing to the court where nine- and ten-year-old girls with pink faces and ponytails played a chaotic game of basketball.

"Mine too, on the other team," Aletta said, trying like hell to regain her composure. She watched her daughter, Ruby, yank the ball from another girl's hands and dribble it furiously toward the goal.

Aletta stood up abruptly. " 'Scuse me,"

she said, and scooped up Gyp. "I gotta go to the ladies'."

With wobbly legs, she made her way down the bleacher steps and found Randy, her chubby, sweet older son, playing underneath them with a couple of other kids. "You stay right here," she said sternly.

"We're just playin', Mama," he said.

Aletta felt her throat beginning to tighten as she rushed out of the gymnasium into the rainy afternoon. She ran to her '57 Chevy, holding Gyp's head to her chest to try to keep him from getting wet, and climbed behind the wheel. She covered her eyes with her hands and saw the plane shatter to pieces again and again. "I can't do this anymore," she said aloud.

Almost two years before, her drunk bastard of a husband had run off on her, leaving her to care for their four children on her own. Out of desperation to keep a roof over their heads and food on the table, she'd put a sign in her front yard on Main Street in Okay, Oklahoma: ALETTA HONOR, PSYCHIC READER. In order to make a living and stay at home with her kids, she'd had to face her own painful past. When she was eleven years old, her father and uncle had been shot and killed when they confronted a man who claimed that Aletta was a witch.

The deaths of her husband and brother caused Aletta's mama, Nadine, to turn bitter and to believe the devil was at work everywhere she turned. Her relationship with Aletta got worse the older Aletta grew, until they barely spoke even while living in the same small town. It wasn't until her mother lay dying a few months after Aletta put her sign out that they were able to make amends. In addition to all of this, she'd also fought a local church for the right to continue her business. After all was said and done, she'd actually become somewhat of a success.

At first, she had thought she was set, that she'd be able to earn a decent living from telling her customers what she saw when she touched them. A little part of her actually thought she could help people. But there was a huge burden in knowing things about folks before they happened or seeing how events in their pasts were affecting them now. How much should she tell them and what should she keep to herself?

One of the first things she had decided was that she'd never tell anyone anything unless they were her paying customer. It was none of her business unless they came to her directly.

With her own family, she didn't get the

visions, but she was careful not to touch other folks. She didn't want to deal with what she saw. Sometimes, however, she couldn't avoid it, and an old friend like Clester Henry would sneak up on her before she could do anything about it.

Aletta forced herself out of the Chevy and back into the gymnasium with Gyp. Randy was still playing underneath the bleachers, so she returned to her seat next to Clester.

"That girl of yours is a real player," he said just as Ruby banked a shot home.

"Thataway, Rube!" Aletta yelled, and pumped her fist.

On the opposite side of the court, Jimmy, her ex, stood up and yelled through cupped hands, "Keep shooting, girl. You're the offense!"

He showed up at every single one of Ruby's games. It was the only thing she could count on when it came to Jimmy.

"She loves it," Aletta said, then continued without taking a breath, "So, you flying airplanes these days?"

Clester grinned like a kid. "You saw my shirt. I been taking lessons for six months. I'm certified since last month and just bought me a real beaut. You oughta see her."

Aletta read his T-shirt. HENRY HAWK'S FLIGHT SCHOOL, it said, under a severe-looking hawk with its wings spread wide. "Maybe you shouldn't fly. It's so dangerous," she said.

Clester's grin faded. "Now you sound like my wife. I've wanted this since I was just a kid, and it makes me happy, Aletta. I work my ass off all week, and this is my reward."

"I just wish you'd take a break or something."

"I believe I will," he answered with sarcasm. "I'm gonna go smoke a cigarette right now. Nice seein' you."

Aletta watched him as he walked down the bleacher steps and out of the gym. Frustration and worry clumped together inside her stomach like curdled cream as she watched the rest of the game.

The young man who sat on Aletta's couch looked like he might burn a hole in her *Elk in the Forest* landscape painting, the way he was staring at it. She didn't always work on Saturdays, but he'd said he wanted to see her right away, and she needed the money, so she booked the appointment. Now she wished she hadn't. This handsome young man with silky brown hair and sad eyes was forcing himself not to cry.

Aletta gazed up at the painting, as she had

so often since she'd set up this office for her psychic reading business over a year before. She'd fallen in love with the piece of art as soon as she'd seen it at Good as New, the thrift store down the street. Even though she knew the sprayed gold frame was a bit tacky, she didn't care. She'd wanted something beautiful in her office, something that would take her away, even if only for a moment, from duty and worry and chores. The painting did that, pulling her into its luminescent sunlight washing over a forest meadow. The elk, with its enormous antlers and gleaming brown eyes, seemed almost mythical to her.

She pulled her gaze from the painting and looked back at her customer. "It ain't that big a deal, Corliss," she said finally. "Sometimes I just don't get anything." She was lying to him. She *had* seen something when she'd taken his hands, but it was something she wasn't willing to divulge. The risk was too high that he would freak out, as her fifteen-year-old daughter, Sissy, would say.

His blue eyes cut at her, then went back to the elk. "You have to help me, Ms. Honor. I feel so different from folks around here, like I don't belong at all. Jenny wants to get married, but I just want to run off

15

and hide when she talks about it."

"Maybe you better not get married," Aletta said, a little too forcefully.

"Why not?" Corliss turned to her hopefully. "Can you see that sometimes I have these feelings . . . ?"

Aletta turned away from his sweet blue eyes. This was breaking her heart, but she couldn't tell him the truth, could she? It might be 1977, but around these parts a man falling for another man was still some serious sinning, and the repercussions she could face for telling this young man that she'd seen him happy, living in California with a man named Scott and a golden retriever, was more than she could risk. She knew darn well that her vision was just one possibility for Corliss, that it was up to him to make the choices to get him there. She'd already fought off the Burning Bush Church just for putting her sign out, and she couldn't be expected to fight another battle. It was just too much.

"Oh, it just sounds like you're not ready for marriage, is all," she finally answered. "Sorry I couldn't help you more."

They walked to the front door, and Aletta kissed his cheek. "I don't take payment unless I get something, so keep your money."

Sissy, who sat in the kitchen eating an

apple, pushed her feathered brown hair back and blinked twice when she saw Corliss. She got off the bar stool and leaned against the door jamb, watching her mother and Corliss say goodbye.

"I want you to remember something," Aletta told Corliss. "I been on the so-called fringes of society since I was yea big, and living there in hiding was the worst thing in the world. If you feel like you aren't like other folks, don't you worry about it. You're all right just as you are."

A tear finally escaped from his eyes, and when one came, the rest followed all too easily. Beginning to sob, he rushed out the door to his El Camino. Sissy came to the door, and she and her mother watched as he sped away.

"Who was that? He's gorgeous," Sissy said.

"Don't even think about it," Aletta answered.

"What'd you say to make him cry?"

"He's a sweet young man tryin' to find his way, just like the rest of us," Aletta said, more to herself than to Sissy. She grabbed her macramé purse. "I got an appointment over at Joy's. Watch Gyp, you hear?"

Aletta said a little prayer for Corliss as she walked the twenty yards to Joy's Femme

Coiffures next door.

"Come on over and take a seat," Joy Trippi said, swiveling around in her rose-colored faux-leather beautician's chair.

Aletta stood where she was, her hand covering her mouth. "Wow," she said finally.

"It's been a hoot just watchin' people walk in the door today, " Darla, one of the other beauticians, said out of one corner of her mouth. The other corner held bobby pins.

Joy laughed, and several of the women in the salon laughed along with her. Joy's hair was in a full Dolly Parton–style blond meringue whip.

Joy started singing in her smoke-scratch voice. "Come on, little dear, and let me cut that head a hair . . ." She started moving her skinny hips and beckoning Aletta toward her with pink-nailed fingers.

Aletta laughed and plopped down in the chair. She eyed Joy with a grin. "You look a lot like her, except for two things."

"So I need about five more cup sizes, and my lyrics stink, but I got the hairdo down," Joy said, lighting a long, thin cigarette.

Aletta relaxed back into the chair and took a deep breath. She figured that how she felt when she got her hair cut was how rich people must feel when they go to Hawaii —

pampered and special.

"Nothin' fancy," she said to Joy. "Just a cut."

Joy sighed her disapproval. "I swear, my mission in life is to get you into a Farrah Fawcett and some heels."

Aletta smiled patiently. This was nothing new. "I don't have time to fix my hair every day for an hour. You know that."

"But it's such a shame. You got the natural looks, with those cheekbones and green eyes. All you need is a perm, a bleach job, and some Maybelline and you'd knock 'em dead."

"Just the regular, please, ma'am," Aletta said, then relaxed as Joy's skilled hands moved through her hair. She'd long since been able to control the visions with Joy, just ignoring anything that sneaked through.

"So how's it going with Eugene? You feel any better about things?" Joy asked.

"I can't tell you how much I wisht I did," Aletta answered. She'd been dating Eugene Kirshka since just after she and Jimmy split the summer before, and at first she'd thought he might be the man for her because he was so kind, responsible, and steady. "I know he's such a good man —"

"Hard to find these days," Joy interjected.

"And he's great with the kids, but the

truth is he doesn't challenge me in any way. Not my brain or my soul."

"Or your body."

Aletta shook her head sadly. "Not that either. Besides, I want to see what it's like not to have a man telling me how to live for once in my life."

Joy hooted. "Now, the first deal I can buy, but don't try to give me that crap about wanting to be alone."

"No, I mean it. I feel so unsure about everything — men, my business, raising my kids even. Maybe being on my own will help me get my footing," Aletta said.

"It sure sounds like we're gonna find out." Joy hummed along with the Merle Haggard tune on the radio as she snipped Aletta's ends.

Aletta closed her eyes and sighed. "My mama would've loved Eugene. She sure did hate Jimmy Honor, though."

"Don't we all," Joy said. "Looks like Eugene's got the credentials but not the chemistry," she continued. "Nothing you can do about that. No matter how much I wish you'd stay with him, you better get it over with sooner than later and let that poor man find somebody else."

Aletta opened her eyes. "Hey, let's change the subject, please. How 'bout I let you roll my hair just this once?"

Joy brightened. "Now we're talkin'."

Aletta looked at Joy's reflection. "Joy . . . I don't think I can do it. Will you call him for me?"

Joy's eyebrows knitted together in disbelief, then she started examining Aletta's neck. "Hmmm. Your head must be comin' loose."

"I'm just kidding." Aletta pouted. "But I dread it so bad. I don't want to hurt him. Who knows? Maybe he'll be relieved."

"Ha," Joy scolded. "Think again."

After getting beautified, Aletta walked back to her house next door. It was April, and the sun was shining for the first time in three days. She lingered outside, standing on her driveway with her hands on her hips, breathing deeply the after-rain smell. To her, the only thing that came close to being as good as the scent of her kids when they were babies was the smell of the sunshine after a spring storm.

She inspected the sign that stood in her yard for damage from the rain. People still occasionally drove by on Main Street yelling threats of hellfire and damnation, and her kids still got teased some at school. But besides Jimmy's small amount of child support, it provided every penny she and her four kids lived on.

Before turning to go inside, she decided it was time for a new paint job as soon as the spring rains were over.

"It's a beautiful day," she said aloud, trying her best to dry up her worry about Clester and Corliss and Eugene like the sun dried up the rain.

Eugene showed up right on time, as usual. He wore pressed Wranglers, a cowboy shirt, and boots, also as usual. They were supposed to go to Oklahoma City for dinner at Steak & Ale, but Aletta asked if they could watch the sunset at Lake Overholser first.

"Whatever you want, sweetie," Eugene said. He drove his souped-up Nova SS through downtown Okay, passing his auto shop on the way to Oklahoma City. They rode the ten minutes to the lake.

He stopped the car under some big elm trees, and they watched a river of light from the setting sun glow across the middle of the lake. Aletta got out of the car and sat on the hood. The wind was cool, and she crossed her arms to warm herself.

She looked back at Eugene through the windshield and half smiled. He caught her gaze for a moment, and surprise and sadness played on his face like the light on the lake.

He got out of the car and sat next to her, crossing his boots. "What's going on, Lettie?"

"Do you know I been with a man, non-stop, ever since I was sixteen and me and Jimmy got together?" She didn't look at him. She couldn't.

"Course I do. I've known you almost your whole life."

"Went right from him to you." Her curls played around her face and shoulders.

Eugene cleared his throat, like he couldn't swallow what she was saying. "Hope you're not comparin' us two."

"No, sir, not for a minute. You have been so good to me and my kids — reliable as a John Deere, putting up with my craziness, doing all sorts a things around the house. Jimmy, on the other hand," she said, waving toward the water, "he'd leave me to drown in that lake if he thought there was a party onshore."

Eugene shifted his weight on the car. "So what're you sayin', Aletta? Might as well let me have it."

She hopped off the hood and stood facing him, putting a hand on each of his long thighs. She wanted to tell him a version of the truth that would make it easiest on him. "I gotta start figurin' out who I am, Eugene. I gotta stop relyin' on a man to decide it for me. It ain't you. It's me." She moved her hands to his shoulders and looked in his gray-blue eyes. Tears were forming in the corners. "I wanna be your friend," she said.

He jumped up so fast, it scared her. "Well, I don't wanna be your friend," he said, wiping his eyes with his sleeve. "I got enough friends. I'm pathetic enough without hangin' around to have you throw me scraps of love every once in a while."

"You're not pathetic, Eugene. Why do you say that?"

" 'Cause I always loved you more'n you did me." His voice broke as he spoke. It bled through pain on its way out of his mouth. "I've tried hard, you know, to be good to you, to treat you right. I thought you wanted someone to take care a you. What's wrong with that?"

"I do. I did. But you treat me more like a child than a woman."

He turned away from her, got in the car, and slammed the door. "I'll take you home now."

She got in next to him. Now it was her turn to cry. "But I don't want to lose you."

He was silent.

Before they even passed Okay National Bank, Aletta could see Jimmy's black Trans Am in her driveway, lit up by her porch light. Eugene did a U-turn and stopped on the street in front of her house.

"Want me to come in and get rid of him?" he asked, his voice hoarse and hurt.

"No, thanks. I can handle it." A lie.

"Oh, right, I forgot," Eugene said flatly.

Just then, Jimmy barreled out the front door, and Aletta hopped out of the car. Sometimes she wouldn't see him for a few weeks. That's when she knew he had a new girlfriend, but then he'd always come back, eating her food and begging her to remarry him.

"Jimmy, you're not supposed to be here," she said, but he ignored her and bent over to look through the Nova's open passenger window.

"Eugene Kirshka, you old son of a bitch," Jimmy said. One side of his face was lit by the yellow streetlight. He was forever handsome, with a square jaw and strong cheekbones, full lips, and heavy eyebrows over mocha-colored eyes. But right now, his skin was flushed red. That and his odor were all Aletta needed to know he had been drinking. "Why don't you just leave her alone?" Jimmy asked.

"Jimmy, shut up," Aletta said.

Eugene shoved the car into gear. "You don't have to worry about me anymore," he said. His tires made black marks that looked like scars on the pavement as he sped away.

Jimmy turned around and smiled at Aletta. He wore cowboy clothes, but unlike Eugene, who worked a small farm on the edge of town in addition to being a mechanic, it was only for show. "You broke up with lover boy?"

"I'm not speaking to you, Jimmy. Go home." Aletta walked across the grass toward the porch. It was still moist from the rain.

Jimmy followed. "I need to talk to you, Lettie. It's important."

"That why you came over drunk?"

"I ain't drunk." He grabbed her arm and turned her around as she opened the screen door.

The door closed hard. "Dammit, Jimmy. Keep your hands off me."

He let her go but reached over her head and held the door shut so she couldn't get inside. "I need to talk to you without the kids around."

She sidestepped him and got out from

under his armpit. "What in blazes do you want?"

"Charlotte wants to live together."

"Charlotte?" Aletta pondered. "Oh, the brunette with the teeth." She put her forefingers to her mouth, making fun of Charlotte's slightly protruding eyeteeth. "I think it's the most brilliant thing I ever heard. Maybe she'll cook for you, so you don't eat all my food."

"I wanted to ask you first, because you know I want to come back, so I can be with you and the kids." Jimmy adjusted his crotch. "And now that you and that redneck have split up, it seems like perfect timing."

"Jimmy, let me get somethin' real clear. You are out of your mind to think I will ever take you back, so you and Charo should go on ahead and live happily ever after."

Just then the door opened, and Ruby, her green eyes wide and scared, looked out through the screen. "Mama, you all right?"

"Yes, baby. I'm comin' in. Your daddy's leavin'."

She went in the house, then shut the screen door behind her. She and Ruby stood there and watched him through it, waiting for him to decide what to do.

Jimmy ran his hand through his black hair,

and his nostrils flared a little. Aletta felt her own fear and the fear coming off Ruby as if it was as solid as the door handle she held closed against his anger.

He pointed at her with a finger, the rest of his hand forming a fist. "You're gonna live to regret this, Aletta. I swear to God."

Aletta wanted to say something mean back to him, something that would pierce into his heart and explode, leaving little shards of pain that he would have to carry around with him like she carried the scar from his fist over her eye. But it was the memory of that fist that made her keep still.

He stood there watching her, waiting to see what she would say, as if he was standing on the edge of a diving board ready to plunge back into the drama they had shared throughout their relationship. Finally, the energy that pulsed between them subsided a little. He took a step backward, dropped his hand, and looked down at Ruby.

"You wanna shoot some hoops, Rube?" he asked.

"It's dark outside, Daddy," she said.

"Well, maybe tomorrow, then," he mumbled, and walked back to his car. And for the second time that evening, a man screeched away from 1110 Main Street.

CHAPTER TWO

It wasn't a whole five days after breaking up with Eugene that Aletta decided to go dancing.

Joy had made Aletta an impossibly tempting offer. "I'll watch the kids Friday night if you promise to go out and have some fun. You work so hard, it makes me tired," Joy said through two sticks of Juicy Fruit gum.

Of course, Aletta had no intention of dating again for at least a year. Just having a good time felt like a betrayal of Eugene. Not only that, she was embarrassed to go out by herself. But she had a powerful urge that won out over shame of any color. She wanted to dance.

Aletta put on a pretty flower-print dress, tied a scarf around her neck, and drove to Jasper, a town east enough of Okay that it reduced the risk of seeing many folks she knew.

She had driven by the Round-Up Club a

half dozen times since it had opened and always wondered what it was like inside. After divorcing Jimmy, she'd stayed away from bars, not only to avoid seeing her ex, but also because his behavior inside them had somehow tainted them all in her mind. Eugene had not been a dancer or a drinker, so he'd never pushed her to go.

It had been so long since she'd been inside a honky-tonk that going to one seemed as far away to her as the Pacific Ocean, but now she was parking her car in the gravel parking lot, feeling as nervous as a teenager.

When she stepped in the door, the music and the smoke hit her first, followed closely by the smell of booze and the wave of energy that she felt from being closed in with all these people.

"Ladies are free. Can I see your ID?" the cowboy who sat on a bar stool at the door asked.

Aletta took a few deep breaths but didn't move.

"Ma'am, are you all right?" he asked.

Aletta finally dug in her purse for her wallet. "I'm fine," she said, trying to sound casual.

He looked at her driver's license and gave her a country-boy grin that made her feel welcome. "You make sure and have a good time."

Aletta walked a few feet inside, then stopped. It made her smile just to see people dance. The music was loud and the laughter even louder. People were drinking and smoking, like having this much fun was the most natural thing in the world. Aletta felt like she could almost cry, like it was too much to handle all at once.

That's when a well-dressed man walked over, his black hair slicked back. He didn't look like he was from anywhere near these parts.

"My God, you're beautiful. Please tell me you'll dance with me," he said, like there was an emergency.

Aletta blushed to her hairline but gathered herself enough to say, "A flatterer is like a cat, don't you think?"

He smiled at her and cocked his head to one side, listening.

"Purrin' at you one minute, then ignorin' you the next," she said. *He sure is handsome,* she thought.

"I tell you what, then. Forget the flattery and just dance with me. I can tell you're dying to." He held out his hand to her.

"Now who're you flatterin'?" she asked, and he laughed.

31

When she took his hand, she saw one image in her mind — a pretty woman slamming down a telephone, anger and hurt playing on her face. But Aletta let it go from her thoughts fast. She just wanted to have a good time.

Charlie Baxter was a fantastic dancer. He led her with a confidence and skill that made her feel like Ginger Rogers. They danced the rest of the night away. She enjoyed all of it, but the real attraction was that he seemed kind of wild and yet sophisticated, like he lived life on the edge. *Not like Jimmy,* she thought. After all, Charlie was wearing a suit and tie, not jeans and boots, and he had only one beer the entire night. He told her he'd been divorced for two years, lived in New York, and was just in Oklahoma working on a real estate deal. To Aletta, that seemed perfect.

Jimmy's latest girlfriend, Charlotte, knew she and Jimmy looked damn good together. Even though he was thirty-four and she was only twenty-two, she had to admit they were a hot couple. After all, everybody out at the bars said so. As Charlotte told her friends from Wewoka when she talked to them on the phone, Jimmy was tall, dark, and handsome.

"Is he good in the sack?" Georgeann asked. It sounded like she was holding pot smoke in her lungs.

"He's an animal, like you'd expect Burt Reynolds to be in bed," Charlotte said with a self-important laugh. "We do it constantly."

Georgeann exhaled. "When do I get to meet this hunk?"

Of course, Charlotte knew Jimmy was full of himself and that he drank too much, but he was also the best time she'd ever had. She figured that with her Elizabeth Taylor looks (everyone said so) and her way with men, she'd be able to handle him no problem.

Tonight, they were two-stepping at Six Shooters, a big new country bar where everybody who was anybody in Oklahoma City went to be seen. Jimmy was already on his fifth vodka, and Charlotte wasn't far behind. They skimmed along the dance floor, boot and heel, Jimmy's arm around her shoulders, then spun and turned till he was pushing her along backward.

After the song ended, Jimmy downed the last of his vodka and slapped her on the ass. "Whew, darlin', I need a drink."

They walked to the bar, which stood three Stetsons deep.

"Goddammit, this is bullshit," Jimmy bellowed.

"Ah, hon, go on, I'll wait for the drinks," Charlotte said.

Jimmy raised his empty glass. "Bartender, I just need a refill! Hey, buddy, just top me off here!"

The man in front of Jimmy turned around. He was shorter than Jimmy but stockier. "Hey, fella, you gotta wait your turn just like everybody else."

"It's okay, Jimmy. Let's go someplace else," Charlotte said, pulling on the sleeve of his black snap-button shirt.

But Jimmy shook her off. His nose flared and his jaw jutted out. He tapped the stocky man on the shoulder, and when the guy turned around, Jimmy's fist landed so true and so hard that Charlotte was sure, as she pulled Jimmy out of the bar, he'd killed the poor son of a bitch.

The day after her mama met Charlie Baxter and her daddy flattened some drugstore cowboy's face, Ruby put her back against the side of the house and shushed her best friend, Micki, who stood next to her chewing a huge wad of Bubble Yum. Pointing with her thumb at the wood-paneled Gran Torino station wagon with the lime green trim that had just pulled up out front, Ruby made it clear who their next victim would be. They ducked behind the bushes that lined the front of the house, mud caking their cowboy boots, and waited.

It was hard to keep an eye on the lady sitting in the car because her head barely cleared the door. After a few minutes of waiting, Micki said, "I'm bored. She ain't comin' out. Let's go kill Randy again."

"You gotta be patient if you're gonna be a outlaw." Ruby was doing her best to teach Micki the ropes, but it was a trying process.

Finally, the tiny lady with the man's haircut got out of her car, clutching her handbag, and walked toward the house.

Just as she passed Aletta's sign, Ruby gave the go-ahead. They jumped out of the bushes, Ruby wielding a pistol in each hand and Micki clutching a rifle. They were about to start shooting, letting the red ribbon go *bang, bang* through the guns, but they stopped cold. It was Mrs. Ledger, the lunchroom lady at Okay Elementary. She could be mean and get you in bad trouble if she didn't like you. And she looked like she'd been crying.

Mrs. Ledger jumped when she saw the two armed hellions coming at her, but when she recognized Ruby and Micki, she hurried to the front door.

They ran back to the bushes as fast as their legs could take them.

"Oh, my gosh, that was Mrs. Ledger. She's gonna kill us. We tried to shoot her *and* we saw her crying." Micki clutched her straight brown hair in her hands. "Do you think we're in trouble at school?"

"Shh, I wanna hear," Ruby said, and moved toward the edge of the house so she could see Mrs. Ledger at the door.

Her mama held the screen door open. Ruby knew she'd been out late the night before; she could see it in the paleness of her complexion. "Come on in, Mrs. Ledger, you're right on time," Aletta said.

"Please call me Bobette."

The girls heard, looked at each other, and could barely keep from laughing out loud. "Bobette?" Ruby whispered, then covered her mouth.

As the two women disappeared inside, Ruby put her pistols in her holster. "I bet Bobette's here to get a readin' from my mama. I gotta hear this."

Ruby ran to the garage, and Micki followed. "Me too. I wanna hear."

Ruby lifted the door, then grabbed a rusted, old folding chair that had been in there since before she was born. She and Micki carried it to the side of the house and, as quietly as possible, set it up below Aletta's office window. Micki kept smacking her gum, so Ruby pulled it out of her mouth and threw it on the ground. Micki shoved Ruby, but this was no time for a fight, so they climbed up on the chair and crouched underneath the open window.

"Come on in. This is my office in here."

Ruby and Micki could hear Aletta like they were in the room with her. They smiled devilish grins and gave each other some silent skin.

Inside, Bobette sat on the edge of the brown velour love seat Aletta had bought, along with her office chair on wheels, from Chuck's Cheap Used Chairs in El Reno.

Aletta sat in the chair and dug her heels in to push closer to her customer. She had one ear trained on the door, as only Randy was watching Gyp in his playpen — Sissy was late again.

"How can I help you today? Anything in particular you wanna discuss?" she asked.

"Well," Bobette offered through a ball of tattered Kleenex, "me and Harley have been separated for about six months now, and I'm wonderin' if we'll ever get back together."

"You mind if I hold you by the hand, Bobette? That's how things come to me." Aletta's voice was calm and reassuring.

Bobette shook her head. She kept one hand with the tissue at her nose and offered Aletta the other.

Aletta closed her eyes and let the images pass through her mind like a swirl of colors while she prayed. "Heavenly Father, we ask you to bless us in this sharing, and we ask that anything revealed here be helpful to Bobette in her time of need. We give thanks for all that we have today, knowing that we live by your mercy and love. Amen."

When she finished, she took a deep breath and focused on the images. When she heard a bang outside the door, all she could see in her mind was Gyp falling and knocking his head on a chair. A moment, then two, no crying, no Randy at the door, so she cleared her throat and started again.

"Well, Bobette, I'll just tell you what I'm seein', and it's up to you to interpret," Aletta said calmly. She'd gotten good at staying composed while people were suffering. "I'm seein' a household without much lovin', I have to say — you and Harley fightin' a lot, even things bein' thrown and busted by both y'all." She paused and watched, trying to decide if she should continue. Something about this woman made her go on. "Is he havin' an affair?"

Outside, Ruby and Micki looked at each other with wide eyes. Micki almost blabbed something, but Ruby covered her mouth with her hand.

Inside, Bobette's little face scrunched up like she'd been kicked in the shin. Tears poured from her lashless brown eyes. "Yes!" she wailed. "But even before that, when the kids were around, we didn't get along. After they left, it got even worse, and now this."

Aletta opened her eyes and considered Bobette. She must be around forty-two, and her nose twitched involuntarily every few minutes. "Do you even like Harley? Outside of him cheatin' on you, a course. Do you like him?" Aletta asked. Aletta had to admit she was feeling a little more confident since breaking up with Eugene.

Bobette stopped crying, the question seeming to surprise her out of her pain for a moment. "Like him? Do I *like* Harley?" She mulled it over, her eyes looking up toward the corner of the small room. "Mmm, not s'much. He's irritable as a mean old dog, not to mention selfish and lazy. And he doesn't like me any more'n I like him, I don't expect, so that's no points in his favor either."

"Well, do you *want* to get back together with him?" Aletta asked.

While Aletta could see some of the pasts and futures of her customers, and even tell what they cared about, whom they loved, and why, what she saw was really no more than a shadow of the whole person. Getting a handle on the intricacies of a human soul was well beyond the reach of even her unusual gifts. So not a day went by that she wasn't surprised, confused, and delighted by the folks who came to see her. It was what kept the job interesting even as she struggled about what to reveal and what to withhold.

Aletta had to admit it was often frustrating when people refused to change even when they knew better. And it was tiresome when they whined, and tedious when they insisted on telling her every detail of their lives. But she saw the good in almost every one of them, so she usually enjoyed it.

"Do I want to live with Harley?" Bobette asked. "Truth is, I love *not* living with Harley."

"Then what's the problem?"

Bobette's tears came again, her chin quivering and her nose turning red. "I'm lonely!" she finally cried.

Outside on the chair, Ruby and Micki both teared up. Ruby wiped her eyes, then mouthed to Micki, "She's lonely."

Micki sniffed quietly and nodded.

Aletta gave Bobette a hug. She'd started doing this on a regular basis with many of her customers because it seemed like what most of them needed more than anything else in the world. What she did next was not something regular, and it surprised her as much as Bobette. "Well, why don't we go out and have some fun together?" Aletta asked.

Bobette hiccupped. "You and me?"

"Sure. Just us girls."

"Hey, whatcha doin'?" Sissy's voice called outside the window.

There was a clatter that sounded like scraping metal.

"What's goin' on out there?" Aletta asked. She stood up, parted the calico curtains, and looked outside. Nothing there.

Ruby and Micki stood just below her with their backs against the house, holding their breath. Ruby motioned to Sissy, who had just been dropped off by her boyfriend,

Rusty, to shut the hell up. Sissy shrugged and walked inside.

The girls didn't move until they heard Aletta and Bobette leave the office, talking about when they might get together.

CHAPTER THREE

Vee Halbert and her boyfriend and comrade, Bo Chartraine, pulled into the dirt parking area of the Tujunga Gun Show. They made sure that the unmarked Chevy with Nevada plates hadn't followed them before they got out of Vee's VW Bug.

Inside the enormous tent, Vee looked around. She wasn't sure what to expect, but what she saw relieved and repulsed her at the same time. Men sat behind tables and display cases smoking and talking while women chatted with each other and watched after their children. There were Confederate and American flags everywhere. It was a scene right out of her hometown of Reedley, West Virginia, except there were just a few more guns.

She was relieved because she was no longer intimidated. In fact, she felt a kinship to these people. The repulsion came because she hated everything about Reedley and had spent her life either planning how to get out or running from the memories once she was gone. This ambivalence had always been there for her when it came to her roots. She felt a deep sympathy for the underclass, the coal miners and their wives who worked themselves to early deaths and their poor, uneducated children. She'd been one of them — even lower than them, actually. Her father had never kept a job, either in or out of the mines, and her mother had died giving birth to Vee.

She also felt a kind of hatred for these people she was seeing now inside this tent, the poor white trash of her past. She wanted to be everything she believed they were not — empowered, educated, important, autonomous. She wouldn't have admitted it and maybe didn't even realize it, but the way she defined herself actually had everything to do with Reedley — both in sympathy with and in opposition to what it stood for to her. The truth was she wanted to rescue not only herself but all the victims of the capitalist male power structures that victimized them.

This thought brought her back to the task at hand, one she hoped would help her achieve her goals. She focused her attention on the unbelievable number and variety of firearms. There were handguns, rifles, shotguns, semiautomatic, sawed-off, military, hunting, pocket-sized, and what seemed to be cannon-sized. The sight of them frightened and thrilled Vee in a way she hadn't expected.

Bo looked at her with his dark blue eyes. She knew he was making sure she was all right, but she didn't need his babying.

"What the hell are we waiting for?" she asked, and walked to a potbellied man who stood beside a display of dozens of weapons.

"Howdy, young folks, how kin I help you?" the man asked.

Vee thought he sounded like he was from Louisiana, like Bo. After dropping out of UC Berkeley two years before to focus her full attention on the cause, she and Bo had traveled around the country together, going to Freedom Revolutionary Party gatherings and movement rallies. She'd gained an ear for accents and usually guessed with amazing accuracy where people were from.

"We need some nine-millimeter handguns and a rifle," Bo said.

"Yessirree, I got everythin' you need rahtchere."

Vee held the Browning 9 mm in her hand. It felt like power. She paid the man in cash for three Brownings, several clips, and a

Winchester rifle with a scope and ammunition. They walked away without a scrap of paper, not even a receipt — yet it was a completely legal transaction.

Out in the bright California sunshine, Vee opened the hood of her VW. She made sure to cover the large brown leather scrapbook that lay amid jumper cables and empty oil cans with an old towel before they put the guns inside.

"Now we can protect ourselves if the fuzz attack us like they did the Panthers," she said.

"Do you think they'll know we're armed?" Bo asked.

"I'm sure they know we have gun licenses, but they don't know what we own, and anyway, it's legal to own a gun. If the military-industrial complex that runs this country can be armed, so can we," she said, and slammed the hood down. "Let's go. I don't want to be late for the meeting."

She pushed her dark brown hair behind her ears and got into the driver's seat. Even though it was only April, the black vinyl burned her legs, but she didn't notice. She had too much on her mind.

The phone ringing sounded like Tinker Bell was calling, what with Aletta's earplugs in, the box fan blowing, and her head under four inches of blanket. But she was a painfully light sleeper and heard it nonetheless. She stumbled out of bed and grabbed the olive green phone on the wall above the kitchen bar.

" 'Lo," she croaked.

"Lettie, I'm sorry to wake you up, but I need to talk." The voice on the other end was unrecognizable, whispered and scratchy.

"Who is this?"

"Betty. It's Betty."

Aletta fell onto the bar stool, but with her satin nightgown on she slid right off. She caught herself before she hit the ground. "Betty. My Lord, you sound like a bad day in hell. What's going on?"

"I asked Frank to move out."

Aletta looked at the clock, more to see if time had stopped than to see how early it was, but the second hand on the baby grandfather was swooping around. It was 5:45. "You better come on over," she said. "I'll put some coffee on."

Aletta and Betty Conway sat at the kitchen bar less than fifteen minutes later drinking Aletta's offer. Betty looked like she hadn't slept all night. Her brown hair, normally done in a "built-up swirl," as Joy called it, was crying out for a tease. Her hazel eyes were rimmed red and her lips were dry.

"You know, ever since you helped free me from the memory of getting molested by my uncle, I been really changin' a lot. Life started seemin' more interesting. There's more things I want to do — travel, dance, live a little. But Frank, well, he's happy doing nothin'. He wants to watch football, have dinner at six, and retire at sixty. That's it. He's not the man I married, Lettie."

"When did this start?" Aletta asked, taking a sip of coffee.

Betty waved a hand in front of her face. "I'm not sure. You know how things can just creep up on you. After he stopped drinkin' five years back, everything seemed great, but now it feels like the more I want to change, the more he wants to stay the same. He was impossible to live with but a hell of a lot more fun when he was still drinkin', I'll tell you that much. He doesn't even take much interest in Rusty or his schoolwork anymore. You remember how he was so concerned about Rusty's grades and all? How he hated him playing his guitar? Now he couldn't care less about any of it. He doesn't even get excited now that Rusty is getting so good at it."

Aletta's stomach felt sour and sinky. She'd told Frank what she'd seen about his son —

he was going to be a country music star. She'd hoped that it would cause Frank to let the boy play his guitar and make them closer.

"Hmmm" was all she could say to Betty, who didn't know anything about what Aletta had told her husband.

"I asked Frank to move out. He's packing a suitcase right now. He's hurtin', but I had to do it. Now that you're single, I figured you could tell me what to do." Betty looked into Aletta's face. Even in hardship, Betty had a candle glow in her eyes. Life flowed full through this woman.

"By the way, where's Frank stayin'?" Aletta asked nonchalantly as she got up to pour some more coffee from the percolator.

"He's stayin' with his brother, Billy, over in Union City till we figure out what's gonna happen."

Just then the front door opened and a shaft of morning light beamed into the house. Sissy, still dressed in the clothes she'd gone out in the night before, walked in. "W-W-What're y'all doin' here?"

Aletta stood up and put her hands on her hips. "What were you *not* doin' here?"

Sissy walked past her mama and sat down at the dining room table. She seemed worn out. "I stayed at Angie's. I been havin' problems."

"You did not have permission to stay at Angie's, young lady. You coulda been anywhere," Aletta said.

Betty shifted in her chair uncomfortably.

Tears plopped out of Sissy's eyes, easy, like they weren't the first of their kind recently. "Rusty broke up with me. Is that why you're here?" Sissy looked at Betty, Rusty's mother.

Surprise and worry crossed Betty's face. "No. I didn't know anything about it. There's been some rough times at home lately," she said. "It's not you, hon."

It hurt Aletta to see her daughter in so much pain, even though she was madder than hell at her. "Sissy, you're grounded for a week for stayin' out, and you never do that again."

Sissy looked defeated. "All right, Mama. Sorry."

"Now come over here and commiserate with us single ladies."

The confusion on Sissy's face prompted Betty to tell her. "Me and Frank are takin' a break. It's been hard on Rusty."

Sissy stood up, put her arms around her mother, laid her head on her shoulder, and cried. "But I love him, Mama. Doesn't anybody stay together?"

Aletta patted her back and held her close. She, of all people, didn't have an answer for her daughter.

Aletta stepped out of the house later that morning to check on her newly planted flags and daisies. Gyp babbled away as she sat him down on the grass. Every time she got all three of her older kids to school on time, fully dressed, with lunch money in their pockets and their homework finished, it felt like a victory.

She looked down Main Street to check on the number of cars parked in front of the shops — Otasco, Ben Franklin's Five and Dime, Bass's Dress Shop, Bud's Tires, and the pharmacy. There were fewer and fewer cars now that Wal-Mart was open out near I-40. She worried about the shop owners and their families, but she knew that trying to keep things from changing was like catching rain in your hands.

Joy stood next to her before Aletta knew what was coming. "You broke up with Eugene and didn't tell me you'd done it," Joy scolded.

Aletta bent over to pick a weed. "We talked about it when you did my hair."

"Yeah, but you never told me you actually

did it," Joy said. Her hair was still platinum blond but not quite as big now.

"How'd you find out?" Aletta asked, more curious than surprised.

"Eugene told his grandpa when they went fishin' at the river. His grandpa told his grandma, and his grandma told her neighbor, Sherry Selby, who told my manicurist, Debbie, and because I'm her boss, Debbie told me." Joy waved at Dolores Knight, her eleven o'clock appointment, as she got out of her car. "I gotta run, girl, but you gotta keep me up on events directly."

"All right, all right, I'll make it up to you." Aletta stood up, weeds in both hands. "Betty and Frank Conway have separated, and me, her, and Bobette Ledger are goin' out on the town Saturday night."

Joy's smile resembled that Grinch character's evil grin from the kids' Christmas show. Aletta laughed.

"You girls aren't goin' anywhere without me there to chaperone you," Joy said.

Aletta laughed harder. "I don't know who'll be lookin' after who, but you're welcome to come along."

Aletta heard her phone ringing, and she jumped up to get it. Maybe it was Charlie Baxter.

■ ■ ■ ■

Somehow, by some miracle, no one had come for Jimmy after he laid the guy out at Six Shooters. It made him even bolder. He'd always known he had a lucky star, but now he was pretty sure he was invincible. Of course, he still wouldn't be going back to Six Shooters anytime soon.

He stood shirtless, looking in the mirror as he got ready to go out for the evening. His chest looked good — hairy but not too much, just enough to show in the V of his shirts. His tight jeans showed off the muscles in his legs and the endowment of his package.

Suddenly, his hands began to shake and he felt pressure in his head. He looked around the small bathroom for the drink he always had with him after five o'clock in the evening, but there wasn't one. They'd run out of booze last night.

"Goddammit, Charlotte," he yelled out the door into their bedroom. "I thought you were gonna get some vodka today!"

"I was workin' till five minutes ago, Jimmy." Charlotte worked at the TG&Y discount store as a cashier. "I came straight home 'cause you were in such a hurry to go out."

"Shit! I was with my kids all day. I can't do everything around here!" He slammed out of the bathroom, pulled his cowboy shirt on, and went into the kitchen. He rummaged through the cabinets for the third time today, looking for a bottle. He knocked a glass off the counter, and it shattered all over the linoleum floor.

Anxiety started to spread throughout his body. It felt like something inside him was trying like hell to bust out. He'd rather get in a ring bare-fisted with Muhammad Ali than feel like this.

He burst out the front door, trying to walk, not run, to his car. He opened the trunk and shoved aside running shoes, maps, empty bottles of liquor, and kids' toys until he found a bottle of old Tickle Pink, the horrible wine that Charlotte liked to drink because she said it tasted like Kool-Aid. He unscrewed the lid and took a long pull on the bottle. It sat in his mouth like warm piss. It had turned to vinegar a long time ago, but he swallowed it down anyway.

Jesse Klesko, the next-door neighbor, stared as Jimmy's face turned sour. Jimmy flipped him off, then walked back inside. He went straight to the bathroom and vomited. It wasn't the first time that day.

The mix of perfumes inside Joy's new brown and tan Buick Riviera made Aletta feel a little high.

"Girls, we are about to paint this town pink!" Joy said to Aletta, Bobette, and Betty as they pulled into Ray's, a small country-western bar on the outskirts of south Oklahoma City.

The gravel parking lot was full of pickup trucks — not the most sophisticated crowd. They sat in the car for a minute, checking out the men and women who came and went.

"They look pretty normal to me," Betty said. "Let's go in."

Joy opened her door. "Well, normal's flyin' right out the window if they let this bunch in the door."

Betty flirted with the cowboy at the door as he told them ladies got in free.

"Getting an early start there, ain't you?" Aletta scolded. She was going to have to watch Betty closely to keep her from ending up with a man.

"I'm just havin' fun," Betty giggled as they walked into the crowded, smoky bar.

Even without touching these folks, Aletta could feel the sexuality, the desire to be noticed, the agendas people came in with. It took a minute before her head stopped swimming and her heart slowed down. By that time, her friends were nowhere in sight.

Aletta scanned the room for them, noticing wagon wheel light fixtures, posters of rodeo stars, and a pretty good-sized dance floor where people moved in one direction like a school of fish.

"You look like you're lost." A large barrel-chested man with kind eyes and sideburns stood next to Aletta.

"I'm just lookin' for my friends."

"I can be your friend," he said too quickly. "Would you like to dance?"

Aletta looked down. She thought of Charlie, his laugh, his hand on the small of her back, but she loved to dance. What harm could it do? "All right, sure," she said to the man.

"My name's Buster," he said, leading her out to the dance floor.

Aletta had been surprised by how strong the images were as people brushed past her, but now she had herself composed and was able to let them float away, barely noticing them at all. She'd gotten really good at this from so many years of denying her gift and from mastering it through her business.

Buster pulled her close and shuffled her

around the dance floor, but there was nothing like the electricity that had flowed between her and Charlie when they danced. As she turned, she saw Bobette on the other side of the dance floor. She was twirling and moving, her patent leather pumps sliding on the floor. For a moment, Aletta couldn't tell if she had a partner or not.

"That's my friend," Aletta said, nodding in Bobette's direction.

When they got closer, Aletta saw that Bobette was dancing her little heart out with a man who had one peg leg, wood from the knee down. He stood pretty much in one place, just turning as Bobette moved around him.

Bobette waved. "Aletta!"

Aletta waved back, then caught sight of Betty and Joy talking to two fairly attractive men at the bar. As soon as the song finished, she left Buster as quickly as she could. He looked heartbroken.

As Aletta walked up, she heard one of the men ask Betty, "So what do you do for a living?"

"I'm a tax accountant," she said.

The man looked at her, puzzled. "What's a tax accountant?"

Betty's mouth dropped open, but nothing came out.

Don't have to worry about that one, Aletta thought. "Hey, girls," she said. "Can I talk to you for a minute?"

Betty and Joy left the men standing there, and they all went to gossip.

"Did you hear what he said?" Betty asked. " 'What is a *tax accountant?* ' "

"How 'bout the Casanova Bobette's dancin' with?" Joy finished the drink in her hand.

"He might be very nice," Aletta said to Joy. "I thought you weren't gonna drink."

Betty rolled her eyes. "That's her second."

Bobette walked up aglow from exertion.

"Did you have a good time?" Aletta asked.

Bobette grabbed Joy's glass and took some ice in her mouth. "It was okay, but I was a little worried."

"Why?" Betty asked.

"With all that turning around and around, I was afraid he was gonna screw himself right into the ground."

They laughed so loud, several people in the bar looked over. Jimmy Honor was one of them.

Joy saw him first as he made his way through the crowd. "Hold on to your butts. Here comes trouble."

"Looks like they should rename this place

the Henhouse," Jimmy said, walking over to them. His drink was full, which meant he'd just arrived.

Charlotte stuck right by his side. "Hi, Aletta." She said the name like it tasted bad in her mouth.

Aletta ignored her. She was sorry Jimmy had broken up with Kathy Kokin after her bout with breast cancer. Kathy had turned out to be an adulterous godsend — not only had she gotten Jimmy out of the house because of their affair, she'd also been real good to Aletta's kids. So now Aletta took out her resentment on his latest girlfriends. "What're you doin' way out here, Jimmy? I thought you liked the glamorous places."

"Slummin' it a little bit, ladies, like yourselves." Jimmy tipped his hat and flashed his gorgeous smile.

"Jimmy, let's go," Charlotte said.

"You wanna dance, Lettie?" Jimmy asked, ignoring Charlotte.

Charlotte's face changed from shock to anger and then back again so fast, Aletta couldn't keep her laughter in. "Don't you have a girlfriend?" she asked, just to make it worse. "I guess I should say a live-in."

Charlotte's lower lip jutted out another half inch, and she stomped away.

"How many guys've you picked up in

here?" Jimmy asked Aletta. "Already whoring around after dumpin' that slob Eugene, aren't ya?" He turned around to follow Charlotte.

"Chase your little bimbo, you lousy drunk," Joy called after him. She'd hated Jimmy ever since he'd started beating up on Aletta when they were still married. Joy had always been the one to clean up the mess.

Jimmy stopped and turned back around. His anger hit Aletta right in the chest, it was so strong.

Aletta took a step back, but Joy walked right up to him, her 120 pounds dwarfed by his 210.

"Joy," Betty called.

But Joy didn't stop. She took Jimmy's drink out of his hand and threw the contents of the glass right in his face. Then she promptly turned around and yelled, "Run!"

The four of them cut for the door.

"You bitch!" Jimmy yelled. He took two steps and caught Joy by her platinum hair. He yanked and brought her to the ground hard.

"Stop it!" Aletta turned around and jumped on Jimmy's back just as he was about to slap Joy's face as she writhed on the ground.

It was like Aletta was no more than a fly

to him, a nuisance to be shaken off. As soon as she was off his back and on the ground, he bent over Joy again. From the ground, Aletta saw Buster push through some people who were watching, a chair held high over his head. As soon as he reached Jimmy, he slammed the chair over his back.

Jimmy stumbled but caught himself before he fell. He turned to Buster, who was motioning with his hand to bring it on.

Two massive security guards, who Aletta found out later were former University of Oklahoma football players, took Jimmy by the arms and pulled him toward the door.

"This guy is beatin' up on women," Buster said, following them.

Betty and Bobette picked their friends up off the ground and followed the four men out the door into the cool night air. Aletta wasn't sure what they'd do to Jimmy and watched as they dragged him to the side of the building.

"Let me go, you redneck assholes," Jimmy screamed.

"This guy needs a lesson in manners," one of the hulking security guards said.

The women got to the car, and while Betty looked for Joy's keys, they were able to pull themselves together a little.

"I can't believe what just happened," Bobette said.

"Where'd those boys take him?" Joy asked.

Aletta sat down on the bumper of the car. She'd had the breath knocked out of her when she hit the ground. "They dragged him to the side of the building."

"What do you think they're doin'?" Bobette asked.

Joy started walking to where the men had gone. "I think they're kickin' the shit outta that bastard. I gotta see this."

Betty looked up. "Joy! Joy! What the hell?"

Betty went after her, and Aletta and Bobette weren't far behind. When the four ladies got near the edge of the building, they got low and quiet. Each of them took a turn peeking around the corner. Aletta stared, her stomach fluttering inside, as Buster and the guards pummeled her ex-husband with fists, knees, and boots. It sounded ugly and mean, but it felt good to see Jimmy get a taste of his own medicine. Aletta had never known him to be on the hurting end of a fight.

"Don't you ever touch a woman again, you low-life son of a bitch!" Buster yelled as he hit Jimmy with a left to the face.

Jimmy fell to the ground, and this time he didn't get up. Rubbing their hands, the men started to walk back to the entrance of the bar.

The ladies saw them coming and fled back to their car.

"By God, they beat his ass," Joy said as she took the keys from Betty.

Aletta grabbed the keys out of her hand. "I'm drivin', but give me a second."

She walked over to the three men as they were about to go back inside. "Thank you," she said quietly. "I been wantin' to do that for a long time."

CHAPTER FOUR

Vee sat on the tattered corduroy couch in the safe house in Venice Beach. The colors of the beaded lampshades around the room reflected off the faces of her comrades; the spots of pink, red, and yellow seemed to mock the serious looks on their faces as they argued with one another.

They had chosen Venice because it was one of the few neighborhoods in Los Angeles where whites, blacks, and Hispanics could be seen going into one house together without arousing too much suspicion.

Carl, a thin, rumpled white guy with endless energy for the cause, led the discussion. "We can use these weapons to really advance our agenda. The movement is losing momentum across the country. People are falling back to sleep now that Watergate and Vietnam are in the past, and we need to do something to show we aren't going away."

Lucius, a black man with an impressive

Afro, agreed. "Let's show the capitalist pigs we mean business. Let's get them where it hurts."

"We need action," Chloe said, nodding. "Rallies and sit-ins are dead."

Vee uncrossed her long legs. "It's the only way to get the message out," she said intensely.

"I'm not sure force is the best way to communicate our position," Bo said.

"Then why the hell'd you get the guns?" Carl asked caustically.

"For protection," he said.

Lucius looked him straight in the eye. "That's bullshit and you know it."

Aletta was still shaking when they pulled into Joy's driveway.

"It don't feel right leavin' you alone, Aletta," Betty said as they got out of the car.

Aletta handed Joy the keys. "I'll be all right," she said.

"Are you sure you feel safe?" Bobette asked.

"I haven't felt safe for a long time, but I can't let that stop me."

"I'm gonna stay with you tonight, hon," Betty said. "Rusty's with his daddy in Union City this weekend, so I don't mind at all."

Aletta started to protest, but Joy put her

hand on Aletta's shoulder. "Just let her," she said.

Inside the house, Ruby and Randy were laughing. They were in the living room watching *Saturday Night Live.* Roseanne Roseannadanna was talking about lint balls in people's belly buttons. Aletta wondered if she should make them turn it off. Whenever she saw any part of this show, it seemed a little too strange for children. Besides, they really should be in bed by now.

Betty sat down next to Ruby on the couch and looked at the TV. "Oh, I love her. She's hysterical," she said.

So Aletta let them watch. "Where's Sissy and the baby?" she asked.

"In her room, I think," Ruby said.

Aletta walked back and peeked into Sissy's bedroom. Gyp was lying on his stomach asleep in the middle of her bed, his chubby legs and arms splayed out. His back moved up and down with perfect baby breath.

Sissy was taking down the RC Cola cans, posters, and signs that filled her room. To her, *RC* stood for Rusty Conway, and she'd put all this stuff up after they got together last summer.

"Hi there. Mind if I come in?" Aletta asked.

66

Sissy turned around. Her eyes were red and puffy. It hurt Aletta to see her daughter so sad. Sissy nodded toward the bed, so Aletta took a seat.

"Not havin' much fun, are you?" Aletta said.

"You could say that." Sissy put the hat made of RC cans that hung on her bedpost into the box with the other things.

"I know it hurts, honey, but you're young. You'll do better'n me at findin' love, I'm sure of that."

Sissy sat down next to Aletta. "Are you still lookin', Mama?"

Aletta patted her daughter's denim-covered thigh. "Sure feels like I'm lookin' for somethin', Sis. I just feel like there's somethin' missing. Love's the only thing I can guess."

Sissy put her head on her mama's shoulder. "I really thought Rusty was the one."

"I know, but maybe this is for the best," Aletta said. "Y'all are too young to be getting serious anyway."

Sissy stood up. "I knew you didn't really care how I felt. At least with Rusty I was somebody."

Aletta looked up at her daughter. She felt tired and sad. "That's exactly what I'm talkin' about, young lady, feelin' like Rusty was why you're somebody. You got a lot to learn before you get serious, a whole damn lot." Aletta wished she knew the words to say to her oldest child to help her, to keep her from making the same mistakes she had. But at the moment she was exhausted, and it seemed that nothing she said was right anyway.

Aletta fell into bed that night feeling as though she could sleep forever, but her worries about Sissy and Jimmy and her own love life kept her painfully awake. As she finally began to doze off, she thought about her mother and how strong she'd been when she was alive. Even though she'd become bitter after her husband and brother were killed and she and Aletta had grown apart, she had always kept her house perfectly clean. She'd made all of her own clothes, baked the best cakes in town, and went to church without fail. Aletta wished she had more of her mother's tidiness and skill at being a homemaker.

When Nadine was in the hospital during her last days, she had acknowledged Aletta for having the psychic abilities that she previously had either condemned or ignored. Mother and daughter had said all the things they needed to say before Nadine died. And now that there was no longer the resentment and blame between them, Aletta wished her mother was here to be with her grandchildren. She also wished she had the support of her mama.

When Aletta finally fell asleep, she had a dream. Nadine was a young woman, before she had given birth to Aletta, which didn't happen until she was over forty. She was walking near a river wearing a dress that was the same rusty brown color as the water. An enormous bird flew over her head and swooped around her. It looked like a golden eagle. Nadine smiled at the eagle and held her hands out to it for a moment.

"Mama," Aletta whispered in the dream. She was watching, not really there, just watching.

Just then, her mother changed. The figure was still her mother, but now she was dark-skinned with long black hair and round brown eyes. She turned to the river and put a metal pail into the water. The wind blew in the trees, and Aletta could tell the mother was listening, understanding.

A shadow fell over the dark-skinned woman, and Aletta felt frightened.

"Mama," she called again. But the shadow grew darker, so dark she could no longer see her mother at all. Aletta looked into the darkness, straining to see, but it was like a cave, deep and black and unknown. Finally, she looked away, and in that moment, the eagle flew out of the darkness toward the light blue sky.

When Aletta woke up, she realized she had been crying in her sleep. The dark-skinned woman in her dream stayed in her mind as she lay under the covers listening to her breath. The woman's eyes had been brilliant and glowing and familiar. Who was she?

Aletta got up and went to the kitchen. Betty had changed out of Aletta's borrowed nightgown and had already made coffee. She poured Aletta a cup. "I guess you're gonna be all right now that the sun's come up," she said. "That ex of yours is like a vampire."

Aletta looked away, trying to keep Betty from seeing the pain on her face. "I'm sorry you had to get involved."

Betty reached out and touched Aletta's arm. "Oh, no. Joy made sure the whole bar got involved." She smiled. "This ain't your fault, girl."

Aletta returned the smile gratefully. "What're you up to today?" she asked.

"Not sure. I got the whole day to myself for the first time in . . ." Betty thought for a moment, looking up at Aletta's collection of cobalt glass figurines that lined the top of the kitchen cabinets. "Well, for the first time in my whole life, it seems like."

Aletta laughed and motioned to Betty to follow her. They walked down the hall, Aletta knocking on the kids' doors. "Time to get up," she called to them.

"Did you see somethin' just now?" Betty asked.

Aletta went into the back room to get Gyp, who was standing up in his crib. He was quiet, but his hands gripped the bars of the crib like he was in baby prison. When he saw his mama, his face spread out in a gummy grin.

"What do you mean?" Aletta asked Betty, then kissed Gyp all over his tiny face.

"When I touched your arm, did you see somethin' about me?"

Gyp fussed as Aletta laid him down on his changing table and took off his wet diaper, but she was lucky. He didn't start crying this time.

"I don't think so. I can't remember really. I let things go so fast," Aletta said, wiping a cloth across Gyp's bottom with one hand and holding both his feet in the air with the other. "I had this crazy dream last night, and that's all I been seein' this mornin'." She put a clean diaper under his bottom.

"You want a readin'?"

Betty waved her hand at Aletta. "Oh, I don't dare. I'm afraid of what you'll see."

"Like what?" Aletta pulled a blue terry-cloth jumper suit out of a beat-up chest of drawers.

"I'm afraid I'll find out that me and Frank are split up for good. I'm scared of that. I love him, but there's somethin' I need that I'm not getting and it's about eatin' me alive."

Aletta looked at Betty.

Betty frowned. "I'm also afraid of finding out that we end up together, me bored down to my fingertips."

"Frank's brother's name is Billy, right?" Aletta asked nonchalantly. She needed to find and talk to Frank Conway, but she didn't want Betty to know.

"Yes." Betty looked at her sideways. "What're you thinkin'?"

"Nothin'," Aletta said, then picked up Gyp and walked out of the room. "Kids! Get on your church clothes!"

"I don't know how you do it alone, Lettie. Most folks'd just stay home from church and rest," Betty said, following her back to the kitchen.

"I gotta go sometimes just to keep my sanity." Aletta pulled a loaf of Rainbow bread and a box of Velveeta cheese out of the fridge. "Want some cheese toast?"

"Nah, I better go start my free day. The Lord only knows when I might get another," Betty said.

The first thing that went across the screen of Jimmy's mind when he woke up on Sunday morning was a flash of fiery light. The light carried a red-hot pain that spilled out into his head like a big rig losing its load all over a highway.

"Son of a bitch," he groaned, and turned over in bed. An explosion of hurt shot through his ribs as he did. He yelled out.

Charlotte ran into the bedroom in her sheer pink nightgown carrying a glass of water.

"Here," she said, holding out the glass. "Take one of these pills the doctor gave you for the pain."

"What doctor?" he asked. He could see her through only one eye. The other was swollen shut, but it took only the one eye to see the fear and disgust on her face.

"I had to take you to the hospital 'cause some big ole boys beat you half to death at the bar last night. Don't you remember?" she asked. A shiver ran through her body, and she looked away from his face.

He struggled to sit up, then took the pill. He remembered being dragged out of the bar but not much else. "I need a drink," he said.

She looked at him blankly for a moment, not believing what she heard. "You got to be kiddin', Jimmy."

The pain truck barreled through his head again, dropping another load. "I need somethin' for the pain, darlin'. It'll help."

Charlotte turned around and went to her closet. "Booze is what got you into this mess in the first place." She dropped her nightgown to the floor.

Normally when she was naked, he looked at her like a hungry wolf, but now he barely noticed. "I need a drink, Charlotte," he said.

She pulled a dress with poofy short sleeves over her head. "It ain't good for you. How 'bout I get you some orange juice and make you some eggs?"

"Goddammit!" he roared. "I need a drink!"

Charlotte walked out of the room without looking back at him.

"Charlotte!" He waited, listening. He heard her keys jingle, then the front door close. "Charlotte!" he screamed.

He realized that he sounded just like a steer he'd found when he was a kid out hunting squirrels for dinner. It had fallen into a ditch onto a steel spike that was sticking up out of the ground. The huge animal lay there dying. The sound it made came from deep inside its belly. It was a wail of desperation and loneliness and terror.

"Oh, Lord," he said aloud.

After church, where Aletta said a little prayer for her and Charlie making it, Aletta piled the kids back into her '57 Chevy, which they'd nicknamed the Pink Pumpkin because of its bulbous build. Then she dropped Sissy off at her best friend Angie's. Sissy had promised to babysit Gyp if she didn't have to go with them.

"Don't leave that baby alone for even an instant, you hear me?" Aletta said as Sissy got out of the car.

"I know, Mama," Sissy answered. "Angie's mama knows he's comin', so she'll help watch too."

"Hey, Sis," Aletta called.

Sissy turned around, Gyp now planted happily on her hip. "What?"

"I love you." Aletta looked up at her, smiling.

"Love you too," Sissy said, then walked away.

Aletta turned to Ruby and Randy. "We're

goin' for a little drive," she said, "If you're good, I'll get you an ice cream on the way home."

She turned the car east on Main Street. On the way out of town, they passed Eugene's auto repair shop. It was closed on Sunday.

"I miss Eugene," Randy said, bouncing up and down on the enormous backseat.

"Me too," Ruby said.

"Well, tonight y'all are gonna meet a new friend of mine who I think you'll like just as much as Eugene. His name's Charlie, and he's real nice." Aletta looked in the rearview mirror as she spoke, but she could see they weren't buying it.

Union City was just thirty miles southeast of town on country roads. She rolled her window down and smelled the familiar scent of farmland as they drove through an endless sea of green pastures and red dirt fields. Cows and horses suckled newborn young, and the banks of the Caddo River could barely hold the rushing brown water between them.

"You feel that, kids?" Aletta asked. "You feel life just bursting out all over?"

She didn't think they'd really understand, but Ruby, who'd had her head out the window, brought it back inside the car. "I feel it, Mama."

"Me too," Randy said.

"Spring is for new beginnings, you know," Aletta said.

"You're not talkin' about that Charlie guy again, are you?" Randy asked.

Aletta turned around and glanced at him for a moment. "No, smarty pants, I'm talkin' about springtime."

When she got to Union City, a poor farming town made up of battered pickups and hardworking people, she went straight for the local diner, Big Jim's. She left the kids in the car and walked inside. The smoky diner was filled with old-timers and families having lunch after church. These folks were right off the farms she'd passed driving in, and she felt she'd gone straight back to her childhood, when she would go to the diner in town for Sunday dinner when her mama didn't feel like cooking.

For a moment, her heart stopped when an older lady came out of the bathroom and looked straight at her. From across the room, she looked so much like her mama, Aletta felt tears burn behind her eyes for a moment.

The lady walked closer, and she seemed to change from her mother into a stranger before Aletta's eyes. "Can I help you?" the woman asked.

Aletta cleared her throat of the tears she'd swallowed. "I'm looking for Billy Conway. His brother Frank's stayin' with him, and I came to visit."

The lady turned out to be the owner of the place along with her husband, and she knew everything about everyone in Union City.

Aletta drove to Billy's place, a mobile home out on a dirt road just south of town. She couldn't stop thinking about her mama. It was almost like Nadine was trying to tell her something.

The mobile home that sat on a brown patch of dried-up land looked like it needed to be put out of its misery. The windows were thick with red dirt, and the whole thing seemed to sag in the center. As she pulled up, a fat, mangy German shepherd appeared from under the wood porch and started barking.

"Kids, you stay in the car," Aletta cautioned.

"Don't worry," Ruby said.

Just then, Rusty Conway walked around the trailer carrying his guitar. His blond hair was longer than the last time she'd seen him, and he seemed two inches taller. Rusty saw the Pink Pumpkin, stopped in his tracks, and turned back around.

Aletta grabbed her macramé handbag and jumped out of the car, facing the dog down with her feet spread apart and her jaw set. She swung the purse and hit the snarling mess of a dog squarely on the head. It whimpered and crawled back under the porch.

"Rusty!" she called, and ran after him. "Sissy ain't with us. I'm here to talk to your daddy."

Rusty stopped and looked back at Aletta. She could still see the little boy in him even as he was turning into a young man.

"She keeps following me around," he said, still holding the guitar. "She's talkin' about getting married, and I don't believe in marriage. Look at my mama and daddy, or you and Jimmy. It don't work." His expression went blank, and he looked past her.

Aletta turned around and saw Frank Conway watching his son. The sadness in his eyes seemed to weigh him down even more than the extra thirty pounds he'd put on. He'd always been a big man, but now he looked fat.

"Rusty, will you watch my kids while I talk to your daddy?"

Rusty nodded and walked past his father, never looking him in the eye.

" 'Lo, Aletta," Frank said after his son was out of sight.

"Frank. Just came out to see how you're doin'. Betty don't know I'm here." Aletta clutched her purse in front of her like a shield against his pain. She felt too much for people sometimes.

"Come sit on the porch," he said, and ran his hand through his black hair. Normally, it was slicked down with some kind of grease, not a hair out of place, but now it looked dirty and unkempt. The stubble on his face only made things worse.

They walked to the front of the trailer and sat down on two rusted metal lawn chairs as the kids followed Rusty to a shabby picnic table near some trees.

"How's Betty?" Frank asked.

"Confused," Aletta said. She studied his face. All together it was attractive in a manly way, but taken alone, each of his features was a little unusual.

"Hmph," he snorted. "Didn't seem too confused to me as she was kickin' me out."

"I think she's confused 'bout why you've changed so much, like you've given up on life. Is it because I told you Rusty's gonna be a country music star one day?" She looked at him. They hadn't discussed this since she'd told Frank about his son. She'd told him the truth so he'd let the boy play his guitar instead of fighting him about it. Frank had believed that the music was a dead end, a hopeless dream, and that Rusty would turn out to be an irresponsible wanderer like his own father had been. So Aletta told him that Rusty would someday beat the odds and make it big. The fighting between them had stopped, but now it seemed Frank had given up not only on being an active father, but also on being a good husband.

He glanced at her, then looked back at Rusty, who was playing his guitar for Ruby and Randy. "I don't mean no disrespect, but I don't want to talk about this with you."

She paused for a moment, trying to keep his words from getting inside and hurting her feelings. She already felt guilty enough. "Well then," she said quietly, "I have a favor to ask."

Frank looked at her sideways, his eyebrows raised slightly.

"My ex-husband got beat up bad last night. He was drunker'n a skunk, and it was real ugly. These three big ole boys at a bar just kicked the holy hell out of him."

Frank shook his head and groaned, "Oh, no."

Aletta went on. "I think he might listen if

you talked to him. He needs a man to talk to."

"I haven't done nothin' like that for a few years," Frank said.

"I know, but he needs your help," she pleaded. "He respects you."

"We played softball together for a couple a summers. He barely knows me. Hell, when I was a drunk, the people I didn't know were the only people I liked too," Frank said. "Why you wanna help him? You ain't married anymore."

She nodded her head out at the kids. They were clapping and dancing while Rusty tapped his toe and strummed his guitar. "He's their daddy, and I'm a big believer in kids needin' a daddy."

Boy, that sounded good, she thought, but she knew it wasn't the whole truth. There was a snake curled up near her heart that she didn't want anyone to see. It was dark and ugly and mean. She realized right then that if there was going to be anything honest between her and Frank now, anything more than skimming along the surface with *How do you do? Oh, I'm just fine,* then she had to be the one to take a risk first. "Besides," she said, clearing her throat, "when I saw him getting beat up last night,

I enjoyed the hell out of it. Now, I know he hit me a few times, and he deserved some of his own medicine, but this ain't about him."

Frank looked over at her but didn't say anything, so Aletta continued.

"I felt hate for the man who killed my daddy and my uncle almost my whole life, and just when that starts goin' away, now I feel that same type of hatred for Jimmy," Aletta said. "It's selfish, Frank. I don't wanna feel this way. It eats me up inside, and the hole it makes lets the life run right outta me."

They sat there in silence for several minutes watching the kids. The wind was up pretty good, and the music made its way across the dirt yard in waves as the wind blew it toward them or away.

"I guess I'll be goin', then," Aletta said finally, and stood up.

Frank stayed seated but looked up at her. "I know what you mean about them holes," he said quietly.

She waited for him to continue, but he shifted his gaze to his boots.

"I know you do. That's why I knew you could help. Jimmy's got 'em too." She stepped off the porch. "He's livin' in the

Cottonwood Apartments on Pershing Street, just so you know. Kids!" she called out. "Time to go."

On the way to Braum's Ice Cream, she drove past a Baptist church just outside of Union City. Out front, there was an announcements sign that read 1 CROSS + 3 NAILS = 4 GIVEN.

Jesus may have forgiven us, she thought. *Now I guess it's up to us to forgive each other.* But she had to be honest with herself — she didn't know how she could ever forgive Jimmy.

CHAPTER FIVE

For Vee, the unsettling, even eerie feeling of waking up in a place she didn't know had been a lifelong experience. As a child, waking up had almost always brought with it an unpleasant surprise. She'd never gotten used to living in squalor with her father. He was always so poor and shiftless that they'd moved to a new shack about every six months to stay a step ahead of the bill collectors. There was always a new, and seemingly more degrading, situation waiting for her. At some level, she believed that this was her punishment for her mother dying when she was born, so she put up with it while bitterness and blame grew inside her heart.

To get through her youth and escape her life, she read. Books were her lifeline to other worlds. The ones she'd loved most were about the downtrodden. She'd read everything she could get her hands on about the Holocaust, American slavery, and the French Revolution. She loved stories of survival and gained courage for her own life from the heroes in those books. When she was in junior high and high school, she'd gone to the library and devoured every magazine and newspaper that reported on the civil rights and anti–Vietnam War movements. She'd fallen in love with Malcolm X and wanted desperately to participate in the wave of change that was happening everywhere, it seemed, but Reedley.

When she finally escaped after high school graduation on Pell Grants and a partial scholarship to Berkeley, she was already angry enough at the world to prevent her from staying in one place very long. She had to make a difference, to find an outlet for her outrage at the treatment of women and blacks and all oppressed people, at their powerlessness in the most powerful society in the world. She knew that if her mother hadn't been so poor and ignorant, she would have been in a hospital and wouldn't have died. Not only that, she believed that saving the underprivileged meant she was somehow saving herself, redeeming her entire life. Besides, the movement gave her something impersonal to pour her thoughts and emotions into so she didn't have to deal with her personal pain.

She'd hooked up with some revolutionaries in Berkeley within a few months of arriving and began working for the movement. Her anger had landed her among the most radical of the many revolutionary organizations. She knew that the oppressors would respond only to violent protest, to a backlash so brutal as to strike terror in the hearts of the capitalists and inspiration in the minds of the people. After nine months of dorm life with Janice, her silly and annoying Tri Delta roommate, where she woke up in the same place every day, she'd dropped out of school to devote her full attention to the cause. She went back to not knowing where she was when she opened her eyes. The disquiet she felt when she awoke, the subtle gripping in her chest and throat, created a habit in her of jumping off whatever couch or futon or floor she was sleeping on, so she wouldn't have to stew in the unwelcome and childish question that crept in if she lay there too long: what would it feel like to have a home?

When she awoke in the enormous brown Buick that she'd traded in for her VW at a shady used car place on Hollywood Boulevard, the sense of homelessness was stronger than ever. As she recalled the day before and the botched bank robbery, the fear clutched at her throat like a frightened kitten, but Vee quickly pushed it away and looked around warily.

Living life on the edge kept her instincts sharp and her mind focused on the task at hand, and that suited her just fine. When she didn't see anyone watching her, she started the car and pulled away from the cul-de-sac where she was parked.

The night before, she'd contemplated going by the house in Venice just to see if she could sneak in and get some of her belongings, but she dared not take the risk. Now, after what had happened on Friday, the only reason she was still in Los Angeles was to see Bo one more time.

She drove to Carol's apartment in Sherman Oaks, where she and Bo had said they would meet if anything went wrong. Carol was a good friend, but she was a junior high teacher and not a member of the organization. The imperialist oppressors didn't have anything on her.

Vee didn't see anyone as she walked to the door of the small fifties-style complex, but she was jumpy as hell. She'd spent a night in jail before, and it had scared her. The cops had picked her up after a rally in Berkeley while she was still a student. The pigs had pawed her with their hands and kept her overnight with a woman who smelled of BO and booze.

"We gotta get outta town now," Bo said as he opened the door for her. He looked like a hunted animal, his blond hair wild on his head.

She agreed. The creases between her eyes were already getting deep, even though she was only twenty-three. "We can't go together, though. We have to split up and hide. We have to go underground."

They agreed to keep in touch through Carol.

Vee had a small army duffel bag that she always kept packed in her car, so she was ready to go.

Bo leaned down to kiss her, but she pulled away when she heard something outside.

"It's Carol's cat," Bo said.

Vee saw the hurt look on Bo's face. She felt his need for her to give him more. This was how it had always been between them. "I have to go," she said, then hugged him and walked out the door.

She got into the Buick and looked in the rearview mirror to see if anyone had emerged behind her. She saw only her reflection. Her brown eyes looked tired and scared, but the anger still smoldered underneath. Her shoulder-length brown hair hadn't been washed for three days, and her skin was pasty white.

"Come on, girl, you gotta get me there," she said, both to herself and to the car. She pulled the shifter down to D and headed toward the freeway.

Charlie Baxter was an hour late getting to Aletta's, but when he finally showed up, he blew in the door like a train to somewhere fun. He handed her a half dozen yellow roses, then picked her up by the waist and swung her around twice before putting her back down. He wore a suit and tie, and his delicious cologne made her think of that silly show *Fantasy Island* for some reason. She was way too distracted to pay attention to any of the images that came to her as he swung her around, and she forgave him for being late before her feet hit the ground.

"My goodness, you're in a good mood," she said, standing wobbly on her cork-soled sandals, not because they were four inches high, but because being around him made her light-headed.

"Well, I get to see you," he said. "You're so beautiful."

Aletta blushed up to her eyebrows.

"Mama, can we go now?" Ruby asked.

Aletta realized that neither of them had noticed when her kids came into the room. She forgot she'd told them to be polite and come introduce themselves when Charlie got there.

"Oh, look at you," she said. Ruby and Randy stood together in the entryway, and Sissy stood in the doorway to the hall holding Gyp. She hadn't really spoken since Aletta told her she'd seen Rusty.

With a cringe, Aletta noticed the cloud that passed over Charlie's face when he saw them all. "Wow, yes, just look at you," he said.

"I told you I had four," she said hopefully.

Suddenly the cloud was gone, and his dark blue eyes sparkled again. "You sure did, and who are these gorgeous children?"

Aletta saw Ruby roll her eyes, surely having seen the same changes on his face, but she wouldn't let that get to her. Four kids was a lot to take in for anyone.

After they told him their names, he reached into his pocket. "I've got something for you, but let me make sure your mama will let you have it."

He turned his closed hand upward toward Aletta, and she noticed there was black under all his fingernails. He opened his hand to reveal four Hershey's Kisses.

"Sure, they can have 'em. Sissy, just make sure Gyp doesn't swallow his whole," she said.

"Yes'm," Sissy said, her voice monotone.

Aletta decided that if Sissy was going to be so polite when she was depressed, maybe it wasn't such a bad thing.

Ruby and Randy grabbed the Kisses from Charlie's hand, then ran back to the living room to watch TV.

Jimmy was almost asleep when he heard the knocking. It was so light, he thought it must be inside his battered head. But when he heard it again, he forced himself up off the divan and over to the door of his apartment. He hoped it was Charlotte, but why would she knock?

It was dark outside, and he didn't recognize Frank Conway until he spoke.

"Hi, Jimmy," Frank said.

Jimmy turned around and sat down carefully at the round oak dining room set he'd bought when he and Charlotte moved in together. Neither one of them had had much of anything, so he'd bought most of the furniture that was now in the apartment.

"Hey, Frank, you look like hell." Jimmy tried to hide the tremors in his hands by keeping them under the table. "What brings you by?"

"Oh, I just dropped off my kid at his mother's. Thought I'd come check on you," Frank said, closing the door behind him. "You look like a truck ran you down, buddy."

"Thanks," Jimmy said. He'd looked in the mirror only once today, and it had made him think long and hard about taking the whole bottle of pain pills. His lower lip was split open and sewed shut. His right eye was still swollen closed. One of those bastards must've been a lefty. He figured at least two of his ribs were broken, and the bandages wrapped around them didn't do anything but make him itch.

"You bring anything to drink with you?" he asked. "I haven't been able to get outta the house."

"You know I stopped a long time ago," Frank said, and leaned against the kitchen counter, crossing his arms.

"Thought maybe you could use one, since I saw your wife out at a bar last night." Jimmy cleared his throat. "Anyway, the pain pills are takin' the edge off."

"You know what I see?" Frank said. "I see myself sittin' in front of me. I used to drink, be a partier like you, kickin' ass and takin' names. But I went to AA, and I got my life back together."

"Okay, preacher man, I got some things to do." Jimmy glanced at Frank with his one eye.

"But I didn't really do the program. I stopped drinkin' and things got a helluva lot better —"

"Then why're you fat and not sleepin' at home?" Jimmy interrupted.

Frank smiled and shook his head. "That's what I'm tryin' to tell you. I stopped drinkin', but I didn't deal with whatever made me start in the first place."

"I don't know what you're talkin' about, man. I need to lie down," Jimmy said, but he wasn't telling the truth. Somewhere in his bones he understood what Frank meant, but he didn't want to think about it. "I can quit anytime, by the way," Jimmy said as he made his way, bent over, to the couch. If he stood all the way up, it felt like he was getting kicked in the ribs all over again.

"That's what I thought," Frank said. "When you try and can't do it, give me a call at my brother Billy's in Union City. There's help for you, Jimmy."

"I remember Billy. He was on our team that one summer." Jimmy lay down with a groan and a chuckle. "Couldn't field a ball on the ground to save his life."

"That's my brother," Frank said. He put a piece of paper down on the counter and walked to the door. "Call me, Jimmy."

Jimmy lay thinking after Frank left. He had to admit his life was pretty screwed up. He didn't know what he was going to say to his boss tomorrow when he couldn't go to work. His girlfriend was nowhere to be found. The ache inside him didn't seem to go away nearly as easily as it used to when he drank, and he was scared to death of being alone.

Just then, Charlotte walked in carrying a bag of groceries. He was so glad to see her, he almost cried for the second time in one day. "Hey." He smiled even though it hurt. "Where you been? I missed you."

Charlotte looked over near him, but not quite at him. "I went out for a while. I needed some air."

The sadness in her eyes went straight inside him. "Come over here," he said, his voice gentle.

She walked over to him, still not looking him in the eye. He scooted over and she sat next to him.

"I've decided something," he said, and took her hand. "I'm not gonna drink no more. I've been getting a little crazy with it lately, so I'm gonna just stop for a while."

Charlotte looked straight at him for the first time since she'd walked in, hope taking the place of sadness in her eyes like a glass filling with water. She touched his face lightly.

He loved that he could have that effect on her. "Can't be harder than driving a tractor twelve hours a day in the burning sun when I was only ten years old. If I can do that, I can do anything," he said.

Charlie took Aletta back to the Round-Up Club in Jasper, where they'd met.

"We can go somewhere in the city if you don't want to drive so far," she'd told him, knowing that she didn't have to worry about seeing Jimmy.

"What's wrong? You don't like bein' in the car with me?" he asked.

He drove a plain white Dodge four-door, and apologized for it. "Company car," he said. "In New York, I drive a Caddy."

They talked all about how he was in charge of buying up land for a big oil company. He wasn't supposed to say which one, because he was doing it secretly so the competition wouldn't find out where they had deals going.

"Enough about me," he said. "You sure

got some brilliant scam going there with the psychic business. People will believe just about anything, won't they?"

She looked over at him, not sure what to say. He looked so put together, so in charge, the way he held himself, the way his hand sat in his lap and two fingers held the steering wheel. She realized she didn't know him and he definitely didn't know her. Not yet anyway. "It ain't no scam, Charlie. I been able to see things about people since I was a little girl."

He looked over at her, the headlights from other cars swiping light across his face. "You really believe in that stuff?" he asked, smiling.

She laughed a little. "Well, no, I don't *believe* in it, Charlie. I *am* it."

"All right, all right," he said, and took her hand. "Whatever you say."

When they got to the bar, Charlie ran around and opened Aletta's door. As he escorted her across the gravel lot to the entrance, a group of five men no older than twenty-one or twenty-two came out of the bar, laughing and stumbling, drunk and rowdy. One of them was so inebriated, he had his arms around the shoulders of his friends, and they dragged him along.

When they got closer, Aletta could see

who the young man being carried was, and she almost gasped.

"Corliss?" she said, and he raised his head, his glazed eyes sweeping over her. He looked so different than he had at her house when he'd come for the reading, and it wasn't just the drink.

"Oh, hey, Ms. Honor . . . ," he slurred. She couldn't understand the rest of what he said.

"Is he okay?" she asked.

"Ah, he's just in shock," the tall, skinny one with the large Adam's apple laughed. "He just found out his girlfriend's pregnant, but he'll be all right."

They started off again, dragging Corliss toward a pickup truck.

Aletta stiffened. She felt as if an electric current was running from her head all the way through her feet down into the ground. Somehow, she knew she was meant to see this, to be here right now.

"You just had to go and knock her up, didn't ya, buddy?" one of them said, laughing.

Paralyzed, Aletta couldn't take her eyes off Corliss as the four guys dumped him into the back of the truck like a bale of hay.

"Poor bastard," Charlie said. "He looks like just a kid."

The sound of Charlie's voice broke the spell, and Aletta turned to him and put her arms around his waist.

"You all right?" he asked.

"He came to me. I should've . . ."

"What?"

"I can't talk about it. Let's go in now."

Aletta looked over her shoulder as they walked in, and watched the red pickup speed out onto the county road until it was out of her sight.

As soon as they were inside, Charlie pulled her out onto the dance floor, and they danced for an hour before taking a break. It certainly helped Aletta to stop thinking about Corliss or anything else for that matter. The images that swirled in her head from all the people around her subsided quickly this time. As they danced, she realized she hadn't had such a good time since . . . well, since the last time they were here. Before that, it had been years.

When he dropped her off that night, he promised to call her the very next day, and kissed her passionately.

"I want to take you to Hawaii," he said as he got into his car. "You'll love it there."

The smell of high school rushed at Sissy as she opened the door of the gray brick building. It was a mix of books, floor cleaner, cafeteria food, and anxiety. The last one wafted off the students, getting stronger with each popularity contest, rejection by this girl or that guy, failed algebra test, and pimple.

Before Sissy even reached her locker, Carrie Jones rushed up to her. "Oh my God, I heard about you and Rusty. What happened?"

"Nothing," Sissy said, wanting to crawl into her locker.

This was how it had been since Rusty had broken up with her. She'd heard the rumors that were going around. She hadn't put out, and that was why Rusty left. He was a senior, and she was too young for him — a prude.

In this, her sophomore year, she had been floating above the panic of unpopularity because of Rusty, but now her safety net was gone. She walked to English class keeping her head down, hoping and praying she wouldn't see Rusty. She ducked into the classroom and sat in her assigned seat near the back of the room, thank God. The bell rang, and she felt the tightness in her throat loosen a little.

Wayne Glaus, a stocky, baby-faced wrestler, tapped her on the shoulder from behind.

"Sorry Rusty dumped you," he said, "but a lot of the guys have been talkin' about you if that makes you feel better."

"Thanks," she said, then turned back around. A warm glow of hope came over her.

CHAPTER SIX

Vee glared at the trucker who sat across from her in the red vinyl booth of a 76 truck stop in Flagstaff, Arizona. He had just walked over and sat down with her like they were old friends.

"Hey, sweetheart, where you headed?" he asked, a toothpick sticking out of his mouth.

She didn't need to hear the accent to know he was from New Jersey or Long Island. His slicked-back hair and open shirt gave him away.

"What gives you the right to come over here and invade my space?" she snarled. "You with your white male superiority complex, brutalizing the underprivileged of the world for centuries."

The trucker looked like she'd just snorted fire out her nostrils. "Fuckin' A, lady," he said, and scooted out of the booth. "You need to get laid or somethin', don't you?"

He walked over to another guy who was

sitting at the counter and motioned toward her with his thumb, then started laughing.

Vee put her head in her hands and stared into the coffee cup in front of her. She'd gone to Phoenix to stay with a fellow member of the Freedom Revolutionary Party, but Shayla knew about the bust in L.A. and was too nervous about the cops finding Vee at her house, so she had made Vee leave.

She couldn't go to San Francisco or New York or Boston, where all her friends were, of course. She was supposed to be underground. The last two nights she'd spent sleeping in her car. But with no cash, she couldn't go on like this.

"Shit," she said under her breath, a wave of loneliness rolling up from her chest, trying to make its way out her eyes.

She got up and went to the bathroom. She looked in the mirror as she washed her face, hands, and armpits with paper towels. Her shoulder-length hair was cut straight at the bottom, and she wore no makeup. She wondered if she should try to look more like a traditional, bourgeois female. She put her hands in her hair and tried to fluff it up, then growled at the mirror, not sure exactly whom she was angry at but knowing that anger was necessary for her survival.

Digging a tattered scrap of paper out of her jeans pocket, she went to the pay phone, slipped some coins in, and dialed the number.

"Hello," the voice of a child said on the other end.

Vee almost hung up, but she looked up and saw the trucker staring at her. "Hello," she said. "May I speak to Aletta Honor?"

"Mama, telephone!" Randy yelled.

Aletta picked up the receiver and tried to sound sweet. "Hello, this is Aletta."

"Hello, my name is . . . um, Vicki Halbert," a woman's voice said. "I'm your second cousin, I guess. We have the same greatgrandparents. Your grandpa was my grandpa's brother."

Aletta sat very still, trying to catch up with what she'd just heard.

"Hello?" Vee said.

"Yes, yes, I'm here," Aletta said. "I'm just surprised."

"Yeah, well, I've known I had relatives in Oklahoma for a while. My dad did this big genealogy of our family . . . seems like the only thing he ever did. Anyway, I'm kinda traveling across the country and thought I would stop in and meet you face-to-face."

Vee paused for a moment to let that sink in.

"If you'll have me, of course."

"Well, of course, Vicki," Aletta said, laughing. "My lands, I can't believe this. My favorite uncle Joe's name was Halbert, and my mama's maiden name, a course. This is mighty excitin', really."

"Yes, it is. I haven't seen any family in a long time. I can show you the book my father made. It's fascinating," Vee said with genuine enthusiasm, surprising herself. "I'm in Arizona. I can be there in a couple of days if that's all right."

Aletta hesitated for a moment. *A couple of days? Company in a couple of days?* "Sure, a few days is fine," she said.

"Great. Oh, by the way, I changed my name from Vicki to Victory, but everyone just calls me Vee. Well, my money's about out on the phone. I'll see you then."

"All righty, see you then." Aletta hung up the phone and sat down to stare at it for a few minutes. She'd been hoping it was Charlie, just as she had every time the phone rang. He'd called her only once since they'd gone dancing, and promised to take her out Thursday night, but here it was Friday and she hadn't heard from him.

Instead of Charlie, it had been a relative from her mama's side of the family who was showing up out of the clear blue.

When Aletta thought about it, she realized she knew very little about her mama's family. Her uncle Joe had been really close to her mama before he was killed, and she'd known her grandparents, Lillian and Franklin Halbert, but they'd both passed on when she was still a child.

She knew her grandpa Halbert had had a brother and three sisters, and she'd probably met them at some family gathering when she was a child. Her parents had had her when they were over forty, though, so many of her relatives were so much older and a lot of them were dead.

After her daddy and uncle died, her mama didn't keep in contact with hardly any of her folks, so Aletta figured they were just lost. But now this lost relative was coming to visit.

Lord above, I hope she likes children, Aletta thought, then looked around the house strewn with toys, shoes, and homework and wondered how she'd ever get it ready for a guest.

On Saturday morning, Randy got up at seven without even trying and dragged his stuffed dog Henry into the living room. For a wonderful half hour, he was alone, but then Ruby came in. It was most fun when they wanted to watch the same thing, because he got to point at the screen and giggle with somebody else.

They laughed at Scooby Doo together until it was over, then Randy got up to get his Cap'n Crunch cereal started. He liked to let it sit in the milk for at least fifteen minutes before he ate it — the mushier the better. But when he was in the kitchen, Ruby changed the channel to Bugs Bunny. He wanted to watch Underdog, so they fought about it until their mama woke up.

"Now listen here," she said, "I won't have this fightin' between you two anymore. I have the black paddle, and I'll use it on you if you can't get along. We got a guest comin'."

That shut them up fast. His mama had gotten the black paddle after his daddy left them because she said she had to keep discipline without a man around to help her. It was a three-foot piece of wood with a carved handle and a leather strap at the end of the handle to give the spanker a way to loop a hand in to get more grip. It was painted jet black and had holes drilled into the ends so it would blister your butt if you got spanked with it.

Aletta had never used it on them and had

only spanked Randy twice in his life with her hand, but she threatened them with it when she was really mad.

After a few minutes of he and Ruby staying quiet, his mama called out from the kitchen, her voice nice now. "Do y'all want pancakes or have you had breakfast already?"

He looked at Ruby, put his finger to his mouth, and slid his cereal bowl full of straw-colored mush behind the couch. "I want some!" he called to his mama.

"Pancakes! Yes!" Ruby yelled.

At noon, Jimmy showed up to take them for the afternoon. Aletta was so wound up with cleaning the house — vacuuming for an hour, dusting and blocking the TV, making Randy get up and take out the trash and pick up his room — that Randy was glad when he heard Jimmy's car rumbling outside.

His daddy walked in without knocking.

"Jimmy, please, I've asked you a hundred times to knock," Aletta said as she turned the corner toward the front door. She stopped cold and put a hand over her mouth. Randy and Ruby just stood staring.

The carnage of Jimmy's face was shocking. It was bruised, swollen, and red-rimmed around his eyes, especially on the left side, and his lip was fat and had stitches in it.

"Y'all look like you've seen a ghost," he said.

"What happened, Daddy?" Ruby asked, her voice breaking.

He put his hand on her shoulder. "Ah, honey, I fell down some stairs. It looks worse than it is, though. I'm healin', and it makes the color come out more."

He looked up at Aletta, and from the look they exchanged, Randy knew his mama was aware of what had really happened.

"What are y'all doin' today?" Aletta asked, trying to sound like everything was fine.

Jimmy walked to the hall closet and opened the door. "It's so pretty out, I thought I'd take them out to see a few of the places where I grew up." He reached into the closet and pulled out a shotgun.

Jimmy pulled back the wood belly of the shotgun and looked into the open chamber. "I'm goin' turkey hunting with a few guys. I figure with a real place of my own, I can keep my gun now."

Randy could see the concern in his mama's face, but she didn't say anything. She just walked into the kitchen.

Jimmy turned away but then stopped. "I quit drinkin'," he said so Aletta could hear him.

Randy felt his stomach flop over. He'd heard his daddy say this before, and each of those times, he'd felt the same thing: hope beyond what he could ever say, like the biggest birthday wish you could ever have. If his daddy really did quit drinking, it would mean everything, Randy figured. He wouldn't have to be scared of him anymore or of him hurting his mama. His mama would be happy and would have more fun. And most important of all, his parents, the two people he loved most in the world, wouldn't hate each other.

Aletta came out of the kitchen carrying a sponge. "Really?" she said, like she didn't believe but wanted to.

"Yeah, so you can stop sending people by to fix me," Jimmy said.

Aletta went back into the kitchen. "I was thinkin' about the kids, Jimmy," she said.

Randy noticed his parents talked to each other from different rooms all the time. His mama would talk, but it seemed like she figured if she was just talking out loud to the air, it was only pretend talking, like she wasn't really giving his daddy the time of day in real life.

"Maybe you'll think about getting back together now?" Jimmy asked. "Or do you have another boyfriend already?"

"Put that gun away before you pick up the baby."

Randy heard the door that led from the kitchen out into the garage open, then slam shut, and knew it was his mama's way of telling his daddy to leave. She was through talking to the air.

Randy bit his lip so hard it made him jump when his daddy didn't make a move to leave but walked to the garage door and opened it instead.

"Now what?" he heard his mama say.

"I just thought you'd want to know that Clester Henry died," Jimmy said, just his head pushed into the garage. "He was flyin' one a them little two-seater planes, and he went down out near Shawnee."

Randy listened to hear his mama's response, but all he heard was Ruby saying, "Come on, let's go if we're goin'."

"Just thought you'd want to know," Jimmy said, then shut the door.

With the big gun in the trunk of his black Trans Am, Jimmy drove Ruby, Gyp, and Randy north out of town. Randy didn't know where Sissy was half the time anymore, and she was gone today. The road they were on was different from the one Aletta took to Union City, but it had the same views.

"Look at the baby horses, Daddy. I want one," Ruby said, looking out the tiny window in the backseat. "You wouldn't ever have to get me another birthday or Christmas present for the rest of my whole life."

Jimmy just chuckled.

Randy looked at Ruby and saw her bright green eyes go dark. He wished his daddy would just get her a darn horse. She'd been asking for one for as long as Randy could remember anything. Her half of their bedroom was covered with horse stuff — posters, blankets, books, and little plastic horses.

"I mean it," Ruby said under her breath, looking down at her lap.

After twenty minutes, Jimmy stopped on the side of a dirt road, and they got out of the car. Just beyond a dilapidated barbed-wire fence was a small, abandoned shack sitting in the middle of a field with a broken-down windmill behind it.

Jimmy held Gyp in one arm, pulled up on the top wire of the fence with the other, and stepped on the bottom wire with his foot. They ducked through the gap, then Jimmy stepped over the top of the wires to get on the other side.

"This is where I lived after we moved from Chickasha when I was about fifteen," Jimmy said as they walked across the wet field toward the little wood structure that looked worse off than most tree houses Randy had seen. "Six of us lived in here until my brothers moved to California."

Randy couldn't believe people could live like this. They stepped into the open door of the one-room shack. It was musty inside, with sun streaming through cracks in the frame. Randy thought the dust motes looked like thousands of tiny flying saucers. The sound of their footsteps was loud on the wood floor as they walked around and looked at the broken-down furniture.

Randy looked out the window. There was nothing but land, the windmill, a little pond, and a few cows in the distance. The sky seemed to go on forever above him, and he felt lonely and sad for his father.

"Look here," Jimmy said, and pointed at a small hole in the wall. "This is a bullet hole."

"What from?" Ruby asked.

Jimmy laughed a little, remembering. Gyp was grabbing at his beat-up face, so he shifted him to the other arm. "Well, after Ray got big enough to stand up to my daddy, the two of them just couldn't be in the same room together. So one night at dinner, my daddy's yellin' at Ray about letting one of the goats get loose that day, and Ray's tryin' to tell him that he didn't do it.

When my daddy wouldn't listen — which he never did, he was a mean son of a bitch — Ray just gets up, pulls the twenty-two rifle off the rack on the wall, and shoots right above Daddy's head. This is where the bullet went in."

"Wow," Randy said. "I bet he was in trouble."

"Yeah, it wasn't too long after that that he and Felton took off for California."

They walked outside again and went around to the back of the shack, avoiding mud puddles as they went. It had rained pretty hard a few nights before.

"I remember hunting all this land," Jimmy said, pointing to a line of trees in the distance that ran along a creek. "It wasn't for sport back then. It's how we survived."

"What did you hunt this time of year?" Ruby asked.

As they walked toward a barn that looked like it would blow over on the next windy day, Randy watched for cow patties and listened.

"The only thing you can hunt in the spring is wild turkey," Jimmy said, and tossed Gyp up in the air as they walked. Gyp laughed harder the higher he went. "All the animals are with their young in spring. I remember shooting a squirrel in the spring once. When she fell, I saw about six or seven little babies look over the branch down at their mama on the ground. Her teats were all big and swollen like she'd just been nursing them."

Randy looked up at his father, wondering if he could really be his son.

"That's so sad," Ruby said.

"Oh, I felt terrible," Jimmy said. "Just awful. I never did that again, that's for sure."

Randy let out a sigh of relief. Maybe he hadn't been adopted after all.

Jimmy stopped in the shadow of the small barn and looked above the large open barn doors. The barn, like the house, didn't have even a hint of paint left on it, if it had ever been painted at all.

Randy followed his daddy's gaze to a piece of round metal that hung limply above their heads.

"What is it, Daddy?" Ruby asked.

Jimmy gave Gyp to her. "It's a basketball rim. The one thing I ever remember my daddy givin' to me was that rim." He pretended to dribble twice to his right, then went up for a jump shot. Before he could let go of the pretend ball, though, he grabbed his side and winced. "Ouch," he said, but continued before they could question him. "I came home from school one day and it was hangin' up there, looking just a little better than it does now. My daddy said it was my ticket outta here. I musta taken fifty thousand shots out here."

"But it's all dirt and there ain't no backboard," Ruby said, looking around at her daddy's impossible ball court.

Jimmy smiled. "I tell ya, I got good real quick because if I missed, the ball would go right into the barn, roll over some hay, and stop in a pile of horse crap."

Randy laughed, and Ruby looked up at her daddy with total admiration. "Maybe you can teach me some more when we get home, Daddy," she said. "I want to shoot better for next season."

Jimmy put his hand on her shoulder, and they all walked into the barn. It was cooler inside, and the sounds of the birds' flapping wings ricocheted off the dilapidated walls, making it a little spooky.

"A lot of times, I'd have animal carcasses hangin' up from these beams, waitin' to be skinned," Jimmy said.

"I bet your mama and daddy were so proud of you huntin' animals for y'all to live on," Ruby said.

Jimmy looked up, then laughed. "I guess they were, but they never said nothin'," he said, then paused before continuing. "I never remember either of them sayin' 'thank you' or 'I love you,' neither one."

"Never once?" Ruby asked.

"Nope," Jimmy said.

Randy looked at his daddy. "Wow, that's weird," he said.

"Yeah." Jimmy's eyes turned skyward again, like he was looking for something in the rotted slats of the barn's ceiling. "You'd a thought it woulda been livin' so poor that was the hardest, but it wasn't the hardest part by a long shot."

Randy didn't know how he knew this, but all of a sudden he realized that his daddy was looking up to keep from crying. He went over and put his arm around Jimmy's waist and leaned against him.

Jimmy messed up Randy's hair. "Y'all are good kids," he said. "I love you."

CHAPTER SEVEN

Aletta yanked on the cord three times as hard as she could, but the damn mower wouldn't start. It had been a few hours since Jimmy took the kids. She knew they'd be back soon, and then her lawn would stay a mess yet another day. It was already an embarrassment to her, overgrown with weeds and tall grass, thanks to the spring rains. She figured all the folks who thought she was off her rocker with the psychic business, and there were plenty, must assume she was poor white trash to boot.

When she caught her breath, she looked down at the rusty old lawn mower and felt grief and anger coming up from her belly, rising into her chest. Ever since Jimmy had told her about Clester, she'd been doing her chores like she was one of Gyp's wind-up toys, her body moving but her head and heart not there at all. It was the damn mower not starting that let her feelings creep in just enough.

She just couldn't believe Clester was gone. She should have saved him. She wasn't sure how, but she knew a smarter or stronger or better person than her would've figured it out.

Just then, all of her anger and emotion swelled up inside her, shot down her arm, and yanked on that cord. The mower belched once, twice, then started with a roar.

Aletta straightened up and stared at the mower. She felt the power of her anger inside her like a strong drink. But there was something else, another feeling that lay below the anger and even self-doubt. Some kind of questioning. It was a sense that what she thought she knew about life and her role in it was on shaky ground.

"Lord," she whispered, "what do you want from me?"

She pushed the mower across the high grass and finally let herself cry about Clester, and then she thought about Corliss and cried for him too. Her sadness turned to guilt, and her tears turned bitter. "I'm not any good at this," she said aloud, her words drowned out by the deafening lawn mower. "I can't do this anymore," she cried, looking toward the cloudless sky. "I don't understand what you want."

Between the roaring mower and her conversation with God, she didn't even notice the pickup truck that pulled up in front of the house. She kept talking out loud and pushing the mower until she finally glanced up and noticed the two people standing in her yard near the sign.

She wiped her face with the back of her hand and stared at them while the mower's engine clamored along. It was an Indian man, probably in his thirties, though it was hard to tell for sure, and a young Indian woman, a rebellious teenager by the looks of her, with her thick eyeliner and black Led Zeppelin T-shirt. They stood watching Aletta patiently, their brown-skinned faces and dark eyes not showing any hint of why they'd come.

The man wore jeans and a cowboy shirt. His black hair was parted in the middle and braids disappeared behind his back. The girl's hair was loose and blew slightly in the ever-present Oklahoma breeze. She seemed to have a little smirk on her face.

I can't deal with this right now, Aletta thought, and pushed the lever to kill the mower's engine.

"Can I help you with somethin'?" she asked, not moving from behind the mower.

"I'm sorry for taking you from your work," the man said. His words seemed chopped off at the ends. "We just went to a celebration with the Cherokee Nation in Tahlequah, and now we are headed back home to Santa Fe, New Mexico. We read about you in *Life* magazine months ago and came to meet you."

Aletta wiped her forehead with the back of her dirty hand. Ever since the article had come out in *Life* magazine about Route 66 and her being a part of it, she'd had folks coming to see her from all over the country, mainly travelers passing through on their way to somewhere else, like these two.

"I'm not really working today," she said, trying to steady her shaky voice. "I got guests comin' in and not enough time to get ready."

"I understand," the man said. "We need to get going anyway, but first, may I give you something?"

"Dad, she doesn't want it," the girl said.

Aletta looked at him, not sure she understood what he'd said, her head feeling light and a little dizzy. Before she could respond, the man went to the white truck and reached inside. The girl climbed into the passenger seat.

Aletta walked closer to the truck as the man turned back toward her. He had a handsome face with high cheekbones and deep eyes. They met at her sign. He held out a piece of cloth that was wrapped around something.

"I believe I am supposed to give this to you," he said.

She took the cloth and opened it. Inside was a feather, about eight inches long and beautiful — white at the base for about two inches and then a deep chocolate brown. Something inside her stirred. That feeling came up again, the one underneath the anger and the sadness.

"This is just lovely," she said, unable to really get a grasp on what was happening.

"It comes from the eagle," he said, and smiled.

Aletta just looked at him.

"It was very good to meet you, Ms. Honor," the man said, and walked to his truck, opened the door, and got in. "You should get back to your grass."

As he started the truck, a question formed in Aletta's mind. "You said you were supposed to give this to me. Why?" she asked.

The Indian smiled again. "I don't know. I thought you might understand." He shrugged. "Perhaps one day." The girl watched her through the rear window, and he waved as the truck made its way onto Main Street and headed west toward the sunset.

Aletta stood there with the feather in the palm of her hand. Suddenly, the image from her dream of the bird flying out of the dark cave where her mother had disappeared came to her. Her mother, she thought, her mind grasping at something just beyond its reach. Then she got it. Her mother in the dream had been dark-skinned, brown like the people who had just left her with this feather. She looked up, searching the street, hoping to see the truck so she could stop the Indians and invite them into her house. But they had disappeared as quickly as they'd shown up.

She looked back down at the feather, and another tear, this time unexpected and unwanted, slid down her cheek. She wiped it away roughly with her hand, smearing dirt all over her face. She went inside, put the feather down on the dining room table, then headed back out to get to work. She might not know how to use her gift right or understand about Indians bringing feathers to her, or why she couldn't just be at peace, but there was one thing she knew and knew well, and that was hard work.

Jimmy and the kids pulled up as Aletta raked cut grass into garbage bags. Her head felt swollen and throbby from crying.

Jimmy carried a stringer of four nice-sized channel catfish, still barely breathing, toward her.

"Mama, look what Daddy's friend at the river gave us!" Randy and Ruby yelled.

"Billy Long was fishin' on the Caddo, and he wanted you to have these," Jimmy said, smiling as well as he could with his split lip.

Aletta walked over, took Gyp from Ruby, and looked at the fish. "Channel cat are the best eatin', that's for sure. How is Billy?"

"Pretty good. He's got another oil well he's wantin' me to invest in. Says this one's gonna be a gold mine."

"Aren't they always," Aletta said sarcastically.

"Can I fillet them in the backyard?"

She hesitated, then kissed Gyp on the head. She didn't have the energy to make him leave right then, so she replied, "Only because I'm a sucker for a fish fry."

Next door, Joy walked out onto the porch of her beauty shop and lit a smoke. She looked over and saw Aletta and waved, then noticed it was Jimmy she was talking to.

"Hi, Jimmy," Joy laughed. "What happened to you? You look horrible."

Jimmy waved back. "At least I got an excuse," he called.

"And what might that be?" Joy responded, then opened the door of the salon and said as loud as she could, "Girls, you gotta come see Jimmy Honor's face."

Aletta threw up her free hand in exasperation. "Don't say anything, Jimmy. Just fillet the fish and go home," she said.

Jimmy started toward the house but looked back at Joy. "Come on, kids, you wanna play with me in the backyard?" he said as loud as he could.

"Why are Joy and Daddy talkin' like that?" Randy asked as they walked inside.

"Because they like to act like they're kids too sometimes, honey," she said, glancing at Jimmy. "Spoilt, back-talkin' kids."

"Maybe they need the black paddle," Ruby said.

Aletta smiled and took Gyp back to lay him down for his nap.

A few hours later, Aletta looked in her freezer at the white fillets of catfish. "We'll have a fish fry when Vicki, I mean Vee, gets here," she said to Sissy. "That'll cheer us up."

Sissy sat at the kitchen bar doing homework. That and the fact she was wearing her old velour sweatsuit and no makeup told

Aletta she was staying in tonight. She knew it was a big deal for Sissy to stay home on a Saturday night.

"Oh, right, a fish fry will solve all my problems," Sissy said. "It may even bring world peace."

"You know," Aletta said, taking a bag of noodles out of the cabinet for dinner, "you got to get over Rusty someday."

"I got other guys who like me, you know." Sissy glanced up from her homework to catch her mother's expression.

"Well, you're a pretty girl. Course you do," Aletta said.

"It takes a lot more than that to be popular, Mama. You got to have the right people like you."

"You just be yourself, and you'll be fine."

Sissy rolled her eyes, like her mother didn't understand anything, and gathered up her homework. She turned to go, then picked up the eagle feather from the dining room table.

"What's this?" Sissy asked.

Aletta was digging for a pot to boil the noodles in, so she had to turn around to see Sissy. "Some Indians gave that to me today," she said.

Sissy set the feather back down on the dining table, then walked toward her room. "I

don't know about you sometimes, Mama,"
she said.

CHAPTER EIGHT

Vee pumped the gas pedal all the way down to the filthy floorboard. "Shit," she said. "Shit, shit."

No matter what she did, the car's engine kept struggling but was losing the battle. The black midnight sky weighed down on her as she willed the car to continue down Interstate 40 just a few hours east of Albuquerque. The next town on her map was Amarillo, Texas, but that might as well be on the moon, as far as it was from here. Wherever the hell here was.

Finally the big engine surrendered, and she pulled over onto the shoulder of the highway, gravel crunching under the tires. The car heaved, made a loud clanking noise, and then went dead. The only thing that had been between her and crushing loneliness had been the hum of the car engine and Bob Dylan in the eight-track player. But without the noise or the passing of the road beneath her, there was no escaping the fact that if she died out here, no one in the world would really give a damn. Bo might be sad for a few days, *if* he ever found out about her. It was so quiet, so dark, she almost screamed.

"Oh, Lord," she said, rocking a little and wrapping her arms around herself. "Please help me. Please help me."

Vee had been an atheist since she was fourteen, having read the existentialists, but she felt much younger than that now. She was broke, alone, and had nowhere to go. Then a thought pierced through the desperation in her mind. *Don't ever be weak. Be angry, be smart, but never weak.*

She reached into the glove compartment and pulled out the Browning 9 mm and put it in her jacket pocket. She felt better already. Just as she opened her car door, a huge eighteen-wheeler blasted by her, blowing her back against the car. "Oh, my God!" she yelled.

She kicked the car with her Earth shoes, then looked around. Except for the single beam of light that emanated from the Buick's one working headlight, there was nothing but black outside. Above her, like pinholes in a black velvet canopy, were a shocking number of stars.

She reached back inside the car and found the hazard lights and turned them on. *Click hum, click hum, click hum.* They were only on for a minute before she saw headlights coming from behind her.

"Okay," she said to herself. "Use the tae kwan do before the gun if you can." She and a group of her revolutionary women friends had taken martial arts so they could defend themselves against rape, mugging, and renegade cops.

The headlights turned out to be an old truck with a dilapidated camper attached to the bed. It slowed down, then came to a stop in front of her car.

Concerned by the looks of the truck already, Vee shoved her hand in her pocket and gripped the gun tightly when she saw the two men who got out of it. This was her worst nightmare — two men, hillbillies by the looks of them, alone with her in the middle of nowhere. She'd have preferred Richard Nixon and Spiro Agnew to these two. At least the politicians might not rape and kill her. They preferred to have other people perform their murders for them.

As the men got closer, she decided they looked like bears, with their beards and large, barrel-shaped bodies. "You got a problem?" the bigger one asked.

"My car died," she said, her voice tight and short.

"I'm Mack. Mind if I take a look?" he asked.

She shook her head. As Mack went to the driver's side of her car and turned the key in the ignition, the other one just stood and looked at her. When he smiled, she noticed he had more teeth gone than he had left in his head. She looked away, making sure not to do anything that might arouse him.

"Sounds like the tranny or maybe a gasket," Mack said, his drawl slow and thick. He walked slowly back toward her. "Nothin' that could be fixed out here."

She stepped back a few feet, making sure to keep them from surrounding her.

"You want a ride?" Mack asked.

The rumble of their truck filled the air as Vee tried to think. There was no way she was getting in that truck with them. "I can't leave my car," she said. "I'm not coming back this way. I'll just wait here for a while."

"We could pull her to Amarillo," the other one said. "We got a chain in the truck."

Mack shoved his hands in the pockets of his overalls. "Bart says we can pull you with a chain, but you'd have to stay in your own car and steer and brake."

Now that was different.

In another ten minutes, they were all moving down the highway going about thirty-five miles per hour, the truck and the two mountain men inside it pulling Vee along in her car. A full moon rose in front of them like an apparition.

After what seemed like an eternity of creeping along, trying to stay awake, staring into darkness, Vee realized the sky was getting slightly lighter.

She watched as the sun crept above the horizon, a glorious flat orange disc. In the rearview mirror, she caught sight of something else. It was the huge full moon, pale blue, almost white, hovering at the exact same place on the horizon, just opposite the sun.

It was a sliver out of time, a holy moment between day and night, darkness and light, as the sun and the moon mirrored each other, sending a silent greeting across the quiet plains.

For Vee, watching the magnificence of this moment as she was being rescued by two men she'd misjudged terribly, everything she knew seemed to melt away, turning the black and white suffering and oppression of the world into some kind of mysterious movement of Nature.

But then the moon disappeared and the sun came up, turning the world into sharp contrasts of darkness and light once again. Her body ached, her stomach growled, and she needed to pee.

She looked around at the endless flat land covered with scrub brush. "Damn, it's ugly out here," she said out loud, and checked the clip on her gun once again.

Seven hours after they stopped to help Vee, Mack and Bart pulled into a service station on the west end of Amarillo. It was a trip that normally took three hours. They unhooked Vee's car, left it for the mechanic to take a look at, and asked her if she'd like to have breakfast at the diner next door.

She was starving and ordered a huge breakfast. She found out Mack and Bart were brothers who came from a tiny town in the Arizona hills and worked on cars and heavy equipment for a living.

When the check came, Vee reached for it, but Bart grabbed it first. "We got it," he said.

Mack just nodded and gave her a slight smile.

Vee couldn't believe their generosity, especially after dragging her through the night already. She thanked them over and over and gave them both a hug before they got in their truck.

Just before they pulled away, Mack winked at her. "Glad you kept that pistol in your pocket," he said, and laughed a little.

Her mouth dropped open slightly, then she just looked at the ground and smiled a little. "Me too," she said.

After they left, she went into the garage of the service station. The man with LARRY stitched onto his greasy shirt walked over, wiping his hands on a red shop towel. "Well," he said, "it sure don't look good."

By Monday morning, Vee still hadn't arrived, Charlie hadn't called, and the house was already getting cluttered again. Aletta thought she might have some time to fold clothes and watch a few minutes of *All My Children* after she got the kids off to school because she didn't have any appointments set, but right at nine, there was a knock on her door.

Aletta opened the door, a laundry basket tucked under one arm. It was Silvia Rivera with her baby, Miguel junior. She had been Aletta's first customer and one of her biggest supporters in her fight against the Burning Bush Church.

"I'm sorry for not calling, but I was driving by and hoped you could see me," Silvia said. She still hadn't lost her weight from having the baby, and she looked tired. Her straight black hair, usually shiny, hung drably around her pudgy face and sad eyes.

"Come on in," Aletta said.

They went to her office and put their babies on the blue-green shag carpet to play with blocks.

"Is there something specific —" Aletta began after she'd said her prayer, but Silvia interrupted before she could even finish the question.

"Oh, *Dios mío,* it's my husband," Silvia said, her voice high and squeaky like she wasn't breathing much. "We've been fighting and fighting. His mother hates me. I don't know what's going to happen, Aletta. I don't know what to do."

Aletta took a deep breath, held Silvia's hands in her own, then closed her eyes. She waited for the images to come, but none did. She took another breath, adjusted herself on her chair, then waited some more. Nothing.

She cleared her throat nervously. "I'm not getting anything right now."

Silvia looked at her as if she didn't quite

understand. "But you always do. You told me where my husband was when he got into all that trouble. You helped me figure out Miguel junior had swallowed a penny when he got sick that time."

Aletta touched Silvia's face and held her breath, waiting. But nothing came. "I know," Aletta said, shaking her head. "I must just be tired. I'm sorry, but why don't you tell me what's happening anyway? Maybe it'll make you feel better."

So Silvia talked and Aletta listened. Silvia told her how she felt like she wasn't good enough for Miguel or for his mother. She started crying when she realized that this was exactly how she felt with her mother when she was a child, like she could never do anything right.

After half an hour, she wiped her eyes and stood up. "Thank you," she said. "I don't think anyone has ever listened to me like that."

"I'm sorry I didn't get any information for you," Aletta said, giving her a hug.

Silvia pulled a five-dollar bill out of her purse and laid it on the desk. "Maybe this is what I needed more," she said.

After Silvia left, Aletta felt vaguely concerned she hadn't seen anything with Silvia. She loaded Gyp in his high chair and fed him some Gerber yams, realizing it was probably because she was tired, exhausted really, from working so hard all weekend on the yard and the house.

When her two o'clock appointment called to cancel a few hours later, however, Aletta felt relieved. She'd get a good night's sleep, then be back to her regular self tomorrow.

The next morning, Aletta dropped Gyp at Silvia's, then drove the mile outside of town to the small brick Methodist church, where it seemed like a hundred cars were parked for Clester Henry's funeral service. She snuck in after the service began and stood at the back of the crowded sanctuary, tears streaming down her face as family and friends eulogized a man who'd been as familiar in this town as the Okay Flour Mills that towered over Main Street. She couldn't bring herself to go to Clester's wife, Rhondalin, or their three children, because she thought she might just faint or start crying uncontrollably, so as soon as the service ended, she bolted for the Pink Pumpkin and drove back.

Once home, Aletta composed herself just enough to be presentable for her eleven o'clock appointment, a man from Blythe whose sister-in-law had seen her the November before. Aletta didn't remember the sister-in-law but acted like she did when Tru Leftwich introduced himself, then sat on her couch, wincing in pain. Tru was in his fifties, a foreman at a mining company who was having stomach trouble.

Aletta said her prayer out loud while praying inside that she'd be able to stay composed and, even more importantly, see something. When she took Tru's hand in hers, she got an image right away — Charlie Baxter picking her up in his arms and spinning her around as they laughed. She opened her eyes, shook her head a little, then smiled at Tru, who was watching her intently, the creases in his forehead like question marks directed toward her.

She cleared her throat, then closed her eyes again. This time, she saw Clester Henry at the ball game, the last time she'd seen him, then an image came of Randy's cereal bowl from this morning as it fell to the kitchen floor, milk and soggy bits of cereal spilling everywhere. She wondered if she'd gotten all the sharp pieces cleaned up. When Tru squeezed her hand a little, she caught herself thinking and almost panicked. Her hands started to sweat, and she was certain Tru would notice.

Finally, she took a deep breath, pulled

herself together as best she could, and opened her eyes. "Where is the pain located?" she asked.

Tru put his hand on his upper belly. "Right here," he said.

"Ulcer," Aletta said. She pulled her hand away, wiped it on her jeans, then took his hands again.

"That's what the docs tell me," Tru said. "None of 'em can do a durn thing about it, though. I been off coffee and spicy food and even fried chicken for a while."

Aletta closed her eyes again and did her best to look like she was seeing something important. She couldn't believe this was happening, but right now it was important not to get caught and blow her livelihood out of the water.

"Well," she said, "this is gonna sound strange, but I'm getting that you need to drink cabbage juice from raw cabbages."

When she looked at him again, Tru had a funny look on his face, a mix of disbelief and hope all at the same time. "Cabbage juice?" he asked. "That sounds horrible."

"But it should help you feel better."

"How do I tell Gertie to make it for me?"

"Now, that I don't know," Aletta answered. She didn't want to act like she'd done it before.

Of course, she had. When Jimmy'd started to get an ulcer back when he first got his job at Southwestern Bell, she'd used a blender, then put the pulverized cabbage through a strainer to get the juice. Her mama was the one who'd told her about the cabbage juice, and God only knew where she'd gotten it from. Seemed like old farm women knew recipes for every hurt or holiday by heart. Jimmy had been like new in under two weeks.

"Been hard on the job lately, lotsa stress?" Aletta asked nervously.

Tru chuckled. "Oh, you bet."

"Problems with the union or new management, somethin' like that?"

Aletta recognized the look in his brown eyes. He was impressed.

"Yeah, the union's pushin' for a new labor agreement, and management's goin' bonkers. I'm caught right in the middle flopping around like a fish on dry land." He put his head in his hands and sighed.

After a few more guesses, close enough to accurate to just get by, Aletta showed Tru to the door.

"I'll try that cabbage juice. Let you know how it turns out," he said as he handed her a check for twelve dollars. "I was sure skeptical, but you're good, I got to admit."

140

She closed the door behind him, leaned her back against it, and groaned. It hadn't been a fluke the day before with Silvia. She couldn't believe it, having had images playing before her every day since she could remember, but the visions were really gone. Now she realized how people could fake this stuff well enough to keep folks wondering, but there was no way she could keep this up. Just then a thought came to her: *Where the hell is that feather? Does this have something to do with it?* She knew just what she was going to do. It wasn't on the dining room table or under it anymore, nor was it in the kitchen, even though she did find a stray piece of cereal bowl and tossed it in the trash.

She started opening drawers and digging through them, looking under chairs and couches, picking up figurines and toys.

Just then, the phone rang. "Damn," she said out loud, then answered it. "Hello?"

"Aletta, hi, this is Vee Halbert, your cousin Vicki?"

Aletta rolled her eyes and put a hand through her hair. "Oh, yes, hello."

"I'm at the downtown bus station in Oklahoma City. I didn't know if it was too far for you to come, or I could hitch a ride to you possibly."

Aletta looked around as if she might find her sanity waiting nearby, ready to be of assistance. "Oh," she said. "You're at the bus station. I thought . . . Anyway, of course I can come get you. You can't hitch a ride. Don't be silly."

When Aletta hung up the phone, she sat down on a bar stool for a moment and closed her eyes. Things were happening too fast. She felt completely out of control, but she forced herself to take a breath. "I need help, Lord," she said.

When she opened her eyes, she looked up and right in front of her was the eagle feather, sticking up out of a small vase on top of the faux fireplace's mantel. One of the kids must have put it there. She went over, snatched it out of the vase, and marched outside.

She took the lid off the metal trash can that sat on the side of the house, dropped the feather into it, then slammed the lid down with a crash. Maybe now things would go back to normal again.

Aletta pulled into the driveway of the Greyhound bus station and looked around. It was a dismal place, gray and sad, with people who matched the décor. She realized she had no idea what her second cousin looked like, but as soon as she stopped in a loading zone right up front, a young woman with brown hair and straight bangs across her forehead peeked into the passenger-side window.

"Are you Aletta?" she asked. She looked like she was weary, and her light brown eyes were ringed with red.

"Yes. You must be Vee," Aletta said, and got out of the car.

Aletta didn't know if she should give her a hug, but when they met at the back of the car, she decided not to try. Not only did Vee look tired beyond her years, but there was a toughness about her that didn't invite much affection.

After stowing Vee's duffel bag in the trunk, they drove away.

"This is a classic," Vee said. "I love these old cars."

"Me too," Aletta said, smiling. "I didn't realize you were taking a bus."

Vee played with a tear in her camel suede jacket. "Yeah, it's easier and cheaper than having a car. I left West Virginia a few weeks ago, and I've been visiting friends in different cities since then. Just wanted to see the country before settling down and getting a job."

143

Aletta nodded as she pulled onto the highway. "Good for you. I never did nothin' like that, and I sure wish I would've. Got married and started havin' babies right outta high school."

"Like most American women. They think that's their only choice."

"I sure love my kids, though," Aletta said, then saw a huge, beautiful bird flying into a stand of trees near the highway. It made her remember the eagle feather and losing her gift. Her hands started sweating. *I don't have time for a houseguest right now,* she thought, then asked, "So where you headed?"

"I don't know," Vee said. "I think I'm just going to see where the road takes me."

"Really?" Aletta started to tap her wedding ring against the steering wheel, a nervous habit. Then she realized, for the thousandth time, that the ring wasn't there anymore.

CHAPTER NINE

Vee had to keep her jaw clenched tight as they drove into downtown Okay so she wouldn't say something rude. She'd been in some pathetic little towns before, but outside of Reedley, this one had to be the worst. A big, defunct flour mill hulked overhead, dwarfing the few worn-out shops on either side of Main Street. She decided she would call the architectural style of the stores and homes she saw post-white-breadism. There was green grass in most of the yards and a few flowers growing in planters out in front of Snyder's Drugstore, but other than that, this place came in shades of brown.

These are the descendants of poor pioneers, Vee thought, looking around at all the conservative-looking white people walking down the street and driving in cars. Their only dream was to own a plot of land and be free to work it. She knew there wasn't a single person she'd be able to relate to, even though she'd come from this very same stock.

Aletta turned off Main and drove down a side street into a neighborhood of tiny clapboard houses. She parked in front of a baby-blue house with two plastic flamingoes in the lawn.

"Wait here. I'll be right back," Aletta said to Vee. She went inside, then emerged with a baby in her arms.

Of course, Vee thought. *One of a bunch, I'm sure.*

"This is Gyp," Aletta said, handing him to Vee as she got behind the wheel. "I hope you like kids."

"Oh, sure," Vee said, then held the baby like he was an explosive as they drove the few short blocks to Aletta's olive-green home. When they turned into the driveway, Vee lost her grip on Gyp, and he tipped sideways. She almost panicked, but he laughed, showing her the nubs of teeth that were just starting to grow in. She looked at him curiously, tipped him the other way, and he laughed again. This time, his dimples and untarnished joy got the best of her, and she gave him a crooked grin in return.

"You're real good with him," Aletta said

as she got out of the car.

"Oh, uh, thanks," Vee replied as she worked her way out of the car with Gyp, making sure to keep both hands tight around his body. She didn't even notice Joy peeking out the window from the beauty shop next door or pay attention to the sign in the yard that Aletta had covered with a tablecloth, since she wasn't open for business.

Inside the house, Aletta mercifully took the baby, and Vee let her eyes adjust to the darkness, but when they did, she wished they hadn't. The place was a nightmare of lower-middle-class Americana. She looked around at the furniture — not a single piece had any character or quality. Most of it was clearly fake wood veneer or plastic. And there were little figurines everywhere. Cobalt blue musical instruments, windmills, cute little people, and shot glasses lined the top of the kitchen cabinets, while animal figurines sat on the fake fireplace's mantel, the center of the dining room table, and the top of the enormous stereo cabinet. The multicolored shag carpet was as worn as the Formica counter in the kitchen.

Compared to her many childhood homes — falling-down piles of junk — this was quite nice. But she had come to believe that being really poor was somehow more honorable than being pathetically on the verge of the middle class.

Vee could tell Aletta had cleaned up for her, because she knew that with a houseful of kids, it had to be more cluttered than this normally. *I'm sure the husband does nothing to help out either,* she thought.

"Your place looks great," she lied. "I really appreciate you letting me stay here," she continued, telling the truth. This little town was a perfect place to hide out. When she'd first thought of reaching out to one of the relatives listed in the family tree her father had compiled, she had two strong feelings come over her. The first was a glimmer of hope, chirping up from inside her chest like a sparrow, that maybe she could find some real family. But she'd laughed the little bird away bitterly and realized that finding some long-lost relative could be the way she could hide from the law with a free roof over her head and food to eat.

"Oh, thanks," Aletta said. "It's humble, but it's home. You'll sleep back this way."

Aletta led Vee down the hall, pointing to the first door. "That's my room."

"You and your husband's?" Vee asked.

Aletta smiled sardonically and removed Gyp's fingers from her mouth. "Oh, no, just me. We've been divorced for over a year now."

"How many kids do you have?" Vee asked.

"Just the four," Aletta said, continuing down the hall.

"You do all this by yourself?" Vee asked.

"Oh, Lord, I do my best, but mostly the days go by and somehow it all happens one way or another."

Vee stopped following for a moment to let that sink in. She was genuinely impressed. She'd figured Aletta was a housewife, brainwashed into a life of subservience and manual labor, taking care of a husband like one of the children as a trade-off for financial support.

Even if she is doing this all alone, Vee decided, *she still probably never thinks about anything more than diapers, dinner, and paying the bills, getting all of her entertainment and passion from watching television.* The lady had gotten herself brainwashed all right, and it had really backfired.

Aletta opened the door to her office. "I'm sorry, it's just a couch, but I hear it's pretty comfortable to sleep on."

"This is fine," Vee said, taking in the *Elk in the Forest* painting.

"Well, make yourself at home," Aletta said.

149

"I gotta change the baby, then we'll sit down for a visit."

Vee sat down on the couch heavily. "Shit," she said under her breath as soon as Aletta had left. She was definitely going to keep in touch with her colleagues so she could get the hell out of here as soon as she thought it was safe enough. Maybe she'd go to Mexico or back to Cuba.

She put her head in her hands, thinking once again how stupid they'd been to try to rob a bank. Their motives for holding up American Federal in Los Angeles had been right on: raising money for the party while doing damage to a stalwart capitalist institution with ties to many top governmental oppressors. But they had rushed it and hadn't done enough reconnaissance to determine how best to handle the job. They had been so anxious to make a real impact, not just a rally or a conference or a newsletter, but something that would get noticed by the top party people. She groaned, remembering what had happened.

She'd been in the getaway car, her VW, in front of the bank, and when she saw the cop cars screeching into the bank parking lot, she sped away. After she left L.A., she read in the *Los Angeles Times* that two of her three comrades who'd been inside had been arrested, but it seemed that Lucius had gotten away somehow.

Bo would've been with them too, but at the last minute, he had backed out because he'd sprained an ankle playing Frisbee on Venice Beach and couldn't run. Of course, he had still been in charge of the guns they used, and his fingerprints were probably all over them. Looking around the small room with its calico curtains, cluttered black metal desk, and ceramic horsehead lamp, she wondered where he was. *Surely it couldn't be this bad,* she thought.

As she looked around, an object on the desk caught her eye. She went over and picked it up. It was a small, round crystal ball that fit perfectly in the palm of her hand.

Aletta changed the baby and pondered her situation. How was she going to entertain a houseguest and somehow avoid having a personal meltdown at the same time? Vee seemed all right — a little stiff, maybe, and kind of quiet, but she'd loosen up after she got settled in. Aletta's brow furrowed as she pinned the diaper. The question was, how long did she plan on staying?

Aletta groaned, put Gyp on her hip, and

walked back to her office. Inside, Vee was holding the little crystal ball in her hand.

"This is beautiful," Vee said. "Where'd you get it?"

Aletta dropped her eyes. "Oh, I've had it since I was a little girl."

There was no way she was going to get into that story right now. But seeing the gift from the old gypsy woman made her think of her mama and how she'd blamed Aletta's gift for bringing evil into the house, visiting death upon her daddy and uncle. These memories always brought a pain that shot right through her heart. Now that she thought about it, the guilt and hurt she was feeling over Clester and Corliss was very similar to how she used to feel around her mama.

Over a year ago, Eugene had helped her find the ball in the old well her mama had thrown it down so many years ago. She'd hoped finding it would bring some kind of closure to her past so that she'd be able to finally live in peace. The peace hadn't come, though.

"How 'bout some lunch?" Aletta asked, trying to sound breezy.

Vee followed her into the dining room, still holding the crystal ball. "You should put this out where you can see it," she said, and placed it on an empty vase that sat on the fireplace mantel, the same one Aletta had found the feather in earlier that morning. The milky white ball fit perfectly on top of the green hourglass-shaped vase.

Aletta put Gyp in his playpen in the dining room, a location that allowed her to see him from the kitchen, and began opening cans of food for lunch.

"I guess your life's pretty mellow, living in such a small town, not much going on," Vee said, looking at the figurines and framed photographs that sat around the house.

"Oh, I wouldn't say that," Aletta answered. Her voice sounded high and strained even to her own ears.

Vee picked up a large frame and looked at the photo of Aletta and her kids with some other adults standing in front of her house next to a sign she couldn't make out.

"What's this picture?" Vee asked.

Aletta looked up from the Campbell's Chicken and Stars soup she was heating. "Oh, that's the day I got my picture taken for *Life* magazine."

"Really? You were in *Life*?"

Aletta wiped her hands on a dish towel and went to the china hutch, which was filled with a mismatched assortment of dishes. She opened a drawer and pulled out a magazine. "Page twenty-eight, I think," she said, and handed it to Vee.

Vee opened the magazine and read. Aletta watched her out of the corner of her eye as she mixed mayonnaise into canned tuna. She knew Vee couldn't have read the sign out front, since it was covered, and she was a little worried how she would react.

"I can't find . . . Oh, here it is," Vee said, then started to read. " 'We also found Aletta Honor, mother of four, who has a homemade sign out in front of her house on Route 66 advertising herself as a psychic. The locals say Mrs. Honor has a gift that is as near as they've come to magic, revealing the pasts and futures of pure strangers as if they were bedtime stories read from a book.' "

Vee didn't look up from the magazine right away but seemed to be reading it over again. Aletta watched her closely now, a fork poised over the bowl of tuna fish. Finally, Vee looked at Aletta, her mouth agape. "This says you're a psychic."

"Yes, that's right," Aletta said, laughing nervously.

Vee went to the front door and walked outside. At first Aletta thought she was so offended she was running off, but then she saw Vee walk to the sign, lift the purple tablecloth, and read. Slowly, Vee walked back toward the house.

Aletta quickly poured the soup into bowls and cut the tuna sandwiches in half. "Lunch is ready," she said when Vee came back inside.

"It's so funny. I thought you were . . . ," Vee said.

"What, hon? Just a boring housewife?" Aletta joked.

Vee half smiled. "Can you, you know, read me?" she asked nervously.

"Come on over here and sit down," Aletta said, placing the food on opposite sides of the kitchen bar. When they were seated, she reached across and took Vee's hands in her own.

Vee pulled away. "Maybe you shouldn't," she said.

Aletta grabbed her hands and pulled them to her. "Oh, don't be nervous. I won't bite," she said, smiling. "I can't usually read family anyway." *Right now,* Aletta thought bitterly, *I can't read anyone.*

After a few moments of listening to her stomach growl, wishing she would see something, she opened her eyes. "Not a thing," she said. "Now I know you're kin for sure."

Vee breathed deeply. It seemed to Aletta

she was relieved. She knew a lot of people felt that way — kind of frightened of her gift, of revealing themselves too much.

As they ate, Vee questioned Aletta about being a psychic, but it made Aletta so nervous thinking about it, she changed the subject to their family. It appeared neither one of them had met many common relatives, because the family was so spread out around the country.

"I think I remember meetin' my granddaddy's brother, Uncle Morris, at a wedding. I musta been real young, four or five, because the only reason I remember it bein' a wedding was the big white cake," Aletta said. "That impressed me."

"That's my Grandpa Halbert, my father's father," Vee said.

"Is he still alive?" Aletta asked.

Vee hesitated for a moment before answering. "No, he died a while back."

"Oh, that's too bad. He was a big man, wasn't he? Real tall, big-boned, with a beard that was dark but his hair was silver."

Vee laughed. "That was him. He really stood out in a crowd. And my Grandma Bobbie was so little, only about five foot two."

Aletta smiled. "Isn't this something?"

Vee finished her sandwich and drank

down her iced tea. "I think I met your mother at Aunt Penny's funeral when I was little. Aunt Penny was Grandpa Halbert's half-sister."

"Oh, sure," Aletta said. "I remember when my mama went to that funeral in West Virginia. I was a teenager, and we weren't getting along very well, so I was happy to have the house to myself."

Vee laughed. "I know the feeling."

"You didn't get along well with your folks?" Aletta asked.

"My mom died just after I was born," Vee said. She'd never told anyone her mother died while having her. "And my dad . . . well, I guess you could say he didn't know what to do with me, so we didn't talk much. He died of a heart attack just a few years ago."

Her daddy had died just like he'd lived — without a fight. When he'd had a mild heart attack, his doctors told him the next one would kill him unless he changed his ways. He'd begged Vee to come back from school and take care of him. She refused, because, having battled to change him her whole life, she knew she could never get him to do what the doctors said — quit smoking, eat right, exercise, take his medication regularly. So he died alone. They'd found him on his couch with a cigarette, burnt to the butt, still in his mouth.

"I'm real sorry to hear that. I guess we do have something in common. We've lost both our parents already." Aletta squeezed Vee's hand, but Vee didn't look up to return her gaze.

"I'm really tired," Vee said. "I think I'll lie down if that's all right."

"Course it is, darlin'. The kids'll be home soon, so rest while you can."

"I'll show you the genealogy my dad did when you want me to," Vee said as she walked to her room.

That evening, Aletta shooed everyone into the living room while she made fish sticks for dinner. Ruby and Randy performed a fully choreographed number for their captive audience, Vee, while they waited. Ruby put the needle to the Elton John album, and they stepped and twirled to "Crocodile Rock."

Vee smiled in spite of herself. She closed her book about Malcolm X because she couldn't take her eyes off these pink-cheeked kids.

Ruby and Randy moved with synchronized arm movements and dance steps, giving it their all until the song was over. When they kneeled with their arms raised, Vee clapped for them, and they took several bows.

Sissy moped in the front door with an armful of schoolbooks, bringing a wave of Love's Baby Soft perfume with her. She stopped when she saw Vee. "Who are you?" she asked.

"This is Cousin Vee — that's short for Victory. Remember Mama told us she was comin'?" Ruby said.

"Hi," Vee said, standing up. "I'm just passing through."

Aletta walked in and saw Vee and Sissy sizing each other up, and she could just guess what they were thinking. Sissy was probably wondering, *Who is this skinny, straight-haired, no-makeup city girl in my house?* And Vee looked like she was trying to figure out how she was going to get along with this voluptuous, feather-haired teenager.

"Well," Aletta said, a little too cheerily, "I see y'all have met each other. I'm sure you're gonna have so much in common."

"I'm going to my room," Sissy said, and skulked off.

"She doesn't like me," Vee said after Sissy was gone.

Randy walked to her and held his hand to the side of his mouth like he was telling a secret. "It ain't you. She doesn't like nobody right now 'cause Rusty dumped her."

Aletta smiled. Her kids always seemed to understand more than she expected them to. "He's tellin' the God's honest truth," she said. "Come on, dinner's ready."

Aletta cleaned up the dishes while the kids took their baths. She'd had to threaten both of them with the black paddle to get them to mind her, because they were so excited to entertain Vee. She'd been embarrassed to pull the paddle out in front of their guest, but it was the only thing that made them get ready for bed.

After the kids were in bed, Aletta sat in the living room rocking Gyp to sleep. She wondered what she was going to do if her gift really was gone forever. Jimmy only paid four hundred dollars a month in child support, and that was about one-quarter of what she needed just to get by. If she had really lost her gift, she was in a desperate situation financially. Working at the 7-Eleven or answering phones at an office just wouldn't provide, especially since she'd have to pay for full-time day care. She looked up at the ceiling. "Oh, Mama, what in the world am I gonna do now?" she whispered.

Just as tears were making their way to her eyes, Vee walked in carrying a large leather-bound book. "Hope I'm not interrupting," she said.

"Oh, no, not at all," Aletta said, composing herself. "Come on in."

"This is the genealogy my father put together before he died," Vee offered. "I thought you might want to see it."

"Now, is that the same as a family tree?" Aletta asked, patting Gyp on the back.

Vee smiled at Aletta like she was a child. "Yes, it's a kind of elaborate family tree."

"Well, you can just leave it. I'll take a look at it when I get him to bed."

After she finally got Gyp to stop fussing and fall asleep, Aletta took the book with her to bed. She was even more exhausted than after a normal day of just taking care of four kids on her own because of having a guest as well, so she just flipped through the book.

On the first page was an intricate web of boxes containing names of people and dates. The boxes were connected by lines. For the most part, it was too much information for Aletta to take in, but she did see her mama's name, Nadine Halbert, near the bottom of the page. It was connected to Al-etta's daddy's box, Clovis Jenkins, and below them she found her name. At the other corner of the page was Vee's name connected to her mama and daddy, Lucien and Carol Halbert. There were names of three other kids, two boys and a girl. Strange Vee hadn't mentioned them.

She opened the book and saw that there were newspaper articles, photographs of people she didn't know, and pages of more connected boxes. *He sure put some time into this,* she thought. Just as she leaned over to turn out the light, she caught sight of a page with her own name at the bottom. It was full of boxes and names like the first page, but this one included only her direct lineage.

She traced the lines up past her mama to her Grandma Lillian and Grandpa Frank. Up from Franklin Halbert was a line to Maxwell Halbert, her great-granddad. But here she noticed something she didn't expect. Her great-grandfather Maxwell had two lines coming from his box, indicating he'd been married twice — first to Adelaide Medina, in 1886, and then to Josephine Connelly, in 1897. Next to Adelaide Medina's name, a word was printed with a star next to it: * INDIAN.

Aletta sat straight up and stared at the page. She read it again. Adelaide Medina, Indian, born 1870, died 1892. No longer tired at all, Aletta jumped out of bed, hurried to Vee's room, and knocked on the door.

"Come in," Vee said.

Aletta entered. "What do you know about this Indian woman who was married to our great-granddad?"

Vee's eyes sparkled. "Oh, you mean Adelaide. If that was even her name — I'm sure some white man gave it to her. Yeah, isn't that wild? She was married to Maxwell Halbert and had two sons, our grand-fathers, then she died, I forget how. Maxwell remarried what's-her-name, Josephine? They had three kids. Aunt Penny was one of them."

"So this Indian is our great-grandmother?" Aletta asked in a whisper, her eyes wide.

"Yes, that's right. Isn't that cool? We have a Native American relative. Must mean we're not all bad."

"Do you know anything else about her?"

"Just that I think she's from New Mexico because that's where Maxwell was from. His father was some bigwig in Santa Fe. I think the story is that Maxwell and Adelaide came to Oklahoma in 1889 in the land rush."

"But they were from New Mexico?"

"Yeah. I mean, I think it was still a territory back then, but that's where they were from."

"Excuse me, please," Aletta said, leaving the room and pulling the door closed. She stood there, staring down the dark hallway in her satin nightgown and pink slippers. She thought about the dream she'd had of the dark-skinned mother and about the Indian man from Santa Fe who had come to see her just a few days before. Maybe somewhere in all this was the answer to her losing her ability. *Oh, Lord above,* she thought suddenly, and bolted toward the front door.

She ran outside, past the garage doors, and around to the side of the house. "Oh, no," she gasped. The trash can wasn't there.

Just then, a window rose next door. Joy peeked out in her curlers. "Girl, what in hell are you doin' out there?" she asked.

"I can't find my trash," Aletta said.

The window closed, and Aletta thought Joy must've decided to simply ignore that she'd even spoken. But a moment later, Joy was walking toward her like a rooster strutting across a barnyard. "Your trash is out at the curbside," she clucked. "I asked Earl to take it out with ours this afternoon. I know you never remember, but tomorrow *is* trash day."

"Oh, thank God," Aletta said. She ran to the curbside, took the metal lid off the can, and looked inside.

Joy wasn't far behind. "What in the name of Elvis did you throw out, darlin'?"

"Oh, I can't see a thing," Aletta said. "I'm gonna pull my car over so I can use the headlights."

Joy put her fists on her hips. "You've done lost your ever-lovin' mind. How 'bout I just go get a flashlight?"

Aletta waited impatiently as Joy stomped inside, then came back out a minute later. "Keep your panties on, Earl," Joy called with a wry look at Aletta. "You got to give me just a minute. Aletta's havin' a break-down."

Aletta tried to grab the flashlight from Joy, but Joy pulled it away. "I'll hold it. You look."

Aletta looked on top, hoping it was there, but no luck. She pulled a paper bag full of trash out of the can, and she swung it out wildly. It seemed like she was going to toss it across the yard. Instead, the bottom of the bag broke open and trash spilled all over the grass.

Aletta didn't even seem to notice. Joy groaned and put the flashlight to her forehead in dismay.

"Hey, hey, I need that," Aletta said, grabbing at the flashlight.

Joy pointed the light back into the can. "Well, good grief," she said. "Whatever it is, it must be worth some change."

Aletta looked into the can again. "Aha!" she cried, like she'd made a grand discovery. She reached in and pulled out the eagle feather.

Joy shone the flashlight directly on the feather to make sure she was seeing right. "A feather?" she asked. She really looked worried now.

"Thank you so much for helpin' me find it, Joy," Aletta said. She gave her friend a quick hug, then walked back toward her house.

"I ain't cleanin' up this trash," Joy called.

"Oh, I'll do it in the mornin'," Aletta said happily, and pulled her door shut behind her.

Joy just stood there with the flashlight poised above the trash and her curlers glinting under the moonlight. "Well, I think she's finally cracked," she said finally, and shuffled slowly back inside.

CHAPTER TEN

When Sissy walked into the kitchen the next morning, Vee and her mama were poring over the big leather book as they drank coffee at the bar.

Her mama's face lit up as she read. "Oh, my Lord, this looks like her obituary," Aletta said.

Vee looked over her shoulder. "You're right," she said. "I forgot about that."

"August twelfth, 1892, from the *Daily Oklahoman*," Aletta read. " 'Mrs. Adelaide Halbert, twenty-two, of Okay County, wife of Maxwell Halbert, died on Thursday. It is believed she drowned after falling into the Caddo River.' " Aletta looked up at Vee, excited and breathless. "That's what I saw in my dream. She was at a river."

"Wow," Vee said quietly.

"What are y'all lookin' at?" Sissy asked, trying to see.

Ruby walked in, her shirt buttoned up wrong. Aletta fixed it as she spoke. "This is our family tree. Our relatives from the past are in here. You have a great-great-grandma who's an Indian."

Ruby beamed. "I knew I was an Indian, 'cause I never want to be the cowboy when me and Micki play cowboys and Indians."

"Well, lookee here," Aletta said, reading a page from the genealogy that had been copied from a book. "It seems like our great-great-granddad, Charles Halbert, was some bigwig judge in Santa Fe. He's mentioned in this book about New Mexico as bein' part of somethin' called the Santa Fe Ring. Sounds like a bunch a rich good ole boys got together to control everything."

"That was Maxwell's father," Vee said. "How happy do you think he was his oldest son married an Indian?"

Aletta looked at her with a sparkle of curiosity in her eyes.

"Why didn't we know about havin' an Indian in the family before, Mama?" Sissy asked, spooning cereal into her mouth.

Vee smirked. "It's because up until recently, with the Native American pride movement, it's been considered a terrible shame to marry an Indian or have Indian blood. It was a total embarrassment to the family, so they kept it hidden like a dirty secret. I mean, whites were considered totally superior to Indians and black people for that matter. Did you all know that the KKK was the only law in these parts for many years before Oklahoma gained statehood?"

Randy walked in carrying his book bag, his shoes still untied. "What's KKK?" he asked. "Sounds like a cereal."

Aletta tied his Converse sneakers. "It ain't a cereal, but we don't have time to go into what it is now," she said. "What do you want for breakfast?"

Sissy eyed Vee as she finished her cereal. She wondered how she knew the things she did. She seemed smart, and that intimidated Sissy.

As she walked out to go to the bus stop, Sissy saw two garbage men picking up trash from their lawn. "Mama!" she yelled.

Aletta came to the front door. "Oh, thank you!" she called to the men, waving.

A few days later, after school, Sissy heard her mama talking on the phone to Betty, and she began to understand her mama's behavior. "I've lost it, girl," Aletta said. "I've been fakin' it for the last week, but I can't keep this up. It ain't fair to my customers, and I'm so nervous all the time, I'm about to get sick."

Sissy felt fear creeping into her throat. Her mama was losing her gift? That was horrible. How would she make a living? She didn't know how to do anything else. And Sissy relied on the income she made from setting appointments for her. Sissy was saving up for a car that she really needed. She'd be even more pathetic to everyone at school if she was still taking the bus after she turned sixteen.

Life sucks, Sissy thought, and turned to go to her room. As she did, she ran into Vee, who was coming out of her mama's office.

"How was school?" Vee asked.

"Awful," Sissy said.

Vee nodded knowingly. "I hated high school."

"Really?"

"I couldn't stand how everyone tried to fit in and be like everyone else. I hung out with the poorest kids, miners' kids. They were never going to fit in, so none of that mattered to them."

Sissy chuckled and nodded like she understood. "I better do my homework," she said, and slid past Vee.

She sat on her bed and thought about

what Vee had said. She decided Vee hated high school because she'd been totally unpopular. Then it dawned on her. *I'm totally unpopular too,* she thought, and started to cry.

On Friday night, Sissy sat in the kitchen, waiting for Angie to arrive and watching her mama twirl around in what she called her "dancin' dress." She and Angie were going to a party at senior Kevin Gilmore's house with Jo Lyn Evers and Sheila Farringer, two girls they would normally never hang out with except that Jo Lyn had a new Datsun 200SX.

Sissy was making herself go to this party. Everyone would be there, and she couldn't let Rusty keep her from having a life.

"I thought Charlie was outta the picture, Mama," she said as she filed her fingernails.

Aletta stopped twirling and began digging through her large denim purse. "He said he's just been real busy with buyin' land and all," Aletta said. "But he apologized a million times for not callin' me sooner. And Lord above, do I ever need to go out and have a good time before I completely lose my marbles."

Finally, Aletta found what she was looking

for — a lipstick and compact. She looked at herself in the small mirror as she applied the Maybelline Peaches and Crème.

"Why're you losin' your marbles?" Sissy asked, both wanting and not wanting her mama to tell her.

Aletta blotted her lips on a paper towel. "We're just a little short on money right now. You should be thankful Vee's here and willin' to take care of these kids or you'd be stayin' home tonight."

"I don't know what they see in her, Mama," Sissy whispered. "She's kind of a weirdo."

Aletta shot her a scolding glance as Vee walked in, holding Gyp awkwardly against her chest.

"Are you sure this is all right?" Aletta asked.

Vee seemed so uncomfortable around the kids, like she'd never been around children in her life. Sissy wondered if Vee had ever even *been* a child. But for some reason, Ruby and Randy didn't mind.

"Sure, I'm fine," Vee said flatly. "When do you think you'll be back?"

Just then, the doorbell rang, and Aletta sprang off the bar stool to get the door.

Charlie Baxter wore tight black pants, a black leather sports jacket, and a pastel shirt with a wide collar. Sissy had to admit he and her mama, in her red scoop-necked dress, looked good together. He carried a bottle of wine in one hand and a bunch of carnations and daisies in the other as he blew into the room. "Oh, my heavens, I've missed you. You look gorgeous," he said, putting both arms around Aletta, careful not to hit her with his gifts.

"Thank you," Aletta giggled.

Sissy noticed Vee roll her eyes.

The girls picked Sissy up a few minutes later, and they walked out with her mama and Charlie. Sissy was embarrassed because she just knew no one else's parents were divorced and going out on the town like hers did.

The girls piled in the car and drove the five minutes to the big stone house with a high entry and fancy front door that was in the new neighborhood near the highway. Sissy already felt intimidated. Several dozen kids stood around outside, most of whom Sissy knew from school. When she entered the house, a guy she'd never met walked up to her smiling. He looked like he was older, maybe even out of school.

"You're pretty," he said.

She smiled back at him. "Thank you." Maybe this party wouldn't be so bad. Just to make sure, she went straight for the keg that was set up on the back patio.

She drank out of the plastic cup, glad that at least the disgusting beer was cold, and adjusted her ruffled peasant blouse to hang off her shoulders. Her mama wouldn't let her wear it that way at home.

"How can you drink that stuff?" Angie asked. "I gotta find somethin' that I can mix with a Coke or I just won't be drinkin' at all tonight."

Just then, Rusty walked out the back door of the house. It didn't matter how many times she saw him, it still almost brought her to her knees. She drained the beer. "That's how," she said to Angie, and refilled her cup.

Angie turned around to find out what had made Sissy go so pale. "Crap, I was hopin' he wouldn't make it."

By eleven o'clock, the party was in full swing, and Sissy was drunk. She stood in the middle of the kitchen, spilling beer all over the floor and telling everyone she saw how much she loved them.

"You know, Jo Lyn," she said loudly to the chubby junior who had brought her to the party, "I never thought I liked you, but you're really great."

Jo Lyn put her arm around Sissy. "I always

174

thought you were a bitch on wheels, but you are so groovy, I can't even believe it."

Sissy held her cup aloft. "I'll race ya," she said. They drained their beers and laughed.

As she went to the fridge to scrounge for more booze, she saw Rusty through the kitchen window. He stood under a tree in the backyard making out with Mary Lou Rudolph, a cheerleader she'd been friends with and had even streaked down Main Street in the middle of the night with last summer. Her first instinct, and it was a strong one, like jumping out of the way of a truck or pulling her hand out of a fire, was to go over to Mary Lou and punch her in the face as hard as she could.

Angie came in from the backyard, having seen the same thing Sissy was looking at. "We should go," she said.

Sissy's next instinct was to break down crying, the hurt inside her blaring like a siren, wailing that there was something terribly wrong. She loved Rusty so much.

Screw him, she thought. She wasn't going to give him the satisfaction of seeing her cry. "No," she said to Angie. "I'm not leavin'."

She took a can of Miller Lite out of the fridge and walked into the living room.

"Don't you think you better stop drinkin'?" Angie asked.

"That's the last damn thing I should do," Sissy said, and spotted the guy who'd complimented her when she first arrived.

"Hey, girl," he said when he saw her from across the room. "Let's dance."

The song "Car Wash" was playing. Sissy loved it. She took his hand and went to the middle of the cleared-out living room with several other kids.

"What's your name?" he asked.

"Sissy Honor," she said. "What about you?"

"Brett Gilmore. I'm Kevin's older brother."

He sure smiled a lot, and now that she really looked at him, he was kind of cute. He had great teeth and lovely light blue eyes. His dark hair was full and kind of shaggy, parted on one side and swept over his forehead.

"You're out of high school, aren't you?" she asked.

"I'm a sophomore at Central State," he said. "I play on the baseball team."

Sissy smiled and put her arms on his shoulders. He just kept getting better-looking. They moved around the dance floor until she had a perfect view of Rusty and

Mary Lou through the sliding glass door that led to the backyard.

She closed her eyes and leaned up to Brett. He kissed her for a long time, his tongue exploring her mouth hungrily.

Several kids — she didn't know who — catcalled and whistled as she made out with Brett. She liked it. Maybe they wouldn't call her a prude so much anymore.

After the song, Brett took her hand and whispered in her ear, "I have something I want to show you."

She stumbled down the hallway behind him and into a bedroom. He shut the door behind them. Even though it seemed like the room was moving as if the house was on turbulent water, she noticed the posters of Jimi Hendrix, Dr. J, and the "Keep on Truckin' " dude in velvet.

"Wow," she said. "You're really cool."

He laughed a little. "Why's that?"

Normally she wouldn't be so truthful, but the drink made it easy. "Nobody else I know has posters of Negroes on their wall."

Brett flipped on a stereo that looked like a large white bowling ball and pushed in an Eagles eight-track.

"Yeah, well, that's because folks in this town are a bunch of rednecks," he said, then went to the double bed and dug underneath the mattress for a moment. He pulled out a baggie with clumps of greenish brown stuff inside. As he held it up in front of his smiling face, Sissy tried to think through the booze.

After a moment, she got it. "Woo-hoo!" she said, raising her arms above her head. She'd only tried pot a couple of times before. It had made her forget everything in her life and laugh uncontrollably. She loved it.

"You may be young, but you're a blast, you know that?" Brett said as he sat on the bed and pulled out a Zigzag paper. "How old are you, by the way?"

"Sixteen," she lied. "What about you?"

"Nineteen," he said.

Wow! Sissy thought. *Nineteen!* "Oh, I love this song!" she shrieked as "Hotel California" started playing on the stereo. She danced with her arms above her head, flipping her long brown hair from side to side.

"Check this out," Brett said, and went to the light switch and turned it off, then turned on a black-light lamp that sat on top of the dresser. Suddenly, the entire room went deep, dark purple and everything that was white, including their clothes and the bedspread, glowed brightly.

"Oh, wow, how groovy!" Sissy cried.

The black-light "Keep on Truckin' " poster was an amazing display of glowing neon color. "Look at your teeth!" Sissy marveled. "They're purple!"

Brett bared his teeth for her, then put a joint between them and lit it. He passed it to her, and she danced around and took the smoke deeply into her lungs. She coughed hard, and the smoke rushed out of her mouth.

"Don't suck so hard," he said, taking another hit expertly.

This time she only took a little smoke and was able to hold it. When she blew it out, she smiled mischievously, then they both started to laugh like little kids.

After her third toke, it felt to her like things in the room were pulsating and the floor below her feet was starting to fall away. She made her way awkwardly to the bed, lay down on her back, and looked up at Brett. He sat down next to her and stroked her hair.

"My boyfriend broke up with me," she said.

"Bummer." He leaned down and kissed her.

She put her arms around him and pulled him down on top of her. He fumbled with her breasts, and she grabbed for the buttons on his Levi's. As she unbuttoned the top one, she clearly heard the lyrics of the song that was playing. The music seemed so close, she thought she felt the breath of the singer at her ear.

"This is wild," she whispered.

Brett put his hand up her blouse. "It sure is."

She felt so alive, so different from her normal self. It was like she was someone else right now, someone older and cooler, like Cher or Farrah Fawcett, someone famous and important who did extraordinary things with amazing people. There was no doubt about it — it was time for her to grow up and learn about life. She had so much to offer.

"Come on," she said to Brett. "I wanna do this."

He stopped kissing her for a moment. "You sure?" he asked.

She pulled him back to her and kissed him again. It felt good and warm, like they really cared about each other. But when he pulled off her panties and entered her, the pressure down there was so intense, it hurt.

As he moved on top of her, she held her breath. The lyrics were close to her ear, so close she flinched a little.

Vee had planned on having a quiet evening, letting Ruby and Randy watch television, while she read and sneaked a few phone calls to Carol and other party members. She hoped Gyp would sleep the evening away, but as soon as the door closed behind Aletta and Sissy, he cut loose, wailing like the night train to hell. Completely mortified, Vee wondered why women did this to themselves. They might as well walk into a jail cell and toss the key out to the closest man.

After a few minutes, Ruby and Randy came in from the living room to help.

"He likes music," Randy said, and put on Elton John.

Ruby took the baby, and she and Randy started dancing with him.

"Come on," Randy said, and took Vee's hands.

Out of desperation to stop the screaming, she played along. Soon they were dancing through the house in a party train, passing Gyp back and forth between them as they twirled and spun. His screams turned to squeals of delight. It felt so good to move her body that Vee didn't stop dancing even as she put the frozen pizza in the oven and poured grape Shasta.

Finally, when the pizza was ready, they sat at the bar and ate, laughing at how Randy ate the crust first, then the toppings, then the doughy triangle underneath.

After dinner, Ruby got out the board game Operation. They all shrieked every single time one of them set off the buzzer by touching the little metal edge that surrounded the bone they were trying to extract.

Vee didn't read anything that evening except the rules for Operation and pizza cooking instructions. She didn't make any phone calls and didn't even worry about her situation. It had been a very strange few hours. She went to bed at midnight after finally getting the kids down, but not long after she closed her eyes, she heard something from outside her room.

"Uhnnn," Sissy groaned as she held the top of the toilet bowl and vomited again.

Vee walked in and wet down a washcloth. "It's a good thing your mom isn't home yet. How much did you drink?"

"I don't know," Sissy whined. Her words came out all blurred together.

"Did you know you have blood on the back of your skirt?" Vee asked, and sat down on the edge of the bathtub.

"What?!" Sissy cried, and looked behind

her. "Oh, my God," she said when she saw the smear of dried blood on the hem of her denim skirt. She sat on the floor and leaned back against the toilet bowl. "I can't believe this," she said, and started to cry.

Vee waited a few moments before speaking again. "Are you on your period?"

"No!"

"You're gonna have to quiet down a little, Sissy. I just got Gyp to sleep. Now why don't you tell me what happened?"

"I — I — I —" Sissy sobbed, but couldn't continue.

"Did you have sex tonight?" Vee asked.

"Yes," Sissy groaned, and hiccupped. Her arms were crossed over her knees, and her head was buried in the circle of her arms.

"Your first time?"

"Yes."

"Did he force you?" Now there was an edge in Vee's voice.

"No. I wanted it."

"Why?"

"Because I'm not a prude! All the popular girls are doing it. I bet Mary Lou did it with Rusty tonight." Sissy unrolled some toilet paper and blew her nose. "Uh-oh," she said, and turned over just in time to throw up again.

"Wait here," Vee told her, and left the

bathroom. She came back carrying a slim, worn book.

"Here," Vee said, and held out the washcloth to her to wipe her mouth. "I want to read you something I've just started. It's from the *SCUM Manifesto,* by Valerie Solanas. Can you listen?"

"Y-Y-Yes," Sissy sputtered, and sat down again, wiping her mouth with the cloth.

" 'Sex is the refuge of the mindless,' " Vee read. " 'And the more mindless the woman, the more deeply embedded in the male 'culture,' in short, the nicer she is, the more sexual she is.' " Vee said the word *nice* like it was poison on her tongue. She looked at Sissy. "Are you understanding this?"

Sissy nodded her head. "I think so."

" 'The nicest women in our "society," ' " Vee continued, " 'are raving sex maniacs. But being just awfully, awfully nice they don't, of course, descend to fucking — that's uncouth — rather they make love, commune by means of their bodies and establish sensual rapport.' "

Sissy looked at Vee blankly. "Are you sayin' that girls have sex because they want to fit in? That it's for stupid girls who don't know any better?"

"Yes. Women who are stupid because they

want to fit into a patriarchal society. That means one dominated by men. Men get exactly what they want from girls who are brainwashed by this society. They have sex to fit in and be accepted, just like you did tonight."

"So Mary Lou and Jill and all those girls that call me a prude are really just stupid, like cows bein' herded to the slaughter?" Sissy asked incredulously.

"That's exactly right," Vee said proudly.

Sissy started laughing. "That's funny," she said. "Oh, boy, that's really funny."

Aletta's head knocked against the door handle, and she felt the plastic of the car seat sticking to the backs of her thighs as Charlie moved on top of her. It felt good, and she really wanted this, needed it in fact, but she was too uncomfortable to relax and really enjoy it. Finally, Charlie climaxed and rolled off her. He zipped up his pants and smiled. "Whew!" he said. "That was fantastic. How'd you like it, hon?"

Aletta sat up and pulled her dress down over her thighs. "I feel like a teenager again," she said. She decided their relationship deserved more than sex in the back of a car. Even if it meant bringing him home to her bed.

They got into the front seat again, and he drove away from the deserted street and headed to her home. "I gotta go back to New York tomorrow," he said as he pulled into her driveway. "But I'll call you real soon."

They sat in his car kissing for another half hour before she finally got out.

"You're glowin', darlin'," he said to her when she leaned back into the window to say goodbye.

"That's what you do to me, Charlie Baxter," she said, then walked her sexiest walk up her porch steps.

She was grateful no one was awake when she went inside. It was late, after two in the morning, and she didn't want to have to lie about what she'd been doing. She smiled as she spread Pond's cold cream over her face, remembering Charlie taking her in his arms on the dance floor and kissing her so passionately. She'd known right then she wanted to sleep with him. Her body ached for a man to hold her and make love to her. Consummating their relationship in the back of a car was not her idea of perfection, but it had still been fun. And now she knew Charlie felt the way she did. Their lovemaking had been so intense, their connection so beautiful.

After checking on Gyp to make sure he was sleeping, she climbed in bed. Even tonight, though, she couldn't sleep. Being with Charlie had given her a break for the evening, but when she was by herself again, it all came back. Her main concern was that she hadn't given a really legitimate reading in two weeks now, ever since that Indian had come by and given her the eagle feather.

She'd hoped that keeping the feather and acknowledging her great-grandmother, even though it sounded like her family hadn't, would restore her abilities. Her gift had been with her since she was a child, whether she wanted it or not. Why would it leave now, just when she was actually using it?

With most of her clients, she was able to get through the appointments by listening and caring about them and giving loving advice. She figured most folks were so unaccustomed to having someone really listen that that's all it took to satisfy them. Every once in a while she would get a hunch about something and share it, and it turned out to be accurate more often than not. *That's probably how it feels for most people,* she thought. *Intuition.*

For other customers — regulars, like Pearl Frye and a few of the ladies from Joy's salon — she canceled appointments, saying Gyp was ill. She knew they'd be able to tell she was faking.

Aletta flopped onto her side and sighed loudly. She couldn't afford to cancel appointments, and she felt guilty as hell about taking people's money like this. She thought about Charlie. Maybe if the two of them worked out, she wouldn't need to have her business anymore. He was so generous and seemed to have so much. She'd be a wonderful wife to him, and he'd have a ready-made family.

As she lay there, her fantasies took them to the wedding chapel and on vacations with and without the kids. She pictured them lying on the beach in Hawaii, drinking pastel drinks, laughing merrily. The new house they lived in was two-story, with a huge master bedroom upstairs, a pool in the backyard, and plenty of room for each of the children to have his or her own bedroom. She didn't work but made sure that the housekeeper kept things nice. Out front, she'd plant the loveliest flower garden in town.

"Oh, my Lord," she said out loud, realizing where she'd just gone. She rolled onto her stomach, buried her face in the pillow, and shook her head back and forth. "I'm losin' my mind," she murmured. But a little voice inside her didn't want to let go of the dream. *Why couldn't it happen?* it said. *Nothing's impossible.*

CHAPTER ELEVEN

Jimmy sat shotgun in the beat-up old van that belonged to Del Walters. He poured coffee out of a thermos into a Styrofoam cup, then handed the thermos back to Del's son, Walt. It was just after five o'clock in the morning, so Jimmy needed the coffee badly, but not as badly as he used to. He took a sip and grinned through the steam. He hadn't taken a drink of booze for three weeks now — proof he could stop when he wanted.

"Think we'll find any birds, Del?" he asked. They were on a seemingly endless two-lane road that headed north toward the Oklahoma panhandle.

Del spit a stream of tobacco juice into a Folger's coffee can that sat on the floorboard between the seats. "If they ain't any turkeys up here, they ain't nowhere," he said gruffly. Pretty much everything he said came out gruffly.

"We'll find 'em," Walt's fourteen-year-old son, Keith, said from his seat next to his daddy.

Keith reminded Jimmy of himself at that age. He loved to hunt and to play ball. But Keith was really close to his daddy, and that part they didn't have in common at all. Jimmy had known Del and Walt Walters since he and Walt had played basketball together in junior high and high school. He loved them like they were family, and they'd always treated him the same.

After another forty-five minutes, Del finally pulled onto a dirt road that paralleled a stand of trees a quarter mile to the north.

"Shit, hell, damn," Del cursed as they hit one bump or hole in the road after another. "My butt's too bony for this. I'm stoppin' here."

Speaking in hushed tones, so they wouldn't scare off the game, the four of them got out of the van and unloaded the shotguns from the back. They wore camouflage from head to toe, because it was necessary for hunting turkeys, which are both clever and fast.

"Got the turkey calls?" Walt asked as he closed the rear doors of the van.

"Yessir, I do. I done told you that already

once," Del said.

"All right, Keith, be real quiet now," Walt said to his son. "These gobblers are smarter'n your grandpa."

Del snorted and Jimmy chuckled as they made their way down and then up a ditch next to the road and started across the open field of prairie grass. The sun was just peeking over the horizon, touching the earth with color and light. Pink and yellow and white wildflowers lay across the expanse like God's own handmade quilt. Jimmy breathed in deeply the smell of the morning, the red dirt, and the growing things.

He loved hunting for this reason as well as for the sport and challenge of it. It got him out into nature, where things made sense to him, and he was in control. It had been his salvation when he was a kid, getting him out of the tiny shack that was filled to bursting with people and their problems.

After about a hundred yards, Jimmy knew they ought to get down, so he signaled to the others. They all dropped to their bellies and began crawling forward toward the trees on their elbows. They had to be careful not to get too close, because if the turkeys heard them, they would fly off.

When they got within about seventy yards of the trees, Jimmy signaled them to stop.

Del pulled out two small wooden boxes that had holes on the bottom and serrated tops. He handed one to Walt. With a stick, they began scraping the top of the boxes, and out came the undeniable sound of a turkey gobbling.

They waited, listening to the sounds of their own breathing, the awakening world, and the high-pitched *gobble gobble gobble* of the turkey calls. Keith got bored and turned over on his back to look at the sky. But just as he did, the flapping swoosh of a turkey leaving its roost sounded.

Keith turned over, "Where is it?" he whispered. "Is it a hen or a gobbler?"

"A gobbler. He just landed up ahead." Walt pointed as he scraped on his box.

A few more turkeys, brown with red heads, flew from the trees and landed in the field around them. The guys carefully rose to their knees and pulled the shotguns to their shoulders. Jimmy could see a turkey that had flown from the roost about fifty yards away on the ground. He waited for it to get closer and watched as its red head darted from side to side. It began prancing and strutting toward them and the turkey calls, doing its mating dance for the hen that was calling at him so loudly to come and mate with her. The turkey got within thirty-five yards and spread his enormous brown wings and black and white tail feathers out wide in a glorious display of his sexual attractiveness. Just before he pulled the trigger, Jimmy noticed with satisfaction how long the red beard that hung below the turkey's beak was — looked like six inches or more. The bigger it was, the larger the bird. He squeezed the trigger, and the turkey crumpled violently onto the ground.

Bam! Bam! Bam! Shots rang out all around him as the men aimed and fired, aimed and fired. Jimmy noticed a gobbler fly from his roost up ahead. He swung his shotgun toward the bird, aimed at the sky just in front of him, and pulled the trigger. The bird turned end over end, tumbling toward the earth. Jimmy made a note of where he landed and turned to find more prey.

After it was all said and done, they had killed six gobblers, and Keith had killed one hen accidentally. They'd leave her on the ground, because getting caught with her meant losing their hunting licenses.

"Now that was a helluva good time," Walt said exultantly.

"Way to go, boys! That's how it's done," Del said.

Jimmy put his arm around Keith's shoulder. "You're almost as good a shot as I was at your age," he said teasingly.

Keith smiled. "If I was a bettin' man, I'd wager I'm a better shot," he said.

Jimmy laughed. They clapped each other on the back and went to find their birds.

At about six o'clock that evening, they all sat down in a booth at Walt's favorite place in Alva, Oklahoma, the tiny panhandle town that hosted hunters from Kansas, New Mexico, Texas, and Oklahoma when they came to hunt quail, pheasant, and turkeys. Woody's was a pool hall that served big, juicy burgers and enormous plates of onion rings and french fries.

Del spat tobacco into a paper cup stuffed with a wad of napkins. "About thought I'd never get up from that nap," he said.

"You're getting old," Jimmy said, laughing.

The waitress, a girl of about eighteen with tight blue jeans and a sweet, open face, came over to take their order.

"What kin I brang y'all to drank?" she asked, a pencil poised above her order pad.

"I'll have a whiskey soda," Del said.

Keith smiled. "Coke, please."

"Let's see," Walt said. "Bring me a draft beer."

"Vodka tonic," Jimmy said. The words came out like they were just his next breath of air, with no struggle or hesitation at all.

After he said it, he looked around to see if anyone was going to stop him, to see if the world was any different from the moment before, to see if lightning might strike or the waitress might protest and not serve him. But everything looked just the same. Walt and Del just scanned their menus. The waitress wrote down his order and walked away.

Jimmy smiled to himself at his concern about having a drink. He'd proven he could stop when he wanted to, that he was in control of the booze, not the other way around. Why shouldn't he have a drink with old friends when he was on vacation? He was a grown man, for God's sake.

The waitress brought the drinks and started taking their food order. Jimmy didn't hear what anyone else was saying as he took a long drink of his cocktail. He felt it warm him, first his mouth and throat, then his belly. His shoulders relaxed a little and his scalp tingled with pleasure. He had a sense, even though it wasn't exactly a thought, that all was right with the world. And this was all with just that first sip.

"Sir," the waitress said. "Sir, excuse me."

Del, who sat next to him, elbowed Jimmy. "Tell the gal what you want to eat."

"Oh, sorry. I'll have the chicken-fried steak," Jimmy said.

After she left, they talked about the hunt.

"Tell us about findin' that gobbler, Jimmy," Keith said.

Jimmy laughed. "Well, I saw him when he flew from the roost, and I shot him still in the air. Y'all know how far away that was."

They nodded.

"I thought I'd tracked him pretty good, but me and Del were havin' a helluva time findin' him."

Del spat his whole wad of tobacco into a paper napkin and stuffed it into the cup. "I finally took a chance he was still alive and used my call," Del said, wiping his mouth with a clean napkin.

"That was smart thinkin,' " Jimmy said, " 'cause that's when I heard him gobble. He was down in this irrigation ditch filled with water about two foot deep. He was just swimmin' around with a broke wing. There wasn't no way I was goin' into that water to fight that bird while he was still livin'."

Walt laughed. "I would've liked to have seen that myself."

"I bet you would." Jimmy smiled and took another long drink. "Course I didn't want to shoot him . . ."

" 'Cause he's harder to clean," Keith said.

Jimmy nodded. "Right. So I grabbed a big tree branch, bigger'n a damn baseball bat." He raised his arms like he was holding the branch. "And I nailed him as hard as I could right on the head."

Del started laughing at the thought of it. "He hit that damn bird with a big ole roundhouse swing that shoulda knocked him clear into tomorrow."

Jimmy cracked up. "It was so funny. That bird just looked up at me like I'd made him mad, like he was sayin', 'Is that all you got, fella?' "

"I thought he was gonna come up outta that ditch and kick your ass." Del snorted as he laughed.

"Finally," Jimmy said, and drained his drink, "I had to shoot him again to kill him. Those turkeys are tough sons a bitches, that's for sure."

They sat in the booth for hours and told stories about their hunting trips, ate too much food, and drank until they were drunk. Jimmy and Walt played pool, but Jimmy didn't remember much of it the next day. He must've blacked out at one point, because he didn't remember how he got back to his motel room or undressed or into bed.

Del beat on the door until Jimmy finally woke up and realized with a pang of shame and sadness that he was hung over.

"Get your ass dressed," Del yelled through the door. "Sun's already up, and the turkeys are flyin'."

Jimmy crawled into the van and pulled his camouflage cap low over his eyes.

"Had a few too many last night, didn't ya?" Walt asked, smiling.

"I wasn't the only one," Jimmy said.

Keith leaned forward. "You beat 'em by about two to one," he said cheerily.

Jimmy groaned. "Shut up, kid."

They went out a different dirt road than the day before, scanning for birds. Jimmy drank some coffee and ate a chocolate-covered donut that Del had brought, and he started to feel better.

They stopped the van and crawled out into a field near a long line of trees where they'd had luck finding turkeys in years past. But today, they didn't see any birds at all for over an hour.

Walt and Del scraped on the call boxes again and again, but nothing happened. The sun got hotter as it rose in the sky, and

Jimmy felt his stomach turning on him.

Finally, they heard the *gobble gobble* of a turkey off to the east in a nearby roost. Out of his excitement, Keith jumped up and swung his shotgun around, looking for the bird. "I heard one," he said loudly.

The turkey, a nice-sized gobbler, flew off before Keith could even bring his gun up to aim.

"Don't shoot!" Jimmy said.

But Keith shot twice, missing badly both times.

"Well that's just fuckin' great!" Jimmy yelled, and stood up. "I guess we can all go home now." He turned to Keith, his face red and angry. "What a dumbass thing to do. I told you not to shoot. There's not gonna be another bird come by all day now."

Jimmy stomped off toward the van.

"Hey!" Walt called. "He's just a kid, you son of a bitch. It ain't that big a deal."

"He's a spoiled brat!" Jimmy flipped off Walt over his shoulder and kept walking.

Keith started crying, and Walt and Del tried to comfort him.

Jimmy didn't hear them anymore after he walked away. The rage inside him was so strong, it was like a wave that capsized his mind and his body. He couldn't believe how stupid the little bastard had been to call out like that, then shoot his gun after the bird had flown away! It had ruined their whole day.

They all loaded silently into the van, and Del headed back toward Okay.

Aletta had intended to go to church, even after she and Charlie stayed out dancing — both on the dance floor and in the car — the night before. But she was so tired Sunday morning, she didn't have the energy required to get the five-headed monster that was her family out the door.

To her amazement, Vee and Sissy asked if she needed anything at the grocery store and went shopping for her. She heard them talking as they walked out the door.

"Why do you stoop to doing housewife kind of stuff?" Sissy asked.

"There's no man here, so there's no housewife," Vee answered. "If there were a man here, he'd have to do his share of the shopping too. Screw the traditional roles."

That tickled Aletta. It was definitely a different era than when she was a teenager. She was also thrilled Sissy and Vee were getting along suddenly. Sissy actually seemed like she had some life back in her. What in the world had happened? When she'd asked about last night, she hadn't gotten information from either of them.

Aletta didn't consider anything but the stack of bills in front of her for long. She spent the afternoon in a state of anxiety while she wrote checks and watched as her checking account went from four digits to three. To relieve the tightening knots in her neck and shoulders, she went outside and worked in her garden with Randy while Gyp crawled around and ate bugs and Ruby rode a path in the yard on her bicycle.

She thought she'd never sleep that night, but when she finally did, the dream that came to her was haunting. In it, she walked into the kitchen of the farmhouse she'd grown up in. Her daddy sat at the big maple table, looking just like he had before he was killed when she was a child. Her mama was at the stove cooking, and next to her stood another woman with long black hair — the dark-skinned woman she'd seen before.

"Mama," Aletta said quietly.

The Indian woman turned and smiled at her. "Well, there you are," she said.

The woman went to the front door of the house and walked outside, hesitating for just a moment, waiting for Aletta to follow her.

Aletta walked after her, but at the door, she looked back at her parents. Tears welled up in her eyes. When she turned around again and looked outside, she no longer saw the dark-haired woman, just an eagle flying toward a low sun that hovered above magnificent purple mountains. She glanced out at the road and saw the Indian man who had given her the eagle feather drive by in his pickup truck.

When Aletta opened her eyes and realized she'd been dreaming, she lay completely still for a few moments, trying to hold on to the feeling of being with her mama and daddy, looking like they had when she was a child, when life seemed like it was safe and happy.

As she put on blue jeans and a striped T-shirt, she realized that neither of her parents had acknowledged her in the dream. It had been the dark-haired woman who had seen her, the same one from her previous dream. Was this her great-grandmother Adelaide? And the man who'd given her the feather was in it too. What in the world was the dream trying to tell her?

In the kitchen, Vee was already making coffee.

Aletta was grateful to see her. Vee seemed so strong and sure of herself, so independent and free. Her presence gave Aletta the courage to see possibilities that she'd never even dreamed of before — even little things like men doing the grocery shopping. *Oh, my,* she thought, wondering when a man in her life would ever do the shopping.

"I'm gonna find out more about her, Vee," Aletta said as she pulled cereal boxes out of the cabinet.

Vee looked startled. "Who?" she asked nervously.

"Adelaide, our great-grandma. I gotta try."

Seeming relieved, Vee poured coffee into mismatched cups. "Another dream?"

"Yes'm, and I gotta figure it out. I gotta know more about this woman." Aletta's eyebrows were knitted together in deep concentration. "Where should I start?"

"This is so cool," Vee said. "Maybe at the library."

Aletta slapped a hand on the Formica bar top. "I'm goin' today. You wanna come?"

"Absolutely," Vee almost shouted. "Let's kick some ass."

"Yes!"

Aletta and Vee drove the kids to school, since they were going out anyway. After dropping Ruby and Randy at Okay Elementary, Aletta turned to Sissy. "Not wearin' so much makeup today, I see. Looks good."

Sissy didn't answer but glanced at Vee, who smiled slightly.

"You still tryin' out for mat maid for next season?" Aletta asked as she pulled into the high school parking lot, teeming with pickups, Mustangs, and Chevy Chevettes. It was easy to tell a kid's family's status from the car he or she drove.

"Mat maid?" Vee asked, a hint of scorn in her voice.

Sissy blushed a little. "It's like a cheerleader for wrestling," she said. "I was just thinkin' about it."

"Mat maid?" Vee said again.

Aletta looked at Vee. "It's a wonderful thing to do, getting involved in something at school." Then she turned to Sissy. "I think you'd have a great time with it, Sis. I know you wanted cheerleader so bad, but this could be even better. The wrestlin' team's the best one we got," Aletta said.

With Gyp squirming between them, Aletta and Vee first drove to the small, musty Okay Public Library and found out from Pearl Frye that they'd need to go to the downtown Oklahoma City library, about forty minutes away, to get any information on someone who went that far back.

On the way to the city, Vee drove and they talked over what they knew about Adelaide Medina Halbert. Since she'd first looked at the genealogy book, Aletta had been too busy and preoccupied to really study it, but now she scoured every line.

"So, we know she married this fella Maxwell Halbert. Maxwell was the son of Charles Halbert, a big shot in Santa Fe in the middle and late eighteen hundreds," Aletta said. "We know she's Indian because your daddy tracked down her enrollment form in this American School for Indians run by Christian brothers. Says here, 'Helping the tribal orphan fit into Christian society.'"

"That's disgusting," Vee said. "They stripped those kids of their culture, their own history. Did you know they wouldn't let them speak their native tongue? If they did, they were beaten."

"Lord above. All you can guess is they thought they were doing good for them," Aletta said. She felt guilty, and she didn't even know why. "Anyway, we know she was an orphan."

She ran her hand over the worn copy of the old and wrinkled enrollment form that had her great-grandmother's name, birth date, June 11, 1870, place of birth, Santa Fe, New Mexico, and enrollment date, January 18, 1882. She stopped Gyp's sticky fingers before they landed on the page, and instead put them around his favorite toy, a stuffed yellow dog.

"This is so exciting — sad but exciting, don't you think?" Vee said. "Finding out more about her is like redeeming her life in some way."

Aletta didn't even hear her. She was too deep in thought. "Now, we also know Maxwell and Adelaide were married in 1886 from the notice in the newspaper here. My lands, she was only sixteen."

"Poor thing," Vee said.

"But she married money, at least."

"But we also know Maxwell and Adelaide and their little baby were in the Oklahoma land rush in 1889. Why would Maxwell go for free land if he had a rich father?" Vee asked.

"That baby they had with them would be my granddaddy, Franklin Halbert, born 1887," Aletta said, looking at his box on the family tree. "Maybe ole Charles was tapped out. Maybe he'd gone broke."

"Or maybe he didn't want them in Santa Fe anymore."

"Hmmm," Aletta said as Vee pulled the car into the parking lot of the downtown Oklahoma City library.

CHAPTER TWELVE

Jimmy sat at his desk at Southwestern Bell Telephone and stared blankly into his coffee. Even though he was in hot water for missing work because of his injuries, he still couldn't get motivated. He should be making calls to his accounts to upgrade them to the new business plan, but his head was pounding from a hangover and from the thoughts that were bouncing off the inside of his skull. He was trying to figure out what had gone wrong with everything — his athletic career, his marriage, the hunting trip, last night.

He'd gotten home from hunting, and Charlotte was cooking fried chicken. She never cooked for him, so he'd convinced her that they should celebrate by drinking a beer with dinner. They must've really tied one on, because he didn't even know what had happened. This morning, Charlotte was already gone and there were pots and pans strewn all over the kitchen with grease and mashed potatoes stuck to the walls, the floor, and the table.

Bill Haywood walked up behind Jimmy. "Hey, champ," he said, and clapped him on the back.

Jimmy's coffee sloshed onto his desk. His first thought was that he wanted to elbow Bill in the gut. He didn't even know why. He liked Bill. "Hey, boss," he said instead. "I plan on winning the sales contest this month."

"That's what I like to hear," Bill said, and walked away.

Jimmy picked up the phone and looked at the typed list of businesses and phone numbers. He started to dial Ace Drilling, but dialed his home instead.

"Hello," Charlotte said.

He was relieved. "Hi, baby," he said casually. "What you up to?"

"Don't you 'Hi, baby' me, Jimmy Honor."

"I guess we got a little outta control last night, didn't we?"

She was silent for a moment before answering. "We? We? You went crazy. Goin' on and on about how you should be playin' for the Celtics, how everyone was against you, even the Walters." She paused and lowered her voice to a whisper. "You said you wanted to kill your daddy like he was one a them turkeys. Then you started throwin' food around, laughin' like you was insane, Jimmy."

Jimmy felt cold suddenly, but he began to sweat under his jacket at the same time. He felt his throat start to close up and the burn of tears behind his eyes. Somehow, he regained control and forced out a laugh. "You musta thought I was outta my mind, sweetheart," he said. "I didn't tell you, but I thought I had a fever yesterday when we were huntin', so I took some medicine that Walt gave me. Those drinks with the drug musta just made me crazier'n a loon. Good Lord, I'm glad you're still there."

He glanced up and saw Bill looking at him from inside his glassed-in office and acted like he was writing something down. "Don't worry about the mess," he said to Charlotte. "I'll clean it up tonight."

"You didn't tell me you took medicine. What was it? You scared me." Her voice cracked a little, and in it, he heard the warmth of affection coming back.

"It was somethin' Walt's doctor gave him," he lied, but it didn't feel like a lie. Lying was just as easy as telling the truth for him. Sometimes easier. "Listen, I gotta get to work now, but I'll see you tonight."

He hung up the phone and gave a thumbs-up to Bill, who nodded his approval. He loosened his tie a little and dialed Ace Drilling. For the rest of the day, he buried himself in work. At lunch, he entertained the other guys with stories from his turkey hunt. They laughed like hell when he told them about killing the half-dead gobbler with a tree branch.

"Why don't you start at the information desk?" Vee said as she and Aletta entered the hushed busyness of the library. "I need to check on something quickly."

"What should I say?" Aletta asked, hitching Gyp further up on her hip. "I haven't been to that many libraries."

Vee smiled. This woman seemed as worldly as a child sometimes. "Just tell the librarian what you're looking for, and she'll direct you."

"All right," Aletta said, and walked away, the leather book under her free arm.

Vee headed straight for the periodicals desk. She asked the plump, gray-haired woman who came over to help her for the most recent *Los Angeles Times* newspapers going back for two weeks. Very slowly, the woman brought them to her, one by one.

"I only have up until last Wednesday. They

come in about three days late," she said, then studied Vee's face for a moment. "You look awful familiar to me. Do I know you from somewhere?"

Vee scooped up the newspapers. "No, not that I know of," she said, and hurried away.

Trying to appear casual, she sat down and thumbed through the newspapers, looking for any information about the attempted robbery. She'd already seen the write-ups from the few days after-ward, and she was hoping there wouldn't be anything else. A headline caught her eye, and she got engrossed in reading about widespread protests against apartheid in South Africa and dissident Steve Biko's murder while in police custody. She also read about the Vatican's decision to bar women from the priesthood. Her blood was boiling by the time she turned to page A16. There was so much injustice to fight. The forces of patriarchy, imperialism, and racism must be defeated. She needed to be out on the front lines, making a difference.

That's when she saw her own face staring back at her. She gasped and looked around, folding the paper closer to her, so no one would see. Her picture was next to Lucius's and Carl's. It was the one that had been taken the night she was arrested for protesting in Berkeley. Her heart beat wildly as she read the short article.

Investigators have released photographs of the alleged perpetrators of an attempted armed robbery at American Federal Bank in Los Angeles yesterday. Several members of the underground political organization, the Freedom Revolutionary Party, attempted the heist to "strike at the heart of the capitalist power structure," said Lucius Denver, one of the group who is awaiting trial. Still at large is Vicki Lynn Halbert, who is alleged to have been driving the getaway car and fled the scene when police arrived.

Vee glanced around and closed the paper. She got up and walked into the women's bathroom with the newspaper folded under her arm. She ripped the page out of the paper, tore it into pieces, threw it in the trash, and piled paper towels on top. She went into a stall and sat on the toilet. "Damn," she whispered. "Damn."

It seemed as if the thoughts that ran through her mind were like sheet lightning on a clear summer night. They obviously caught Lucius, and she was going to be next. She thought about stealing Aletta's car and driving straight for the Mexican border, or maybe she could borrow enough money from Aletta to get on a flight to Canada, then make her way to South Africa or Cuba. What if the feds were on their way here now? What if they were waiting outside? How had they gotten that picture? Had Lucius and Carl given her up?

She needed some money. She grabbed a fistful of her hair and pulled. She had to get it together or she was going to end up in jail.

She felt like vomiting, but nothing came, so she folded the paper under her arm and went back out into the library. She felt as exposed as if she were naked.

Aletta had a stack of books on a table in front of her and was wrestling Gyp with one arm to keep him in her lap while turning pages with the other.

"Oh, this is so excitin' and frustratin' at the same time," she whispered to Vee when she walked up. "They got some information on this Santa Fe Ring and how they ran everything. Charles Halbert's name is in those. There's some books here about Indians around Santa Fe too. Mostly, they're Pueblo and Navajo. But nothin' on Maxwell Halbert, and definitely nothin' on Adelaide

Medina. I feel like I haven't got a hoot's chance in Hades of findin' anything on her. I'm guessin' orphan Indian girls don't get much attention in history books."

"You guessed right," Vee said, looking around nervously.

"But I can't tell you how fun this is. I never even went to college for a day, and the only thing I ever researched in school was for a paper on Thomas Jefferson or the like." Aletta grabbed Vee's hand. "Thanks for suggestin' we come here —" Aletta stopped cold, holding tightly to Vee's hand.

The wave of images that came over her almost knocked her off her chair. Before her eyes, the library transformed into a dark, earthen room. In the center of the room stood an Indian child, a girl of about seven or eight with long braided hair. She was surrounded by dancers wearing amazing and terrifying masks, their long black hair flowing down their shoulders and backs. The masks had large features and were adorned with feathers and fur and horns. Two of the dancers chanted words that Aletta didn't understand. Aletta could hear drumbeats, and the words themselves sounded rhythmic and steady.

The young girl stood upright, her shoulders back, listening carefully. Behind her, a man and a woman watched with pride. Somehow, Aletta knew these were the girl's parents. Two elderly men, the leaders of these people, also watched. One of the men leaned toward the other and remarked, "She has the medicine of a seer, just like her grandfather." Aletta wasn't sure how, but she understood these words, each one dropping into her mind like a cube of ice into a glass.

"Aletta," Vee said, and pulled her hand away from her cousin's grip. "Aletta."

The dark of the ceremonial room faded away, and the library returned. "Oh, my Lord," Aletta said, her breath shallow, grateful that Gyp was still sitting snugly on her lap.

"What happened?" Vee asked. She looked pale and frightened. "You wouldn't answer me."

"I saw some things, Vee. It was so strong. I saw images when I held on to your hand." Aletta steadied her breathing and blinked her eyes to make sure she was seeing right again.

"I feel sick," Vee said. "I need to go."

The wave had passed for Aletta, so she drove, letting Vee slump in the passenger seat. "That's the first time anything's come to me in weeks," Aletta said.

"Was it about me?" Vee asked glumly.

"No, no, that's the strangest part. It was about Adelaide, but she was just a little ole girl. She was takin' part in some dance type a thing," Aletta said, then thought for a moment before adding, "Like a ceremony."

Vee's expression changed in an instant from deeply upset to intensely interested. "Tell me everything," she said.

Aletta told her about the vision, describing the masks and the dancers and the little girl. Finally, she told Vee what she understood the old man to say at the end. " 'She has the medicine of a seer, just like her grandfather,' " Aletta said. "It wasn't the words he said that I understood, but more like his thoughts."

She looked over at Vee and couldn't help but laugh a little, her eyes were so wide.

"You know what that means, don't you?" Vee asked.

"I think I might," Aletta said, staring hard at the narrow blacktop road. She was taking the slow way through the countryside home instead of the highway.

Vee's voice was low and quiet. "Adelaide was psychic too. And so was her grandfather."

For a moment, Aletta just stared out at the flat Oklahoma landscape. Oil derricks lined the road on either side of them, pumping up and down like enormous water birds searching for food with slow precision.

Finally, a single tear streamed down each of her cheeks.

"What is it?" Vee asked.

"Well, I don't quite know," Aletta said, and wiped her cheeks with the back of her hand. "I guess I don't feel so alone for some reason."

Vee reached out and touched Aletta's shoulder but pulled her hand back quickly.

It was so subtle, her pulling away, but it was the very type of thing that made Aletta feel the way she did. She tried to ignore how folks reacted differently around her, but how could she help but notice? Aletta had spent her life avoiding touching others, so she wouldn't see things about them. Now, many people avoided touching her in return. She had felt isolated and alone her whole life, but today she had found out that there were people who were like her, and they had been in her very own family.

"I need me a pop somethin' desperate after all this," Aletta said, turning off her feelings as best she could. "Mind if I stop?"

Vee shook her head and sank lower into the seat of the Pink Pumpkin. She held Gyp while Aletta went into the 7-Eleven.

Aletta's mind was so full with all that had just happened, she didn't notice anything about the store. Not who was inside or how big it was or even if a clerk stood behind the counter. She went straight to the Icee machine and started filling a large cup with Pepsi and cherry mixed. She couldn't get those haunting and beautiful masks out of her mind as she watched the foam spill into the cup.

Just then, some guys came into the store, laughing and carrying on with each other. She looked around and noticed they were roughnecks from the oil derricks. It was easy to tell oil workers from their grease-lined faces and dirty shirts. They went to the refrigerated drinks and started pulling out Cokes.

"What I really want is a beer," one of them said.

"Little early for that, don't ya think?" another answered.

Aletta jerked her head toward them. This time, she looked closely. She closed her eyes, took a breath, then looked again.

"Well, son of a bitch," she said. "Charlie Baxter, what in hell are you doin' here?" It was as confusing to take this in as what she'd seen in the library

Charlie looked over at her and just

dropped his chin to his chest when he saw her. One of his buddies looked from Aletta to him, then back again, and started laughing. "Uh-oh, boys, Charlie's done it again," he said.

They all laughed like crazy at that.

Aletta's Icee started to spill onto her hand. It felt just like the cold that was pouring over her heart.

Charlie pushed his buddies away from him and walked to Aletta, smiling. "You gotta admit we had a helluva time," he said.

"You ain't a businessman from New York?"

He chuckled, looked at his blackened hands, at the wedding ring that was clearly visible, and shook his head.

"You're married." She remembered the only image she'd gotten when they met: a woman, hurt and angry, slamming down a telephone. When he'd told her he was divorced two years, she figured that must've been his ex.

"Oh, now, don't go and spoil the whole thing," he said, and reached out to touch her.

She took a step backward and threw the drink all over his chest.

"Goddammit!" he yelled, and she ran toward the door.

As the door closed behind her, she heard him calling, "You know you loved it!"

Aletta got in the car, yanked it into reverse, and squealed backward out of the parking lot.

"What happened?" Vee asked.

Aletta couldn't look at her. "Nothin'. I'm just still feelin' off from them visions. I need to get home."

Vee sat in stunned silence for a moment, then asked, "Did those men bother you?"

Aletta pulled up to a stop sign at one of those Oklahoma junctions that cuts a perfect cross into farmland and prairie for miles in every direction. She put her head down on the huge steering wheel of the '57 Chevy and let out a wail. It was a guttural sound that came from her belly.

Gyp whimpered and started to crawl toward his mother, but Vee pulled him back. "Aletta, what's going on?" she asked, concern making her voice trembly.

Aletta was too humiliated to tell Vee about Charlie Baxter, so what she ended up saying came out as a surprise even to her. "I want to go to New Mexico. I need to find out about Adelaide, but I can't. I'm stuck here. My life is stuck. I'm stuck right here at this stupid stop sign for the rest of my whole life!"

She glanced into the rearview mirror and saw a highway patrol car coming up the road behind them. Vee followed Aletta's glance and slid even further down in her seat. "Christ, Aletta," she said, "we should go home and talk about this."

"Nope. I'm stuck right here." Aletta shook her head back and forth on the steering wheel. "My sorry life has come to a standstill, and there ain't nowhere left to turn."

Now the cop car was right behind them, and Vee seemed about to squirm out of her seat. "I'll watch the kids while you go to New Mexico," she blurted.

"This ain't your problem. You can't do that," Aletta said.

"I swear, I'd love to. You go. I'll stay. But I really need to go home!"

Aletta sat up, cleared her throat, and smoothed her hair very carefully. It looked like she could've been preparing to go into a job interview, the way she was so particular about it. Her thoughts, normally buzzing along like a beehive in summer, seemed to shut completely off. The combination of the Indian ceremony in the downtown library along with seeing her New York businessman as a roughneck in the 7-Eleven had been too much. Finally, she drove on.

Vee seemed to relax when the police car

turned right instead of following them. The regret was tangible in her voice when she spoke again. "So, you really want to go to New Mexico?"

Aletta shook her head in defeat, her thoughts revving up again like an old engine. "Forget I said anything," she said. "It could never work."

Vee was silent. She looked out the window, thinking. Then, suddenly, her tone of voice changed completely. "You know what? I really, really think you should go. You leave me a car and a little money, and it'll be no problem at all."

Aletta shook her head. "I've never left my kids, and I can't see it happenin' now."

"Aletta, seems to me like you're about to have a nervous breakdown," Vee said. "What if the only thing that'll help is to go to New Mexico and try to find out about our great-grandmother?"

Aletta looked up and saw Jimmy's Trans Am in front of her house. Instinctively, she tapped the brakes, but then as her heart sank, she realized there was nowhere else to go. "Well, somebody please just put me outta my misery," she groaned.

Vee hadn't met Jimmy yet. They'd missed each other on a few occasions, and she wasn't upset about it. She knew he had mistreated Aletta, and it was self-important white men like him that she wanted brought to justice, not just for their woman hating but for their chauvinistic sense of entitlement to all the power and wealth in society. Besides, for her, Jimmy was just another complication in an already complicated situation.

She and Aletta went inside the house and found him drinking milk out of the carton. "Well, if it ain't Psychic Susie," he said playfully.

"Don't you have a job?" Aletta asked as she put Gyp in his playpen.

"I left for a meeting right after lunch." He extended his hand to Vee. "I've heard all about you."

Vee shook his hand, then skulked off to her room. She sat on the couch and put her head in her hands. God, what a mess she was in. She tried to figure out just how she was going to get out of it, but within minutes, she heard Aletta and Jimmy shouting.

"You shoulda never left me, goddammit!" Jimmy yelled. "I was there for you all those years, then I needed you, and look what you did to me!"

"I won't even listen to this bullshit, Jimmy! Are you drinkin' again?"

"Hell, no. Not a drop. Don't you accuse me!"

Vee heard a loud noise and jumped several inches off the couch. She reached inside her duffel bag, pulled out her gun, and stuffed it in the back waistband of her pants. By the time she reached the kitchen, Jimmy and Aletta were on to something else.

"I need more child support," Aletta said, her hands on her hips.

Jimmy threw his head back and laughed sarcastically. "You divorce me, then you want me to pay." He kicked the cabinet behind him with the heel of his shoe, then spat on the floor.

As Vee walked close to him, her mouth went dry and her stomach flipped over. All her put-on strength and bravado seemed to drain out of her. But something willed her forward, and she spread her feet beneath her and put her hands up in fighting position. "I know tae kwan do," she said.

Jimmy's mouth dropped two inches, then he looked at Aletta and laughed. "Where in the hell did you find her?"

"She's my family," Aletta said, like they'd grown up together. Vee saw Aletta glance at her, then back at Jimmy, before continuing. "And guess what? She's gonna be watchin' the kids while I take a little trip." Aletta's eyes glowed.

"You ain't takin' a trip," Jimmy said, and picked up his jacket off the bar stool where he'd left it.

"Oh, yessir, I sure am. I'm goin' on a huntin' trip, like you have been for years and years."

Vee didn't move a muscle. She was frozen in place with fear, but she glared at Jimmy like she'd take him down in a heartbeat.

Jimmy started to walk to the front door. "I tell you one thing for sure. She ain't watchin' my kids."

Aletta smiled. "All right, then, you take them."

That did it. He walked out the door.

Aletta turned to Vee. "Tae kwan do?"

Vee was speechless. She was so relieved she didn't have to fight huge, muscular, mean Jimmy Honor. She fell onto one of the green plastic bar stools, and when she did, the gun clanked on the backrest. She bolted straight upright, then off the chair. Backing her way out of the room, she said, "I need to lie down for a while."

She went into her room, closed the door, and hid the gun in her duffel bag. She collapsed on the bed, realizing that the only thing that had made her stand up to Jimmy was her concern for Aletta. Was that what they meant by the power of love? She groaned and turned onto her stomach. That might have been the corniest thing she'd ever thought.

Chapter Thirteen

When Jimmy got home, Charlotte was wiping down the countertop in the kitchen. She had cleaned up everything, and the place looked great.

Jimmy went to her, picked her up at her waist, and kissed her on the mouth. "Oh, you gorgeous thing. I'm gonna have to give you a little present." His hand moved down her waist to her round buttocks.

She swatted him with the kitchen towel but couldn't help smiling. "You better mind your p's and q's from now on, mister. No more crazy, all right? You wanna tell me what you think happened?"

"Nothin' happened," he said, and kissed her again, gently moving his hand to her crotch. "There's nothin' to talk about."

After they made love, he ordered pizza, and they sat eating and watching a news program on TV. The show was about a new disco called Studio 54 that had opened in

New York City. Seemed it was the place to be for all the celebrities. They watched as people like Liza Minnelli, Mikhail Baryshnikov, Mick Jagger, and Rod Stewart made their way into the club with fans screaming and cameras flashing. Inside, everybody danced and drank and looked gorgeous.

"Oh, wow," Charlotte cooed. "Wouldn't you just *love* to be there? Look at how glamorous they are."

Jimmy made a noise that could've gone either way. He wasn't going to admit it to her, but not only did he want to be there, he thought it was the kind of place he *belonged.*

Just then, the phone rang. It was Frank Conway. "Hey, Jimmy, I'm headed out to a meeting over at the VFW and thought you might want to come along," he said.

"Don't know what would make you think that," Jimmy said, his voice flat.

"Who is it?" Charlotte mouthed.

"It's Frank Conway," Jimmy said.

"What's he want?"

"Nothin'. He's goin' to one a them AA meetings."

Charlotte jumped off the couch. "Oh, Jimmy, you should go. Yes, yes. You go with him."

"Darlin', I don't need that voodoo bullshit."

"After I cleaned up all this mess, it's the least you could do, Jimmy Honor," she said, her hands set firmly on her hips.

Jimmy glared at her for a moment but knew he'd lost this one. He groaned and put the phone to his ear. "I ain't goin' in Okay," he said.

"No, sir, the VFW's over in Jasper," Frank said. "I'll meet you there at nine o'clock."

Charlotte hugged him around the neck when he got off the phone. "It'll be my turn to give *you* a nice present when you get home," she said.

Jimmy smiled and kissed her, figuring one meeting couldn't be all that bad, but by the time he pulled into the dirt parking lot of the small, isolated building off Route 11, he'd changed his mind. How the hell had he gotten roped into this?

Frank was waiting for him outside the door, holding a Styrofoam cup of coffee. He shook Jimmy's hand and smiled. "Thought I'd meet you out here. This is where a lot of folks turn around and head in the other direction."

"I'll bet it is," Jimmy said, "Especially when this ain't their problem."

They walked inside, where several people

stood around talking. Jimmy didn't look at any of them directly. But he did notice how much better Frank was looking. He'd lost some weight, and the dark circles under his eyes were gone. But more than that, there was just something different about him that Jimmy couldn't put a finger on.

"What'd you do? Start jogging?" Jimmy asked. He himself jogged five miles almost every day.

"Nope, just started comin' here again," Frank said, and poured Jimmy a cup of coffee.

Just then, a thin man with even thinner hair said, "All righty, y'all, let's get started."

Three tables with folding chairs were set up in a U shape in the middle of the room. The thin man sat in the center. Behind him, on an exposed brick wall, hung a poster listing the twelve steps of Alcoholics Anonymous.

Fifteen or twenty people including Frank and Jimmy sat down at the tables. Jimmy couldn't believe this many folks were here, admitting they were losers. He felt embarrassed for them.

"Welcome, everyone, to the nine o'clock meeting at the VFW. My name's Norm, and I'm an alcoholic," the thin man said.

Jimmy jumped a little in his chair when

everyone in the room said, "Hi, Norm."

They said a prayer, which made Jimmy even more uncomfortable. He was squeamish as hell around religion.

"Anyone here attending their first meeting of AA?" Norm asked.

Jimmy started to sweat but refused to raise his hand, even though it felt like they were all looking straight at him. After that excruciating pause, it got even worse. They all started to introduce themselves one at a time.

"Hi, I'm Tammy, and I'm an alcoholic."

"Hi, Tammy!"

"I'm Ron, and I'm an alcoholic."

"Hi, Ron!"

Jimmy wanted to run out of the room, but that would be even more embarrassing than sitting here. He just glared at a little heart that was cut into the wooden tabletop until it was his turn. All he could manage was saying his name under his breath.

"Hi, Jimmy!" they called.

He raised his eyes, and to his surprise, they were all now looking at the old lady who sat next to him as she proclaimed her belonging in this weird club. He let out a sigh of relief, and Frank gave him an encouraging smile. The next hour seemed like the longest one of his life. He shifted in his chair, stared at the ceiling fans circling lazily above them, and tapped his foot on the floor. He made sure not to take anything he heard seriously, or he might get sucked into this pathetic crowd.

He didn't relate to any of these folks anyway. They weren't like him. Just like this guy, Oren, who was talking. He was a redneck if Jimmy ever saw one.

Oren was saying, "You know, my days now are good. I get up and go to work if I'm on a job. I go see my mom and take her some dinner, make sure she's all right. I talk to my girlfriend on the phone. You know, normal stuff." Oren took a sip of his coffee, then continued. "But that ain't how it used to be. I used to wake up vomiting. When I got it together enough to get dressed, I'd act like I had some kind of big important business, of which I had none, to take care of. It was just an excuse to go to a bar."

The people who sat around the tables laughed and nodded.

"Just to go to relatives' house a few blocks down the road, I'd fill up a big container with whiskey. I almost killed three human beings in two different car wrecks, and you know what my only thought was? 'How am *I* gonna get outta this?' " Oren paused and looked around the room for a moment. "My days used to be only about myself, and now they're a lot more about other people."

Jimmy had no idea what this guy was talking about. He didn't wake up vomiting or almost kill anyone or do any of the things Oren had mentioned.

Tammy talked about how she'd never had any friends until she started coming to AA. "My sponsor told me, 'You can't pet a snarlin' dog,' and that's exactly what I was until I admitted I had a problem and began asking for God's help. I was friendless and alone."

Jimmy's mind flashed on Del and Walt Walters looking at him with such disgust after he'd screamed at Del's son. *But the kid deserved it,* he thought, and remembered all the guys surrounding him at lunch, listening to him and laughing at his stories. He remembered Bob Blylevin signing that contract today. People admired him. They always had.

After it was over, Jimmy shook Frank's hand and headed for the door. Outside, he took a deep breath of night air. He'd felt like he might suffocate in there from all the honesty and cigarette smoke. He used every horse the Trans Am had under her hood to get out of that parking lot. His anger rose up in him as he sped along in the night. *How dare these people think they know me?* he thought. As he went through Jasper, he caught its only two stoplights on green and didn't slow down from the seventy he was pushing.

On the other side of town, however, he found himself easing off the gas. The neon lights of the Round-Up Club caught his attention. He'd heard of the place, that it was a lot of fun with a good crowd, but he always went to the city instead. Studio 54 flashed in his mind, and he had a powerful urge to feel young and sexy and attractive like the celebrities he'd seen on TV. It was only a Monday night, but there were still four or five cars out front. He braked and pulled in next to a white Mercedes-Benz. *Nice,* he thought. He already liked the place.

When Aletta told Joy about going to New Mexico to try to find her great-grandma, Joy decided to call an emergency meeting. Aletta knew it was in part because of her breaking up with Eugene, the trash can incident, and Joy's general concern for Aletta's mental health that she'd asked Betty and Bobette to come by after the salon closed one evening to figure things out. So here they sat, Aletta, Betty, Bobette, and Sissy, in Joy's Femme Coiffures watching Vee have her hair done.

Joy finished applying the color, put a plastic bag on Vee's head, and sat her down under a dryer. Vee looked so pitiful, slumped in the mauve chair, it was as if Joy had performed surgery to remove a limb.

She tried to smile. "Thanks. I promise I'll work as long as it takes to pay you off."

Aletta had been surprised when Vee said she wanted to change her look completely and asked if Joy could do her hair and makeup, but it was clear Vee wasn't enjoying the process. Of course, Joy was thrilled to get her hands on the girl and let her work off the cost by doing chores around the shop. Joy's life's work was to keep women looking beautiful, and when she'd met Vee, she whispered to Aletta, "Are you sure she was actually *on* that bus or was it draggin' her behind?"

"All righty," Joy said, and lit a Capri cigarette. "Let's talk."

"Well, y'all know why we're here. I've been thinkin' about goin' to New Mexico to find out more about this lost relative of mine, but I keep goin' back and forth," Aletta said. Watching Joy inhale made her want desperately to smoke, but Ruby and

Randy were playing barber in the chair next to her and Sissy sat across the room.

"We don't want you to go," Ruby said as she rubbed pomade into Randy's hair.

"Oh, now, we talked about this, Rube," Sissy said. "If she wants to go, she oughta be able to go. Me and Vee'll take care of y'all. Mama needs to express her independence a little bit."

Betty swiveled around to face Sissy. "Well, you sure have grown up since . . ." She didn't finish, but everybody knew what she was going to say.

"Since Rusty and me broke up," Sissy said to Rusty's mother. "It's more than that, though. Vee's been tellin' me about women needin' to stand up on their own."

They all looked at Vee, who managed to look proud even under the circumstances.

"By the way, Mama, I ain't gonna be a mat maid," Sissy added.

"What?" Aletta exclaimed. "You been wantin' that so bad. Now, this is goin' too far if it means you can't have some fun."

Joy cleared her throat to bring the meeting back to order.

Aletta glared at Sissy. "We'll talk later," she said, and Sissy shrugged.

Bobette's face did a full twitch, including mouth, nose, and a radical blinking of her eyes, before she spoke. "I for one agree with Sissy," she proclaimed importantly. "In fact, I've been thinkin' on it, and I believe that Aletta's in no state to be goin' out drivin' to Moses and back by herself. So I've decided. I wanna go with her."

Betty slapped both hands on the armrests of her salon chair. "I was thinkin' the same damn — sorry, I mean darn — thing!"

Joy smashed her cigarette butt into a beanbag ashtray and exhaled smoke. "Well, y'all ain't leavin' me here to watch the paint dry on the walls while you're out chasin' down Indians, I can tell you that for damn sure."

Randy giggled. "They keep sayin' *damn.*"

"Yeah, damn," Ruby said under her breath.

Aletta turned to her children. "That's adult language only, you two."

She turned back to the ladies, who were watching her with anticipation. They could see the moisture gathering in her eyes. "Y'all are the best friends a person could ever want," Aletta said, and couldn't hold back the tears.

"So we're goin' to Santa Fe?" Bobette whooped.

Aletta cast her eyes down and shook her

head. "I just don't think I can do it," she said.

The whole room erupted in protests, everyone adding her two cents until Joy's timer rang and brought them all to silence. Bobette and Betty looked so disappointed, Aletta started feeling guilty.

Joy went over and checked Vee's hair. She pushed the drier dome back and walked Vee over to the shampoo sinks, and still they all stayed as quiet as chastised children. Joy began rinsing the color out of Vee's hair, then looked up at Aletta. When she spoke, Joy's voice had a rare and meaningful sincerity in it that made Aletta listen not only with her ears but with her heart too.

"Lettie, this is bigger'n you, and you know it," Joy said, her hands taking care of business on Vee's head without needing her brain at all. "You ain't like the rest of us. Things happen for you that we never experience and can't even understand. God's got some kinda plan for you, girl, and you better darn well listen or this thing's liable to chew you up and spit you out."

There seemed to be a single breath among them as all eyes turned from Joy to Aletta, and the truth of Joy's words sank deep inside her.

"Well," Aletta sighed finally, "if y'all are

all comin' with me, who's gonna help watch these kids? There needs to be a responsible adult involved, and we all know that ain't Jimmy Honor."

Betty leaned forward in her chair, excitement playing on her face. "Silvia Rivera will be happy to help out. She worships the ground you walk on."

"Do you think so?" Aletta asked.

Joy dried off Vee's hair with a towel. "Let's give her a call right now."

Bobette was at the pink wall telephone with the ten-foot cord in seconds. "What's the number?"

Joy removed the towel from Vee's head, and Vee ran to the mirror. Her tousled, still-damp hair was a light strawberry red, almost blond. "Oh, God," she said.

"It's gonna be gorgeous," Joy commanded. "Now sit down."

By the time Joy had cut Vee's hair and begun a lengthy blowdrying process, Silvia had agreed to help take care of Aletta's kids while she was away. Bobette had a calendar balanced on her lap and was circling possible departure dates.

After ten minutes of compromising, Bobette exclaimed, "So the twelfth it is. We got just ten days, then it's off on an adventure!"

At that moment Joy turned off the blow

dryer and swung Vee around in her chair so everyone could see. A single collective gasp filled the air before the women barraged her with compliments, oohs, and aahs. Joy had done her hair in a shoulder-length sassy shag. Parted in the middle, it feathered down each side of her face in layer upon layer. Vee sat there looking like one of Bobette's twitches had frozen onto her face, she seemed so uncomfortable.

It wasn't until Aletta said, "You look like a completely different person," that Vee managed a slight grin.

As they walked back over to her house later, Aletta heard Sissy and Vee talking.

"I thought you didn't want to do things just to look good for guys," Sissy said. "This is sure the kind of thing they like."

CHAPTER FOURTEEN

On Thursday, May 12, Bobette pulled into Aletta's driveway at exactly seven-thirty in the morning. They were going to take Bobette's lime green Gran Torino station wagon, so they could fit all the luggage in the back. Bobette threw the car into park, bounced up to Aletta's front door, and rang the bell. Then she ran next door to Joy's and did the same.

After ten more minutes and one last check of the tire pressure, status of the spare, and engine oil by Bobette, Aletta finally came out her front door with two Naugahyde suitcases that had been her mother's. Randy and Ruby trailed behind her, both of them whining at her not to go.

"Well, you ready to have some fun?" Bobette said before she looked up from the car's engine and saw the distressed expression on Aletta's face.

Aletta dumped her suitcases next to Bobette's orange vinyl one in the back of the car. "I hope it's worth all this."

Vee and Sissy walked out the front door at the same time Earl and Joy came out of their house. Vee carried a notepad in one hand while Earl lugged Joy's massive pink suitcase. Joy's hair was still platinum blond, but she had it done up in a twist. She wore dangling turquoise earrings with matching pumps, purple-hued sunglasses, and tight capri pants. Carrying a matching pink makeup case, she walked to the wagon and sat inside while Earl heaved the suitcase into the back.

"Mama, I don't want you to go!" Ruby yelled.

Aletta ignored her and called to Sissy. "You make sure that percolator's unplugged, and I want you helpin' Vee out around here."

Sissy put a hand on her hip. "I know, Mama."

Joy stuck her head out the door and let Earl give her a kiss on the cheek, then held up a finger. "Excuse me, but can we just keep it down a little bit? It's godawful early in the mornin'."

Bobette's face twitched, then settled into a smile. "Why, this is the best time a the day, you ask me. I'm ready to get on the road!"

Joy closed her door.

Aletta went over her list with Vee one more time. "Now, you got the money I gave you for groceries. Make sure they eat their real food, not just candy and pop. Here's Dr. Lowrey's number. Don't hesitate to call him if anything comes up."

"Aletta, I got it. I got it," Vee said as Rusty Conway drove his mother to the curbside.

Aletta glanced at Sissy, whose face drained of color. "Uh-oh," Aletta said.

"Who is it?" Vee asked.

"Rusty. Sissy's old boyfriend."

Rusty got out of the car and carried his mother's luggage to the wagon.

Betty practically skipped up the driveway. "Isn't this wonderful?" she said.

"Well, that's what I thought." Bobette crossed her arms and legs and leaned her butt against the car.

Rusty put his mother's suitcase in the wagon, then glanced at Sissy. "Hey," he said.

"Hey." Sissy looked at the ground, clearly trying to hold back her tears.

Vee walked up to her. "Sissy, I need you to help me with my master's thesis on patriarchy in the media. Can we do a little bit more before you go to school?"

"Oh, uh, sure," Sissy said, noticing the surprised look on Rusty's face.

Just then, Jimmy rumbled up in his black Trans Am and got out of the car, keeping the door open and a hand on the roof.

"Mornin', folks," he said.

"You got to be kiddin' me," Aletta groaned, then leaned in to tell Joy, "Just stay in the car."

Bobette and Betty scowled but didn't say anything since the kids were there.

"Goodbye, Jimmy," Aletta said.

Jimmy took off his mirrored sunglasses and glared at Aletta. "I don't think you oughta be leavin' these kids like this."

Aletta glared at Ruby and Randy, shutting them up, before answering. "I'm outta here, Jimmy. I know you're gonna help Vee out takin' care of your children while I'm gone."

Rusty said goodbye to his mother, then left quickly without looking at Sissy again.

Sissy rolled her eyes at her parents. "Y'all are embarrassin'."

Jimmy ignored her. "I got a sales conference all day tomorrow and Saturday, so they're on their own. If anything happens, it's your fault, Mama," he said, then got back in the car and drove away.

Aletta hugged and kissed Ruby and Randy and Gyp, assuring them nothing was going to happen, then got into the front passenger seat. "Let's go now," she said, "or I'm gonna chicken out."

Bobette hopped behind the wheel and started backing out of the driveway before Betty had her door closed all the way.

Aletta waved to her kids, but they all just looked at her with the saddest faces she'd ever seen. She knew Sissy's attitude was because of Rusty, but the two middle ones were upset because she was leaving. Vee was the only one waving. She was smiling too, but behind the smile Aletta could see the fear.

As they lost sight of the house and turned off Main Street toward the highway, Aletta turned to the ladies. "Oh, my lands, I can't believe we're actually doin' this."

Betty laughed. "We're free!"

"Like the wind!" Bobette cried.

"Like a bird," Aletta said.

"Like a pack a dogs," Joy answered. "But I'm a dog on a leash."

Bobette drove up the ramp onto Interstate 40. "What's got into you today?"

"Did you and Earl get in a fight last night?" Betty asked.

Joy crossed her legs and looked out the window. "He didn't want me to come."

"Oh, now we know why you're so pissy,"

Aletta said for the three of them.

"Yeah, you're not used to havin' a leash of any kind, are you?" Bobette asked.

Betty laughed. "Joy fancies herself footloose and fancy free with Earl wrapped around her little finger, don't you, darlin'? But he didn't play by the rules."

"He knew 'em when I said yes, so I don't know what's changed now," Joy said, lighting a cigarette. Everyone knew Earl worshipped the ground she walked on, taking orders and accepting a backseat to her flamboyance. He rarely questioned her on anything.

"Maybe he just doesn't wanna be away from you. He's a good man," Aletta said.

"Hmph," Joy grunted.

"A lot more'n you can say for some I know," Aletta said quietly.

Joy exhaled. "But you know the worst."

"Yeah, I do."

Betty stared at Aletta, knowing something was wrong. "What happened?" she asked finally.

"Well, I was too embarrassed to tell y'all before, but I saw Charlie Bastard — oh, I mean Baxter."

She told them about running into Charlie at the 7-Eleven and how he was an oil worker, not a businessman, how he was married and had her on the side, how she had fallen for him and never seen who he really was. There was so much female righteous indignation in that car by the time she was finished, any man unfortunate enough to be riding with them would've probably choked to death from the fumes.

"I'm so damn humiliated," Aletta said finally. "Not just because he had me fooled, but because I'm such an idiot for this type of man. He couldn't have tricked me if I didn't wanna be tricked in some way. It's like I feel unworthy of a good man or somethin'."

"Well, that's just hog pee," Joy said.

Bobette kept her eyes on the road. "I feel the same way as Aletta. That Harley keeps comin' 'round, and I don't know why I can't just tell him to get lost for good."

"Why do y'all think you like the bad boys?" Betty asked.

"I thought with Jimmy, it was punishment for how my daddy was killed by Johnny Redding, but then, after all that, I do the same damn thing again and start up with Charlie Baxter," Aletta said.

Bobette nodded. "I grew up thinkin' women just put up with men no matter what. That's what my mama did, and that's what I've been doin'."

Joy leaned forward and looked at herself in the rearview mirror. "You think that's what this Indian lady we're chasin' did, Lettie? You think she got herself in with a man that was no good for her?"

"Well, she was forced to go to that Indian school, where they just sucked the life right outta the kids. Did I tell y'all their slogan? 'Kill the Indian, save the man' — or woman, as it turned out," Aletta answered. "That was actually the slogan for how the government chose to deal with the Indian 'problem,' as they called it."

"My Lord, that's just awful," Betty said.

"Unbelievable," Bobette exclaimed, but added, "What does it mean?"

"It means they thought if they stamped out the Indian from a person, then it would save him from being a heathen, a savage," Aletta answered. "They just crushed their whole Indian culture and language and history. Did it all over the country too. It was a whole policy back then."

Bobette looked at Aletta with admiration. "You sound like a historian."

Aletta laughed. "I'd have to guess what that is, but it sounds good. Anyway, she went to that school, then she married a white man, the son of a rich judge whose job was to enforce all these policies. Sounds like a bad choice to me, like one that denied her true self."

"Is that what you do with these men you choose, Lettie?" Betty asked.

Aletta looked out the window at the passing flat Oklahoma landscape as she spoke. "It's funny, but I can look at my greatgrandmother and see who she was, an Indian who belonged to a tribe and had special abilities and a history in her family of it. There was a place for her even though she did lose it so young. But for me, I don't even think I've ever known what my true self is."

"Lord, do I know what you mean," Bobette said.

"What woman really does, for that matter?" Betty asked.

"Well," said Joy, "I know my true self perfectly well. This month it happens to be Dolly Parton."

They all laughed. "I guess you better inform your breasts," Aletta said.

"They've been thinkin' about an enhancement," Joy said, pushing them up.

"No!" they all cried in unison.

"Did y'all see Marilyn Crudup's new pair? She went off to Los Angeles and came back a D cup," Bobette said. Miss Crudup was one of Okay Elementary's second-grade teachers.

"You shoulda seen Principal Power's face when Marilyn got back from Christmas break and her new rack entered the room well ahead of the rest of her."

They talked about boobs for another thirty miles before the conversation turned back to men. Aletta was thrilled to hear Betty was thinking about taking Frank back.

"He's started goin' back to AA. He's lost some weight and seems a lot happier. He and Rusty are doin' a little better too. He ain't really pushin', but I figure I better take him back 'fore some other woman takes him away."

Bobette glanced at her in the rearview mirror and grinned. "Marilyn Crudup's sure lookin'."

"Exactly," Betty said. "So, ladies, this may be my last weekend of bein' single, and you better watch out, 'cause I'm gonna live it up."

Joy dug in her purse and pulled out a small flask. "On that note," she said, and tipped the flask to her pink rose lips.

They sped down I-40 at seventy-five miles per hour, and the further west they got, the more relaxed Aletta felt. She was as worried as she could be about having left her kids, but now that she was here, she was enjoying the hell out of it. They passed a big rig, and Joy, who had had more than one pull at the flask, rolled down the window and waved at the driver.

"Hi, sweetheart!" she called.

The driver, a thick-necked man with a mustache, sunglasses, and ball cap, waved back, then blared his horn three times. This thrilled the ladies, and they all had to turn and wave.

"Must be my sexy car," Bobette chuckled.

They made it to and through Amarillo flirting with truck drivers the entire way. After a while, they didn't even have to try. As soon as a trucker saw the Gran Torino coming in his rearview mirrors, he was honking his horn and waving like crazy.

Just after they passed the New Mexico state line, Bobette saw a patrol car with its lights on behind them. "Oh, shit," she said. "The fuzz."

The next exit was just ahead, so she pulled off and into the parking lot of a worn-out adobe building that was home to the Navajo Indian Store and Café.

The patrolman approached them, hitching up his heavy belt on his hips.

"Just act calm, y'all. Nobody flip out. Just stay cool." Joy was so nervous, she could barely sit still.

"Driver's license and registration, please," the big blond cop said as he leaned toward Bobette and checked out the other women.

"What was I doin' wrong, officer?" Bobette asked.

He looked at her paperwork, pausing for effect. "Did you know the speed limit is fifty-five miles per hour?"

"That's what I was doin'," Bobette said. "I know 'cause I was sittin' behind one a them truckers who wouldn't get outta the fast lane."

Aletta and Betty giggled.

The cop leaned down and eyed them again. "Well, I been hearin' y'all have been doin' seventy-five and up."

"Hearin' from who?" Aletta asked, leaning over Bobette to look up at him.

"Well, ma'am, I been listenin' to truckers from Oklahoma all the way through the Texas panhandle and into New Mexico talkin' about you on the CB. I guess I just had to see for myself."

Betty rolled down her window all the way. "Are you sayin' you stopped us 'cause you heard about us on your radio?"

"What're they sayin'?" Bobette asked.

The policeman grinned and looked at the ground. "Well, they're sayin' you ladies are real nice to look at and burnin' rubber like you're headed to Vegas."

There was a pause for a moment in which nobody knew quite what to say next. Finally, Joy's car door opened and she got out, patting her hair into place. "Well, ain't that the nicest thing I ever did hear. What's your name, Officer?"

They chatted with Officer Brody for several minutes. When he had to take off on a call from his radio, they decided to eat at the Indian Store and Café.

"Bye now!" Joy called sweetly to Brody as he pulled away. Then she added under her breath, "I should report that son of a bitch."

They all laughed. "Why were you so nervous around him?" Aletta asked.

"I've always been nervous around police. I guess it's my guilty conscience," Joy said. "Oh, and maybe that time in high school I got thrown in jail had an effect on me too."

They stopped in the middle of the dirt parking lot. "You were thrown in jail?" Aletta asked.

Joy walked away from them. "I ain't sayin' another word."

"Can you believe that cop stopped us so he could get a good look?" Betty asked as they followed Joy.

"Men!" Bobette shouted as she pushed open the door to the café. The entire room of about a dozen people turned to look.

The ladies all busted up laughing as a shy young Indian woman with big eyes and long black hair took them to a booth. Aletta stared at her as she slid across the red plastic, taking the menu from the girl. Her name tag read TERESA.

Teresa returned to take their order, and Aletta couldn't stop looking at her. Before she walked away, Aletta got up her courage. "Excuse me, how old're you?"

"Eighteen," Teresa said, her eyes avoiding Aletta's.

"You live around here?"

"On the reservation," she said. "Only place I've ever lived."

Bobette put her iced tea down. "Oh, is this reservation land? How fascinating."

The girl smiled slightly, amused by these women.

"Do you live in a pueblo?" Aletta asked.

"No, we're Navajo," she said. "I'll be right back with your food, okay?"

As soon as she left, Joy leaned forward. "What does that mean?"

"Well, Navajo's a tribe," Aletta answered.

"I've heard of the Navajo tribe, but what's a pueblo?" Betty asked.

"As far as I can tell, it's a small Indian village made of mud buildings. Pueblo Indians have lived in them since long before white men came here," Aletta said quietly. For some reason, it seemed rude to talk about the Indians right in front of them like they were animals at the zoo.

"What about teepees?" Bobette asked.

"That's different tribes," Aletta said, then looked at Teresa, who was carrying a tray of burgers to another table. "She's so young. Adelaide was settlin' in Oklahoma with a two-year-old at her age. Can you imagine?"

"Those pioneer women just amaze me at what they went through," Joy said.

"And she had it worse than most, bein' an Indian," Betty said.

Bobette shook her head. "Oh, my lands, the prejudice was just awful, even when I was growin' up. I don't remember anyone ever callin' an Indian just an Indian. It was either 'dirty Indian' or 'drunk Indian,' and sometimes both."

"That's why I never knew she was in my family or I was part Indian myself. Seems like the whole family was ashamed," Aletta said.

"Lord above, that musta been a hard row to hoe for her," Joy said.

Just then, Teresa came over with their food. They all bent over backward acting nice to her and then left her a big tip. It was all they could do to make up for a past none of them had any control over but wished they did.

Aletta and Betty went into the Indian store next door when they finished eating. It was full of cheap things like plastic tomahawks and bows and arrows. There were flint arrowheads and leather bullwhips and little statues of the sad Trail of Tears Indian slumped over on his horse with his spear dragging next to him. The overweight Indian woman behind the counter was drinking a huge Coke, eating cheese fries, and watching *All My Children* on a small black-and-white TV.

Aletta's throat started closing up on her in the middle of this place. She stepped outside and stood under a huge gathering of dark clouds.

"You all right?" Betty asked, following her.

"That place makes me sad," she said. She couldn't quite understand why it bothered her so much, but there was something unnatural about the whole thing. She also felt that this was probably as close as she was going to get to finding out about real Indians. She was on the outside — a white woman, a tourist — and this was what people like her got to experience: the sad, fabricated Disneyland version of Indians.

Bobette started the car when she saw them. "Come on, girls. It's about to dump on us."

They drove straight into a wall of black clouds and got another twenty miles down the road before it opened up on them like a torrent from an angry God. Bobette strained over the steering wheel, trying to see the road, but they had to go painfully slow. The highway became a river within half an hour, and the big trucks that had been their entertainment before became dangerous obstacles as they tried to pass.

"How you doin', Bobette?" Aletta asked nervously.

"Oh, well . . ." Bobette's voice trailed off.

Just then a big rig cut over in front of them, clearly not seeing them because of the rain. Bobette slammed on her brakes, and the massive station wagon begin to fishtail down the road, skimming on top of a layer of road grease and water. Bobette's face twitched wildly as she turned the steering wheel back and forth, trying desperately to regain control.

The other three women grabbed on to whatever they could to stay upright, the panic and fear closing their throats against screaming. Finally, Bobette got the car straightened out, then she pulled over onto the shoulder of the highway. They sat in silence for a moment as the rain pounded on the car, drumming and drumming like it was coming to get them.

"Anyone for stoppin' in the next town for a while?" Bobette asked.

"Get us outta here!" Joy cried.

Betty put her hands to her face. "I thought we were goners."

Bobette pulled onto the highway again, this time going about forty miles per hour.

"I know this storm's goin' east, but you don't think it'll hit Oklahoma, do you?" she asked.

None of them answered her. They all were thinking the same thing, though. A big storm in May in Oklahoma was more than likely to mean one thing — twisters.

"Here's an exit," Bobette said. "I'm getting off this godforsaken interstate."

They pulled into the parking lot of the Wild West Motel, a clean and friendly-looking place with large images of cowboys painted on every room door.

"Let's just wait it out for a little while," Bobette said. "It'll pass soon."

Joy got out her nail file, and Betty pulled a deck of cards from her purse. "How 'bout some gin rummy?"

"I'm gonna go call my kids," Aletta said,

then got out of the car and ran toward the little lobby of the motel.

"They're fine," Joy called after her, shaking her head. "It's us that need help."

Aletta was dripping water when she walked through the door that had a cowboy on a rearing horse, his hat in his hand. A little bell rang as she entered, and a woman wearing a denim skirt, turquoise jewelry, and a white cowboy hat walked out from a back room.

"Well, you poor thing, out in this crazy weather!" the plump older lady said warmly.

"We had to pull off the highway, it was so bad," Aletta said. "Can I use your phone to call my kids? I'll call collect."

"Well, sure," the woman said.

Aletta got through to the operator, who dialed her number. It rang three times, then a flash of lightning struck right outside the motel, followed by a huge thunderclap, and the phone went dead.

Chapter Fifteen

Vee ran to answer the phone, thinking it might be Bo or Carol returning her call, but when she got to it, there was nobody on the other end.

"Damn," she said under her breath.

She was planning to leave town Sunday, the day before Aletta returned, and she wanted to have a plan. At the moment, she thought she would go south to Mexico, even though driving all the way through Texas scared the hell out of her. At the moment, she was surprised at how calm she felt, considering what she was going to do in only a couple of days. It was the same kind of numb feeling she'd gotten before they pulled the bank job.

Vee carried Gyp outside to check on Ruby and Randy, who had gone to play with the neighborhood kids. Clouds were starting to gather overhead, and she hoped they'd be ready to come in soon.

Just then, Sissy walked up the street, a sullen look on her face.

"Hey, how was your education in imperialist power structures today?" Vee asked, smiling.

Sissy shrugged. "There's nothin' I care about anymore, so it's boring."

Vee shifted Gyp to her other hip. "What did you care about before?"

Sissy sat down on the porch steps and Vee sat next to her, allowing Gyp to crawl free. "Well, Rusty, a course. That was funny what you said this mornin'. I don't think he understood a word of it, but it sure made him think."

Vee smiled. "Good. Probably the first time in his life."

"Another thing I was into was bein' a mat maid, but I see how degrading that is and all."

"Okay, show me what the hell a mat maid does. Just those words make me cringe."

Sissy tossed her book bag aside and sat cross-legged on the cement porch. "Well, it's just a cheerleader for wrestlers. But since they're on the ground, you have to sit on the edge of the mat, on the floor like this, and cheer."

Vee tried to keep from rolling her eyes.

Suddenly, Sissy started slapping the

ground in a rhythm like she was playing the drums, then she slapped her hands together, then her knees. Ground, slap, hands, clap, knees, clap, slap, tap. It was some fancy handwork with a great beat. The cheer Sissy did went perfectly with the rhythm.

"Put his back, back, back on the mat, mat, mat. Put his back" — *slap, slap* — "on the mat" — *clap, clap.* "Put his back on the mat. Lay him flat!"

Vee's eyebrows stayed raised throughout the entire performance. When Sissy stopped, Vee said, "You must've worked a long time on that."

Sissy shrugged. "Angie and me practiced every day after school."

"I just wonder what would happen if you put all that energy into something that would empower you instead of empowering those boys." Vee picked up Gyp, who was about to reach the driveway and its grease stains, then she continued. "You don't have to be trapped in this little town and live a life of marriage and childbearing, Sissy. You can get out of here and make a difference in the world."

Sissy stood up and picked up her book bag. "You're right," she said, even as her head was hanging. Vee could tell Sissy wanted to impress her.

An hour later, Vee went outside to find the kids so they could do their homework. The sky was now a deep blue-gray, and the air seemed weighted down with the heaviness of a coming rain. She went through the gate of the rotted wood fence that bordered an open field behind Aletta's house. Crossing the field, she came out on the street behind Main, where half a dozen kids lived.

Vee saw Ruby and Randy just as the wind kicked up. They were playing with an older girl in her front yard several houses away. "Ruby! Randy!" she called, but they didn't hear her voice because of the wind.

By the time she reached them, the rain was coming down in drops the size of half dollars. The other girl's mother called her in from outside as Ruby and Randy ran to Vee.

"Did you all ever think about heading home before it started to rain?" she asked as they turned up the street and started running home.

"We were havin' fun with Kendra. She has lots of toys," Ruby said.

"Yeah, Tonka trucks and Barbie dolls," Randy said, his stout little legs running as fast as they could go.

"Oh, well, that makes perfect sense, then." Vee couldn't help but smile.

The rain started to come down heavier, and by the time they crossed the field, went through the gate, and got home, they were soaked through. Vee made them take their shoes off in the garage, then undressed them when they got inside.

"Go get yourself changed, Ruby," she said as she pulled Randy's shirt over his head.

His smooth, brown belly pooched out a little, and his home-cut bowl-shaped hair was a mess on his head. His smile was big and wide and missing two teeth as she rubbed him dry with a threadbare towel.

She smiled back, kneeling in front of him. "What're you so happy about, mister?" she asked.

"I'm glad you're here," he said, then hugged her around her neck.

Vee held on to his little body. She felt a melting sensation in her chest, but she had no idea what to say or how to handle such affection.

"I better get out of these wet clothes," she said finally, and pulled away from him.

"Lord above," she said as she walked into her room. *Lord above?* she thought. She'd never said that in her entire life. She thought about Sunday and felt relief that she was going to get out of this Podunk before she turned into one of its inhabitants. But relief was followed by dread, and for that, she didn't have an explanation.

Jimmy left work and was going to go check on his kids, but when he passed the VIP Lounge on the way home from the city, the heavy rain gave him an excuse to go in and have one drink until it lightened up a little. Jimmy liked the VIP, an upscale, modern bar that had its fair share of leather, velvet, steel, and mood lighting from hanging stained-glass balls. Even though he desperately wanted to feel he belonged in a place like this, he didn't come that often because he felt insecure around people with money who knew more than he did. But sometimes, when he'd had a good day, this was his first choice for a watering hole.

As soon as he walked in, he knew he was in for a good time. Chuck Everage and Luke Plummer, guys he'd played baseball with at Central State University, sat at a table drinking cocktails.

"Well, if it ain't the gunner from Okay," Chuck said as Jimmy walked up and shook hands with them.

Luke motioned to the waitress. "Sweetheart, bring this gentleman anything he wants."

"Anything?" Jimmy asked, looking the blonde up and down.

Chuck and Luke laughed as the waitress blushed. "Well, almost anything," Luke said.

The rain started to pound against the windows of the club, so the owner turned up the disco music. Jimmy took a drink of his vodka, and they started in talking about the old days, when Jimmy was throwing ninety-mile-an-hour fastballs and his nickname on the team was Gunner. This was Jimmy Honor's version of heaven.

The sweet but extremely chatty owner of the Wild West Motel was about halfway through with her life story when Betty honked the Gran Torino's horn, letting Aletta know it was time to come on.

They got back on the highway, which was almost empty now. It seemed they weren't the only ones beaten by the storm. Aletta switched on the radio and twisted the dial, trying to find a weather report, but all she found was a Mexican station, so she turned it off.

"Put this in," Joy said, and handed Aletta an eight-track tape. Elvis's luscious voice seemed to smooth out the drive.

They watched the sun stream through indigo clouds rimmed with orange and pink as it set over the changing desert landscape. Before they knew it, they were turning off I-40 onto the state highway that led to Santa Fe. It took another hour of steadily gaining elevation before they saw signs telling them they were entering Santa Fe, the oldest city in America. By that time, it was pitch black, the clouds keeping any light from the moon hidden away.

Betty drove down Cerrillos Road while Aletta gave her directions to the El Rey Inn, their home for four nights.

Aletta and Joy checked into one room with two double beds, and Bobette and Betty took the other.

Aletta threw her suitcases onto the bed and grabbed the telephone. She dialed her number, but all she got was a weird, fast busy signal.

"What the hell?" she said out loud, and dialed again, but got the same thing. She dialed the operator and told her what was happening.

"That number is out of order at the moment, ma'am. It seems they're having some weather in the area that is causing some problems," the operator said.

Aletta put the phone down and sat on the

edge of the Southwest-print-covered bed. She stared at the painting of coyotes baying up at the moon that hung over the cute little adobe-style fireplace. "I can't believe this," she said.

"Oh, now, have a cookie, hon. Don't worry so much," Joy said, then promptly got on the phone to call Earl. But her phone was out too.

Betty and Bobette walked in. "Ain't these the cutest little rooms with all the Santa Fe décor?" Bobette said.

"What's wrong?" Betty asked, noticing that Aletta and Joy weren't looking too good.

"The phones are dead back home. Weather problem," Aletta said.

Joy went to the mirror and took her hair down, letting it fall around her shoulders. "I guess there's only one answer to this problem."

"What's that?" Aletta asked.

"Margaritas, of course."

Bobette's face did a little dance before lighting up in a smile. "Will you tell us about getting arrested?"

Joy didn't turn from the mirror. "Not on your life," she said.

Vee stood at the window with her arms

crossed, looking out at the rain coming down from the sky like it was trying to beat the hell out of everything, like it was mad at the world. It was still early evening, so she could see the damage it was causing pretty clearly. Ruby walked up and stood next to her, mesmerized by the movement.

Suddenly, a blinding flash of lightning struck the elm tree right outside, causing an entire limb to crash to the ground and the lights to flicker out. The thunder that followed was so loud, both Vee and Ruby ducked down like it was coming through the roof to get them.

"Oh, man," Randy whined from the living room, where the TV had just gone out with the rest of the electricity.

Vee went to the kitchen to try to find candles and flashlights as Sissy stood holding Gyp, looking out the kitchen window at Main Street flowing by like the Caddo River.

Vee found a flashlight, but it didn't work, so she began to dig for batteries as she thought about calling Jimmy. Even though it was a loathsome idea, she felt like she was in over her head, and she didn't want to be responsible for all these kids in this crazy weather. They *were* his damn kids, after all.

"Uh-oh," Sissy said, so low Vee almost

didn't hear her. She figured Gyp must be wet.

"Um, Vee . . . um, I think, um . . . ," Sissy muttered, her eyes transfixed on something outside.

"What is it, Sissy?" Vee asked, and went to look.

An enormous black cloud had descended from the sky like a wall coming down from heaven. But this cloud looked more like it was from hell.

"Do you see that little, um, tail kind of thing coming out of that cloud?" Sissy whispered, not wanting Ruby and Randy, who were standing behind them, to hear.

Vee strained to see what Sissy was talking about.

"Right there," Sissy said, and pointed.

Vee went to the front door and opened it so she could get a better look than the view through the dirt- and rain-streaked window. All four kids gathered around her out on the covered front porch. She looked again, and now she saw it so clearly, her heart stopped for at least two beats. A slim funnel was curling out of the cloud, pointing its way to the ground. Suddenly, it stopped raining and the wind quieted down.

"Oh, shit," Sissy said. "That means it's comin' right at us."

"How do you know?" Vee asked, her face stark white.

Just then, a tornado siren started blaring. Vee pushed everyone back inside and closed the door. By now, Ruby, Randy, and Gyp were crying. She ran to the phone to call Jimmy, but of course, it was dead.

She slammed the receiver down, then turned to Sissy. She had to yell to be heard over the siren and the crying. "All right, now. Let's not panic. I've never done this, so what are we supposed to do?"

"You're supposed to go in a basement," Sissy called. "We used to go to my grandma's house."

"Fine, let's go!" Vee grabbed the keys off the counter.

"She died in February."

"Oh, my God! I don't know what to do!" Vee screamed, panic trembling in her voice. The wailing of the siren blared so loudly, she couldn't even think.

"We have to get into the shower. All of us. Right now," Sissy said.

"What about openin' the windows? Mama always opens the windows," Ruby said as they hurried toward the back of the house.

"Why?" Vee asked.

"They say that if you don't, it causes too much pressure to build up inside the house

272

and it busts all the windows and doors open. That's even if the tornado doesn't hit us directly," Sissy said, handing Gyp off to Ruby.

Randy screamed, "I'm scared!"

Vee and Sissy pushed the kids through Sissy's bedroom and into the tiny bathroom. She and Sissy ran around the house, opening windows a crack in every room. Finally, they ran back to the bathroom and squeezed into the tile shower with Ruby and Randy and Gyp. There was really only enough room for one person to take a shower, so they stumbled on one another's feet until each found a place to stand.

Vee closed the opaque plastic door, realizing how ridiculous it was to do so, like that little sheet of plastic could do anything to protect them against a tornado ripping through the house. The showerhead dripped and the smell of mildew and greasy kids' hair filled her nose. The siren wasn't as loud anymore since they were in the back of the house, so she could hear the sniffles and ragged breathing of the children. It seemed like all of her senses were heightened, like the possibility of death made everything stand out as something important and meaningful.

Gyp sneezed all over her neck, but she just

wiped his nose with a tissue from her pocket without paying much attention. As the light faded completely away, she could no longer see the faces of the kids clearly, but she reached out and touched each one of them, squeezing a shoulder or caressing their hair.

"Let's sing a song," she said finally, unable to stand the fear and the fact that she was helpless to do anything.

Randy started to sing "Jesus Loves the Little Children," and the rest of them joined in. Instinctively, Vee rolled her eyes and kept her mouth shut tight against the religious brainwashing.

"Jesus loves the little children," they sang, their small voices high-pitched and sweet. "All the children of the world. Red and yellow, black and white, they are precious in his sight. Jesus loves the little children of the world."

Something just cracked open inside her listening to them sing in the face of such danger. They were singing about the very things she cared about — racial equality and the fair treatment of every person. It just came in a package she judged to be inferior and simple-minded at best, dangerous and idiotic at worst. But listening to this sweet song, Vee realized that she so often lost the compassion of her beliefs in the anger she had for the bullies of the world. Somehow, anger just didn't make sense right at that moment.

They started the second verse, and she did her best to sing along with them. Just as it ended, the siren faded out, indicating that the tornado had passed, and all that was left was a profound silence. They waited in the silence and darkness for a moment, the realization that they would live washing over them. And then the moment was gone, and they were hustling out of the bathroom, whooping it up and laughing as they barreled down the hall.

Jimmy and Luke and Chuck sat on the carpeted floor of the VIP Lounge underneath their cocktail table, laughing and telling dirty jokes, smashed from three hours of drinking. Finally, the damn siren stopped blaring outside, and they did their best to make it to their feet.

"We're alive!" Chuck shouted.

"Better have a drink to celebrate," Luke slurred.

"I gotta go check on my kids," Jimmy said, pushing himself off the floor, then falling back down again.

"You ain't drivin' anywhere, buddy," Chuck said, and had the bartender, the only other person left in the place, call Jimmy a taxi. The phones in Oklahoma City were still working.

The taxi driver helped Jimmy to his front door and pushed the bell. Charlotte answered, her face red and angry. She took Jimmy's arm and led him to the couch, where he lay back and put his arm over his eyes.

"We were just in a goddamn tornado," she yelled. "You better be glad we got a basement over in the rec room. I mean, did you even consider what I might be goin' through? Do you ever think about anyone but yourself? Jimmy? Jimmy?"

He had passed out, and she left him there snoring away.

CHAPTER SIXTEEN

Aletta pulled the earplugs out of her ears and grabbed the telephone. She hadn't slept much at all, but she was wide awake at seven-thirty, hoping the phones were back on. She let it ring until the answering machine picked up.

"Hello, this is Aletta. I'll be out of town until Monday, so I won't be doing readings till I return. You can leave a message, and I'll call you when I get back. Have a great day." *Beep.*

"Sissy! Vee! Ruby!" she called into the machine as loud as she could.

Joy rolled over and put her pillow over her head.

Finally, Vee picked up the phone, her voice croaky and tired.

"Oh, my Lord above," Aletta sighed. "I've been so worried."

Vee told her the whole story as Aletta held her breath.

"I don't even know what to say," she said when Vee finished. "I'm sorry as hell you had to go through all that."

Vee laughed nervously. "It's the least I could do," she said.

"I can't believe that bastard of an ex of mine didn't even come by. He's really gone even lower than I thought he could with this. I mean, I know he gets so much joy out of making my life miserable, but at the expense of his kids? I'm just in shock."

Joy flopped over again. "That man is conscience-free. How can he still shock you?"

"All right, Vee. Well, call me if you need anything at all. I'm glad everyone's okay," Aletta said, then hung up the phone.

As Aletta let water trickle over her in the pink and turquoise shower, she decided she needed to go back home. As she dressed in her Chic jeans and denim shirt with embroidered flowers, she considered the words she would use to let her kids know she meant what she was saying. She pulled on her cowboy boots, thinking she'd let them know at breakfast, then opened the door and stepped outside.

The light of the dazzling sun, warm and soothing, was the first thing to fill her senses. Then the smell of piñon and sage accompanied the fresh, crisp mountain air into her nose and lungs. She looked up, and her breath was snatched away. Just over the roofline of the hotel, a line of magnificent deep purple mountains muscled their way into the bluest sky she'd ever seen.

As she stood there, she felt her entire body tingling, but not only from the fulfillment of her senses. It seemed as if the ground itself was vibrating slightly and sending its current through her. There was something about this place, there was no doubt about that. She looked around and noticed a bumper sticker on a car parked at the office. NEW MEXICO: LAND OF ENCHANTMENT, it read. A little laughter escaped from her.

Just then, Bobette and Betty turned the corner into the parking lot. They were so happy, they looked just like two little girls. They'd been taking a walk and were thrilled with the mountains and the fresh air and the cute adobe architecture.

"Let's eat," Betty said. "There's a place with somethin' called huevos rancheros just across the street."

"What in creation is that?" Aletta asked, but they didn't know either.

Joy walked out into the morning sun, wearing a white dress with a ruffled neckline and hem and royal blue cowboy boots. She covered her eyes to adjust to the light.

"Well, Earl was over at Sam Blunt's last night playin' poker. I guess he survived. . . ."

Finally, she looked up and saw the mountains, and they laughed as the grumpy look on her face turned into awe.

"Wow" was all she could say. It was the first time Aletta remembered Joy not having words.

As Aletta ate her eggs on corn tortillas with red sauce and rice and beans, she decided there was no way she could leave Santa Fe yet. After all, Vee and her kids had made it through a tornado back home. There couldn't be anything worse than that. Besides, she felt more compelled than ever to find her great-grandmother. She felt deep down — beyond her gut or even her bones, down into her soul — that she had a connection to this place, this land of enchantment, and it made her so excited, it was hard to get her food down.

She looked around the hole-in-the-wall restaurant to see if she recognized the man who'd brought her the feather, but of course he wasn't there. When they went out to get in the car, she scanned the area and the road for his white pickup truck. She did the same thing as they drove down Cerrillos

Road toward the historic and beautiful central plaza in downtown Santa Fe to see the sights. This became her habit. Everywhere they went, she looked.

Even with a map from the El Rey Inn, it took them getting lost a few times before they finally found the plaza. It seemed that all the streets kind of zigzagged or went in circles, changing names at the strangest places. Throughout it all, they oohed and aahed at the charming authenticity of the place.

"Feels like we've stepped into another time," Aletta said as they got out of the car.

They walked past the Hotel St. Francis with its large tiled lobby and enormous fireplace, down a narrow street, and onto the plaza — a town square with grass and trees in the middle and restaurants and shops on three sides. On the fourth side was a large sidewalk area where Indian folks laid out blankets and showed their handmade jewelry to passing tourists. The women were drawn to the gorgeous silver, turquoise, and beaded jewelry like little girls are drawn to princess dresses.

Aletta particularly liked the shiny silver pieces that were etched with animals and totems. But what she was really looking at were the faces of the people doing the selling. They sat on lawn chairs, not making much eye contact with the people walking by. The men wore jeans and boots for the most part, while the women wore long, flowing skirts.

Aletta approached a man who resembled her mystery man with the feather. He had the same long hair, strong jaw, and kind eyes. She bent over and picked up a lovely silver ring with a pale blue turquoise stone.

"This is just gorgeous," she said to the man.

"Found that stone myself," he said, and nodded at the ring in her hand.

"Really?" This truly was an amazing place. It had gorgeous stones coming right out of the land, so anyone, at least anyone who knew where to look, could pick them right up and make something beautiful and lasting.

Aletta put the ring back down on the wool blanket. "We don't know each other, do we?" she asked quietly.

The Indian looked at her straight on for the first time and pulled the toothpick from his mouth. "No, ma'am, not that I know of."

She squatted down in front of his blanket, so she wouldn't be towering over him. "This may sound a little insane, but there was this man from here who came by my house in Okay, Oklahoma — just a little ole town outside Oklahoma City. Anyway, he came by and gave me this feather."

She took the feather, still wrapped in cloth, out of her purse and handed it to the man.

"Eagle," he said.

Aletta nodded and smiled. "I'm trying to find him. He didn't leave me his name or anything, but he drives a white truck and looks kinda like you."

"Did he say why he was giving it to you?"

"Just that he was supposed to, but he didn't know why."

"Well, there's a lot of guys that look like me and drive white trucks around here. Just because we're Indian doesn't mean we all know each other," he said, and chuckled a little. "Maybe you could check out on the pueblos. Not that all of us live in them. In fact, a lot of people have left," he said. "I live in Albuquerque."

Aletta stood up and smiled. "Well, thank you."

"The eagle feather is used in most of our ceremonies. Do you know why?" he asked, looking up at her.

Aletta shook her head.

"Because the eagle flies closest to the sun.

The sun is a source of great power. I hope you find what you are looking for," he said, and put the toothpick back in his mouth.

"Thank you," she said. "Thank you so much."

Joy and Betty bought turquoise necklaces from a plump Navajo woman with a sweet smile, then the four friends toured the rest of the plaza. They saw galleries with paintings of sunsets and Indians on horseback racing across the high desert, and sculptures of animals and people and mythical beings. Aletta loved all the art. It stirred something in her that made her want to create something beautiful too. Whether it was a painting or her life, it didn't seem to matter. She just wanted to make a lovely offering to the world and move people the same way she was moved when she gazed at these creations.

At the Loretto Chapel, just off the plaza, the ladies went inside to find out about the advertised "miracle staircase."

It was a charming chapel with arched beams leading to a high ceiling above. In the rear was the choir loft with a rose window behind it. There was a deep silence in this small church that settled into Aletta and gave her a sense of peace. She sat in one of the pews and began reading the little pamphlet about the staircase that went from the chapel up to the loft in two perfect spirals, and her peaceful feeling turned into excitement.

In 1872, Bishop Lamy of Santa Fe commissioned a convent chapel for the Sisters of Loretto to be built. During its construction, the architect died, and it was discovered that he had made an error and didn't provide for a staircase to the choir loft. The worst part was that there was no room to build a staircase now that construction was almost complete. The nuns prayed for nine days in honor of St. Joseph, for he was a carpenter. The day after their novena ended, a poor-looking man appeared at the door and, after seeing their problem, assured them he could build the staircase they needed. For three months, he locked himself into the chapel, permitting no visitors. When the mother superior finally saw his creation, she stared in amazement. The staircase was a beautiful freestanding structure rising in a double spiral to the choir loft.

Aletta looked at the staircase again, then kept reading.

There is no central pole, no wall attachment, and not one nail or screw used in its construction — only a few wooden pegs. The wood used is so rare, people disagree on its origin. The fact is, the carpenter had brought no wood with him at all. Architects from all over come to inspect its incredible craftsmanship.

When the work was complete, the mother superior attempted to pay the man for his services, but he was nowhere to be found. No one had ever seen him come or go. It is thought that the unknown carpenter was none other than St. Joseph himself.

Aletta walked over to Bobette, who was running her hand along one of the steps.

"Ain't it somethin'?" she asked.

Aletta pointed at her pamphlet. "This bishop they talk about in this story is the one who opened the Indian school my greatgrandmother went to. It's real. He was really here, and so was she."

"That's really amazing. Just think about it, Lettie. Jesus's daddy was here too, at the same time your great-grandma was livin' right here in this town," Bobette said, her eyes wide.

They walked outside, where Joy and Betty

were waiting for them. Joy inhaled on her cigarette. "Well, that was cool," she said. "Kind of reminds me of when I got arrested."

Betty laughed.

"Excuse me?" Aletta asked.

"Divine intervention and all," Joy said nonchalantly, and walked away.

"You better just tell us the story," Bobette said, rushing after her.

They spent the rest of the day on the trail of Adelaide. At the Native American History Museum, Aletta stared into a display case showing small figurines of dancing Indians with masks like the ones she'd seen in her vision. KACHINA DANCERS, the placard read.

"Kachina," she whispered to herself as she read about them.

Kachinas are supernatural beings who come through masked dancers impersonating them during ceremonial dances and rituals. They have many functions such as bringing rain, promoting the growth of crops, curing sickness, and helping childless wives become pregnant among others. One of the rituals is an initiation of children into the secrets of the kachina.

Aletta read the last line on the sign several times, her heart beating a little faster. That was what she had seen in her vision at the library — Adelaide's initiation into the secrets of the kachina. She wondered why this was what had come to her.

Next, they went to the *New Mexican* newspaper office, where a woman with long gray hair and bifocals helped them locate a microfiche newspaper from 1885 that showed a picture of a group of Indian girls standing in front of Lamy's Indian school, wearing long skirts and white shirts, their hair pulled back.

"They look so sad," Betty said, leaning over Aletta's shoulder.

Aletta scanned each dark face, trying to see if she recognized her great-grandmother from her dreams. But she couldn't see their faces very well. The picture was old and fuzzy. Finally, she read the short article, claiming how the school was these girls' salvation.

"Says here most of them were orphans. I wonder why."

"Back then, mainly from tuberculosis and smallpox," the woman said.

Bobette's face convulsed once. "Wow."

The woman raised her eyebrows and nodded. "Times were tough back then."

"Especially for these girls," Aletta said.

They also found a picture of Aletta's great-great-grandfather and the Santa Fe Ring, eight white men, all with facial hair of some sort, stern expressions on their faces and hats on their heads. Four were seated and four stood behind. Aletta found Charles Halbert in the back row. He had long sideburns and a mustache. His face was impossible to read except for a smugness at the corners of his mouth. It was clear not only from the company he kept but also from the way he held himself that he had power and influence, and he knew it.

Aletta couldn't help but wonder how this man must've felt about his son marrying an orphaned Indian girl.

They drove out to a nearby pueblo that seemed almost deserted. The dirt road led them to a group of adobe buildings, some old and crumbling, some newer-looking, situated around a central square. The pueblo seemed as natural to the land as the juniper, the coyotes, and the cottonwoods.

"Well, this place is party central," Joy said as they got out of the car.

Aletta desperately wanted to talk to someone, to have one of these people invite her in for an iced tea. For some reason, she felt like she needed to get inside of this world and be a part of it, but as she walked around and read the signs that warned against picture taking and watched as the villagers walked from one place to the next without so much as looking her way, she realized she never could. She was an outsider, even though this land, with its arid majesty and vibrant history, seemed to be in her bones. But this was a very insulated world, and she didn't belong with these people, no matter if she had an Indian ancestor or not. The only way she could even get a faint sense of their lives was through books, display cases at museums, and pictures in newspapers.

She felt foolish that she wanted this so much, like a kid who wanted Santa Claus even after knowing the truth. She'd never felt like she fit in anywhere, not during her childhood, her marriage, or even running her business. She recalled the vision she'd had in the library of the ceremony for the little girl, the seer. The child's gift had been not only accepted but celebrated as well.

Aletta walked to a tree stump in the middle of the pueblo's central square and sat down. The dark mountains in the distance seemed to brood right along with her. However begrudgingly, she had to admit that just because her business was pretty successful didn't mean she knew how to use her gift well or responsibly. She felt in over her head, and maybe that was why she had lost her abilities.

She looked around at the nearly empty pueblo, raising a hand to shade her eyes. Surely someone here could tell her how to deal with having this gift — her curse, she'd often called it. In the ceremony, the Indian had called it the "medicine of a seer." He'd been excited and reverent when he said it, like someone nowadays might talk about the "mind of a genius." She laughed a little at that. She felt as close to a genius as the stump she was sitting on.

She stood up and walked back to the car and sat in the backseat. Her friends got in, and they drove away from the pueblo in silence. Finally, she spoke up. "I'm sorry I brought y'all all the way here. I ain't gonna find anything out here. I don't even know what the hell I was looking for. I feel like a damn fool."

Each of them took a turn telling her she was being silly. They were having a great time. She shouldn't give up hope. But she just looked out the window and stared blankly at the terra-cotta landscape dotted with green scrub.

That night and the next day, Aletta stayed

quiet. She went along wherever her friends wanted to go and stopped searching for the pickup truck. Betty insisted they go up into the mountains, and they found a trail just off the road that followed a beautiful little stream through aspen trees that rose thin and white and tall out of the rich, moist earth. It was spectacular, and they walked for over an hour before realizing they'd gone so far. By the time they got back to the car, Joy was nearly screeching about a blister on her left foot and Bobette's face was just twitching away from the exertion in that altitude.

Betty could have stayed out the entire day, she loved it so much.

"I want to move here," she said as she got behind the wheel, her cheeks flushed and her eyes bright.

"It's almost too beautiful," Aletta said quietly as Joy pulled off her dirt-covered pink Keds sneakers and groaned.

Aletta turned around and forced a smile at Joy.

"You sure wouldn't make much of an Indian," she said.

"Not on your life, sister. That's your fantasy," Joy said playfully.

Aletta's smile faded away as she turned around. There was a painful silence in the car as Betty backed up, then pulled onto the road.

"Hey, kiddo, I didn't mean nothin' by that," Joy said.

Aletta waved a hand through the air without turning around. "I know. It's fine." But she stayed quiet the rest of the way down the mountain.

Jimmy woke up on Friday morning to the phone ringing. He rolled off the couch and stumbled to the phone in the kitchen. His mouth felt and tasted like it had been stuffed with feathers that had been dipped in rotten eggs. His head was worse off than that.

" 'Lo," he croaked into the phone as memories of the night before with Luke and Chuck lumbered across the fuzzy gray screen of his mind.

"Daddy?" Ruby said on the other end.

"Hey, sweetheart," he said, and pulled the phone cord as far as it would go to reach a glass and the sink.

"I thought you were in the tornado last night."

He forced a chuckle. "Oh, no, peanut. I was busy at work." That's when he remembered work and frantically glanced at the Budweiser clock that hung over the oven.

He was going to be late for the damn conference.

Ruby's voice sounded like hurt outlined with anger. "That's why you didn't come get us." It was more of a statement than a question.

"Listen, babe, I gotta get to work, but we'll do somethin' just great this weekend."

"I don't want to," Ruby said, and hung up.

Jimmy pushed down regret and guilt along with a desire to throw up and rushed to the bedroom. "Charlotte, honey, you gotta take me to get my car," he said, leaning over to stroke her hair before heading to the bathroom.

She fought him, but in the end, Charlotte took him to his car at the VIP Lounge, and he was only a half hour late to the sales conference.

"Aletta's gone off and left me with the kids while she's on vacation with her friends," he told Bill Haywood as he poured himself coffee from an urn at the back of the hotel ballroom where the conference was being held. "Ruby was throwin' up this mornin' and couldn't go to school, so I had to get a sitter at the last minute."

He did his best to look worried and haggard.

"Don't worry about it," his boss said, and clapped him on the back. "It's a big job bein' a parent, ain't it?"

"Oh, yeah." Jimmy nodded and laughed knowingly.

He was starving from not eating last night and stuffed down two donuts and another cup of coffee, but they came up on him during the presentation entitled "Closing the Deal." He closed the deal over a toilet bowl, grateful no one else had been in the bathroom when he did. By the time he went back to his seat to try to stay awake through the "Avoiding Cancellations" talk, he felt much better.

By the end of the day, when Ann Flowers walked over to him smiling that gorgeous smile and showing that French-vanilla cleavage, he was almost back to normal. She had softly curling auburn hair, full, sexual lips, and curves that his hands ached to explore. He'd been so attracted to her since he met her last year at one of these things, he could barely speak in her presence.

"Well, if it isn't Ann Flowers," he said, grinning and sucking in his gut to enhance the size of his chest.

"Ann Carver," she corrected, pointing to her name tag. "I'm divorced since January. I hear you've dropped your ball and chain too."

"Oh, yes." He smiled. His stomach started to flutter and he had to force himself to keep his eyes from wandering down to her breasts. He couldn't think of anything else to say except, "How 'bout a drink at the bar?"

After dinner and several drinks washed down with flirtation that turned to innuendo, they started groping each other like high school kids. They sneaked up to Ann's room, and their sex was acrobatic and muscular, a combination of dancing and smash-mouth football. At midnight, Jimmy rolled off Ann for the seventh time (he was keeping count) and reached for the phone.

"You didn't tell me you had a girl," Ann said, teasing.

"You didn't ask."

"I didn't ask 'cause I don't care, darlin'. I just needed to get laid somethin' terrible, but I go home to Tulsa tomorrow, and so do you," she cooed.

He put the phone back down. "You have someone back home?"

"A fiancé," she said, smiling. "He's not as hot as you are, hon, but he's got way more money."

Jimmy grabbed the phone again. He felt

angry and ashamed for some reason. Because of that, he was going to tell Charlotte he'd be home soon and leave Ann lying there, but just as Charlotte answered, Ann began to massage him under the covers. Even though he was exhausted, he was standing straight up again under her devilishly skilled and sexy hands.

He gave Charlotte some pathetic excuse about working late and being too tired to drive home and told her he'd see her tomorrow after the conference was over. He hung up as Charlotte was still screaming, freed himself from Ann's grasp, and stood up. He grabbed her by the ankles and pulled her to the edge of the bed as she squealed with delight. He turned her over, slapped her ass hard enough to leave a handprint, then gave it to her from behind, pretending the whole time he was the one in charge here.

After the storm Thursday evening, Friday was one of those Oklahoma spring days that seemed scrubbed clean and spit-shined, so that all the colors of the land were much more vivid than the usual drab browns and greens of late winter through early spring. The animals — dogs and cats, horses and cows — seemed as happy to be alive as the still shaken but grateful townsfolk.

After Aletta's frantic phone call that morning, Vee got the kids out of bed to go to school. She couldn't help but notice that all the complaining they did about having to go to school when their mother was around didn't happen with her. Somehow, after being crammed into a shower with their little bodies, waiting to see if they'd live or die, it seemed normal for her to give Ruby and Randy and Gyp kisses on the forehead as she roused them out of bed.

"Thanks for your help last night," she told Sissy as the younger girl applied mascara. Vee hadn't broken her of that yet. "I was just about to panic, and you acted like a real grown-up."

"Sure," Sissy said with a teenager's shrug. "No prob." But Vee saw a smile play across her face just as she left the room.

Vee promised the kids they could do something fun on Friday night. She felt bad for them that their daddy hadn't even called, especially when she heard Ruby on the phone with him before she went off to school. Even after he'd left them for dead during a tornado warning, Ruby was worried about the son of a bitch. Vee couldn't believe how much parents could get away with and still have their children's love. She set her jaw as she poured milk over their

Count Chocula cereal. She'd been the same way with her dad when she was a kid, but now it was different.

Despite the hard thoughts and clenched jaw, a hurt arose in her chest and throat that she didn't want to even think about. Instead, she considered when she should try to call Bo to finalize their plans. It was high time for her to get out of what just a few months ago she would have considered to be a living hell and back to her life of trying to change this goddamn, crazy world.

She still had a few days left, though, and she wanted to make the best of it — keep herself and the kids as busy as possible. That evening, she took the kids to the drive-in movie, sneaking Randy and Ruby through in the trunk to save money. They watched *Pete's Dragon* and ate Jiffy Pop popcorn and drank Shastas from home. There was no way Vee was going to spend money at the snack bar — she was going to need every penny she could find. But the kids were just happy to be here, and they all had a great time. Vee couldn't remember the last time she'd laughed so much.

Jimmy spent all day Saturday avoiding Bill Haywood's glare and laughing off the jokes and winks from the guys. He'd bought a tie from the hotel's gift store, but everything else he wore was the same as the day before. Ann disappeared before lunch, and he never saw her again.

He was so damn happy to get out of that hotel at four-thirty that he grabbed a cute pink teddy bear for Charlotte, who collected stuffed animals, in the gift shop, then sang along to Waylon Jennings on his way home. He thought of an intricately detailed story to tell Charlotte, and he decided to take her out to a nice dinner in the city and to never cheat on her again. Ann was a good lay, but she was the kind of woman you could never count on for anything. Charlotte had stuck by him through a lot, and she deserved to be treated better.

Jimmy walked to his apartment, loosening his tie and humming to himself. As he approached his front door, he smoothed his hair back and worked his face into his most charming smile.

"Honey?" he called as he pushed the door open. "Honey?" He stepped into the apartment, and for a brief moment, he was confused. The smile dropped from his face. "Honey!" he yelled.

He cursed from deep in his belly as he stomped from one empty room to the next.

"Goddammit! I'll be go to hell!"

She'd cleaned out everything except for his clothes, his shaving kit, and his painting of two bird dogs pointing down a pheasant. She'd taken all the furniture he'd bought to furnish the place and even the few pieces he'd had before they met. She'd even taken his new banana lounge from the tiny balcony that overlooked an alley off the living room.

He slammed every door and threw the teddy bear across the room. "Bitch!" he screamed, but the violence in it trailed off into a whimper.

His rage turned from Charlotte to himself then. He ripped the tie off his neck and threw it near the bear. His jaw worked back and forth as his face turned crimson, and the veins in his neck bulged with self-loathing.

"You fucking idiot!" he yelled through clenched teeth.

He turned over an empty plastic milk crate that lay in the middle of the living room floor and sat down. It had held Charlotte's romance novels before, but she must've decided she didn't need it with all her new furniture. He put his hands to the sides of his head and rested his elbows on his knees. But there was nothing restful about him. His fingers began to knead his cheeks as if he were trying to pull them off the bone. Then he ran them up the sides of his head and grabbed his hair, cursing under his breath.

The emotions inside his body were so strong that his thoughts got caught in them like a flock of birds in a storm. And the storm was fed by the alcohol that was still running through his veins and the constant craving he had for that first drink of the day. *I'm gonna kill that bitch. I hate this shit. How stupid can I be? What'd you expect, Jimmy, idiot farm boy loser Jimmy? I'll fucking kill her. She had to have help. I'll kill them too. Or maybe just myself.*

He jumped up and went to the kitchen, slamming through empty cabinets, searching and searching. Finally, he glanced in the sink and saw that she had poured his new bottle of Smirnoff out, then left the empty bottle to torment him. He picked it up and threw it against the wall, which didn't break it, but hitting the linoleum floor did, and it shattered everywhere.

He looked over at the milk crate sitting in the middle of the old, stained carpet covered with food crumbs and dirty pennies and fallen nails. Somehow, his mind made a connection. The milk crate had been in the hall closet. He walked to the closet and opened the door. Inside the small, dark space hung a few of his jackets and a box of Charlotte's stuffed animals she must have forgotten. Reaching behind them, he found what he was looking for. He pulled the shotgun out, tucked it under his arm, then went back to the crate and sat down. He pulled the belly of the shiny wood and steel gun back to check its load, but he already knew he'd find the red shells with gold butts lined up and ready to go. He'd left it loaded on purpose, for security.

He clicked off the safety, then gently pushed the barrel tip into his mouth. As his hand moved down to find the trigger, he thought of the huge turkey he'd shot a few weeks before, flapping around in that ditch while he bashed it in the head over and over with a tree limb, until he finally had to shoot it for it to die.

Vee was starting to feel nervous. It was already Saturday afternoon, and she couldn't get hold of either Silvia or Jimmy about tomorrow. Silvia's phone just rang and rang, and Jimmy was at a conference. Aletta wouldn't be home until Monday evening, so Vee wanted to have both of them lined up for Sunday after she left, in case the kids needed something. She interrupted Sissy, who was talking on the phone, and asked her if she'd keep an eye on Gyp, who was sleeping in his playpen, while she went out for a few minutes.

She asked Ruby and Randy to come along, because she had no idea where she was going. She went in the bathroom before they left and put two cotton balls into her mouth, stuffing them into her cheek like a wad of chewing tobacco.

"What's wrong?" Randy asked as they got into the Pink Pumpkin.

"I've got a screaming bad toothache. I gotta get it taken care of tomorrow. I need to talk to Silvia Rivera to make sure you'll be watched while I'm at the dentist."

Ruby and Randy directed her to Silvia's house, where she knocked on the front door. She had to knock twice more before Silvia's distressed face looked at her through the glass. Silvia saw her, then the kids, and shook her head violently and wagged her finger at them.

"I just wanted to see if you could watch them tomorrow," Vee shouted.

Silvia stepped out of the house and closed the door behind her quickly. "You can't have them here," she said, nodding to the children. "My *estupido* cousin brought over her little boy who had chicken pox, and now my baby has it and my husband. They've both been very sick." There were dark circles under her eyes as she spoke.

Vee backed away, pushing the kids back with her. "I've had it," she said. "Have you had chicken pox, kids?"

"I don't think so," Ruby said.

"No, but this kid at school was out a whole week last year, so I wanted to get it too," Randy said.

"I'm sorry," Vee said, then rushed them back to the car. "We should go."

Silvia went back inside as Vee pulled away.

"What's chicken pox?" Randy asked. "Does it make you sick?"

"It's a disease, dummy," Ruby said.

"It's something we want to stay far, far away from," Vee said. She couldn't believe this.

Ruby directed her to Jimmy's place next. It was now five-thirty, so he should be home.

"There's his car," Randy said, pointing out the Trans Am in the parking lot.

They walked up the steps and went to his door. Vee knocked lightly, but there was no answer. She knocked again, but this time, Ruby turned the knob and walked inside.

"Hey, we should wait . . . ," Vee said, then looked up and noticed the empty apartment and the broken glass all over the floor. "Kids, I want you to stay right here." She walked slowly toward the living room. "Jimmy?" she said, her voice shaking. The guy gave her the creeps anyway, but this was too much.

She turned into the room. In the middle of the floor was a blue plastic crate. She looked up and saw Jimmy out on the little balcony. He held a shotgun in his right hand, and with his left he was swinging a stuffed animal of some kind around and around over his head.

She stepped toward him, her fascination overcoming her fear. Finally, Jimmy let the bear go and it flew high over the alley below. Jimmy pulled the gun to his shoulder, aimed, and fired. *Blam!* Pink cotton exploded overhead.

He reached down into a box that sat next to him and picked up another stuffed animal, a purple pig. He threw it, then raised the gun again and *blam!* The pig spun sideways crazily in the air, and he reached immediately into the box again.

"Daddy," Ruby whispered.

Randy burst into tears.

Vee turned around. They had seen the whole thing. "Come on, you guys. Let's go."

She herded them out the door as fast as she could before Jimmy saw them. The last thing in the world she wanted to do right now was face Jimmy Honor when he was shooting stuffed animals out of the sky.

On the way home, she explained to them that it looked like their daddy was upset because he and his girlfriend split up. She assumed the girl had had enough and cleaned him out. Served him right. But the timing couldn't be worse for her. There was no way she could change her plans now. She and Bo had arranged to meet, and besides that, Aletta was coming home. She knew she'd stayed in one place long enough, and she was pushing her luck by staying any longer. It was time to go. Now.

That evening, she stuffed another cotton ball into her cheek and winced in pain as she spoke to Sissy. "I found this dentist in Edmond who can do it tomorrow, but he said it could take all day long."

"I guess I can babysit all day," she said unenthusiastically.

"You don't have plans tomorrow night, do you?" Vee asked.

"I do, but you'll think it's stupid."

Vee waited.

Sissy flopped down onto one of the dining room chairs. "I was invited to toilet-paper some football players' houses."

"Oh," Vee said.

"I know. I know. I told them I'd go only if we could do Rusty's house too. I know his daddy will make him clean it up, and he hates housework." Sissy laughed a little.

Vee pulled a chair close to Sissy and looked her in the eyes. "Remember, don't do anything stupid that's going to get you in trouble, so you end up stuck here, all right?"

Sissy nodded.

"Anyway, you probably won't be able to go," Vee said, and stood up again.

"You'll be home before tomorrow night, won't you?" Sissy sounded worried now.

"I will, but I'll need your help since I'll just be off anesthesia."

Sissy's shoulders dropped.

"All right?" Vee asked.

"All right," Sissy answered glumly.

Vee spoke to Aletta that evening when she called. She told her she had to go to the dentist for a few hours, but she didn't say anything about Silvia or Jimmy except that they were available if they were needed. She told Aletta the kids were in the middle of a TV show and that Sissy was out.

"Oh, well, don't bother them, then," Aletta said. "I'm just glad to hear everything's fine. I hope you can get that tooth taken care of. It's amazing you found someone to do it on a Sunday."

"I know," Vee said, hoping she sounded convincing. Just to be sure, she added, "Don't worry about anything. Everything is just fine."

CHAPTER SEVENTEEN

Aletta hung up the phone and walked outside the hotel room. Even in the middle of town, the stars were bright and twinkly and beautiful, and it was still early. The crisp, cool mountain air was a lovely contrast to the heavy humidity of Oklahoma. She breathed in deeply and tried to relax, but the sadness and disappointment still hung around her like a bad head cold.

She was worried about her gift and about what she was going to do with the rest of her life. Having had a taste of working for herself, she couldn't stand the thought of getting some stupid job, like being a secretary or receptionist. Hell, she couldn't type anyway. More than likely, she'd end up on her feet at the 7-Eleven or the IGA grocery store, working on enhancing her varicose veins. And the money she made wouldn't even come close to what they needed.

She tried to put all of this aside so she

could just have a good time for the rest of her trip, possibly the last one she'd take on her own until Gyp was out of the house. She got into the Gran Torino, where her friends waited. They were perfumed, coiffed, dressed, and accessorized for a night on the town.

They drove up Canyon Road and ate at a local place where two hippies played guitar and sang and a bear head hung over the fireplace.

Once they had their drinks in front of them, Betty raised her glass to toast. "Here's to good times and good friends."

"Hear, hear," they answered.

Bobette drank, then raised her glass again. "Oh, I have a toast," she said. "Here's to good friends who tell stories about getting arrested."

Joy set her glass down. "You're a bulldog with this thing, ain't you?"

Aletta and Betty chimed in. "Come on, just tell us."

"Oh, all right, but I'm blamin' y'all if I get indigestion." Joy took a long drink, tapped a cigarette out of the pack that sat next to her on the table, lit it, and inhaled deeply. "Well," she exhaled finally, "it all started when I went to visit my wild cousins down in Dallas."

Aletta noticed that Bobette had different facial twitches for different moods. Her happy twitch was more mouth and chin, but if something bad was happening, her eyes and nose were like moths in a jar.

"How old were you? What year was it?" Bobette asked, her mouth working away.

"I was seventeen, so that would be 1956," Joy said. "Anyway, my cousin Marilee was one of those girls who looks like this sweet little angel, but she had the devil in her, I tell you. If that girl wasn't in trouble, she was lookin' for it."

"Oh, and you were Miss Innocent, I'm sure," Aletta said.

Joy just grinned.

"How old was she?" Bobette asked.

"She must a been eighteen or nineteen. She said we were country mouse and city mouse, and she was gonna show me what city folks did for fun. Anyway, so Marilee takes me out to this dive bar on the outskirts of the city where the clientele was as rough as the booze they drank. She even knew some of the people in there, and at one point went outside with this man who I saw going out with other folks one at a time, too. Well, I was young and a fool, so I just drank the moonshine they served while I pinched my nose — it was the worst rotgut you can imagine — and danced to Elvis Presley."

Joy took a sip of her margarita and put out her cigarette before continuing. "At one point, Marilee comes over and says we're gonna take a ride with some friends of hers. I walk outside, and there's these two characters in a beat-up old Chevy. The driver was bald as a melon, and the other one was Mexican and barely spoke any English, as far as I could tell. Marilee got in the backseat, so I did too. Well, it wasn't till we were out on the road that I asked how long did she know these men. 'Oh, we just met,' she says. 'They want to show us somethin',' and that's when she pulls out this reefer and lights it up."

Betty gasped. Bobette put a hand to her heart, and Aletta said, "In 1956? You couldn't get marijuana back then, not that I knew of."

"City mouse could," Joy said flatly.

"So did you smoke it?" Betty asked.

"I was seventeen. Take a guess," Joy said, and smoothed her hair back to maintain her dignity even after such an admission. "I have to tell you, I was havin' a damn good time after that little magic cigarette passed by me twice. Anyway, those boys took us way out into the countryside, and I was so high, I didn't even protest, can you imagine? The big bald one finally stopped the car in the middle of this deserted road. There was a good moon out that night, 'cause I could see not half bad. In front of us was a small rise, and on the sides of the road was a thicket of trees. It was a real spooky place."

"Lord above, Joy. You coulda been killed," Betty said, finishing off her gin and tonic. The girl hippie sang a Grateful Dead tune in the background.

"Tell me about it," Joy said, and lit another cigarette. Storytelling required a prop. "So we're sittin' there, and Baldy starts tellin' us that this place is haunted. He says at the top of that little rise are railroad tracks, and this is the spot where a busload of school-children got hit and killed by a train. Well, I don't know if it was the reefer or what, but I get a chill up and down my spine that about had me sittin' in my cousin's lap. Course, she's over there lovin' the whole thing. The Mexican guy laughs like it's some big joke, and I'm thinkin' I'm with some real nut jobs. Well, that's when Baldy turns off the car and the headlights, and I'm thinkin' we're done for one way or the other."

"He didn't," Bobette gasped.

Joy nodded. "Oh, yes, ma'am, turned off

the car and we're sitting there in the dark. He puts the thing into neutral, makes a big show of it, raises his feet up and takes his hands off the steering wheel."

Aletta shook her head in disbelief. "What were you doin'?"

"I was about to wet myself is what I was doin'. I thought about runnin', but where the hell to? Well, you can't even imagine what happened next." Joy paused, drank the last of her margarita, fished out a cube of ice, and popped it in her mouth.

"Joy!" Betty said so loud that half the restaurant turned and looked.

Joy grinned and batted her Maybelline-enhanced eyelashes at them before continuing. "The damn car started to move! Those boys said it was the dead children pushing us over the tracks so we wouldn't get killed like they did."

"Oh, my God," Bobette whispered.

"Now, I remind you," Joy said, "this is going uphill at this point. Well, I'm stone cold sober from all this goin' on, and I'm yellin' at Baldy to stop, while Marilee is clappin' and sayin', 'Ain't it creepy? It's so creepy,' over and over. Baldy keeps tellin' me he ain't doin' anything, that it's the dead children. The Mexican is laughing and tokin' away on the rest of that joint. Finally, we get up to the top of the rise, pause just a second on the railroad tracks, then keep movin' till we're goin' down the other side."

Joy motioned to the waitress for another margarita, then continued. "Now, you'd think that goin' downhill, we'd just keep rollin'. But no! Once we were across and safely on the other side, we stopped. Not a roll to a stop but a stop like with brakes. Now, I was lookin' at Baldy's feet every few seconds, and I never once saw him put them close to the gas or the brake."

"Wow," Bobette said as the waitress came over with their steaks.

As the waitress served them, Betty whispered to Joy, "Are you pullin' our leg, Joy? That's hard to believe."

"I'd swear to it on my grandma Dossie's grave," Joy answered.

"I believe it," Aletta said, and they all looked at her. "I sure know things happen in this world that we can't explain."

"Isn't that the truth," the waitress said, and smiled. "Enjoy your food."

"But I got one question," Bobette chimed in. "What does this have to do with you getting arrested?"

Joy began cutting her steak as she spoke. "Well, once we get stopped and Baldy starts the car, I think I'm safe and we can get the hell outta there now. But he pulls forward, then stops again. He and the Mexican point over at this railroad crossing sign that's kinda leanin' funny outta the ground like it's not put in real good. They get out of the car and go to inspect the damn thing. As I'm doin' my best to convince Marilee to make them take us back to our car, they're diggin' the sign outta the ground and carryin' it over to us. Now, I gotta tell you, this is a steel pole about seven feet tall with a big ole yellow railroad crossing sign on top and a concrete base."

"What in the world?" Aletta asked, taking a bite of a french fry.

Joy rolled her eyes. "That's what I was askin'. I guess they wanted it for a souvenir," she said. "Course, Marilee's delighted. She says, 'Are y'all takin' that sign?' and they say yes! I was tryin' to convince them to leave it, but then Marilee asks me if I ever had anything so interestin' as the crossing we just did ever happen to me before, and I have to admit no, so she hands me another reefer to shut me up. Those boys take that huge sign and put it on top of the roof, 'cause it won't even fit in that big ole car, that's how big it was, and Baldy holds it with one hand out the window, keeping it balanced on the roof of the car, and drives with the other. We drive down the back roads for a while toward the city, them adjustin' that sign so it's secure, if you could ever call it that. Then — I am not lyin'— we come up to the highway, and Baldy gets on and speeds up to about fifty miles an hour."

Joy paused and took a bite of her steak. "Well, you can guess how long it took for a patrol car to see us," she said, chewing. "About a minute and a half. They stop us, line us up on the side of the road like criminals, find the bag of marijuana in the car under the passenger seat, stupid Marilee, and start getting in our faces. 'Whose is this? Whose is this?' I couldn't breathe, let alone speak, and Marilee's over there lookin' innocent and sweet. Finally, the Mexican says, 'It's mine.' And you know what they did? They dumped it out! They said, 'If any of y'all would've said it was theirs but him, we'd take y'all in for drug charges.' "

"But it was Marilee's," Betty protested.

"Ain't that a bitch?" Joy asked. "Those cops were so sure that it was the Mexican guy's pot that if any of us white kids said it was ours, they woulda been mad at us for lyin'. He saved our ass, that's for sure. And for no reason than to protect us. He coulda been in some damn serious trouble. As it was, they took those guys in for stealin' that sign and me for underage drinkin'."

Joy took a long drink of her margarita. "And that's how I got arrested. My aunt and uncle came and picked us up at the jailhouse, and I got out of it with a fine. They never did tell my parents. I think they knew how bad an influence their daughter was."

Bobette clapped her hands together. "Now, that was a great story," she said.

Aletta groaned. "Lord above, I can't help but think of Sissy. She's as crazy as you were, Joy. But I think Vee's havin' a good influence on her."

"Sissy'll be just fine. She's just at that age," Joy said.

Betty clapped for the singer. "I like her voice so much," she said.

After they finished eating, Aletta went over to the hippie duo and chatted with them for a few minutes. When the girl started singing Carole King's "You've Got a Friend," Aletta told the ladies she'd requested it for them. The singer had long braids, a headband, long flowing clothes, and a voice as sweet as peach cobbler. Afterward, the ladies had to dab their eyes with their napkins.

"I know this has been the most ridiculous wild-goose chase the world has ever seen, but I'll never forget it, and I'll never forget y'all comin' with me," Aletta said, and they all held each other's hands in the middle of the table.

They barreled out the restaurant door laughing and ready for some more fun. "It's time to dance!" Joy called to the moon, which hung overhead like a half-closed but watchful eye.

"Woo-hoo!" Betty howled at it.

Then they all started howling at the moon, standing there like bejeweled, half-drunk coyotes, unconcerned by what other people might think. Aletta realized as she bayed at the moon how wonderful it was to not have everyone know who she was for a change.

Still howling and laughing, they packed into the station wagon. Bobette, who had had only one drink, got behind the wheel and pulled onto the dark and narrow Canyon Road.

Betty tapped her on the shoulder. "We gotta get turned around somehow. The honky-tonk those folks at the museum were talkin' about is back the other way."

"I wish this night would never end," Aletta said.

Bobette turned the giant car into a dark driveway, then put it in reverse. As soon as she backed out onto the road, the Gran Torino jumped sideways, jolting them the other way, and the harsh and eerie sounds of crunching metal and breaking glass pierced the air. Someone had hit their car.

"Oh, my God, are y'all all right?" Bobette cried.

"I'm okay," Aletta said. Her right arm hurt from getting jammed into the door, but after moving it, she knew it was just going to be bruised.

"I'll be fine, but I ain't happy," Joy groaned

"Me too," Betty added.

Just then, a man walked to Aletta's window. She looked up at him but couldn't see him very well, because it was so dark. Another figure held back in the shadows. Slowly, the four women got out of the car.

"I'm sorry," the man said. "I couldn't see you backing out when I came around the corner. Are you okay?"

"I think we're all fine," Aletta said. "I don't know about the car, though."

They went back to inspect the damage. When the man leaned over to look at the cracked rear light, Aletta saw him in the red glow of the light and her heart stood still for a moment. He had long black hair, a high forehead, a strong jaw line, and a thin, straight nose. She looked over to see what he was driving — a white pickup truck —

and recognized the teenage girl skulking near the truck too.

"No way," Aletta whispered as the man talked to Bobette about the damage, kneeling on one knee to inspect the dented bumper.

He stopped when he heard Aletta speak and looked up at her. "What'd you say?" he asked, and stood up. They looked at each other for a long moment, so long that her friends finally noticed and glanced at each other with raised eyebrows.

"You brought me a feather," Aletta said finally. She felt like she was looking at an apparition, like she'd made this man up in her mind, and now he was standing in front of her.

The man smiled, then laughed a little, his teeth white in contrast to his brown skin. "Well, isn't this an interesting coincidence?" he asked, then turned to the girl. "Maria, this is the woman Senda sent us to."

"Really?" The girl stepped forward to look at Aletta.

"This is the Indian who brought you that damn feather?" Joy asked, incredulous.

Aletta forced herself to stop staring at him and looked at Joy. "This is him."

"I'm Julian Moquino," he said, and shook hands with each of the women. "This is my daughter, Maria."

"You've got some explainin' to do, Julian Moquino," Joy said as she took his hand.

"I tell you what," he said. "I have a friend with a body shop. I can try to get him to fix your car tomorrow. It's not much damage. Why don't you give me a call in the morning, and if he can do it, we'll drop it off."

"What are we gonna do for transportation?" Bobette asked.

Julian put his fingers to his chin, thinking. It was something Aletta would come to get used to. "Well, if you don't have plans for tomorrow," he said, "I could take you on a tour of my pueblo and maybe some ruins. Have you seen any petroglyphs?"

"Ugh," Maria groaned.

"Petro who?" Betty said.

"Art carved into rock by Indians beginning hundreds of years ago," Julian answered.

"Oh, that sounds exciting," Joy cooed. "Let's do it."

Betty and Bobette agreed, then looked at Aletta, who was still in a bit of a daze. "Sure," she said. "Sounds great."

Julian gave Aletta his phone number on a crumpled piece of paper from his truck, and underneath it he wrote, TESACOMA PUEBLO.

As they pulled away, Betty rolled down her window. "Hey, if you don't have plans," she called to him, "come join us at the Bull Ring."

He just waved and smiled, then drove away.

Betty, Bobette, and Joy sounded like sparrows chattering and chirping at each other all the way to the bar. They couldn't stop talking about Julian. Aletta stayed quiet for the most part, just trying to get her mind around what was happening. She had so many questions for him, so much she wanted to know, and tomorrow was their last day.

They shoved their way into the bar at the packed Bull Ring. It was the kind of place where you might see biker gang members having a drink with rich tourists wearing furs and diamonds. There were Mexicans, white people, and hippies who looked like they lived in tents. It was a heady mixture of folks — most of them out for fun, and some out for trouble.

The ladies pushed over to the bar, but before they could order, a fancy-looking gentleman in a big felt cowboy hat and snakeskin boots asked if he could buy them a drink. Within minutes of getting their cocktails, all of them except Aletta were off on the dance floor. She found herself a corner to watch the action from and sipped her beer.

She turned down the guys who asked her to dance but tapped her feet to the music, smiling as she saw Joy and Betty flirting with their partners while Bobette tried to get rid of the short, balding man who'd latched on to her. When someone tapped her on the shoulder, she immediately said, "No, thanks," then turned to see Julian standing there, smiling.

"Come on," he said. "I'm not that great, but I won't step on your feet."

She felt her face flush with excitement as he led her to the dance floor.

By the time the two cops arrived, Jimmy was sitting on the plastic crate, the shotgun lying on the ground next to him. He cried like men sometimes do, his shoulders moving up and down, but without the accompanying tears, just a misty glaze over his eyes. He looked up at the policemen who walked toward him carefully, their hands hovering near their revolvers.

"Hey, Jimmy," the older one said. He moved toward the shotgun, then picked it up.

Jimmy wiped his nose with the back of his

hand before answering. "Leave me alone, Hub," he said.

Hub, barrel-chested with sticks for legs, chuckled. "Well, I'd like to, but we been getting complaints you're shootin' your gun out the window. Can't do that, Jimmy."

"Wasn't me. I was just cleanin' it," Jimmy said halfheartedly, nodding toward the shotgun in Hub's hand.

The redheaded kid who was with Hub checked the other rooms, then came back. "Looks like somebody cleaned you out," he said.

Jimmy's face contorted in pain. "Yep," he spat.

"A friend of yours?" Hub asked.

"I'll take care of it," Jimmy said.

Hub handed the shotgun to his partner, then walked over to Jimmy. "Listen, buddy. We've known each other a long time," he said, then turned to his partner to explain. "We used to work together at harvest time, balin' hay and drivin' combines."

Jimmy smiled sadly. "Those were the good ole days," he said.

"The hell they were." Hub laughed. "We were up at dawn and worked our asses off in blisterin' heat for twelve hours and got paid shit. You start wishin' for them days and I'll really be worried about you."

Jimmy shrugged. "It was simpler times."

"Jimmy, I'm afraid I'm gonna have to take you in," Hub said, his voice serious and stern. "I don't know what the hell's happened here. You were shootin' target practice out the window. And it sounds like you're makin' threats at whoever done this to your place. Come on, let's go." He leaned over and took Jimmy by the arm.

"Come on, Hub. I ain't gonna do nothin'," Jimmy said, and pulled his arm away.

"Yeah, but if you did, it'd be on me for the rest a my life, so let's just take a ride."

Jimmy didn't have any fight left in him, so he got up and went along. They drove to the new police station out on Route 66, a place with shiny linoleum floors and unhappy customers. Hub sat Jimmy in an office and got him some coffee.

"Now listen," Hub said as he shut the door. "I talked to the captain and told him your, um, situation. Gene agreed we don't need to book you, but we don't want you to be alone right now. Do you have anyone who could come pick you up and stay with you for a while?"

Being forced to drive over here in the patrol car had been a slap in the face for Jimmy. He'd always felt like he was immune from this kind of thing because he knew most of the cops. He'd either grown up with them or played ball with them or both. "I could call my kids," he said.

Hub shook his head and tried to hide the smile that came across his face. "I don't think so. I mean someone responsible, someone you could lean on while you're getting through this thing."

Jimmy thought about it. First to his mind was Walt Walters, but then he realized they weren't talking anymore. He thought about the men at work. He was friendly with them, but they'd never been more than acquaintances. Anyway, he didn't want this to get out. Then he really racked his brain. All his old ball-playing buddies, like Chuck and Luke, were fun to have a drink with or talk about old times when he happened to see them, but they weren't people he called on the phone or knew in any real way. That was certainly true with his drinking pals out at the bars too. He'd had one real friend besides Walt, but Vic had moved to Broken Arrow, and they had lost touch.

As the realization that he had no friends sank in, the color drained from his face. He'd felt helpless and afraid in the past, but these feelings had always been accompanied by anger or machismo that covered any hint of vulnerability. But just now, all he felt was alone, and for once he didn't fight it with meanness or try to laugh it off. For just a moment, his mind became quiet, and in the stillness, he heard himself say, "Call Frank Conway."

By the time Frank got there, it was already eight o'clock. He came in acting like this was the most natural thing in the world. No panic or judgment in his voice. "You wanna get something to eat? I bet you're starvin' " was all he said when he saw Jimmy.

"Sure," Jimmy said, not looking Frank in the eye. He had no idea how to act when a man was being kind to him. Friendly, like buddies, or haughty, like competitors, these he understood. But kindness from a man made him feel small and somehow indebted to him. He didn't trust it in men, so he didn't really trust Frank. He got up and mumbled, "Sorry to bother you like this."

"Hey, I'm hungry too, and you're buyin', so I figure I'm comin' out on top here," Frank said, following Jimmy out of the office. He winked at Hub as they left the building.

They went to Ken's Pizza and sat in a corner booth. Jimmy, his brown eyes dark and hurt, told Frank about Charlotte cleaning him out. He told him the truth about staying out drinking at night, not calling her, lying, and finally cheating with Ann.

Frank listened without interruption. When Jimmy was finished, he took a drink of his Coke before speaking. "I've heard a thousand stories like yours, Jimmy. Seen men stronger and even better-lookin' wind up worse off than what you done told me. I just hope for you that you've hit your bottom."

"What does that mean?"

"It means that drinkin' and the consequences of it are more painful than not drinkin'."

"I never wanna drink again in my life," Jimmy said. "It's ruinin' me, Frank."

"Yessir, it is, and on a day like today, it's easy to swear off the bottle. You see what it does to your life, but the next time that ole anxious, crazy feelin' starts up in your gut, and you wanna do anything in the world but face whatever's in there makin' you feel that way, and you know that first drink's gonna calm it down like a mama talkin' sweet to a cryin' baby, well, that's when the time comes that you find out how powerful the drink really is." Frank's gray-blue eyes were serious but warm.

Jimmy knew Frank was telling him the truth. He knew it, and he was scared as hell. "So, what do you do?"

Frank chuckled. "You get your ass to a meeting or you call your sponsor or both. It's the only thing ever worked for me."

Jimmy's elbows were propped up on the table. When he thought of AA, he dropped his head and held it in his hands. "It makes me feel like a goddamn loser. I oughta be able to do this on my own."

Frank reached across the table and held Jimmy's forearm.

It surprised Jimmy, and he looked up, thinking Frank must be angry or at least frustrated with him, but what he saw was a tenderness in Frank's eyes that touched him deep inside.

"Listen," Frank said. "If you want me to be your sponsor, I'll be right there with you, but you gotta decide."

Jimmy swallowed hard. He was afraid tears were going to come up on him. "Well," he said finally, his voice quivering a little, "I guess I'd be an even bigger jerk than everyone thinks I am if I said no." He laughed nervously. "I'd sure appreciate it, Frank."

"All right, then, but this is completely up to you. I can't do it for you."

"Okay. But hey, I got one problem."

"What's that?" Frank answered, concerned.

Jimmy paused for a moment, his expression becoming very serious. "You said you knew guys in AA who were better-looking than me?"

Frank smiled and shook his head. "By a long shot," he teased.

Julian was right. He wasn't a great dancer, but Aletta couldn't have cared less. Being with him felt about as likely as having a movie star walk off the screen and start talking to her. He had been in her thoughts so much, and now here he was in a cowboy shirt, jeans, and boots, smelling like wood smoke and honey.

They danced for two rock 'n' roll songs like teenagers. Then "How Deep Is Your Love?" by the Bee Gees came on, and Aletta started to walk off the floor as couples began to hold each other close.

Julian took her by the hand and turned her to him. "Now this I can do," he said.

She smiled and put her left hand in his and her right on his shoulder, but Jimmy and then Charlie Baxter crossed her mind and she flinched a little.

"You okay?" Julian asked.

Aletta's body was stiff in his arms. "Where's your daughter?"

"I dropped her off at her punk rock boyfriend's house. That's where we were headed when we ran into you," he said. "I have to pick her up soon."

"I got so many questions for you," she said.

"It was my grandmother who sent me to your house with the feather," he responded.

Aletta blinked her eyes, letting that sink in. "Your grandmother?"

Julian turned her, then dipped her slightly. He smiled, and Aletta felt her body relax into his. It seemed to have a mind of its own.

"My great-grandmother, actually, but I call her Senda. In my language, it means 'grandmother' or is an endearment for one who is wise. Indian languages aren't so picky as English. The entire village calls her Senda, because she is the grandmother of the pueblo. She saw your picture in the magazine. She loves the pictures in *Life* but still won't look at television. Thinks it's got bad spirits in it. She's the one who told me to bring you the feather when I was in Oklahoma," he said.

"Why?"

"She didn't say. She's very old, ninety-six, and she doesn't talk much, but when she does, I listen. She's a storyteller among my people and is very respected."

Aletta was fascinated with what he was

saying, but she was also acutely aware of his thighs against hers. "Storyteller?"

"She holds the stories of the tribe. They have been passed down for generations."

"I lost my psychic abilities after you gave me that feather. That's why I'm here," Aletta said. "I found out not long after that *my* great-grandmother was an Indian from these parts. I don't know what all this means, but I need to find out. I been lookin' for you."

He looked at her with a caring she wasn't prepared for. "I'm glad you found me," he said.

"Me too. You're a terribly interestin' man, Julian Moquino," she said.

"And you are just lovely." As if they had one mind, at the same moment, they put their arms tight around each other and held on in a close embrace. They moved slightly to the music as Aletta felt Julian's breath on her neck. She felt like she was floating above the dance floor, and they were the only two people alive.

However, when the song came to an end, she pulled away and quickly walked off the floor. He followed her. "Aletta, what's wrong?"

"I said I had questions," she responded,

pulling her arm from his hand.

"Ask away."

"You married?"

The smile on his face flickered out. "Widowed. I haven't seen anyone since my wife died a few years ago."

"I'm sorry to hear that," Aletta said, then walked over to the wall, leaned back against it, and crossed her arms in front of her. She wasn't going to let feeling sorry get in her way. "Let me just tell you somethin', so you know who you're dealin' with, okay?" She couldn't believe she was being so direct with a man like this.

"Okay," Julian said.

"I am a divorced mother of four. I just went from one low-down son of a bitch, my ex, to a man I tried to play safe with, to another that I just split with. I actually thought that these guys were gonna save me, make my life worthwhile somehow."

Aletta shook her head and put her hand to her eyes, like she didn't want to see what was right in front of her, but now was the first time she was admitting this, and it was coming out no matter what. "Even after the first one blew up in my face," she continued, "I just fell right into the same old deal of believing it was some man who made me what I am, so I gotta tell you, not only don't

I trust you, but even more important, I don't trust myself."

She took a deep breath before dropping her hand from her eyes and looking at Julian. "What in the world are you smilin' at?" she asked.

"I just like you," he said.

Aletta put her hands on her hips, "Now you're makin' fun," she said angrily.

He put a hand on her shoulder. "No, I'm telling you what I'm feeling. I'm not good at pretending to be aloof or not care when I do. As far as what you just said, I read most of it in the magazine, about you being divorced with four children. I looked at your picture a lot after Senda showed it to me. There was just something about you. And about the men in your life, I would appreciate it if I didn't have to carry them around on my shoulders, because they could get very heavy."

Aletta cocked her head to one side in a question. "What do you mean?"

"Well, I see these men around you," Julian said. He moved his hands around her head and shoulders. "You carry them here, and you think it will protect you from others like them, but it won't. The only thing that will is believing you deserve better. But here they are on your back like a quiver of arrows and then you try to shoot them at me, but I don't want them."

"So you're sayin' you're not like them?" Aletta asked.

"I'm saying I just want a chance to be myself with you, and you can see if you approve, but I don't want these other men hanging on my neck. Otherwise I have no chance no matter what I do," he answered.

Aletta looked away, considering. She'd never had a man speak to her with such frankness or insight. It caught her off guard, and she figured that she could turn her back on this man to prove a point, but then what if he was for real? That would prove something too, wouldn't it? Finally, she answered, "I guess what you say is fair, and anyway I'm only here through tomorrow, so how bad could things get?"

Julian nodded and smiled. "Let's just enjoy the time we have."

"All right, then, but don't you dare try to get lucky," she said, wagging a finger at him.

"I want you to know, I won't be taken advantage of," he answered.

She smiled. "I mean it."

"Me too. No funny business, or I'll have to say goodbye."

"Julian!" She laughed, then kissed him quickly on the cheek.

"Hey," he said, leading her to the dance floor by the hand. "What do you think I am, easy?"

Chapter Eighteen

Vee woke up to the sound of Aletta's Mickey Mouse alarm clock at seven o'clock on Sunday morning. She took a shower and packed the rest of her bags, then loaded them in the trunk of the Pink Pumpkin. She drank coffee and waited anxiously for the kids to wake up.

Randy came in first in his Underdog pajamas, his belly sticking out a little underneath the shirt.

"You want scrambled eggs?" Vee asked him.

He climbed up onto a bar stool. "Sure, but I thought you don't cook."

Ruby walked in with Gyp, her long blond hair going in seven or eight different directions and the baby with the hiccups. "Hey, whatcha makin'?" she asked.

"Eggs," Vee answered.

Ruby looked at Randy, and he shrugged.

"So y'all are gonna be good kids today,

339

right?" She couldn't believe she'd started saying *y'all.* It had just happened in the last few days. "You're gonna mind Sissy and help her out?"

They were completely noncommittal.

Vee served them scrambled eggs and biscuits. "You know, I've really liked staying here with you. You should let your mama know that when she comes back," she said. She didn't want to talk too much around Sissy, because she was afraid she'd guess what was up.

"Okay," Randy said.

Ruby kissed Gyp's forehead. "Sure."

Vee was supposed to leave by nine, and she still wouldn't make the border until the following day, so after feeding Gyp his bottle, she woke Sissy up. "I gotta go to the dentist," she said. "You're going to be all right, aren't you?"

"We'll be fine," Sissy said, and rolled over in bed.

"Sissy, I can't leave until I know you're awake."

Sissy sat up in bed. "I'm awake. I'm awake. Tell the brats I'll be out in a sec."

"Sissy, don't worry me. You have to be responsible for them," Vee said, exasperated.

"Oh, I'm just kiddin'," Sissy laughed.

Vee hesitated at the door.

"Go on and go. You're worse than my mama."

Vee walked to the kitchen, hugged Ruby and Randy, and kissed Gyp on those rose-petal-soft, round, wonderful cheeks until he started to squirm. She had to admit to herself that not only had she been frightened of him in the beginning, but she'd also considered this most kissable little sweetheart a sign of Aletta's imprisonment.

Finally, she went out to the car and backed away from the house. She put the car in drive, then glanced at the house one more time. The four Honor kids stood on the porch, waving goodbye. Vee stopped and waved back at them. They looked so beautiful standing in front of the slightly dilapidated olive-green house, the only place she'd ever felt even close to home. She felt an ache in her heart that she knew would turn into tears if she stayed much longer, so she pushed the gas pedal down hard and drove away fast.

As she got on Interstate 40 going east, headed toward I-35, the road that would take her straight down through the heart of Texas, she realized she didn't have a picture of the Honors. It made her slow the car down at the first exit she came to, but she looked up at the freeway extending out in front of her like an invitation and steered the car straight.

Maybe one day they could forgive her, and then she'd ask Aletta to send her a picture wherever she was — Nicaragua, South Africa, Cuba, or even back in the States fighting her home country's capitalist machine. No, she wasn't going to go back. She leaned back in the Chevy's enormous seat and put her left foot up on it, leaning her knee against the door. The wind tossed her hair across her forehead, and she glanced in the rearview mirror to look at herself. Smiling, she wondered what Bo, who was waiting for her in Nuevo Laredo, would think of her new look.

She turned on the radio and smiled again when she heard the Crosby, Stills, Nash, and Young anthem against the U.S. military and its killing of the four students at Kent State. She cranked up the volume, even though the old speakers vibrated in protest, and sang as loud as she could about the soldiers and Nixon. An exhilarating sense of freedom replaced any guilt or remorse she'd had a few miles back.

Jimmy slept so deeply on Frank's couch, it took Frank three tries to get him to finally open his eyes.

Jimmy wiped a hand down his face and cleared his throat. "Couldn't get to sleep last night," he croaked, and sat up. "Only drifted off a few hours ago, I think."

Frank poured three bowls of cereal in the kitchen. "You're used to havin' the booze put you to sleep," he said.

Rusty walked in. "Hey," he said to Jimmy.

Jimmy didn't look at the teenager. He felt ashamed and wished Frank wouldn't be so blabby about everything. "Howdy" was all he said.

They ate Grape Nuts standing around the kitchen. "I'll pick you up to go to Grandma's after my meetin', all right, Rusty?" Frank said between bites.

"We gonna get to ride?" Rusty asked.

"We'll have to see," Frank answered, then turned to Jimmy. "You still comin'?"

Jimmy hesitated, looking out the window so they wouldn't see the fear in his eyes. "I don't wanna be in the way."

"You ain't, and besides, if I was you I wouldn't wanna be alone."

Rusty dropped his eyes when Jimmy glanced over at him.

"Well," Jimmy said slowly, "I guess I'll come along then."

Before the ten o'clock AA meeting, they loaded up a twin mattress set, a rickety card table, and a metal folding chair from the Conways' garage. Frank tossed in a set of sheets and a pillow, and they took it all to Jimmy's apartment.

"I still have time to see my kids this mornin'," Jimmy said as he carried the mattress and Frank followed him with the box spring up the stairs to his place. "I'll take my car and see you at the meeting."

He was glad he couldn't see Frank, because he knew he'd see the doubt in his eyes, but all Frank said was "Suit yourself."

Jimmy walked into the kitchen of his former home half an hour later. The warmth and clutter and that particular smell that he only found there filled him with a mild sense of well-being. It was a calm he hadn't felt for a long time. The only thing that he'd found to replace it was a belly full of booze.

He took a deep breath, then called out to his kids.

They stood dutifully in front of him a few minutes later. "Hey, kiddos," he said. "How's it goin'?"

"Fine," Ruby said.

"Fine," Randy said.

Sissy handed Gyp to his daddy. "We're getting by," she said.

Jimmy looked at his watch. It was ten minutes to ten. He sat down and kissed Gyp on the cheek. Maybe he should just stay here. Aletta was out of town, and he could even sleep over, like old times. That way, he wouldn't have to go back to that miserable, lonely apartment, but he could be here with all this life and living. Maybe he could even convince Aletta to let him stay when she got back. He had a family, people who loved him and needed him. It was here with them that he could get his life together, not with some cult of strangers in smoke-filled church meeting rooms.

His heart beat faster, an excitement filling him, but then as he was about to announce his new plan, he looked at his children, really looked at them for the first time since he'd gotten here. What he saw in their eyes was unmistakable. Their disappointment and even fear drove away the contentment and excitement he'd felt moments earlier, like a hunter flushing a covey of quail from the ground.

The flurry of emotions continued as he handed Gyp back to Sissy. "I gotta go, but I'll call y'all later, all right?"

"Fine," Ruby said.

"Fine," Randy said.

"See ya later," Sissy said, and shut the door behind him.

■ ■ ■ ■

Jimmy showed up a few minutes late to the meeting at the Disciples of Christ church, an old brick building near Main Street that embodied both the holy and flawed sides of the folks who passed through its doors. It was run-down, to be sure, but of excellent pioneer-style Victorian construction. The floors were worn-out linoleum and stained carpet, but the lathe-and-plaster walls were in good shape. The fellowship hall was just four walls and folding tables, but its sanctuary was one of the prettiest in three counties, with a stained-glass window of the Last Supper that inspired parishioners and made prayers more fervent.

Jimmy found his way to the fellowship hall and sat down. He couldn't believe how many people were here — must be over forty, he guessed, about thirty-five of whom were men.

Frank saw him and nodded his way. Jimmy nodded back, then looked around to see if he recognized anyone else. He saw Bill Orcutt, owner of Bill's Tires on Main Street. He'd never have guessed it. There was a lady who was a cashier at the 7-Eleven, one of those people he saw probably three or four times a week when he went in for gas and beer and the newspaper, but he'd never once considered her personal life or even that she had one. He had always felt himself a little better than folks like her.

The former football player who'd introduced himself as Warren at the other meeting Jimmy had gone to sat across the room. When Jimmy looked his way, Warren waved and Jimmy nodded in return. *God, I hate this,* he thought.

The leader finished the reading out of the Big Book, then asked if anyone had anything to share, especially any newcomers. To Jimmy, it was like his body separated from his will, and before he knew what was happening, his hand was in the air. He didn't even notice if the leader, a jowly-faced man with thinning hair and a wide middle, called on him or if anyone else had their hands up. He just started talking to his lap.

"I guess I never figured I'd be here. I never thought I really had a problem, you know?" He glanced up and then back down without really looking at anyone. "Hell, I wasn't gonna show up today either, but I was cleaned out by my girlfriend last night. I knew she really hated me when she poured out my bottle and left it in the sink. I guess that's the worst thing she could think of to do to me." He chuckled sadly. "But even this mornin', I was thinkin' I wouldn't show, even though Frank over there's been helpin' me a lot, but the truth is I didn't come for him. I came because I just saw my kids. . . ."

He stopped and raised his eyes to the ceiling, holding on with all his might to keep the tears from coming. "I don't know when it happened, if it was last year or yesterday, because I been way too busy thinkin' about myself to notice, but I saw it today, them standin' there in their little pajamas and my oldest lookin' anywhere she could but at me. They don't respect me. Hell, I don't even think they can stand me anymore. I guess when you've lost the love of your kids, in addition to every other thing in your life, including your goddamn dignity, it's time to swallow your pride." Jimmy wiped his eyes with his fingers and shook his head. He waved his hand toward the leader to show he was finished.

The meeting leader waited. There was a pause in the room, and finally Jimmy realized no one else was speaking, and looked up.

"Thank you," the leader said when Jimmy's eyes met his.

Jimmy nodded slightly, then glanced around at the faces looking at him, these folks who were his neighbors. He saw the opposite of what he felt about himself. He saw respect and encouragement and even love coming at him. From the seen-it-all old-timers to the young outcasts, they all were acknowledging him.

The humility and gratitude he felt were like a tingling that went all the way down into his toes. It was strange and beautiful and made him feel lighter in his chair, like he could lift right up out of it. It lasted for only a few seconds, and then he remembered his empty apartment and his busted marriage and his desperate need for a drink, and the lightness and tingling drained out of him right into the ground under his feet.

He sat shaken by what had just happened, lost in his own thoughts, trying to hold on to some idea or feeling that had been in his grasp for just a moment but then was gone like a dream that he couldn't remember. Finally, when he came out of his reverie, he heard someone speaking.

It was Warren. "I remember when I first started comin' here, I thought I was so much better than y'all." Warren laughed, and so did everybody else. "I thought I'd come until I could control the drinking, then stop. Well, I tried it, but finally, I gave in, just surrendered to y'all and to this program, and the funniest thing started happening. I'd actually have a good day here and there. I remember at first, I'd be nervous as hell 'cause I knew somethin' bad must be comin', but then I'd have another one. Finally, when I started doin' the steps, I started havin' more good days than bad. For a long, long time I felt like I didn't deserve 'em 'cause of what I'd done when I was drinking, but now I've even forgiven myself for most of that. I owe my life to this program, and I know it can help. That's all I got for today," he finished, and glanced at Jimmy.

Jimmy dropped his eyes to the floor. Warren's story had a ring of truth to it, and the anxiety that had been creeping into his chest and throat, the sense of being out of control that had come up after he finished talking and all the good feelings had left him, started to retreat a little again. Hope, or something like it, started to wedge its way in. He took a deep breath, and the next person to speak was the flamboyant old woman he'd seen at the other meeting. Today, her bleached blond hair poofed out on the sides but was flat on top, and along with a purple headband, she wore white go-go boots and a full-length pink polyester jacket with a sheer white scarf around her neck.

"Hi, I'm Zelma," she said.

"Hello, Zelma," the room answered.

Jimmy forgot and mumbled "Zelma," after they did.

Her voice grated like an emery board. "I'm eighty-one years old this week, and that right there is a damn miracle after all I dragged myself through. I'm seein' miracles all the time now," she said, then raised a bony finger. "Now, don't get me wrong. It wasn't till about ten years ago I even started believin' in God and that was after nine years of comin' here. Hell, if I'd a come up in here and they'd a made it sound like church, quoting scriptures and all, I'd a run right outta here and died drunk."

Jimmy looked around expecting to see scowling, disapproving looks at what she'd just said, but mostly he saw people nodding or smiling.

"But they didn't. Nobody forced anything down my throat about any of that," Zelma continued, "and like they say here, I came to my own understanding of God, and now it's just there with me all the time. Thanks for listenin'."

For the rest of the meeting, Jimmy listened intently to each person, and with every single one of them, he felt they had something in common. It didn't matter if it was an eighty-one-year-old woman in go-go boots or a fat cigarette-smoking truck driver — they had all had the same experiences as Jimmy.

Afterward, he walked out of the church into the warm spring sunshine and waited for Frank. Several people came and shook his hand and told him they were glad to have him there. When Zelma came out and started talking to him, he found himself glancing around to see if he recognized anyone driving by. He didn't want to be seen talking to her, and then he got self-conscious about being seen outside an AA meeting.

Finally, Frank came out and clapped him on the back. "How do you feel?" he asked.

"I'm not sure," Jimmy said. "Shaky."

They started walking toward the parking lot on the side of the church.

"I'm glad to hear you say that," Frank said. "A lot of people go to one meeting or two and think they're cured. I stopped going and you saw what happened to me."

"I can't imagine havin' to go forever," Jimmy said. The thought of that struck fear in him. It was like considering something like living without a limb for the rest of his life. He couldn't get his mind around the idea of sitting in these meetings when he was fifty or even older. It made him want to throw up.

Frank stopped and turned to Jimmy, who knew Frank could feel the fear coming off him like waves of heat. Frank looked Jimmy straight in the eye. "Just take this one day at a time, fella. Just one day at a time."

On Sunday morning, Aletta called home and Sissy answered the phone. "Vee's gone to the dentist, but everything's fine," Sissy said.

"All righty, I'll call you tonight, then," Aletta said.

"You don't have to, Mama. We're doing fine. There ain't a thing happenin' here. We're bored outta our minds, so you know we're bein' good."

The ladies pulled into Martin's Auto Shop on Don Gaspar Avenue half an hour later. Aletta hadn't let herself think much about Julian since last night, and she refused to talk about him at all with her friends. She had to admit he was a fascinating man, but she wasn't going to let herself get all moony or ridiculous. She wanted to keep her feet on the ground and practicality ruling over her untrustworthy heart.

All of this made her completely unprepared for what happened when she saw Julian standing in the parking lot of the body shop, wearing blue jeans and a black T-shirt, holding a Styrofoam coffee cup in his hand, his black hair pulled back into a ponytail. She got out of the car, and he walked toward her, smiling like it was his job to keep the sun shining with his grin.

Aletta stopped and stared at him. All around Julian, she saw a shimmering glow, kind of a silvery gold that moved with him as he moved. Her heart sped up, and excitement fluttered in her stomach. Just then, Maria stepped out of the pickup and stared at Aletta.

Julian spoke to her friends, but he never took his eyes off her. "Welcome, ladies. Come in and meet my friend Martin. He's going to make your car just like new." He put his hand on Aletta's shoulder. "It's good to see you again. You look great."

"You too," Aletta said, giggling at how strange she felt.

Martin was a very hairy white man with long sideburns and a beer belly the size of a beach ball. He inspected the Gran Torino, grunting when he had to stoop to see underneath. "I can fix the bumper, and I'll have to replace the rear lights on this side, but you're damn lucky. I got the parts in the garage," he said.

Bobette cleared her throat. "Um, how much is this gonna cost?"

"It's fine," Julian said, and clapped Martin on his large back. "We got this covered."

"You're gonna owe me now, Moquino," Martin said, and held out his pudgy hand to Bobette for the keys.

As Martin pulled the station wagon into his garage, Julian escorted the ladies to his truck. He touched Aletta's hand as they walked, and the thrill of it coursed through her body.

"So you decided to join us after all?" Betty asked Maria as they approached her.

Maria, who was wearing tight jeans and another concert shirt, this time Pink Floyd, stretched her arms in the air and yawned. "Like I had a choice," she said, smiling.

"Well, I hope we won't bore you too much," Betty replied.

"It's not you that's boring," Maria said, cutting her eyes at her father, then pushing him on the shoulder.

"There's a little problem with the tour, besides Maria's attitude," Julian said. "My grandma's car had a flat this morning, and there was no spare, so all we have is my pickup. I thought we could maybe go to some of the museums here in town instead of driving all over."

Joy stomped her sandal-clad foot. "But we've already done the boring inside stuff."

They were like little girls being told they weren't going to the circus. "Oh, my heart was set," Bobette said.

"I wanna be out in nature so bad. I wanna see the peter . . . you know, the petra . . . that art on the rocks," Betty whined.

"What about meeting your grandmother?" Aletta asked quietly.

Julian held out his hands. "Just in case you insisted, I brought some blankets to put in the back if you all wanted to, you know, get some fresh air."

Joy walked to the back of the truck, put her foot on the bumper, and climbed over the rear gate. "Did somebody forget we're a bunch a farm girls?" she asked, standing in the back of the pickup. "Let's quit pussy-footin' around and go see some Indian stuff."

Betty whooped loudly and climbed in, then Bobette followed. Aletta put her hand on the rear gate to pull herself up, but Betty slapped it away. "You get up there with him right now."

Aletta looked at them. "Are you sure?"

"Ain't enough room for you back here."

Joy smiled. "We don't want you."

"Now go have fun," Bobette said.

Julian put the blankets down in the bed of the truck as Aletta climbed into the cab next to Maria. "You are some classy women," he said to Aletta's friends.

"That should tell you a little about that lady up there," Betty said, nodding toward Aletta, whom they could see through the rear window.

"Yes, it should," Julian said. "Now get comfortable. It may be a little bumpy, but I'll try to take it easy."

They sat down with their backs against the cab of the truck and their legs stretched out in front of them. "This is so much fun," Bobette squealed.

"Just like when I was a little girl," Betty said.

Joy took the scarf off her neck and tied it around her hair. "Tell the chauffeur I'm ready to leave," she said in her best snobby-sounding voice.

Julian pulled the truck onto Don Gaspar, then headed south. Aletta hoped he felt the same electricity filling up the cab of the truck as she did, in spite of his daughter sitting between them. She wanted to ask him if he felt it, if he saw the shimmer around her too, if he was real or if she was dreaming. She wanted to turn his face toward her and look into his eyes and see if she could understand what was happening from reading his soul. Instead she asked, "So what do you do?" in a barely audible voice.

He drove the truck out of town on a road that cut straight through flat, high desert. "I carve animal totems, for one. I'm involved in tribal activities like ceremonies and politics."

"He's a shaman," Maria said.

Julian continued, "I take care of my kid and Senda. I like to fish when the creeks are high and the trout are biting. I read a lot."

"What's a shaman?" Aletta asked. Just the word sounded fascinating.

"I study and practice the medicine of my people, trying to help out in whatever way I can — with the sick or dying or if someone is on a spiritual quest. I'm not a master, though, just a dabbler."

"What about you, Maria? Are you a shaman too?" Aletta asked.

Maria shook her head. "No, I'm a black sheep."

Julian put his hand on her thigh. "She'd make a great shaman."

"Come on, Dad," Maria protested.

"No, really, she remembers all the ceremonies after seeing them only once. Anytime I am with someone and she's patient enough to stick around, she always has good advice."

"You're embarrassing me now," Maria said, and turned on the radio.

Julian turned to Aletta. "Is that what you meant by 'what do you do?' " When she hesitated, he continued. "No, you meant what do I do for a living. I'm a high school teacher. I teach history and Native American studies."

"He's a nerd," Maria said playfully.

"How wonderful," Aletta answered. "I bet that's so fulfilling. I could never teach, I don't think."

Julian paused before asking, "Isn't that what your job is? Teaching people about their lives and dreams?"

"Hmmm," Aletta said, thinking hard. "I do tell people the visions I get, but it's more like a . . ."

He turned east on a road that cut toward a far-off mountain range and waited for her to continue, but when she didn't, he asked, "Like a what?"

"Nothin'," she said. Knots of self-doubt tied themselves together in her chest and throat, not allowing her to see herself as anything other than a struggling mother of four.

"Where I'm from, there's a name for someone like you," he said.

"Are you really psychic?" Maria asked. She sounded interested for the first time.

Aletta shrugged a little. "I was. Before y'all brought me that feather."

Maria looked at Aletta. Under all the makeup, Aletta saw that her eyes were gorgeous. A light shone in them that she hadn't noticed before, a spark of intelligence hidden beneath her sarcasm and eyeliner.

"That's cool," Maria said with admiration.

"Oh, that's me all right. Cool as can be," Aletta said, smiling.

Julian slowed down to drive across steel bars in the road that prevented cows from crossing.

"Hey!" Betty called. "My butt may be wide, but it's flat!"

"She's also got a hangover!" Joy yelled.

"Sorry!" Julian called out the window. "It's a dirt road now, so brace yourselves."

Aletta watched the strange and beautiful landscape pass by. Ranch houses sat way back off the road every so often, but mostly there was red earth polka-dotted with green juniper and sage. Rock formations pushed out of the ground in no real pattern or regularity. Aletta was surprised at how different this place was from her home.

Both New Mexico and Oklahoma had red dirt, but New Mexico's was different from Oklahoma's. It was lighter, more golden than rust. It was drier too from the high desert air and the near-constant sunshine. Here, the earth smelled like pine and sweet herbs, while Oklahoma earth smelled musty and warm. She rolled down her window and breathed in the difference.

In front of them was a long line of rock outcroppings rising from the earth. "Looks like a dragon's back, doesn't it?" Julian asked.

"It does," Aletta marveled. "It's so unusual."

"It's called an escarpment. It was formed by earthquakes."

Aletta's eyes followed it as it cut across the flat land for miles. "It goes on so far. It's like the earth crashed together and pushed all this straight up out of it."

When they got to it, Julian pulled the truck to the side of the road and stopped. The ladies got out of the truck a little wobbly.

"Feels like we're still movin'," Bobette said.

"I'm gonna listen to the radio," Maria said, still sitting inside the truck.

Julian leaned down, his hands on the top of the door, to talk to her in a quiet but firm voice. "Come on now," he said. "Don't be like this."

Maria turned the dial on the old radio without looking at him. "Like what? I've seen this stuff a hundred times."

Julian gave up with a sigh. He walked to a barbed-wire fence and put his foot on the middle wire and pulled up on the top one. "Don't worry," he said to the ladies with a smile. "This is state-owned. If they catch us, at least they won't shoot us."

Betty was the first one through. They had quite a time getting Joy through. First she caught her hair, then her jeans, then her sandal on the barbs.

"Oh, for the love of God!" she yelled before finally stumbling onto the other side.

As they walked toward the escarpment, Betty charging out front and Joy straggling behind, Aletta spoke with Julian. "I have a teenager too. They're hard to figure sometimes."

"Most of the time," he agreed. "She used to love when I brought her to the sacred places, but not anymore. It's been really tough since her mother died. It was a car accident, so . . ."

Aletta waited for him to finish, but when

he didn't speak again, she took his hand and said, "I'm sorry about that. I think you're doing great with Maria, by the way."

He laughed slightly, a nervous and uncertain chuckle with his mouth in a tight, straight line.

By then, they were standing under the escarpment and looking up at the flat-faced rocks at the top of the hill.

"What're we lookin' for?" Joy asked, coming up from behind.

"It's higher than it looks from the road," Aletta said.

Betty pointed. "What's that?"

Above them, carved into the rock, they could see a spiral winding around. "How cool," Betty said, and scampered up the hill to get a closer look. She was always so athletic and full of energy, even with a hangover.

The rest of them followed. Joy kept slipping in her sandals, so Julian held her arm. By the time they reached the rock, which was almost as tall as they were, Aletta realized what they were looking at. For as far as she could see along the escarpment, there were carved images. There must have been hundreds of them. A thrill went up her spine and goose bumps rose on her arms.

"Oh, my," Betty said in a reverent whisper.

"This is the most amazing thing I ever saw," Bobette said.

They moved along the rocks, and Julian explained what they were looking at. "This is the way ancient people told their stories. Some of these are hundreds of years old and some from the last century, but they all tell the stories of this land and its people." He pointed at animal images. "You can see these deer and elk here. Hunters would carve them to help them on their hunt. Look at this." He pointed at a round face with huge eyes and dagger-like teeth. "This is a warning. If you see a face like this, you're supposed to look at what it's looking at because there's danger there."

They looked over their shoulders at the flat land rolling away from them. The sun shone down hot and bright, and the air was still, almost stagnant.

"This particular drawing tells a lot about this place," Julian said, still pointing at the warning face. "This became a very dark place, a sad place for my people."

"What happened?" Aletta asked.

"Let's keep going," he said.

They walked some more and saw pictures of coyotes, lizards, suns, and squiggly lines, of upright, elongated figures with horns and no arms. "What is this guy?" Joy asked.

"That's a depiction of a shaman," Julian said. "A powerful medicine man. They needed a lot of medicine here."

"How long did these take to make?" Aletta asked.

"Some of them took many years," Julian answered. "Many of them would've been done by more than one person and were added on to over the years."

Betty, who was in front, stopped and looked at some carvings. "What are these?" she asked.

The carvings were of small people with sticks for arms and legs. Spots were carved inside and around them.

"What does it look like?" Julian asked, just like a teacher.

"It looks like people, children maybe, but what are these?" Bobette started to touch the spots.

"Don't touch them," Julian said. "The oil from your skin damages the petroglyphs."

Bobette jerked her hand back guiltily.

"It's okay." Julian smiled, but then his smile faded. "These are children — babies, actually — and the dots represent small-pox."

"Oh, my God," Joy said.

Julian walked a little further, then pointed out some larger figures with the same spots.

"These are elders with the smallpox." He hung his head a moment before continuing. "The white man brought many diseases that Indians had never seen. Smallpox alone killed thousands and thousands of people. In order to try to stop the infection from spreading, the healthy people would have to kill the babies and the old people, the ones who would die anyway because they couldn't resist it, so there would be fewer infected people. This is where they did it."

Aletta felt dizzy for a moment, as if the ground under her feet was moving. Sadness and hurt filled the stillness, and the hot sun felt mean on her neck and shoulders.

"They killed the babies on top of the rock with the pictures of children, and they killed the old people here, on top of this one," Julian said. "They did it with respect and as a ceremony."

"I can't believe it," Bobette whispered.

Aletta couldn't stay there any longer. She ran down the side of the hill, back to flat ground, and covered her eyes with her hands. As tears trickled through her fingers, she suddenly saw an image of her great-grandmother at the riverside, bending over to fill a pail of water. The shadow came over the young Indian woman as it had in Aletta's dream, but this time Aletta saw the image of the scary face, the warning, behind her grandmother, looking at whatever was making the shadow.

Just then, Julian walked up and put his hand on Aletta's shoulder. She started a little. "Are you all right?" he asked quietly.

Aletta shrugged and nodded slightly. She looked up at him and noticed the rain clouds creeping their way over the escarpment above. Suddenly, a cool, soft breeze whispered across her face and through her hair.

"It's going to rain," she said.

"It does that in the afternoons here. Sometimes it lasts only a few minutes," he answered. "Maybe we should try to outrun it. There's somewhere else I want to take you."

A few minutes later, they were all racing toward the truck. They piled in, and Julian took off, headed away from the fast-moving clouds.

"What did you think?" Maria asked Aletta.

"It was amazing. . . ."

"And sad." Maria didn't look at Aletta, but her slumped shoulders and bowed head told Aletta how much she felt about this place.

Aletta nodded. "And very sad, yes."

They rode south along a smooth dirt road that followed the line of mountains in the east. The ladies in the back were quiet for the first time all day as they watched the wake of red dust kicked up by the truck and the blackening sky behind them.

Inside the truck, Aletta was still shaken from the story Julian had told and from the vision of her dream and the warning face. "My great-grandmother was put in one of the Indian schools, because she was an orphan," Aletta said. She needed to talk about what was happening, to try to make some sense of it. "She married a white man and moved to Oklahoma during the land rush. She died when she was very young, after having my grandfather and uncle. Something happened to her there. They said she drowned. . . ."

Julian drove with one hand and his arm on the seat behind Maria. He touched Aletta's hair with his fingers. At first, she felt nervous, not sure if she should pull away. The energy between them was so strong, it scared her a little, but when she saw the kindness in his eyes, she relaxed. "I've had visions of her, dreams at night. Just now . . ." She stopped and wiped the moisture from her eyes with her free hand.

"That's a powerful place. I'm not surprised," Julian said.

Maria stayed quiet, but Aletta could tell she was listening intently.

"When I was a kid, there was this family with about a dozen kids who lived on a farm in the country. My uncle Joe took me over there one day, because he was looking to buy a truck from their daddy. Those kids were playing cowboys and Indians. They made me the Indian, because nobody wanted to be, and they'd heard I had . . ." Aletta paused and looked out the window. "They'd heard I had seen things, visions and all. They called me 'Indian witch' and chased me down and tied me up with rope. They were gonna throw me off the hayloft until my uncle interrupted."

Julian shook his head. "That sounds scary as hell."

Aletta nodded. "It's the same feeling when I see the vision of my grandmother by the river. The same feeling I got back there looking at those carvings."

Just then, large drops of rain spattered on the dusty windshield. From the back they heard squeals of protest.

"We're here!" Julian called out his window.

Aletta looked around as he pulled to the side of the road. She didn't understand where here was. There was nothing around except a line of trees about a hundred yards away beyond a barbed-wire fence. The ladies scrambled out of the back, ready to find cover, and looked around, as bewildered as Aletta. The rain came a little harder, but it was still gentle, not a thunderstorm but a shower.

"Come on!" Julian called to Maria, who was holding back again. "You love it here." He went back to the pickup, took her hands, and pulled her out of the truck.

She smiled in spite of herself but rolled her eyes to show she was an unwilling participant.

Julian walked to the barbed-wire fence and did the same routine as before. As Betty headed through first, he said, "Now, here we could definitely get shot."

She stumbled a little and fell on her butt on the other side. "Excuse me, sir?" she said as she got up and wiped off her jeans.

"Let's just say we need to keep moving," Julian said. "It's private property, and the owners have been known to be a little cranky."

"Screw 'em," Bobette said, and bent over to climb through after Maria ducked under.

As they walked toward the trees, they just gave in to the rain. Betty stuck her tongue out, and Aletta raised her hands to the sky.

"It feels wonderful, doesn't it?" she said to Maria, and put an arm around her shoulders for a moment.

"We must have danced well," Maria answered.

Julian smiled and nodded.

Bobette, who was never afraid to ask a question, looked at them. "What does it mean?"

"It's a saying among my people," Julian said, the rain glistening in his black hair. "If it's a good rain or a bountiful crop or a healthy baby, we say it's because we must have danced well. It's for anything that is good for us together."

"I love it," Bobette said.

The others agreed. "It musta been all that dancin' we did last night," Joy said, and laughed.

"You all are kinda wild for old ladies, aren't you?" Maria asked, smiling.

Joy shot the girl a look filled with daggers. "You better put a muzzle on your little rock star, Julian," she teased.

Aletta looked at Maria, concerned her feelings might be hurt. Joy could do that to people, even if she was just playing, but Maria started running ahead, jumping like a gazelle every so often, her legs open mid-stride for a moment in the air. Then she ran into some trees, and they couldn't see her anymore.

As they reached the tall pine trees, Aletta saw that behind them was a large rock formation gently sloping up out of the ground. "What is this place?" she asked.

"It's called the Blessing Way," Julian answered. "It's a sacred ceremonial site for native people all over this area."

Walking through the line of trees was like entering a passageway. They went through the natural entrance between the trees and climbed until they were standing on top of a huge rock formation that stretched on for about fifty yards.

"I would've never guessed this was here," Joy said. "It's wonderful."

As they walked across the smooth surface, Aletta realized this place was the opposite of the escarpment. Where that had been rough and exposed, with straight lines, this was smooth, round, and enclosed by trees and by the walls of the formation itself. In the rock here, there were small caves and holes. Aletta laughed a little as she felt the soft rain cooling her off. It had been so hot and arid and still at the escarpment, while this was moist and mild and breezy.

"What?" Betty asked when Aletta laughed.

Aletta shook her head a little, unable to

explain what she was feeling. "It's so wonderful here," she said.

Bobette's face twitched happily. "I feel kinda tingly," she said.

Julian walked across the rock and pointed to a shallow pool of water. Its surface rippled with the raindrops, but as they watched the pool, it became perfectly still. The rain stopped, and the sun broke through the clouds.

Julian kneeled down next to the pool. "This place has been used for many ceremonies, but the most important ceremony performed here is inducting the youth into the tribe as adults when they turn a certain age. This water is always here, and it is used during the rituals." He put his fingers in the water, then stood up and walked to Aletta. He touched the water to her face and drew his fingers down each cheek, then kissed her cheek softly, hesitating a moment before pulling away.

She cocked her head to one side and smiled at him, a little shy, her cheek still tingling where his lips had been.

Julian and Aletta followed the others toward the dark openings in the rock wall. The first one they came to was low and wide, like a large mouth in the rock. Above the cave was an etching in the rock of a rudimentary face. They looked at Julian.

"You all can go in there, but I can't. It's called the Cleansing Cave. It's only for women," he said.

Maria walked over and pointed at the face over the cave's entrance. "That is the Corn Mother. She watches the women enter and keeps men out."

The women entered the cave one by one, bending over to get inside as Maria hovered near the entrance, watching. Aletta stood up inside the cave and felt something move within her, a deep sense of the importance of this place and its history. It was larger than she had expected from the outside, and its smooth walls were carved with symbols. Openings near the top of the cave let in shafts of light, and the cave seemed to be awash in a soft, almost magical glow. All she could hear was the breathing and footsteps of herself and her friends as they lingered in this holy place.

Aletta examined the carvings on the wall and noticed two handprints that were about shoulder height — a black one on the left and a white one on the right. Even though Julian had said not to touch the carvings, she had an overwhelming desire to put her hands over these. She reached up and put her hands on top of the carvings. They fit perfectly.

Just as she was about to remove them, she heard a woman's voice from behind her. She turned around, but her friends were on the other side of the cave. The voice became clearer, and she realized it was in a language she didn't understand. She closed her eyes, her hands still on the carvings, and just allowed it to wash over her, a woman's voice, deep and warm and encouraging. The words sounded like music to Aletta, and she realized they were being sung, slowly and rhythmically.

She took a deep breath. Just then, she heard footsteps behind her, and then she felt someone's breath on her neck. She turned around to see Maria standing right behind her, so close that they were touching.

"The white hand is to release bad energy, sadness, and painful emotions," Maria said in Aletta's ear as the other women gathered around them. "The black hand brings power and love into you from the earth mother."

Maria took Aletta's right hand in hers while Aletta kept her left hand on the black carving, and began to speak quietly. "Oh, Old Woman Earth. Oh, Old Father Sky." As she spoke of the earth, she pointed Aletta's arm to the ground, and when she said "Father Sky," she raised her arm toward the ceiling of the cave. "Your daughters are we, with tired backs and weary spirits. We bring you our gifts of love. Weave the warp of the white light of morning." Maria continued to speak in a rhythmic, gentle cadence, and Aletta felt the song within her, in her bones and her flesh and her soul.

"Let the warp carry us in your garment of brightness. Let the weft be the red light glow of evening. Let the fringe bring the moisture of falling rain. Let the border be the standing rainbow of love."

Maria placed Aletta's right hand back on the white hand on the wall and traced the line of a rainbow with Aletta's other arm. "Thus weave for us your ways of brightness, that we may walk the path that is green, green with life. Oh, our Old Mother Earth. Oh, our Old Father Sky."

Maria finished by bringing Aletta's hand to her heart, and they stood this way in a silence that was full and deep and rich. A tear dropped down Aletta's cheek as she turned and put her arms around Maria.

"Thank you," she said, and looked at her friends, who were watching intently.

Maria shrugged a little as she pulled away

from Aletta. "That was the prayer that's said when your hands are on the carvings, so it just came out."

"It was so . . . beautiful," Bobette said.

Joy looked at Aletta. "I've never seen you look so lovely, girl," she said.

Betty smiled radiantly. "Your eyes are glowing, Lettie."

Aletta felt like her body was filled with a warm glow, and her green eyes shone.

"If you want, I can do it for all of you," Maria said with another shrug. And right then, Aletta felt love for her, for her shiny, straight black hair and brown skin, but also for her Pink Floyd shirt, heavy makeup, and rings on every finger. She thought of Sissy and decided to try to accept her more, to try to listen better.

Her three friends hung back shyly after Maria's offer, so Aletta took Betty's hands, led her to the wall, and placed them on the carvings. She stepped out of the way and let Maria take over, first with Betty, then with Joy.

When Maria was finishing with Bobette, Aletta realized that Bobette hadn't twitched the entire time in the cave.

After Maria stopped speaking, they all stood in a circle, the shafts of light criss-crossing their bodies and faces.

"I loved that," Joy said finally.

Betty, who was glowing herself now, she was so happy and excited, said, "That was the coolest thing that ever happened to me."

Maria laughed a little. "It was no big deal, but you can't tell my father. You have to promise," she said, looking straight at Aletta. "Men aren't supposed to know what happens in here, and we can't know what happens in their cave. Besides, I don't want him to know."

"I promise," Aletta said. She looked toward the mouth of the cave. "I guess we better not keep Julian waiting."

They walked out of the cave into the bright sunshine under an enormous sky dappled with white cloud puffs departing after the rain. Julian was leaning against a boulder with his ankles crossed, watching swallows dart in and out of holes and crevices high up on the rock formation. When he saw the ladies emerge, he looked at Aletta and smiled.

"Did something happen in there?" he asked. "You all look . . . different."

Betty wandered away, looking up at the swallows.

"Thank you so much for bringin' us here," Aletta said to Julian.

He looked at her sideways, a crooked grin

on his face. "I'm glad you like it," he said. "You're not going to tell me, are you?"

Aletta shook her head.

"But it ain't because you're not cute as a bug's ear," Joy said.

"I agree," Bobette said.

"It's true," Aletta said, and smiled.

"Oh, well." Julian blushed a little and put his hands in his back pockets. "That's not a bad consolation."

Maria rolled her eyes. "I'm gonna throw up."

CHAPTER NINETEEN

On the way out to the old Conway place, Frank tried to make small talk, but neither Jimmy nor Rusty was taking the bait. Jimmy looked out at the passing fields and farmhouses, pretty much feeling like he was the unluckiest son of a bitch alive. If he hadn't been injured playing baseball, he'd probably have been a professional pitcher. He'd gotten weeded out from becoming a pilot in the army because of bad timing; they weren't taking any more men into training even though the recruiter had promised him. Now it turned out he couldn't have a damned drink like every other man in the entire world without it messing up his whole life. He was pretty certain that if he wasn't here with Frank right now, he'd be finding an excuse to drink away his sorrows, and that scared the hell out of him.

He was still brooding as Frank turned into the long dirt drive that led to the Conways' — a white two-story farmhouse with a big front porch. In its day, it had been one of the nicest homes in Okay County, but now it looked worn and tired, a little like the woman who came out on the porch to wave at them. Mrs. Conway, Frank's mama, wore an old dress and sturdy black shoes. Her white hair curled around her face. She'd never been a pretty woman, but her face was kind and open and invited anyone in her presence to relax around her, even if they didn't know why.

Frank's daddy had died several years back, but his mama refused to move off the land.

"She says even the thought of livin' in town makes her feel claustrophobic," Frank said as he stopped the truck. He said it with pride in his voice, and Jimmy could see him light up as he gave her a kiss on the cheek.

They went inside the house, and Mrs. Conway served them peach cobbler and coffee, then Rusty went out back to feed Tillie, the eighteen-year-old mare, an apple. Jimmy sipped his coffee as Frank and his mother discussed all the work that needed to be done around the place.

"I can mow that field out back if you want," Jimmy said after a list of chores had been compiled.

Mrs. Conway got up to get him another

piece of cobbler. "Why, Frank, you didn't tell me you brought a man who could drive a tractor."

"You remember Jimmy's daddy, don't you, Mama?" Frank said. "Burl Honor used to drive the gas truck around these parts. Sharecropped too."

Jimmy saw the cloud that passed over Mrs. Conway's face when she remembered his daddy. He'd been a hard man, and mean, and unlike Mrs. Conway, Burl Honor made you think you'd done something wrong.

"Course I remember him," she said. "He was very . . . reliable."

"He was a bastard," Jimmy said.

Mrs. Conway lingered over the cobbler, and Jimmy knew she was uncomfortable. She was a real lady, a woman with morals from the old days. In her presence, even though she was kind, he felt somehow soiled, forever stained by his past, his heritage. "Excuse my language, ma'am. My daddy and me just didn't get on," he said.

Mrs. Conway put the cobbler down in front of him. "Well, I'm sorry to hear that," she said. "Sometimes it's hardest to love the ones closest to us, isn't it?"

"Sure is," Jimmy said.

Half an hour later he was sitting on an old

tractor with a mower attached to the back, headed out to clear the field that had once been alfalfa but had gone fallow. As soon as he rumbled out into the open with the tractor belching along beneath him, the memories started coming. He looked out at the eight acres of overgrown weeds. But in his mind, he saw three hundred acres, spread out before him as far as the eye could see, the stubble from cut wheat waiting to be plowed underneath him one row at a time.

He'd started driving a tractor for pay when he was ten years old, at his daddy's insistence.

"Time to make yourself useful" was all his daddy had said one night at dinner, without even looking at Jimmy. "You start Monday."

Jimmy felt angry and ashamed. Ashamed because he believed his daddy thought he was a burden, just another mouth to feed, and angry because he worked so hard already. Three or four nights a week, it was a kill he'd brought home that they'd eat for dinner.

After his daddy's pronouncement, he started working other folks' land too. One of the farm hands would pick him up at around five o'clock on Monday morning from his parents' shack, where he lived with his sister and two brothers. By six o'clock, after a breakfast of eggs and hash browns, biscuits and gravy, he was out on the tractor, where he'd stay, except for a half-hour break for lunch, until sundown.

In the morning, it wasn't too bad except for the boredom, which didn't let up no matter what time of day it was. But then the burning sun got up in the sky, and it was usually near one hundred degrees by ten o'clock. Then the bugs came out, and the tractor's engine would get hot, blowing blasts of scalding air back into his face along with dirt and grit. Thirteen hours later, he'd climb off the tractor, having earned five dollars for the day.

On Saturday nights, he was driven back home to spend Sunday with his family. He didn't like religion except that the churches had enough influence to make sure he never had to work on a Sunday.

Jimmy hated that his mama insisted he go to church with her half the day on Sunday and hear how bad he was, how sinful, how doomed to hell. He could almost hear Reverend Pike railing against the devil who just lurked around the corner, waiting to take advantage of a weak sinner like him.

Being back on a tractor at the Conway place, making himself useful and working up a sweat, made Jimmy feel much better.

The memories of his folks and his childhood were bittersweet: bitter because it had been as hard a life as he could ever imagine, sweet because he'd made it out of that hell and had made more money than his father had ever seen in his entire life. His mama had desperately wanted him to be somebody famous, a big star, better than everyone else at anything he did. He hadn't been able to live her dreams, but he wasn't a complete failure, was he?

The desire for a drink crept up on him so quietly, so slyly, like just another thought passing through along with the thousands of others that came and went. But it was more than a thought. It was an urge that he felt deep in his bones, down into the dark places of his flesh and his mind. It seemed to grow inside him suddenly when it came, and it wouldn't stop until he fed it, calming the fire with more fire. It held a power over him that it seemed he could never shake, like being born with a handicap, something you might dream you didn't have, but every morning when you woke up, it was still there, twisted and deformed.

He started to sweat, and his hand shook as he wiped it across his forehead to keep the moisture from his eyes.

He turned the tractor onto the last row,

not really even seeing where he was going anymore. Finally, he drove back to the house and turned off the tractor. He felt shaky and weak as he climbed down.

He eyed Frank's pickup truck, wondered if the keys were in it, then shook away the crazy thought.

"Frank," he said, but there was no answer.

"Frank!" he yelled through the screen door of the house.

He tramped, wild-eyed and sweating, out toward the old barn. "Frank. Goddammit, I need to go!"

Frank walked out of the barn wiping his hands on his jeans. He took one look at Jimmy and the smile dropped from his face.

He took Jimmy by the arm and led him to a wood bench under a cottonwood tree near the house. "Sit the hell down here. I'm gonna get you a Coke."

Jimmy slumped over on the bench, his stomach cramping and his mouth watering. All he could see was the cottony white puffs falling in front of his face, coming down like snow from the cottonwood tree behind him. They landed on his hair and his eyelashes as he sat there, frozen like he was in a winter storm.

As Frank walked toward him, Jimmy finally couldn't hold it in any longer, so he stumbled away from the bench and vomited near the base of the tree. Frank held out a cold can of Dr Pepper, but Jimmy didn't take it.

"I can't do this," Jimmy said, looking up at him as he held his belly with his hands.

"Folks a whole lot worse off than you have lived to see the other side of this disease, Jimmy," Frank said. "This ain't no kind a way to live. And you don't have to."

Jimmy stood up, feeling the grip loosening on his stomach. He took the Dr Pepper and drank half of it in one pull. "I've stopped before, Frank. For a few days or even the last time for weeks. But it always pulls me back in. Every damn time." He shook his head and took another drink of pop. "I just can't do it."

"Come sit down," Frank said, and sat on the bench, which was littered with white from the cottonwood. He took a pill bottle out of the breast pocket of his cowboy shirt and showed it to Jimmy. "This here is one thing that can help."

Jimmy sat down next to him. His eyes lit up a little. He'd taken some pills in the past and liked them. Various girlfriends had given him a Valium or a Quaalude or a tranquilizer. They didn't take the place of booze, of course. They were way too mellow for him. The booze felt like a big party; the pills just made everything kind of dull. But they were a whole hell of a lot better than nothing.

"What are they?" he asked.

"They're called Antabuse. They ain't nothing unless you drink. It's like you haven't taken a thing. But if you drink, it'll turn you inside out."

Jimmy's expression turned from hope to shock. "What the hell do you mean?"

"If you drink, you'll get sick as a dog. It'll be like you drank poison."

"Well, son of a bitch, Frank," Jimmy said. "I'm already sick."

"But that'll pass if you can get through the detox. With this here Antabuse, going to ninety meetings in ninety days, and lettin' me help your sorry ass, I know you can do it." Frank put his hand on Jimmy's shoulder and squeezed it a little.

"So, you're tellin' me to take somethin' that'll make me wish I was dead if I take a drink."

"Yessir, I am. It's helped a lot of folks I know. Me included. This ain't gonna be easy, Jimmy, no damn way you look at it."

Jimmy grabbed the bottle of pills, opened it, and put one of the tablets in his mouth. He swallowed it down with the last of the

Dr Pepper. "God help me," he said.

"He'll help those who help themselves, and you just have," Frank said.

Jimmy turned away from Frank's gaze. He wasn't a believer, not after the hellfire God his mama had forced on him, not after all the pain he'd witnessed in this life. All he knew was that if anything good ever happened to him, it was because he'd made damn sure he was looking out for himself.

"Come on," Frank said. "You should go lay down inside."

Jimmy stood up and wiped his face with his hands. "Nah, I'll help clean the barn. I don't think . . ." He paused before continuing. "I don't think I should, you know, be alone much."

"Betty don't get home till tomorrow evenin', Jimmy. Stay with us tonight at the house, all right?" Frank said.

"Yeah," Jimmy said. His hands still shook a little, and he wished he could just go to sleep and not wake up until he felt better, but he was sure he'd kick this thing's ass this time. He'd bite the bullet and just do it, by God.

Sissy picked up the telephone on the first ring. She and Angie didn't want the baby to wake up, because they were in the middle of making a collage of the cutest guys out of Angie's *Teen Beat* magazines. Sissy had resisted the idea until boredom got the best of her.

"We just have to put the stuff away before Vee gets home, okay?" she'd told Angie.

"Why?" Angie had asked.

"Because it's stupid girl stuff."

When Sissy heard Vee's voice on the other end of the line, she glanced guiltily at the magazine clippings on the dining room table. "You sound real bad," Sissy said to Vee.

"Yeah, I'm in a lot of pain and there were some problems with the . . . procedure, so the doctor wants to keep me overnight here," Vee said, sounding like it was a struggle to speak.

Sissy's eyebrows rose. "Oh. What about school?"

"You can get Ruby and Randy off in the morning, then I guess you'll have to stay home. I'm sure your mother will understand. It's an emergency. Can you handle it?"

"I guess so," Sissy said. She had an uneasy feeling about skipping school. That was a big deal, but she wanted to sound grown-up with Vee, like she could handle anything, even though keeping the baby overnight by herself scared her.

On the other end of the line, Sissy heard Vee talking to someone. "I'll be off in just a minute," Vee said, sounding like the pain must be subsiding. "Has your mother called?" she asked.

"This mornin'," Sissy answered. "I told her not to worry about nothin'."

"Thanks a lot, Sissy."

Sissy hung up the phone and immediately wished she'd asked Vee when she would be home. If she'd let herself feel her feelings, she would have been wanting her mama. Instead, she buried her fear, smiled at Angie, and went back to pasting a picture of Leif Garrett onto purple construction paper.

When her daddy called a few minutes later, she grabbed the phone again. "Oh, hi," she said. For just a moment, she was happy to hear his voice, but then she remembered. This wasn't the daddy she needed right now. This was the monster she couldn't stand.

"Hey, hon, just wanted to make sure y'all are doing all right," he said.

"Just fine," she said, trying to sound breezy. The last thing she wanted was him coming over here. Keeping the kids overnight made her nervous, but he and his boozing and his temper scared her to death.

"Everything's great. No problems at all."

"I'm gonna be, um, not around much tonight, but you'll be all right? That girl's taking care of y'all, isn't she?"

He sounded so strange, his voice sad and tired, even vulnerable, but Sissy didn't want to know what he was doing or going through. Each time she let herself get hopeful that he was changing, he seemed to figure out a way to disappoint her worse than the time before. "We're doing great, Daddy. Don't worry about anything."

When she hung up the phone, she went to the kitchen window and looked out. Ruby and Randy were on roller skates they'd borrowed from the neighbor kids, skating circles and figure eights in the driveway. "Everybody sounds so weird," she said.

"People *are* weird, Sis," Angie said.

Sissy had told her mama not to call, but now she was sorry as hell she had.

Aletta hung up the pay phone outside the gas station where Julian was filling up his truck. It was late afternoon, and they'd driven over fifty miles to get to Chimayo, a tiny village famous for its chapel and the dirt located inside that was said to heal the sick and grant miracles to the needy.

They had dropped Maria off at her boyfriend's house after she begged Julian, and then they'd had lunch near the plaza before coming out here.

"The phone's busy," Aletta said when she returned to the truck.

Betty, Bobette, and Joy were stretching and trying to walk off the stiffness from riding in the back for so long.

"If she's anything like Rusty, she's on the phone all the time," Betty said.

Aletta smiled. "I'm sure that's it. Vee's back home by now, so Sissy's probably back in her room talkin' to Angie or somebody. She told me I didn't need to call, that I was worryin' too much."

"She's right. Just relax," Joy said.

Julian came out of the station stuffing his wallet in his back pocket. "You ladies ready to get healed?" he asked.

"As long as I still get to have fun," Joy said.

Bobette climbed into the back of the truck, groaning. "I wouldn't mind sheddin' about fifteen years."

"How 'bout fifteen pounds? And my buns could use a healin' too, that's for sure," Betty said.

They drove a few miles and then Julian pulled into a dusty parking lot. Just beyond them stood a charming Mission-style chapel with two square spires on either side of the modest entrance and an arched adobe gate out front.

They climbed out of the truck and walked toward the gate.

"I read about this place in town somewhere, but I can't remember the whole story," Betty said.

"Come," Julian said, directing them to some shade under a large oak tree. "I'll tell you about it before we go in."

Like excited schoolgirls, they gathered around Julian, Aletta standing as close as possible while he spoke.

"It started on the night of Good Friday in 1810," he began. "A local friar was performing penances and saw a light coming up from the ground, so he went to it and began digging there. In the dirt he found a crucifix. It was a big deal around here, so they sent for the priest, who took the crucifix to his chapel in Santa Cruz. But the next day the crucifix was gone. They found it right in the same spot where it had been found by the friar. They did this two more times, and it returned here again and again. It was evident the crucifix wanted to be only in this place, so they built the shrine you see here." He waved his hand toward the Santuario. "That's when the miracles started, and really it's better known now for the healing dirt in which the crucifix was found than the crucifix itself."

"Is the crucifix still here?" Joy asked.

Julian put his hand out, inviting them to enter the gateway to the chapel. "Right inside."

When she walked inside the sanctuary, Aletta felt the silence wrap itself around her like a warm blanket. A few pews lined either side of an aisle that led to an unassuming altar, which stood alone beneath a crucifix where Jesus hung, his crown of thorns atop his thin, bare body. On either side, candles burned for the loved ones of visitors who had been here before.

"That must be the crucifix," Bobette whispered.

Aletta nodded, then bowed her head slightly to say a silent prayer. *Lord, I guess I better start praying about this situation I'm in. I haven't been wanting to admit that I've lost my abilities, that maybe I haven't been able to live up to your expectations, but I gotta feed my family, so I'm asking you for help with this. Thank you, God.*

She opened her eyes and saw her friends kneeling around a small pit in the ground just beyond the altar. Bobette and Joy put their fingers in it but after a few moments got up and left. Aletta glanced over her shoulder as she approached the dirt and saw that Julian was standing near the entrance to the chapel, watching.

She kneeled beside Betty. "I guess this is the healin' dirt," she said in a whisper.

"I guess so," Betty answered.

"What do you think you're supposed to do with it?"

"I'm not sure."

Betty bent over and touched the powdery dirt again. She dipped both hands into it, then allowed it to run through her fingers.

Aletta joined her, and together they covered their hands with the cool earth.

"I want to do somethin' more with my life, Lettie," Betty said. "Comin' on this trip has made me realize it ain't Frank that's the problem. I mean, I won't settle for givin' up on life like he seems to have done, but at the same time, it ain't his responsibility to keep me fulfilled in every damn way. I been unsatisfied for a long time, and it's because I'm sellin' myself short. Frank's just been a handy excuse."

"What are you thinkin' you want to do?"

"Well, I don't know. I wanna have a purpose like you do, helping people in some way, with my own kind of abilities and talent. I don't wanna only be an accountant the rest a my life, I know that much."

"You think I have a purpose?" Aletta asked, surprised.

"I don't think, I know," Betty said, her voice filled with gratitude and sincerity. "You helped me more than I could ever say when you let me talk to my daddy after he died. Turned me around and led me right to this point here where I'm thinkin' I could do more with my life."

Aletta felt a stirring inside her, almost like someone or something was nudging her a little. A thought that had been coming stronger and stronger since she'd been in New Mexico, this haunting, otherworldly place, slipped in again. The idea seemed self-important and silly, so she had been pushing it away, but now she let it come on out. *Maybe there's more to my gift than making a living. Maybe I'm supposed to use it for something bigger.*

"I don't feel like I know my purpose, either," Aletta said, and took Betty's dirt-covered hands in her own. "So let's send out a prayer, then, and ask that we know what our purpose for this life really is."

"Amen," Betty said.

When she touched Betty, an image came into Aletta's mind, fast but clear and colorful. It was only there for a few moments, but it was something. Aletta inhaled deeply and closed her eyes. Still on her knees, she swayed back a little from the impact of the vision.

Betty looked at her intently. "What is it, Lettie?" she asked.

Aletta waited until the wave passed, then opened her eyes. "I saw something when I touched your hands."

"Praise the Lord," Betty said. "Maybe it's comin' back."

Aletta's knees were hurting, so she stood up and wiped off her jeans, then took Betty's hand and helped her to her feet. "Didn't get nothin' that time," she said.

"What'd you get the first time?" Betty asked as they walked out of the room.

Aletta didn't answer, just smiled at Betty.

They looked into a small room off the sanctuary where crutches and braces of every size leaned against or hung on the wall.

"Looks like folks got healed and left their crutches," Aletta said.

Betty nodded, her mouth agape. "Looks that way."

They turned and walked outside into the late afternoon. The air was so crisp and clean and the sky so blue behind the deep, dark green of the pine trees that Aletta had to stop and take it in for a moment. All day she'd felt that something special was happening, something important, even holy, and she knew a big part of that was because of the sacred land they were in.

Betty put her arms out to her sides. "My Lord, I love it here," she said, then turned to Aletta. "Are you gonna tell me what you saw or not?"

"I saw you standing inside a bus full of people, all dressed for winter, like they were headed out to play in the snow. You were up at the front, and it looked like you were telling all those folks something. The bus was driving up a beautiful mountain. That's all I saw," Aletta said.

Betty stood there, thinking. "Huh," she said finally. "That one's hard to figure."

Aletta spotted Julian walking toward them, and she went to meet him.

"I just called Martin. He's done with the station wagon," he said.

"Julian," Aletta said, "I need to meet your great-grandmother."

Julian drove across a bridge that spanned a flowing creek lined with oak and cottonwood trees. The entrance to the pueblo just on the other side of the bridge was marked with a faded sign that read WELCOME TO TESACOMA PUEBLO. PLEASE, NO PHOTO-GRAPHS. The truck bounced over rutted dirt roads circling the village of small adobe buildings.

Aletta recognized poverty when she saw it, and this place had all the signs. Everything — the people, the houses, the cars — all sagged a little, worn down by hardship, like they'd been pushed past the point where they needed some upkeep and care. Lack ate away the newness of things like locusts in a wheat field, leaving it ravaged and bare.

Julian stopped the truck in front of one of the squat houses that stood with its door open. An old, rusted Chevy with a flat tire was parked next to it.

"I'll be right back," he said, and looked at Aletta. "I want you to know she may not wish to see visitors. She almost never sees anyone outside the pueblo anymore."

Aletta nodded, and Julian went inside the little house.

Aletta stepped out of the truck and looked around. This pueblo was a lot like the other one they had visited, and she felt as much an outsider here as she had there. The beauty she associated with Indian life — freedom, living off the land, a deep, mysterious connection to the earth and its creatures — all seemed laughable as she watched a skinny, sad-looking dog trot across the dusty road, past old cars on blocks, junked-out appliances, and tattered sheets and towels hanging on a clothesline next to an adobe house across the way that had a definite lean.

Aletta looked up at the mountains, dark now with clouds brushing over the peaks, and realized they had known this land and these people before the white men came, when this village was thriving, before this squalor and sadness.

"Man, this is some rough livin'," Betty said as she stood up in the back of the truck and put her hands on her lower back.

"It's all the color of dirt," Bobette added.

"Except for the mountains," Aletta replied. "No matter how bad things get, I bet these folks always take comfort in lookin' up at them."

"It smells wonderful," Betty said, inhaling the aroma of baking bread.

Joy grunted as she rolled onto her hands and knees. "At least they still live where the damn white men found 'em, unlike the poor old Cherokees and Choctaws and them, getting drug off their land on the Trail of Tears."

Julian walked out with his hands in his jeans pockets. He scanned the ground as he spoke. "I'm sorry, Senda isn't up for visitors."

Aletta's mouth dropped open. She couldn't believe what she was hearing. "But I have to see her. I leave tomorrow."

"What do you think she'd tell you?" Bobette asked.

Aletta put her hands to her face and stared at the mountains. "I don't know, but I know I'm supposed to talk to her. She left me the feather. I lost my gift. She's the reason I'm here."

Before she finished the last sentence, Aletta turned and walked straight through the front door of the house. She didn't know if Julian tried to stop her or not, but it wouldn't have mattered if he had.

Once inside, she had to stop abruptly because she couldn't see a thing. It was so dark after the bright sunshine that her eyes took a moment to adjust. After they did, she saw that she stood in a tiny living room with a worn green carpet. A single lamp lit the room, which was sparsely furnished with a small couch covered with an Indian blanket and two wooden rocking chairs that looked homemade. In one of these chairs sat the tiniest woman Aletta had ever seen.

The woman, her silky, thin silver hair flowing down past her shoulders, stared up at Aletta, a slight grin on her face and a definite spark in her rheumy eyes.

Aletta backed up a step when she saw the old woman and stammered, "E-Excuse me, but I've come a long way to see you."

"Senda, this is Aletta Honor," Julian said from behind her.

The old woman stood up, and Aletta figured she was well under five feet tall, even if she hadn't been stooped. She looked at Julian and pointed a finger, "I told you, De-ce-eh," she said.

"Yes, you did," he chuckled.

"Told him what?" Aletta asked, looking back and forth from one to the other.

"My name is Rafaelita Pijoan," the old woman said to Aletta. She pronounced her last name "pee-hwan," and Aletta couldn't imagine how that might be spelled. "But you may call me Senda, like everyone else does. Would you like some coffee?"

Aletta looked at Julian, and he nodded. "Yes, ma'am," she said finally. "So does that mean I can stay for a bit?"

Senda did not answer but walked into a tiny kitchen next to the living room and began filling a percolator at the tap.

"I'll take the others to town. You can meet

up with them later," Julian said to Aletta.

"What did she mean about telling you no?" Aletta asked.

He leaned close to her ear. "She said only if you refused to leave would she see you. She bet on you."

"And you bet against me?"

"I thought you were too polite," he admitted.

Aletta smiled. "Not when I'm desperate I'm not."

They heard Joy call from outside, "Hey, kids, we've decided we've had enough of this truck bed. We're ready to get back to town. I got a margarita with my name on it."

Julian brushed his lips against Aletta's cheek. "I'll be about forty-five minutes."

Aletta stared at the place he'd left, fighting back an urge to follow him and go find a margarita with her friends. She felt nervous around this old Indian woman, and she didn't know why.

CHAPTER TWENTY

On the outskirts of Laredo, Texas, just a half hour or so before the Mexican border, Vee pulled into a filling station to put gas in the car even though there was still a quarter of a tank left. All she had remaining of Aletta's money was eighteen dollars and change, and she took her time at the pump, putting in five dollars exactly.

She went to pay the attendant, but as soon as she stepped into the run-down, hole-in-the-wall gas station, she stopped and listened. Elton John was belting out "Crocodile Rock" on the grease-covered radio behind the cash register. Vee smiled to herself, then laughed aloud as she remembered Ruby and Randy singing every word to the song as they performed their very own dance moves for her.

She stood there, lost in the memories, until she realized the gas station attendant was staring at her with heavy-lidded eyes.

Without thinking, she grabbed a few dusty candy bars, some pretzels, and a bag of potato chips, and dumped them onto the counter. She paid the man as she sang along to the song, then walked back to the Chevy and got behind the wheel.

She drove to the I-35 access road. One sign read I-35 SOUTH — MEXICAN BORDER, the other I-35 NORTH — DALLAS. As she turned the car north and merged onto the freeway, all she could think was that she had to go get a picture of those kids.

Aletta sipped the watery coffee and looked sideways at Senda. They had been sitting like this for at least five minutes, silent but for the slow, methodical *ree ree ree* of Senda's rocking chair. To Aletta it seemed like it had been over an hour, but she didn't want to be rude or pushy. She would've liked for Senda to start the conversation, but it looked like she might wait forever for that to happen.

"Did you know my great-grandmother, Adelaide Medina?" she ventured meekly.

"No," Senda said.

"Oh." Aletta wondered what in God's name she was doing here with this ancient woman who probably couldn't remember yesterday, let alone something from almost a century ago.

Just then, Aletta heard footsteps and conversation outside. Suddenly, there were several people standing at the front door.

"*Sing-giddy-ho,* Senda. Is it time?" It was a man's voice.

"Yes," Senda said. "Come in."

The door opened, and one by one, three men and two women filed in. They were all older, anywhere from fiftyish to possibly in their seventies. Their presence filled the little house completely. Aletta caught herself staring at them as they filed in. Everything from their Indian jewelry to their quiet manner fascinated her.

"Hello," Aletta said with a question in her voice.

They either nodded or said hello but didn't pay much attention to her. The three women sat on the blanket-covered couch, while the two men dragged chairs in from the little kitchen table. They looked at Aletta after they sat down, their dark faces impossible to read, and she figured this must be what it felt like to be a monkey in the zoo. They had to be here for her, didn't they? No one spoke for several moments, so she sat nervously, wondering what the hell was going on, but she didn't dare speak first. They seemed to be sizing her up, glancing her way, then looking at their hands or the floor. Aletta didn't know what she was supposed to do, but she decided to just stay quiet and wait it out.

"She is Eagle Clan?" one of the men asked finally. He was older but handsome. His short hair was jet black, and his eyes shone under heavy eyebrows.

Senda replied, "She is the one from my vision."

Aletta turned to Senda, goose bumps prickling on her arms. "You had a vision of me?"

Senda didn't answer her. She stared straight ahead as if she hadn't heard. Aletta had to know what was going on, so she turned to the others. "My great-grandmother was Adelaide Medina, who came from this pueblo," she said. "My great-grandfather was Maxwell Halbert, her husband. Their son is . . . was my grandfather, Franklin."

They were all looking at her intently now. One of the women, the oldest of the group other than Senda, spoke up. "So Adelaide had a son? There were rumors she was pregnant in the Indian school, but no one was allowed to see her."

Aletta's brow furrowed. "She had two

sons, actually, my grandpa and my great-uncle Morris, but I'm sure they were after she was out of the school and married to Maxwell Halbert."

"They were just rumors, but my father didn't believe it. My mother and father were very close to hers," Senda said. "We all have relatives who knew her. She was Eagle Clan, the clan that our greatest medicine people have come from. They were said to have the wings that could fly us home, which we need now more than ever."

The others nodded in agreement.

Aletta saw sadness in her eyes, but Senda didn't speak again, and Aletta couldn't decipher the expression on her face.

She looked around for help, but everyone just sat there, stone-faced and quiet. "So what did they say about her?" she asked, pressing on.

"They said the medicine ended when she was taken away." Senda's voice was so quiet, Aletta had to strain to listen.

"The medicine ended? What does that mean?"

"This village, these people, always had strong medicine, help from the spirit world through a *tcaiyanyi,* but your great-grandmother was the last one, and she was taken before her initiation."

Senda looked into Aletta's eyes for the first time since she had entered her home, and her gaze was piercing, like she saw into Aletta and knew more about her than she knew about herself. "We haven't had strong medicine since. She was the last of the Eagle Clan. It died out when she was gone."

Aletta tried to understand everything Senda had just said, but there was so much, and it seemed so important. "This *tcaiyanyi*," she said, struggling to pronounce the word, "what is it?"

"During the emergence of our people from the lower world, Utctsiti, the mother of the Indians, chose Tcaiyanyi to be her representative in this world. She is the daughter of the supernatural being Bocaiyanyi." Senda spoke as if she were telling an old story. It had a rhythm to it, like she had told it many times. "A *tcaiyanyi* has the power to bring about things that are unexplainable to help his or her people, and she has visions to explain the unexplainable. She is here to watch over her people. She is our medicine woman, our spiritual leader."

"And my great-grandmother was supposed to be this person?" Aletta was completely enthralled, in part because she loved learning about history and people and their cultures. But this wasn't just something she read from a plaque in a museum next to a case full of arrowheads and pottery. This history was her history too, and somehow her entire life began to make more sense.

Senda continued. "Yes, she would have become *tcaiyanyi* after her father, but he caught the tuberculosis, along with his wife, and they both died while Adelaide was still a child, only twelve years old. That's when the white men took her away." She looked down at her hands with their prominent veins.

"To the Indian school?" Aletta said, now sitting at the edge of the rocking chair's seat.

"Yes," Senda replied. "All of the orphans went there, and some of the other children were even taken from their parents. Our people were so poor and sick from the white man's diseases and ways, we couldn't fight to keep the children. We never considered them orphans, because they belonged to us all."

Aletta looked at the faces around her. Lines of pain and loss and hardship creased each of them, but she also saw dignity there, in their eyes and the way they held themselves. "Do you know what happened to her after that?" Aletta asked.

"That white man stole her," one of the women answered bitterly. She was plump and wore her hair, which was black with streaks of dark gray, pulled back in a bun. She looked at Aletta directly, and Aletta knew this woman didn't want her here.

"They got married and went to Oklahoma together," Aletta said defensively. She didn't want it to be true that her great-grandmother had been forced to marry Maxwell Halbert.

"She did not want to marry that man," the plump woman insisted. "He just wanted a slave to cook and clean for him in Oklahoma."

"And to anger his father — that was a big part of it," the thin man added without the bitterness.

"How do y'all know this? You weren't even alive yet," Aletta said, her voice small and weak. A hard ball of hurt rolled up from her chest into her throat. It was the sense of shame she'd lived with since she began telling others about her gift when she was a child and realized they did not approve. Her visions were as unwelcome to many folks as her having an Indian in the family.

"My father spoke to her just before she was married," Senda said. "But she warned him not to try to prevent the marriage. We were fighting to keep our land at that time, and she felt if she married this man, this son of the most powerful judge in the territory, we would have a better chance. There was nothing my father could have done, and she knew it. I think she was trying to make him feel better about the marriage."

Aletta felt a chill on her arms, and she rubbed them with her hands. "But why didn't the judge prevent it if he didn't want them to get married?"

The man who hadn't spoken yet smiled slightly. He had scars on his face that made him look mean, even frightening, but when he smiled, his eyes softened. "A father cannot control what his son chooses to do," he said knowingly, "especially when the son is doing what he is doing to get back at the father for some wrong he felt was done to him. This son felt his father never loved him, never approved of him, so he did what he thought would hurt his father: he married an Indian girl and left his home. This was the worst thing he could think of to do, and to white people at the time, it was the worst thing he could have done."

The thin man added, "He also wanted to prove himself to the judge by making his own fortune in Oklahoma, without his father's help. He left for the free land he could find there."

The group nodded their agreement.

Aletta felt like she was at Joy's salon when the old ladies got together and debated and discussed events from the faraway past. She knew these dark-faced, quiet folks had been talking about the judge and his son and his Indian wife, their precious *tcaiyanyi,* since they were children and had listened to the same stories told by their parents.

"I lost my psychic abililties after you gave me the eagle feather, Senda," she said, believing this was the reason she was here, to retrieve her gift and learn about her great-grandmother and father. "Can you help me get it back?"

Senda shook her head a little. "Will you leave us for a few minutes?" she asked.

Aletta wasn't expecting this, but she nodded and went to the door. "I have to leave in just a little while," she said, but it was as if she hadn't even spoken, because no one even looked her way.

She stepped outside into the lavender twilight and shut the door behind her. It was almost dark, and the pueblo had no lights except for those coming from inside the houses. She dug blindly in her purse for a cigarette and found one, misshapen and falling apart, at the bottom. Nervously, she smoked and looked up at the stars appearing in the darkening sky.

She wondered if she had lost her psychic ability as punishment for her great-grandfather taking her great-grandmother away from these people. Were they deciding if she could have it back now? She thought about the way she had come to be standing here in this Indian village in New Mexico, and she couldn't believe any of this had happened.

She remembered Julian showing up at her house with the feather. Where was he anyway? He'd said he'd be forty-five minutes, and it had been well over that. Aletta realized that he must have told the elders that she was at Senda's and to go there. She wondered if Julian was part of some scheme to get back at her family.

She put out her cigarette, grinding it beneath her shoe, and decided that if these Indians were trying to get back at the judge, who had taken their land and sentenced them all to poverty, and at his son, who had taken their precious girl from them, she could understand it, but it wasn't *her* fault. Maybe Julian didn't care about her at all. Maybe he had just lured her here so his people could take out their anger on her.

It's not as if I don't deserve it, she thought. *Even my mother was prejudiced — against gypsies, Negroes, Indians.* She knew she still held some remnants of the bigotry she'd grown up around, not only in her own family, but also in the folks in her community and her life. Because of her gift, she'd seen from a very young age the pain bigotry could cause those who were being judged. It had made her sensitive to folks looking down on others, but she had to admit that when she was faced with someone she'd never been around much, like a Negro, she'd find herself clutching her purse tighter or watching over her shoulder. It embarrassed her, and she didn't even know where it came from, so she tried real hard to be friendly. But the whole thing seemed forced, and she wished she could just be natural.

The only person she'd ever been friends with who wasn't white was Silvia, and she was so grateful for their friendship. Now here she was with these Indians, wanting so badly to be accepted by them, but she just knew she was about to get told off.

Aletta tried to remember if anyone in her family had ever spoken of her great-grandmother, but she knew they hadn't. She remembered the grown-ups were always telling stories about the old times, but when anyone asked about Grandpa Halbert's mama, they'd talk about Josephine, his daddy's second wife.

The door opened behind her, and the man with the scars on his face nodded for her to come back in. Aletta felt like she was going in to be sentenced, but she walked back into the room and faced her accusers. She chewed on a fingernail and glanced around at the old faces staring at her so intently. Senda was standing near the others, and she looked up at Aletta.

"In my vision, the one that I had after I saw your picture in *Time* magazine —"

"*Life,*" Aletta interrupted, and regretted it the moment the word left her mouth.

But Senda just nodded. "I was looking at the pictures, sitting here in my chair, and that's when I had the vision of you with the eagles flying and holding the *tcaiyanyi*'s *yapi* in your hand."

"What's that?" Aletta asked.

"It is the staff he or she carries," the man with the scars answered, and stood up. He cleared his throat before continuing, "My name is Eliseo Salas, and I am the war chief of this pueblo. I am the one to choose a *tcaiyanyi*. Right now, we have an acting

417

tcaiyanyi," Eliseo glanced at the thin woman who sat near him. She nodded gravely. "But we have not had a full *tcaiyanyi* since the time of Adelaide Medina. When Senda told me of her vision, we decided to send you the eagle feather from the *tcaiyanyi*'s prayer stick to see if you would respond. And now, since you are here, it has been decided that you should go into the mountains."

Aletta stopped breathing, and her eyes darted from Senda to Eliseo to the plump woman who glared at her. "What do you mean?" she said, her voice like a scared little girl's.

"We believe you can help return the medicine to our people," Eliseo answered.

"Me? I thought y'all were . . . I thought y'all were mad at me," she said meekly.

"You are a descendant of the Medinas. You have been touched with the gifts from the spirits already. You must fast and pray and ask the Great Spirit for a vision to guide us so that we may find a full *tcaiyanyi* who has the medicine of the Eagle."

Aletta took two steps backward, then sat down. "But you don't understand. I have to leave in the morning. I can't go into the mountains. I don't have any idea how to do what you want." She shook her head and laughed. "I thought you were deciding if you were going to give back my psychic ability or not, if I deserved it because I'm related to that judge and his son."

"We did not take away your gift, miss. We cannot give it back, either," Senda said. "I did not choose to have a vision of you, but it came to me, so we must pay attention to what is given us —"

"I told you she wouldn't do it," the plump woman interrupted. "She's not Tesacoma. She's not Indian."

Senda glanced at the woman, then back at Aletta, "Dominga thinks you are afraid. She thinks a white woman is too weak to perform the ritual."

Aletta wanted to agree, to walk out the door and keep walking until she found her friends in another world drinking margaritas and flirting with a bartender. She stood up and moved toward the door, but something made her stop.

Just then, the door swung open and Julian walked in carrying a bag of groceries. "*Sing-giddy-ho,* Senda," he said.

"De-ce-eh, did you get my ice cream?" Senda asked.

"Of course," he said, then looked from Aletta to the group and back again. "Did I interrupt anything?"

"You know exactly what's going on here," Aletta said impatiently.

"You asked me to bring you here, remember. You wanted to come."

"You could've told me," she said, but he just smiled slightly, and she knew it hadn't been decided if they would ask her to do this until just now. That's when she realized how much of an honor this was. They had decided she was worthy of their quest, a quest they hoped would bring a renewal to this village and its people.

She went to Julian and whispered in his ear. "How long will this take?"

He shook his head and smiled at Senda, who was watching them. "I don't know. A few days, maybe. I will pay for you to fly home," he whispered back.

Just then, a loud thumping came from outside, and the sound of a souped-up car coming to a stop, followed by what sounded like screaming but which Aletta knew was some kind of crazy rock music.

Senda watched the open front door, looking as if she was trying to create silence with her glare. "Julian, will you please shut the door? Your daughter is disturbing the peace again," she said, exasperated and annoyed, raising her voice to be heard.

When the door clicked closed, Aletta

dropped her head, then turned around to look at this council of elders. She knew now that's what they were.

She couldn't read much in their faces. In the very short time she'd been around these people, she had come to know that they didn't show much emotion, at least not around her. There was certainly no desperation coming from them, and she knew they would never beg her for help, but she did see, or maybe sensed, that they needed her. And she knew for certain that she needed them.

When she came here, she had just assumed it was to regain her psychic abilities so she could continue to provide for her family, but now she knew it was more than that. She needed to know how to use her gift, and unlike the folks back home, these people weren't frightened, intimidated, disbelieving, or in awe of her. They honored her and her gift as a normal and important part of their lives. Hell, they even had names for people like her — shaman, medicine woman, *tcaiyanyi* — and, amazingly enough, none of them meant "crazy person." Suddenly, a question, clear like a chiming bell, came to her through the fog of confusion she'd felt since coming here: *What good is it to have a fancy guitar if you don't know how to play?*

Finally, she looked at the elders, put a hand on one hip, and with the other pushed her hair behind her ear. "You know, if we're gonna get real technical about it," she said, "I ain't completely white, and even if I was, I've been told I'm pretty darn tough." She glared at Dominga, the plump woman, who glared right back.

"So you will seek the vision?" Eliseo asked.

"Lord help me," Aletta said. "What do y'all want me to do?"

Sometimes, usually when he was about halfway through his first drink, before drunk but after sober, Jimmy felt special. He felt the world was special too, like it was a magical place, and it was important that he was in it, that there was some reason for his being here that he couldn't quite grasp but was true nonetheless. Things and people seemed to sparkle just a little bit, and his chest would swell with the sweetness of possibility.

As he sat in the AA meeting that Sunday night after he and Frank and Rusty got back from the Conway farm, he thought about that feeling, how distinctly different it was from his usual state of confusion, anger, and boredom. He sat slumped in a brown metal folding chair, and suddenly realized he'd had that same feeling when he was a little kid. The thought went through him like cold water and turned him pale.

He hadn't remembered this feeling, this childhood experience, until now, but when he did, the memories came flooding in. He had believed he was special when he was little, that he was important to the world and that he mattered.

He stood up while a guy was talking about his jail time last year, and walked outside into the early evening. Leaning a hand against the brick building, he inhaled deeply to hold in the tears that came with old feelings that had been buried under hardness and anger.

"Dammit," he said, and leaned over with his hands on his knees.

He was there again, walking in the woods with his dog, stopping every so often to listen to the world around him. He felt like he was part of everything in those moments, like the trees and the animals and the earth itself were his friends, his life, his breath.

Jimmy had locked away this part of himself to protect it from the ridicule of his father and the pain of the world, but when he drank, almost every time, it crept out for a few minutes. It was one of the reasons he loved drink so much. He'd heard folks talk about their first hit on a cigarette and how satisfying it was, and that was how he felt about drinking. It was that first drink that he loved the most, because it gave him the feeling that there was something more to life, something he wanted so badly but never thought he could have, never thought he deserved.

The problem was that he could never stop after the first drink. He always wanted more. Always more. Always more.

Jimmy stood up and rubbed his face with his hands. He choked back the tears that seemed just on the verge of breaking through, like there was a crack in the dam around his heart. "I can't believe this bullshit," he said under his breath, then yanked up his jeans and smoothed his hair.

Jimmy had survived his sensitivity by kicking tail and not giving a shit about anyone but himself and by always having a woman around to do his feeling for him. He wasn't about to give in to this pansy-ass stuff now. He laughed at himself and the little boy he used to be who thought he was so great because he liked trees and animals. He went back in to the meeting but didn't pay attention. He just sat there, numb and unfeeling, trying to make it through.

That night at Frank's house, Jimmy lay on the couch trying to sleep, but emotions, like wild animals snarling and running loose, catapulted him off the couch and out of the house. His shirt still unbuttoned, he got into his Trans Am and raced down the street. He decided he would find Charlotte, that she was the cause of him getting taken to the police station and ending up in Frank's house. She had ripped him off and lied to him, and he wasn't going to let anyone screw with him like that.

As he passed the 7-Eleven on the corner of Cornwell and Vandament, he heard a distinct voice in his head. *You deserve to have a drink. Look what that bitch has done to you,* it said. Jimmy was angry now, his jaw set and the veins in his neck bulging. He yanked hard on the steering wheel and roared into the 7-Eleven. He left the motor running and went inside. They didn't sell vodka, and the liquor store was closed, so he bought a jug of bad wine, took it out to his car, unscrewed the cap, and took a long pull on the bottle.

Yes. Now things are okay again. This is good. This is right, the voice said. He took another long drink and backed out of the parking lot. He headed across town to drive by Charlotte's sister's house to see if her car was there, taking drinks from the bottle as he raced down empty streets. He felt powerful behind the wheel of the sports car. He loved the way it sounded and the way it rumbled beneath him.

He would try to find Charlotte, then he would go out to a bar in the city. He was itching to fight, to test his manhood against any asshole who looked at him sideways. He clenched his fist and pounded it on the steering wheel, and that's when his stomach clenched too. He yelled out and held his belly as pain shot through him and a wave of nausea drenched him in sweat. Blindly, he pulled off the road into a parking lot, put the car in park, then opened his door and fell out onto gravel and dirt.

On hands and knees, he vomited over and over until there was nothing coming out of him except bile. Water streamed out of his eyes, and saliva dripped from his mouth. He didn't remember the pill Frank had given him earlier that day until the nausea hit him. It had seemed like a week ago that he'd been out at the Conway place. He cursed Frank, Charlotte, Aletta, and the world as a headache tightened like a ring around his skull.

"Oh, God," he said aloud, crawling backward to get away from the puke that stained the ground beneath him.

He rolled on his side and pulled his legs up to his stomach and held himself with his arms as the pain and the nausea washed over him. After a few minutes, he opened his eyes and saw a sign lit up in front of him, not twenty feet away. In large block letters, it read: THE SON CAN DO NOTHING OF HIMSELF, BUT WHAT HE SEES THE FATHER DO: FOR WHAT THINGS HE DOES, THESE ALSO THE SON DOES LIKEWISE.

Jimmy closed his eyes and inhaled deeply. That damn sign was talking to him. He read it again and realized what it was saying. *I'm no better than my father,* he thought. *He was a bastard, and I'm a bastard too.* He'd turned away from the kid he used to be, and turned into his daddy instead. He broke down crying, lying there with gravel digging into his face and tears turning the gray rock black.

When he finally got up and dragged himself behind the wheel of his car, he saw that he was in a church parking lot. CHURCH OF THE REDEEMER, the sign said. And beneath the quote, he read JOHN 5:19. He sat there with the car rumbling, his eyes bleary, and his mouth dry, and thought about the sign in front of him.

He realized that he'd read it to mean that when a child sees his parent acting a certain way, the child acts the same. His father had been mean and self-centered and hard-hearted, and that's what he'd become too. But now Jimmy read it again — THE SON CAN DO NOTHING OF HIMSELF — and he realized it meant something else for him as well. It meant that he, of himself, was powerless. That's what they said in AA, wasn't it? Alcoholics are powerless over alcohol, and he knew that not only was he powerless over alcohol, but all of the things he'd thought were powerful — his anger, his looks, his willpower — were really nothing at all.

He realized there was a power that was bigger than him, something greater to rely on than his ability to manipulate the world and control people to get what he wanted. He knew he *needed* that something, and the yearning was sweet inside him.

Suddenly, the thoughts left his mind, and all that remained was a desire to sleep. He drove slowly away from the church back toward Frank's house.

■ ■ ■ ■

The landscape in front of her blurred, melting together headlights and highway and a big rig that barreled down the road ahead of her. Vee's head sagged forward, then she snapped awake, looking around to make sure she wasn't driving off the road or cutting in front of another car. She'd been driving since nine o'clock that morning, starting south toward the border, and now it was after ten at night, and she was still in Texas headed north. Nothing made any sense to her anymore. All she knew was that she was going to get a photograph of the Honors, and then she'd decide what to do next.

Her eyes began closing again, and this time she didn't wake up until the sound of the car tires cutting through gravel hit her ears. She pulled the car straight again, steering it off the shoulder of the road. Just ahead on the highway was a sign that read DEAD HORSE ROAD NEXT EXIT. *The road to nowhere,* she thought. There was nothing at the exit but unmarked blacktop that cut east and west across scrub brush, not a gas station or house, not even a sign to indicate if there might be anything waiting beyond the horizon.

She drove east on Dead Horse Road

about a half mile, then pulled the car over into the weeds. She locked the car doors, took her pistol out of the glove compartment, lay down on the enormous seat, tucked the gun close, and pulled her jacket on top. She was asleep in seconds.

CHAPTER
TWENTY-ONE

Aletta lay in Julian's bed, her eyes wide open but seeing nothing at all. It was so dark in Julian's small adobe home on the far edge of Tesacoma Pueblo that she couldn't see her hand when she put it right up to her face. Her doubts and worries made sleep seem about as likely as . . . well, as her lying in some Indian's house the night before a vision quest. How in hell could she have agreed to this craziness?

Julian was on the couch in the living room. She wondered if he was awake too. Of course, he wasn't about to be sent off to the mountains before dawn looking for a vision.

And besides all of that, Aletta was hungry. The elders had said no food and no sex. She blushed when they told her, and Senda snickered and clapped her hands twice. Dominga had laughed too and given Aletta a look of superiority.

It had annoyed her to no end. She wasn't planning on having sex with Julian — not tonight, anyway, for heaven's sake, especially with Maria in the other room — but now that it was off-limits and those old farts were tickled about it all, she really had the urge to go crawl under his blanket with him.

Julian had told Maria about Aletta accepting the elders' request, and to Aletta's dismay, Maria had laughed. "I can't believe they talked you into that," she said, and went to her room.

Aletta was also worried that she was being selfish and irresponsible and a bad mother to her kids. When she spoke to her friends on the phone, they had encouraged her to stay, that this might be the reason she'd come all this way. Joy said she'd check in on Sissy and the kids when she got home, and that had made Aletta feel better. She knew she was supposed to be serious and reverent about this whole vision thing, but she just felt put upon and irritable.

She finally fell asleep in spite of herself, and the next thing she knew, Senda was standing over her.

"Come," Senda said. "It's time."

After she dressed, Aletta walked outside into the final darkness before the new day, leaving Julian asleep on the couch. She pulled close the denim jacket he had loaned her, because the mountain chill was trying to crawl underneath her clothes. She followed Senda away from the village, feeling achy and tired and hungry. They walked to a small hill where Eliseo Salas stood holding what looked to Aletta like a walking stick with feathers hanging from it.

Senda and Aletta climbed the hill, and Senda turned Aletta to face the east. Aletta knew it was east because the sky was just revealing a hint of soft pink in that direction. Senda and Eliseo stood in front of her.

Senda took Aletta's hand and held it up to her own. She closed her eyes and leaned her head back slightly. "Here is this woman's hand on your hand," she prayed. "May she have good thoughts and know the power of the earth."

As Senda prayed, Aletta felt the hair on the back of her neck stand up. She took a deep breath and realized this was an important moment, something to remember.

Senda let go of Aletta's hand and opened a small leather pouch that hung around her neck. She put two fingers inside the pouch as Eliseo put his hand on Aletta's shoulder and said, "These ashes from the cleansing fire are to make good medicine for this woman."

Senda took her fingers, now covered with ash, and dragged them along Aletta's right cheek.

"Please receive her into your arms, our arms. We give her strength and wisdom for her journey," Eliseo continued as Senda smeared more ash on Aletta's left cheek and forehead with her gnarled brown hands.

Eliseo held out the walking stick to Aletta. "This is the prayer stick of the *tcaiyanyi*," he said. "Walk with it today."

"Thank you," Aletta said, and took the smooth wooden staff. The feathers that hung from it moved gently in the slight breeze. She noticed that they were eagle feathers and realized that this was where her own feather had come from.

Senda reached into a paper grocery bag she'd brought and pulled out an animal skin pouch on a leather strap. "This is made from the kidney of a doe," she said as she put it over Aletta's shoulder. "It is water for you and represents a circle of spiritual energy for your journey."

Finally, Eliseo gave her a handful of jerky. "This is elk jerky. When you eat it, you accept the spirit of the animal into you."

As she stood there, Aletta was overwhelmed with a sense of the power within and around her — not a physical strength, but something more, something she couldn't explain. She could see that Senda and Eliseo felt it too, and she was humbled to be in their presence. In fact, she was humbled by this entire experience, and she said a silent prayer for strength and guidance.

Senda turned and looked at the brightening sky. "After you watch the sun rise, walk into the mountains," she said, waving her hand toward the nearby mountain range, which was just turning from black to green as the light touched its surface.

Aletta looked at the mountains and shivered a little. "How will I know where to go or what to do?" she asked.

Senda had to tilt her head back to look up at Aletta, because she was so small. "Do not worry," she said. "You will know."

"I have one more question. You call Julian something. What does it mean?"

Eliseo and Senda smiled. "Oh, I call him De-ce-eh," she said, pronouncing it "DAY-SAY-eh." "It means 'rooster,' I guess you would say."

"Oh," Aletta replied, not understanding.

"Basically, it means someone who rises with the roosters," Eliseo said. "She calls him that because he struts around knowing everyone's business like he's in charge of the henhouse."

Aletta giggled. She'd thought it was some kind of sacred shaman name. She couldn't wait to tease him about it. Suddenly, however, she realized what lay before her, and she wondered if she'd ever even see Julian Moquino again.

Senda and Eliseo walked down the hill, and Aletta watched them until she knew they would not turn around. She turned to the rising sun as it peered over the horizon, watching the birth of a brand-new day. Despite her worries, she smiled as the earth awoke, birds singing and insects busy with their important tasks. The sky seemed bigger than she'd ever experienced it before. It made her feel both small, as infinitesimal as one of the fire ants crawling at her feet, and also enormous, like she was part of everything, like she was the sky, watching it all.

Just as the sun rose beyond the trees, Aletta walked toward the mountains in the north. She turned back to the pueblo, expecting to see the elders watching her, but the only person there was Julian, standing in his socks and jeans. He raised his hand to her and she raised the prayer stick in return, resisting the urge to run into his arms and let him take her back inside. She turned her eyes to the mountains and didn't look back again.

At first, she had to keep her eyes on the ground and pick her way past rocks and cactus and sagebrush, and she was grateful for her comfortable shoes and her favorite pair of jeans. But then she found a nicely worn trail that led directly to the mountains, and she was able to watch the morning happen around her. The ceremony she'd just experienced made her feel a sense of purpose and put a bounce in her step.

It took only half an hour before the trail began to ascend and trees replaced the flatland bushes. As she began the climb, she thought about her friends and how they must be packing to leave right about now and how upset her children would be when she didn't come home. She thought about Julian and her attraction to him, and she smiled at the scandal it would cause in Okay if she were to shack up with a full-blooded Indian.

After several minutes, she realized she should be trying to come up with a vision, not thinking about her life, so she concentrated on the path in front of her, not knowing what else to do. The trail became steeper and began following a beautiful creek that gurgled its way downward, and the trees became thick.

When the creek eddied into a clear pool just below some fallen logs, she stopped beside it and drank from the kidney pouch, trying not to think about how it had been obtained. Her thirst was intense in this altitude anyway, and the hiking made it even more so. The water tasted like none she'd ever had before. It was sweet and creamy, and she drank until it ran down her chin and onto her shirt. She decided to stay close to the creek so she could refill the water bag often, realizing how much better she felt when she drank.

Soon, she was walking through aspen trees, their slender white trunks like thin columns from some building in Europe, someplace fancy and old. The sun danced with the brand-new green leaves overhead and made the creek sparkle and glint in the light.

Aletta had never felt more wholesome in her life. The air, the water, and the light were all clearer than she'd ever known, and she breathed deeply, not only because of the effort of climbing, but also because it felt good. She smiled to herself every so often and shook her head, not able to comprehend how she'd come to be climbing this mountain, ash smeared on her face, enlisted by a bunch of aging Indians.

She walked and walked, noticing large deer tracks and small ones nearby, a mother and fawn. Birds flew overhead, chattering in the aspens, and squirrels darted here and there. The trail began to narrow, and in places it was hard to distinguish as the ascent became steeper. Aletta began to feel tired. Her legs and feet hurt, and she fought for enough air. She was also getting more and more hungry, her belly gnawing at her, growling for food.

She stopped and sat on a fallen tree trunk, looking around for something she might be able to eat, but she didn't know what any of the plants were, so she dared not try them. Then she remembered the jerky, took a piece out of her pocket, and gnawed some off. As she chewed the salty meat, she thought about staying here for a few hours, just passing the time until she could head back down with some of her dignity intact.

But determination forced her to her feet and further up the mountain. She would climb until the sun was directly overhead, she decided. She wondered what would happen to her if she passed out — if someone would come looking for her, or if they would think she was up here for days working on this vision thing.

It was the last clear thought she had

before pure will took over, and the climb became a matter of simply putting one foot in front of the other. At times now, the trail was gone completely. She had to cross the creek on rocks and logs and use the prayer stick to lean on as she traversed rocky or narrow sections. In the steepest places, she threw the stick up the trail, then bent over and used her hands to climb. Her hands and knees were covered in dirt and mud.

Every so often, she would stop, catch her breath, and take a drink from the bag, checking the sun's position in the sky. It seemed not to move at all. Her thighs screamed with pain, and she knew there were blisters on her feet because they hurt like hell, but she didn't look, knowing there was nothing she could do for them.

I'm walking to the sun, she thought as she climbed. And this became like a song in her head. She stepped to its rhythm, bringing the walking stick and one foot down then the other foot down after. *Walking, walking, I'm walking to the sun. Walking up, walking up, walking straight up to the sun.* This single-minded focus on the task at hand kept her going, even when she felt dizzy with hunger and wrung out with fatigue.

After almost six hours of this, the jerky

long gone, Aletta was so exhausted and hungry that she didn't notice she was in a meadow until she was almost halfway through it. She was dragging the walking stick now, her gait slow as an old woman's. The sun on her face made her realize there were no trees around her. She looked around, and even through her overwhelming fatigue, she almost started to cry, this place was so beautiful. It was a small mountain meadow ringed with tall, perfect aspen trees. The grass was deep and thick, and yellow and purple wildflowers created a tapestry of color among the green. Somehow, she had veered away from the stream, but right then, she didn't care.

This was a place that made her think of heaven. She wanted to stay here with a deep longing that came from her bones. She looked to the sky and saw that the sun was already on its way down toward afternoon. How had it gotten so late? Unable to get her body to stand up any longer, she finally crumpled to the ground and sat cross-legged, holding the walking stick across her knees. It seemed to her she could be dying, she felt so light-headed and weak, but that was just fine with her. She lay back in the grass and closed her eyes. It wasn't just the climb and the hunger that had brought her to this place, she knew. The exhaustion came from deep inside her, beyond just her body. Her mind was tired too, her soul worn out from fighting with life.

Ever since her gift came to her when she was a child, she had been wrestling with the demon of being different. She'd married a man who proved that she wasn't worth a damn, and she'd hidden her abilities up until his leaving forced her to try to make money off them. She was tired all right. Tired of fighting, of trying to make things work that didn't, tired of working so hard just to get through the damn day.

Lying there in this mountain meadow, a million miles away from everything she'd ever known — the worry and fighting and just getting by, the trying to fit in and find her place in the world, the daily battles with self-doubt and sadness — she felt free. She was ready to be lifted from the earth and taken in some other form or to simply stop existing. Either way would be just fine.

She relaxed then, allowing her body to sink onto the grass completely. The sun warmed her and loosened her muscles until they stopped hurting so much. She let out a sigh and gave in to the sleep that overtook her like a drug seeping through her veins.

■ ■ ■ ■

When Vee opened her eyes in Aletta's Chevy, the feeling of homelessness, the ungrounded displacement she experienced so often, was more intense than ever, so she sat bolt upright, then let out a yell. Grabbing her sore neck with her hand, she groaned and tried to turn her head from side to side, but it was stiff as hell, and she couldn't turn it to the right at all. She looked in the rearview mirror, noticed a truck coming up the road behind her, and smoothed her hair. She fished the key out of her jacket, then put it in the ignition and turned. The sickening sound of the engine trying to turn over made her heart sink. Frowning, she turned the key back toward her, then pushed it forward again, this time pumping the gas. Again the engine labored to start, but nothing happened.

"Shit!" she yelled, then realized that she was on Dead Horse Road in Nowhere, Texas, and that the truck she saw might be the only one the entire day.

She shoved her gun into the glove compartment, then jumped out of the car. Holding her neck with one hand, she waved desperately with the other just as the truck sped past her. To her relief, she saw brake lights then the truck backing up. The side of the truck said PRETZEL TOW AND AUTOMOTIVE in faded letters, and she was amazed at her luck.

The man inside the truck wasn't as promising, but she hoped he was as kind as the brothers who had towed her to Amarillo when her Buick had broken down.

"How do?" he said. "Wassa problem?"

This guy looked like a mess. His shirt was grease-stained; his blondish gray hair grew only on the sides of his head, not on top, and stuck out crazily. One eye drooped lower than the other, and he had no front teeth at all.

"Um, my car won't start," Vee said, waving toward the Chevy.

"Well, you done found the right place." He laughed. "Found the right place. Let's get it on the truck. I can, you know, take it on in and take a look. I sure can. I can take a look."

Vee smiled nervously, then looked up and down Dead Horse Road, hoping to see another option. "How much will this cost?" she asked.

The man got out of the truck. "Oh, don't let's talk about dirty ole money. Money's the root, you know. Don't you know?"

Vee didn't have any money left but six dollars and some change. She didn't even know how she was going to buy enough gas to get back to Okay, so this answer made up her mind.

"Sure," she said weakly.

He backed the truck up to the front of the Chevy, and after ten minutes of work, it was ready to go. The whole time he worked, he talked to himself, a stream of comments about what he was doing or seeing. It seemed that every thought that came into his head, he spoke aloud, then usually repeated. It unnerved Vee, because she realized this was what most people's minds sounded like, including her own.

He waved at her to join him in the cab of the truck. He had to move beer bottles and candy wrappers, greasy gas receipts, and old engine parts out of the way for her to get in.

"Name's Pretzel," he said as he drove toward the highway.

"That's . . . unusual," Vee said. "I'm, um, Joan."

"You gonna be jist fine, Joan," he said. "Joan's gonna be fine, jist fine."

He reached over and patted her leg with a hand boasting the blackest fingernails she'd ever seen. Did he paint them? She moved her leg away.

"How did you get the name Pretzel?" she asked, trying her hardest to be pleasant.

He stuck his tongue out and grinned a gummy grin. He put his left arm behind his head, keeping his right hand on the steering wheel. His arm sank lower and lower behind his head, bending at his shoulder at an impossible angle. He reached over so far with his left hand, dangling off the arm that was behind his neck, that he actually grabbed Vee's nose and pretended to have stolen it by sticking his thumb between his first and second fingers.

"Got your nose," he said, and laughed.

She shook her head away and rubbed her nose with the palm of her hand. "So you're double-jointed," she said, irritation creeping into her voice.

Pretzel unwound his arm, then grabbed his left foot, which sported a work boot with the sole flapping off on one side. He pulled the boot straight up above his head.

"Um, you don't have to show me," Vee said, watching the road nervously.

He laughed a little, stuck his tongue through the space where his teeth should have been, then went ahead and pulled his foot all the way behind his head, still driving, right hand on the wheel and right foot on the gas. Finally, he let go and went back to sitting normally.

"That's really something," Vee said, scooting so far toward the passenger door that her right cheek was off the seat.

"That ain't the half of it. Not even half a what I can do. Not half even," Pretzel said proudly as he turned onto the highway.

They rode in silence for another ten minutes then he got off at an exit that said STROUD LAKE 5 MILES, with an arrow pointing east. Vee was relieved when Pretzel pulled the truck into a dilapidated service station that sat only a few minutes off the highway, the only thing around except for a boarded-up building across the road that looked like it had been a restaurant a long time ago.

The plastic Mobil sign in front of the station that had probably lit up at night was in shards on the ground, probably shot out. Only one gasoline pump seemed to work — the other two had canvas draped over them with rope tied around the bottom. Over the doors of the garage, someone had hand-painted PRETZELS' AUTO & TOW in black on top of peeling white paint.

"This here's my kingdom," Pretzel said as he hopped out of the truck. "King of this castle. My daddy used to own it, but he died 'bout eleven years back — the ole son a bitch." He laughed merrily at that.

"I need to go to the bathroom," Vee said as she watched him begin unhitching the Chevy.

"Sure, sure, sure," he said, loosening straps and chains. "Outhouse is out back."

Vee walked to the back of the small building, stepping around rusted car parts and rotting lumber.

"Great," she said out loud when she saw the pathetic wooden structure, leaning at quite an angle to the north with gaps two fingers wide between each slat.

She went behind it and squatted, not daring to even open the door. When she finished, she walked back toward the station, but she had a funny feeling. Looking around, she saw two badger-like eyes watching her through a small window in the back of the station. A creepy feeling crawled up from her toes all the way to her head, making her scalp tingle.

When she looked back, the eyes had disappeared and back around front, Pretzel was leaning over the engine of the Chevy, prodding it here and there. "Well, looks like the starter. Starter ain't startin'," he said. "See, this here armature ain't engaging the flywheel, see, and the flywheel's what engages the spark plugs and them's what starts the engine."

"Can you fix it?" Vee asked.

Pretzel stood up straight and put his fists on his hips. "Damn right. Right as rain. I can. Yes, I can. Got the part too."

"That's great. I'm in kind of a hurry," Vee said nervously.

Pretzel eyed her, looked her up and down twice then smiled, the cavern of his mouth black and seemingly endless. "I'm gonna need some payment," he said. "Got to get paid some way, some how."

"I told you I don't have any money," Vee said, her voice sounding weak, which she hated.

Pretzel smoothed his crazy hair back, then rubbed the top of his bald head. "I don't need money," he sang in a warbly howl. "All I need is love."

He walked over to her and kissed her right on the lips, stroking her hair with one of his greasy hands.

She shoved his hand away and stepped backward. "Don't!" she screamed.

"It's either lovin' or I'm leavin'," Pretzel said, unfazed and smiley. "I'll jist get in my truck and take off, then you can leave me that sweet ole Chevy, and you can go up on the highway up yonder and hitchhike with some devilish truck driver, lot meaner'n I ever been."

He turned and walked into the garage, leaving Vee standing there staring at the spot he had occupied. For a moment, she was frozen, and then she bolted for the car. She got in, grabbed her Browning 9 mm pistol, then stood near the car and waited for Pretzel to come out, holding the gun behind her.

He walked out of the garage holding a small car part with wires hanging from it.

"Is that the part for my car?" Vee asked sweetly.

Pretzel held it up. "This here's the one," he said, holding it up. "This is the one. This is the very one."

In that moment, Vee changed her mind and shoved the gun into her pants at her back. "You get it put in right and show me the car will start, then I'll give you some love. How does that sound?"

Pretzel looked at her sideways, suspicious.

"You were right. I don't have any choice," Vee said. "And besides, I like you, Pretzel."

He stood there, blinked and licked his lips. "You like me?"

"Sure. What's not to like? You're a nice guy, and I bet you're a great mechanic."

He turned to the engine with gusto. "That

I am. I am that," he said, and went to work.

Vee came to believe otherwise, because whatever the hell he was doing, it took forever. Every once in a long while a car would pull in for gas. Many of them turned back around and left, but when they didn't, Pretzel would go pump the gas for them, talking the entire time. He and Vee ate stale peanut butter crackers from the vending machine inside, and he opened a can of Spam, but she wouldn't touch it.

When he was close enough, he'd try to kiss her or lay his hands on her, so she kept her distance, talking sweetly to him but never letting him close enough for contact. Finally, at about two-thirty in the afternoon, Pretzel declared he was finished. He got into the car and started it, beaming with pride.

"Guess what time it is?" he asked over the sound of the engine. "What time is it, pretty girl?"

Vee pulled the gun from behind her back and held it with both hands, just as she'd been taught when they'd started buying weapons. "It's time for you to get your greasy, nasty, disgusting ass out of the car," she said, and then she added sarcastically, "Out of the car. Out of the car."

Pretzel grinned that infuriating grin of his and dropped his head. He turned the ignition off and stepped out of the car with the keys dangling from his hand.

"Drop the damned keys," she said through clenched teeth.

His eyes narrowed and his grin broadened. He reached back like he was going to throw the keys as far as he could.

So she shot him in the leg. *Bam!* The gun exploded in her hand, then a burst of red exploded on his thigh. The keys skipped across the pavement, landing just a few feet from her. She picked them up, then ran to the car. As she backed out, she heard him groaning and saw him writhing on the ground in pain, holding his leg with his hands.

For an instant, she felt sorry for him, unsure whether she should leave him, then she thought of those eyes watching her pee, and she stepped on the gas. Before she got half a block, though, she slammed on the brake and made a U turn. She pulled up to the pump, got out and filled the car with gas as Pretzel cried out from ten yards away.

"I wasn't gonna touch you," he pleaded. "I was bein' nice, helpin' you. No money, I says, remember, no money. Just help me, Joan. Joan."

"You're a predator," Vee said as she got

back in the car. "I should've shot you in the crotch."

This time, she drove away and kept going.

At first, Vee felt numb — driving, watching the road, checking the rearview mirror, wondering what Bo was doing right then and if he had left Nuevo Laredo yet. But five miles or so down the freeway, exhilaration began to take over.

She had shot someone! That bastard had treated her like an object, a piece of meat, forcing sex because she was stranded — a rapist. Because she was a woman, smaller than him, not strong enough to resist, and he knew it. So she'd done what she'd always wanted to do to men like him. She'd hurt him and showed him what it felt like to be a victim, to be overpowered by someone who didn't give a shit about his feelings or his rights or his humanity.

This lasted for another five miles or so, and then exhilaration was replaced with terror. She checked behind her every five seconds or so, certain a cop would be on her tail. What if she had killed him? What if he was lying there dying right now? She hadn't wanted to kill him, just to hurt him and get her keys.

She didn't know how she'd gotten herself into such a horrible mess, but the only thing she knew to do, the only thing that made any sense at all, was to keep driving until she got to Okay.

In the dream, Aletta wore a beautiful wedding dress and walked down the aisle of the Resurrection Lutheran Church. A lovely pearled headpiece held a veil that trailed down the back of her hair and rested lightly on her bare shoulders. Julian, who was wearing full ceremonial Indian garb, with leather-fringed leggings and vest, escorted her proudly. On one side of the aisle sat folks she knew from Okay, her friends and family, and on the other side sat the Indian elders, the Indian waitress from the diner, and the man who sold jewelry at the plaza in Santa Fe.

Julian took Aletta to the front of the church, where Reverend Mueller stood waiting, along with another woman who stood with her back to Aletta. *That must be my maid of honor,* Aletta thought. But then Julian stopped and took Aletta's hand off his arm. She looked around, confused, and noticed that Jimmy, Eugene, and Charlie Baxter all sat in the front row on the Okay side of the aisle, and a young Indian woman sat on the other next to Julian's daughter.

Adelaide, Aletta thought.

That's when the maid of honor turned around and Aletta was shocked to see that it was Aletta herself, but she was dressed in a beautiful Indian dress, with a handmade silver and turquoise belt and a headdress of feathers and stones. Julian smiled and invited the Aletta who wore the wedding dress to join her counterpart at the altar. When they stood together, Aletta looked around and saw that the people in the pews were smiling, their eyes glowing with love and approval.

Reverend Mueller opened an enormous Bible that was bound in gold.

Aletta's eyes opened, and she blinked, trying to take in her surroundings, but it was already almost dark. She sat up slowly, her body stiff and weak. Her mind stayed on the dream, and she tried to remember all of it, but even as she did, it made no sense to her. This wasn't a vision about the *tcaiyanyi* at all. It seemed like a wacky blending of her life lately — Okay and Indian people, Charlie and Julian and Adelaide.

She must have been sleeping for hours, completely exhausted from not sleeping the night before, from hiking, from hunger, and from being overwhelmed. As she shook off the sleep, she began to realize the situation she was in. It was getting dark fast, and she had no shelter or food or warm clothing. It would be freezing cold up here in no time, not to mention so dark she'd be blind.

She rolled onto one side and pushed herself up with a groan, her body sore and stiff, panic starting to take over her mind. She stood in the middle of the meadow, shadows and light crisscrossing it this way and that. She had no idea which way the sun was or the direction to get down the mountain. A swell of fear came up from her belly, burned into her throat, and came out as tears from her eyes.

Just then, she saw something out of the corner of her eye, and she jumped, terrified. She hadn't even thought of all the wild animals that were lurking in the darkness, hungry and mean. Once again, she saw something move near the edge of the trees. A huge bull elk with an enormous rack of antlers raised his head and looked straight at Aletta. Instantly, her tears stopped and her heart beat faster as this magnificent animal and she watched each other. When she realized that the elk standing there in the meadow with the forest behind him was the same image as in the painting in her office at home, a thrill passed through her, and goose bumps stood out on her arms.

The elk blinked his huge eyes, then began walking slowly toward her. Her heart beat even faster as he got nearer and nearer until he was standing only a few feet away. He sniffed the air, then began eating grass as if she wasn't there. She watched his muscles quiver slightly under the thick tan fur that covered his chest.

After several minutes, Aletta realized he wasn't going to leave, and she knew she had to stop watching the elk and do something to try to survive the coming night, but she couldn't think of a thing. She looked around and started walking away, spooking the elk a little, but he only raised his head and looked at her warily, then went back to eating.

Even though she was frustrated and disappointed she hadn't received a vision, she began looking for a trail to take her back down the mountain. The reality of spending a night out here alone was more than she could deal with now that the prospect of it was really upon her. Surely Senda and the elders didn't expect this much of her. She was sorry she hadn't found what they were looking for, but she'd done all she could do.

Carefully, she walked the edge of the

meadow, looking for a trail or even her own tracks, so she would know which way she came from, but she found no trail and no sign of tracks. Her face and hands were sunburned, and she was hungrier than she'd ever been in her life. She leaned on the walking stick and looked back at the elk. She felt light-headed and weak, and she knew she wasn't thinking clearly. Her strongest desire was to simply lie down and go back to sleep, but she knew if she did that . . . She shook her head, unwilling to even think about it.

Once again, the elk stared at her.

"What?" she asked. "Do you have somethin' to tell me, or are you just here for the buffet?"

The elk blinked again, then turned and walked the other way. She watched him go, his gait elegant and strong. Without thinking, she began to follow him, hurrying after him until he walked into the forest. Straining to see the magnificent animal among the trees, she walked as fast as she could until she could no longer see him at all. She looked back to where she'd come from, breathing heavily, completely unsure which way to go.

She felt scared and helpless, and her breath was shallow with worrying, but she didn't move. Instead, she glanced around at the forest, thick and close, with a lush forest floor covered with pine needles and mulch from dead trees. Silence, wave after wave of it, washed over her, and she felt like crying again as desperation began to build inside her chest and throat.

After a few moments, as her breath slowed and began to quiet down, she thought she heard something, and looked to her left, where the sound came from. In the dimness of the forest, she thought she saw a figure walking away from her, and fear leaped into her throat. *Who the hell would be up here? Some madman, some mountain lunatic,* she thought.

She strained to see, but when she couldn't make out anyone, she decided that maybe it was just a hiker who might know where the trail was, or maybe it was no one at all. A chill trembled through her as she realized how cold it was already becoming, and she pulled the denim jacket closer around her body.

She walked in the direction of whatever it was she'd seen, and within ten yards or so, she heard the sweet murmuring of a stream. Not knowing what else to do, she began following the creek down, struggling through dense underbrush of fallen logs, ferns, rocks, and roots. No hint of a trail was apparent, and the going was excruciatingly slow. Tree limbs kept slapping her in the face, so she used the prayer stick as a shield, holding it in front of her as she stumbled along.

After an hour of battling to get anywhere, the last hint of daylight faded completely, and she couldn't see at all, but she decided to keep going as long as she heard the water running next to her. She pushed on until her right foot landed on something slippery, possibly a moss-covered stone, and she fell wildly, arms and prayer stick flailing as she tried to stay upright. She smacked the side of her head on a rock as she landed facedown in the water, half in the creek.

She lay there, unable to move, as pain shot through her cheek and left knee. As tiny pings of light played in front of her eyes, she tried to lift her head, but the effort was too much, so she set it back down in the water, her face turned to the side. When she did, she noticed something even through the dizziness and pain: the water she was lying in was warm.

She reached out with a groan and put her hand deeper into the water and further into the stream, but the biting cold that she expected wasn't there. It was warm, like bathwater. She pushed herself up and strained to see. She noticed something that looked like smoke rising from a fire — was she crazy? She also noticed a peculiar smell — almost like rotten eggs — that seemed to come from somewhere nearby. Nothing was making any sense to her at all, but she knew her body ached, and the cold night air was doing its best to work its way under her skin.

As she sat there shivering, she remembered Hot Springs, Arkansas. She'd had several friends who'd been there and told her about the sulfur-laden hot water just coming right up out of the ground. She looked at the smoke again and realized it was steam rising from a small pool of water about ten yards downstream.

Aletta's mind was surprisingly clear. The need to survive seemed to sharpen her senses and her thinking. She made a decision not to cry, knowing it would exhaust her even further. Although the only thing she could think about with any fervor was food — roast beef and mashed potatoes, to be exact — she tried to maintain her determination to find her way back. After trying in vain to warm up by hugging herself, Aletta struggled to her feet and stumbled through the shallow creek, carrying the prayer stick, to the edge of the pool of warm water.

She pulled off Julian's jacket, then glanced around at the dark before stripping naked. Making sure to pile her clothes close to the edge of the pool, she dipped her toes into the water first, then, squatting down, dunked the whole foot, holding herself up with her hands under her buttocks. The gloriously hot water went just past her knee before her foot hit the mulchy bottom of the creek. It seemed to her that just as she started into the pool, the moon shone through the trees, providing a dim glow of light over her, the water, the forest.

"Oh, my God," she sighed, an ecstatic, tingling sensation crawling up her neck and head as she lowered her body completely into the water.

The water was much warmer than she expected, hot in fact, and her sore leg muscles pulsed slightly as they released in the heat. Just then, she heard something in the woods beyond and looked in that direction. In the moonlight, she could see the outline of the enormous elk moving through the trees.

That morning, Sissy had pretty much tossed Gyp into his stroller. She grabbed Randy by the shirt and Ruby by the hand and ran out the front door. They were late, having dawdled with getting out of bed and making their lunches and eating breakfast and getting dressed, and she was damned if she was going to let them miss the bus. They jogged the block to the bus stop, Randy and Ruby complaining the whole time.

"Where's Vee? Where's Mama?"

"I don't like you babysittin' us, Sissy."

Sissy hadn't said a word but shoved them onto the bus with a little extra oomph as its doors were about to close. Now it was after noon and she was bored to death. Of course, there were dishes and laundry piled up. The kitchen floor needed to be swept and mopped desperately, and all the beds were still unmade.

She had sometimes wondered what her mama did at home all day besides taking care of Gyp and giving readings. She figured there must be a lot of TV watching and talking on the phone involved. But now she realized just how much it took to keep a house and a family and run a business, especially alone.

While her admiration for her mama was growing, so was her resentment at being forced to take care of everything. There was no way she was going to do housework in addition to babysitting her siblings and missing school. So she loaded Gyp back into his stroller and went for a walk, leaving the housework for somebody else, anybody else, to do. Not wanting anyone to see her down at the shops on Main Street, she turned the other way.

Before she knew it, she was near the high school, near enough to see the cars in the parking lot. Most of them belonged to the seniors, and the nicer ones, like Jed Hovdy's Mustang convertible and snotty Becky Wadsworth's preposterously large and grown-up Cadillac, she recognized.

For the first time since Rusty had broken up with her, Sissy wished she could be inside the charcoal gray high school. She wanted to hang out with her friends, especially Angie, and laugh and have fun. Since her mama had left and Vee had vanished, she'd begun to appreciate her life a whole lot more. She thought about how miserable she'd been the last few weeks, and she vowed not to be that way anymore. She thought of Scarlett O'Hara in *Gone with the Wind* and her dramatic vow never to be hungry again. Sissy giggled at herself, but deep down, she knew Vee was right about boys. It was ridiculous to let anyone ruin your life.

Just then, a red VW bus puttered toward her, slowed, and then stopped. Inside, Brett Gilmore, the boy she'd had sex with, beamed at her. Sissy blushed so red that her scalp tingled from it. She hadn't seen Brett since the night of the party, and frankly, she hadn't wanted to.

"Hey," he said through the open passenger window, "I thought you were supposed to be in school."

"My mama's away, and I'm havin' to babysit," Sissy said, and glanced down at Gyp. "I thought you were supposed to be at college."

Brett leaned on the steering wheel with both hands. "I came home this weekend and only had one class today, so I blew it off," he said. "Get in. I'll give you a ride."

Sissy relaxed a little. Brett was being nice, not teasing her as she'd feared, and she had to admit he was cute. Anyway, anything was better than what she was doing now — nothing.

Brett jumped out of the VW and loaded the stroller while Sissy got in the passenger's seat with Gyp in her lap. He had been so good, but just then he started crying, wailing as if his entire little life had just gone wrong.

Brett got back behind the wheel. "What's wrong with him?"

"He probly needs a new diaper," Sissy said, a little embarrassed.

Brett couldn't hide his dismay. "Oh."

"If you take me home, I can change him."

Brett smiled, and Sissy couldn't help but think how nice it was. "Is anyone else there?" he asked nonchalantly.

"No, just me and Gyp," she said.

"Great." He put the bus into gear and headed toward Main.

CHAPTER TWENTY-TWO

The huge, pink '57 Chevy made Vee feel like she was driving a flashing sign that screamed, *Look at me!* She had passed the Oklahoma state line a half hour before and was getting closer and closer to Okay, but every time a trucker or some old geezer or a station wagon full of little kids stared at the car as she drove up I-35, she scrunched a little lower in the seat until now she could barely see.

Just as she was contemplating trading the car for something less conspicuous, she saw flashing lights up ahead. Peering through the steering wheel, she strained to see what it was. Cops. It was definitely cops, more than one car, stopped on the side of the road. A roadblock for her, she was certain. Surely, the creep she'd shot had called the police by now. Her face drained of color and sweat instantly poured down her skin.

At the last second, she yanked the car across two lanes of traffic, horns blaring angrily at her, and shot down an off-ramp, the last one before the roadblock. She sped west, away from the cluster of roadside restaurants and gas stations, toward open pastures. Gripping the steering wheel so hard her knuckles shone white through her skin, she chastised herself for not just meeting Bo in Mexico. What in the hell had she been thinking? But now it was too late, and with no money, her only hope was getting back to Okay and regrouping.

At the first road she came to, she turned north again, passing farmhouses and cornfields. After ten minutes or so, she figured she was now north of the roadblock, if that's what it was. Now that she had some room to breathe, she considered the possibility that maybe it had just been an accident. Either way, she didn't want to go anywhere near the fuzz.

Up ahead, she saw a black man in overalls chopping weeds down with some kind of hoe. When she pulled up beside him, he whistled and grabbed his lower back. "Whew-ee, that's one fine automobile," he said.

"Thanks. Um, do you know how to get to the freeway from here?" Vee asked nervously.

"Sholy do," he said kindly. "Up yonder two more stops is all. Then head back east."

"Thank you."

Vee sped off again, grateful for regular people. *That guy would probably understand me,* she thought. He was among the downtrodden of the world, and that's who she'd been fighting for. Surely he would understand why she had participated in the bank robbery, why she had dedicated her life to defeating the imperialist machine of this country. How dare the politicians and the corporate fat cats who paid them off keep that poor man uneducated and powerless. Her anger began to rise at the injustices she hated so much, but then it faded, because right then, all she really cared about was going home.

Aletta leaned back against the rock ledge she'd chosen as her seat. Sweat trickled down from her hairline onto her forehead, then took a detour at her eyebrows and streamed down her cheeks. She'd been sitting in the hot spring for what seemed like an eternity. Alternating between submerging herself up to her neck and then taking a break on the edge of the pool to cool off, she finally gave in to the dizziness and hunger pains and just lay in the water without moving. Lying there naked, she began to feel like a baby wrapped in the warmth of its mother's womb. She let out a sigh and relaxed completely.

Overhead, stars were bursts of impossibly bright light. As she stared up at them, she became certain that she'd been here watching the stars as long they had shone. She felt like a newborn and at the same time older than the trees that plunged into the night sky. Her body was like one of the smooth stones that lay at the bottom of the stream, warm, smooth, and unmoving, while her mind seemed like the sky itelf. Open, spacious, embracing everything.

A laugh escaped from her as she realized that losing her sense of being herself was one of the best things she'd ever experienced. The sound of her laughter as it cut through the silence seemed foreign to her. *Can a mountain laugh?* she wondered, then laughed again. She was sure the Indians would think so.

"*Sing-giddy-ho,* Senda," she whispered.

She didn't know what it meant, but she loved the sound of it. Then she remembered Senda's words. *Give this woman good thoughts and make her know the power of the*

Earth. Give her good medicine.

It seemed to take all the strength Aletta had to reach out with her right hand and take hold of the prayer stick that lay on the ground nearby. She pulled it closer, feeling the smooth wood under her hand and the eagle feathers brush lightly against her wet skin.

"Help me, Great Spirit," she said.

She closed her eyes and began to see things. Her mother on the edge of the stream, sitting in Senda's rocking chair. Julian walking toward her with that glow around him. She heard the voices of her children and her friends murmuring things she couldn't understand.

She knew she should get out of the water, but she couldn't move. She tried to focus, tried to pray, but she couldn't fight off the sleep that overtook her.

She started dreaming as soon as her eyes closed, a dream like no other she'd ever had before because during the entire thing she knew she was dreaming. She knew she was sitting in a mountain stream and could watch what was happening in another place and time as if the veil that had kept it separated from her had dropped suddenly away.

■ ■ ■ ■

Adelaide is walking along the river with her pail, just as she had in Aletta's previous dream. But this time, Adelaide stops and looks back where she came from, and suddenly, Aletta is watching her as a younger girl, dressed in a long skirt and white cotton shirt with a scarf tied around her hair, just like the other girls around her in the bleak, spotlessly clean school.

Adelaide sits on the edge of a thin cot, holding the hands of another of the girls, and Aletta knows she is seeing images about the girl.

"I also see that you will leave this place and live back in the pueblo one day," Adelaide tells her, and the girl smiles, tears welling up in her eyes.

"But there are other things I see that I cannot tell you," Adelaide continued. "They are not bad or good, but just what happens. My father said to always listen to the spirit guides about what to share, and they are telling me that there are things it is best for you to just live without knowing about before."

Tears come to Aletta's eyes, mix with the sweat, and run down her cheeks as she sleeps.

Just then, a nun stomps into the room, which is lined with cots on each wall, and takes Adelaide with her. She walks her out to a small two-story house behind the school and locks her into a second-floor bedroom. That's when Aletta sees that Adelaide is pregnant, her belly pushing out under her clothes.

Adelaide looks out the window, sadness and defeat playing on her face, until a teenage Indian boy jumps the fence encircling the school's grounds.

An Indian man, a gardener who is raking leaves, sees him but says nothing.

Adelaide smiles and waves at the boy frantically, but he doesn't see her or hear her through the locked window, and after looking in the windows of the school's main building for a few minutes, he jumps back over the fence and disappears.

Just then, the scene changes to Adelaide delivering her baby. She bears the physical pain stoically, but when the nun takes her daughter from her without letting her hold her, she cries from the hurt in her heart. Aletta feels her pain and cries with her.

Now, Aletta sees the nun, a big-boned woman with close-set eyes and a large, round nose, getting out of a carriage with the baby wrapped in blankets. She walks up to a tiny adobe house on a narrow street and knocks on the door. An Indian man and woman answer. It's the same man, the gardener from the school.

The nun gives the woman the baby girl, "Here is your daughter. Tell no one where she came from or I will be forced to take her back."

The woman holds the baby, tears in her eyes as the man tells the nun, "We'll tell no one. That is a promise."

"What will you name her?" the nun asks.

"We are her refuge and she will be ours," the woman answers, not taking her eyes from the baby. "We will call her Refugia."

The door closes and the scene shifts again. Adelaide is older now and stands in the door of a small farmhouse on the plains of Oklahoma in the early morning, a toddler at her feet and a baby on her hip — Aletta's grandfather Franklin and great-uncle Morris. They are beautiful boys, olive-skinned with green eyes.

From old pictures, Aletta recognizes the tall, broadshouldered man who walks to Adelaide and kisses her on the cheek. It is her great-granddad, Maxwell Halbert. Adelaide puts her free arm around his waist and leans into his chest. *She loves him,* Aletta thinks. *They love each other.*

Adelaide leaves the boys with her husband and takes a pail from the porch. She walks down to the river, her dress the same color as the muddy brown water. She kneels to fill the pail, and once again, Aletta sees the shadow cross over her. Adelaide looks up and sees two men on horseback, both wearing white hoods on their heads. The whites in Adelaide's eyes show clearly as fear grips her heart. Aletta wants to scream but nothing comes out.

"You sure we should do this?" one of the hooded men asks the other.

"This is how we keep our purity," the other answers. "No more mixed babies."

He takes out a pistol from a holster at his hip — a revolver with a long barrel and a mother-of-pearl handle. He pulls the trigger, point blank, and Adelaide falls backward into the river, her brown dress blending with the water, her hair splayed out around her head.

Aletta's whole body flinched when the gun went off, and her eyes opened with a start. Sobs, great, heaving ones, shook her to the core. She rolled her head slightly from side to side, her hair dangling in the water, as she stared up into the darkness. There had been so much in the dream, she didn't know what to think of it all.

She'd sensed that something had happened to Adelaide, something dark and frightening and horrible, but now she knew for sure, and it made her feel sick. *How could this have happened?* she thought.

Slowly, her sobs died down, and she knew how it could have happened. She remembered her daddy telling her that during Oklahoma's territory days, before there was any organized law enforcement, the Ku Klux Klan had been the law. Most of the white men were members, and they used the organization to keep the peace and punish criminals. He'd told her his daddy and uncle had been members, but they had never lynched anyone or burned any crosses. But it seemed that some of the Klan were as violent and hateful as they were in the deep South, and they had killed her great-grandmother for being an Indian married to a white man. She wondered if they had also known about her gift.

She closed her eyes, but there were no more images, just blackness with squiggly, rods of light swimming in it. Sleep crept up on her again despite her trying to figure out what she'd just seen, and this time it was black sleep that stayed with her until she woke up, her naked body somehow draped on the edge of the pool, her feet dangling in the water. The slightest trace of light illuminated the forest, and as she shivered violently from the cold, she realized that she'd made it through the night.

Aletta slipped back into the water to think. She had no idea where she was in this huge mountain range, no idea how to get out of it, and no food for her weak and ravenous body. If she stayed here, maybe someone would find her. If she left, she could pass out and end up out here in the mountains for another night, and she knew she wouldn't be lucky enough to find another hot spring.

The only thing that made her choose to get back on her aching feet and fight through the forest was the thought of her children.

"Okay," she said aloud. She clenched her jaw and stood up in the stream. She stepped onto the ground, already shivering, and pulled her clothes onto her dripping body. After nearly falling over three times from trying to balance on one foot, she finally got her shoes and socks on. Her thirst was almost overwhelming, so she filled the kidney bag right from the pool, and drank warm water. Finally, she grabbed the prayer stick and started out, deciding to head downstream. It seemed as good a plan as any.

She took two steps and would have fallen right on her butt like a toddler trying to go too fast, except she held on to the prayer stick. She stumbled and grunted loudly but somehow kept her feet. She carefully made her way over the pine-needle carpet of the forest, the downed logs, the heavy underbrush. All she could think of was her kids, their bright eyes and suntanned skin, their need for her and hers for them.

After what seemed like hours, but must have only been about thirty minutes, she had to take a break. She sat down on a log with a groan. Her stomach growled so loudly, she reached out, plucked a leaf from a tree and put it in her mouth, but after two chews, she spat it onto the ground. She sat there for at least fifteen minutes before trying to move again, and when she stood her head swam around in a circle so fast, she had to hold on to the prayer stick with both hands. Finally, the world stopped spinning, but as it came to a stop, something else knocked her off balance — a figure standing in the diffuse light of the woods, watching her. Her heart leaped in fear, and she instinctively started to run, but after a few yards, her foot caught on a tree root and she fell right onto her chin.

She heard the figure running toward her, and she turned over to shield herself with the stick. Since she'd started up this godforsaken mountain, she'd thought about all the animals that could rip her apart with razor claws and teeth, and she'd decided she'd fight to the death.

Finally, the footsteps stopped and the only thing she heard was the sound of her own blood pulsing in her ears.

"Are you okay?" a woman's voice called from nearby.

Aletta, still lying on her back and wielding the prayer stick, looked around but didn't see anything. "I don't think so," she said weakly.

A woman emerged from behind a tree just a few feet away. "I'm sorry to frighten you, but I won't hurt you."

Aletta didn't move.

"Maybe you could put that stick down," the woman said as she came closer.

She was Indian, in her thirties, dressed in jeans and a navy corduroy jacket.

Aletta realized she looked like she was going to bludgeon the woman to death and put the stick on the ground. She sat up and put her arms around her knees. "What are you doing up here?" Aletta asked.

The woman smiled. She had dimples in both rounded cheeks. "Just walking," she said.

"Did Senda and Eliseo send you?"

"No."

Aletta shook her head a little, unable to comprehend. "But it's the crack of dawn. You walk before dawn?"

The woman smiled. "It's the best time of day, don't you think?"

"I can't say that I do, unfortunately. Are we far from, you know, people?" Aletta asked, her breath starting to slow down. Her own voice sounded strange to her, different somehow.

The woman reached down to help Aletta to her feet. She was strong. "A few hours' hike at least," she said. "Looks like you could use some help getting down."

Aletta got her balance, then put her hands on her hips and laughed. "I must look like a drowned rat that's been dipped in cow manure."

The woman just smiled. She was pretty, even without a hint of makeup, because her skin was so clear, like a child's, and her eyes were almond-shaped with long black eyelashes.

Aletta put her hand on her growling belly. "You don't happen to have any food, do you?" She couldn't believe she sounded so polite. The truth was she might have mugged this lady for a piece of bread.

The night before, Jimmy had gone back to

Frank's house and slept a dreamless, black sleep that he didn't want to wake up from when Frank shook him at seven-thirty.

"Jimmy. Jimmy," Frank said, finally pushing on Jimmy's shoulder to try to rouse him.

Jimmy opened his eyes. A soft light was shining around Frank's head from the sun pouring in the living room window behind him. "You look like an angel," Jimmy said, laughing a little.

Frank stared at him. "What?"

Rusty walked into the room, still in his pajamas, on his way to the kitchen. "Hey," he said, his eyes red and his hair a shaggy mess.

"Rusty, don't your daddy look like an angel? Do you see it?" Jimmy called out.

Rusty walked over and looked at his dad — burly, 230 pounds, hairy forearms and all — and then at Jimmy. "Did he say you look like an angel? He's freakin' out."

Frank shook his head a little and shrugged.

Rusty moved closer to Jimmy and looked down at him curiously.

Jimmy sat straight up and pointed at Rusty. "You look like one too," he said. He waved his hands behind his head where he saw the light around Frank and Rusty's heads. "Y'all should see yourselves."

"I heard you leave last night, Jimmy," Frank said. "It really ain't none of my business, 'cause you're goin' home and you can do what you want, but what did you take last night?"

Jimmy laughed, and he had to admit he sounded a little strange, but he felt strange, kind of giddy, like a huge fist that had been pressing down on him for years had let up a little. "I went to find Charlotte, mad as hell, and I just had to have me a drink. Course, I forgot about that damn pill you gave me, and I just about died in some church parkin' lot."

Frank took a chair from the dining room table, turned it around, and sat down. Rusty crossed his arms but remained standing.

"The drink is cunning and baffling, just like they say, ain't it?" Frank asked.

"Oh, God, yes," Jimmy said. "It was like a voice was in my head tellin' me to drink, that I deserved it, that it would make everything all right again. It was so powerful I forgot I took that pill. Man, that pill just about killed me."

"Did you throw up?" Rusty asked, like it was a cool thing.

Jimmy shook his head, "First I upchucked my lungs, then up came my guts next."

Rusty loved it. "Gross!" he said enthusiastically.

Frank put his head in his hands. "Dammit, Jimmy."

Jimmy rubbed his face with his hands, trying to wake up. "No, it's okay. I think something happened to me. I think I'm gonna be all right."

Frank looked at him warily, "Now, don't get too confident, bud. That's when it'll sneak up on you for sure."

"But I think I hit the lowest place I could've ever imagined goin' in my life last night. I think I hit bottom of the barrel, like they say at the meetings." Jimmy smiled, remembering the sign at the church and the feeling he'd had driving home. "And then I bounced on the bottom and saw outta the opening at the top for a second." He looked at Frank. "Do you know what I mean?"

"I don't," Rusty said, bored now that the vomit talk was over, and walked into the kitchen.

"I know what you mean, and I'm happy for you. But I'm tellin' you . . . ," Frank said in warning.

And of course he was right. The moment Jimmy stood up, he felt like he had the worst hangover of his life. In the past, his cure for a hangover had of course been a hair of the dog, so naturally, the thought of a cold beer crossed his mind. On his way to work, he decided to drive by the church and read the sign again, and he was shocked to see that it had been changed.

There was one car in the parking lot, but how could they have done this so quickly, and on a Monday? The new sign said, CAN'T SLEEP? FORGET THE SHEEP. TALK TO THE SHEPHERD.

Jimmy didn't get it, and by the time he got to work, he was feeling even worse. In the parking lot, he turned off the engine and sat there with his eyes closed. He tried to think of something positive — the feeling he had when he was a boy, hunting in the woods by himself. He knew that this sense of connection, that everything is just right at least for this moment, was what would see him through.

He smiled a little, resting his eyes, until there was a loud knock on the window next to his ear.

"Hey, Jimbo, dreamin' of Playboy bunnies?" Carl Yates, one of the guys Jimmy talked about babes and baseball with, stood outside with a ridiculous grin on his pudgy face.

Jimmy got out of the car and smiled at Carl, trying to seem normal, but he didn't feel normal at all. He felt like hell, couldn't quench his thirst, and couldn't eat because he knew it would just come right back up. He wanted to go to a meeting for the first time ever, desperately wanted to talk to the folks there about what he was going through. He needed someone to listen, to understand. He thought about his kids and almost cried, he wanted to see them so badly. *What is all this weepy shit?* he thought, beginning to beat himself up, but then he pictured the little kid he once was, and stopped.

Sitting at his desk, his tie loose around his neck, sweat darkening his shirt under his arms, Jimmy felt like he was falling apart. He just couldn't do this here. Finally, at about three o'clock, he went to his boss and told him he thought he was coming down with something. He got in his car and headed straight for Main Street.

Vee drove into Okay so excited to see the little town, she laughed a little to herself. Just weeks before, it had seemed like a prison, and now it felt like her escape. She drove down Main Street relishing the sight of the old flour mills, Snyder's Drugstore, Bass's Dress Shop. She waved at Eugene as she passed his auto repair shop, and he waved back, a surprised look on his face. She had never said more than two words to him before.

She saw Randy and Ruby walking home from school with their lunch boxes (*The Bionic Woman* for Ruby and *Bewitched* for Randy), and her heart soared.

"Hey!" she called out to them, pulling over and honking the horn.

"Vee!" they yelled when they saw her.

"Wait right there," she said as she got out of the car and crossed the street. "I'll come get you."

When she reached them, they hugged her around the waist, burying their little faces into her. She stood there, holding both of them in front of Okay National Bank, not wanting to let go. Finally, she held each of the kids by the hand and walked them across the street to the Chevy.

Brett's tongue just wouldn't stop. He and Sissy sat on the couch in the living room while Gyp took a nap, and the making out had turned into a panty, wet, crazy thing. Sissy felt like she was standing on the edge of a precipice with one foot dangling off the side, he was so out of control. Brett had started out sweet and soft, but after a few

486

minutes, he'd gotten more and more intense, pushing his body against hers, and putting his hands anywhere and everywhere she'd let him.

Sissy loved kissing. She'd found that out with Rusty. It was so intimate and sweet and intense, and it made her feel dizzy in the best way. But with Brett what she felt was how much he wanted her to give in to him, and part of her just wanted to let him have his way. It would be so much easier than fighting him, than dealing with him not liking her.

She let him unbutton her shirt finally, after he tried and she resisted three times before. He was just so insistent, so relentless. He slipped his hand inside her shirt, then inside her bra and touched her nipple, and she almost knocked him to the ground, she jumped up so fast and so high.

"No!" she yelled, standing over him, pointing down at him with her forefinger. "I'm not gonna do this no more! I don't give a shit if you hate me and you tell all your friends and the whole damn town to hate me, this isn't me."

Brett smiled up at her, shook his head, and laughed a little. "Sorry," he said shyly, smoothing his hair back, trying to regain control of himself. "I just completely forgot my manners with you, and I apologize."

"Oh," Sissy said, unsure how to take this.

Brett stood up and adjusted his corduroys. "Young guys, um, you know, we get a little crazy around such a pretty girl like you, and we stop thinkin' straight. Hell," he laughed, "I stopped thinkin' at all there for a minute. So I hope you won't hold it against me."

Sissy looked at her feet, then back up at him, feeling her power returning to her. "I guess not," she said, trying hard not to smile.

Outside, she heard a car pull up. She went to the window and saw the Pink Pumpkin with Vee and the kids inside, and she sighed in relief. Thank God she hadn't let him go all the way. She also saw Joy walking up her driveway next door with her suitcase. Where was her mama?

"You need to go now," she said to Brett, and walked him to the door.

Outside, he bounced down the steps, calling, "See ya later," and jumped in his VW bus.

Vee put the car in park and saw Brett. She turned to Sissy, and for a moment the two of them shared a look, smiling at each other knowingly. But Sissy's gaze was distracted by two men in suits getting out of a white sedan across the street.

With their hands hovering inside their jackets, they started toward the Pink Pumpkin, where Randy and Ruby still sat in the back-seat. Vee glanced in the rearview mirror, then turned and looked at them directly. Suddenly, she put the car in gear again and, without looking back, screeched down Main Street.

"Vee!" Sissy called, and ran down the porch steps into the yard.

The men scampered back to their car, and Joy turned to Sissy after watching the Chevy drive away.

"What the hell's goin' on?" she called to Sissy, setting her luggage down.

Sissy ran over to Joy's. "I don't know," she said, her voice full of fear. "Vee was gone since yesterday morning."

Joy fished in her purse and pulled out her keys, "Those men were chasin' that little alley cat."

"You think?" Sissy asked. Joy went to her Riviera, and Sissy ran after her and jumped inside.

"She sure as shit was runnin'," Joy said. She yanked the car into reverse, then backed out of the driveway, almost hitting ancient Pearl Frye on her way from the library.

Joy waved out the window in apology and took off after the Pink Pumpkin.

"Where's my mama?" Sissy asked, holding on to the handle above the car door.

"Don't ask," Joy said. "She's just fine, but I can't think good enough to explain it right now." She saw a flash of pink turn a corner ahead, then the white car fishtail after it. She yanked the steering wheel left, and the Riviera seemed to Sissy to rise up on two wheels. A little yelp escaped her lips.

"Vee, why're you runnin' from them men?" Ruby asked, looking through the back windshield at the two men in the white car. She was sure their hair was made out of plastic, and the dark sunglasses they wore made them look mean and scary.

"They're bad men," Vee said, her foot pressing the gas pedal all the way to the floor as she raced through town, blowing through stop signs. "They hurt people like us real bad for thinkin' the way we want to."

Randy started to cry a little. "They look so mean. What're they gonna do to us?"

Vee didn't answer because she was swerving to miss a school bus.

The hiker Aletta met on the mountain had only two strips of jerky, and Aletta had eaten them both, feeling like a ravenous wild dog as she did. After she ate, the woman had taken them to an actual trail that she said went down to the south end of the Tesacoma Pueblo. They'd been walking for almost two hours, and in the steep parts, she let Aletta lean on her arm.

Aletta had been focused on getting down the damn mountain, but every so often, she asked a question. "Are you from the pueblo?"

"No," the woman said, but that was it.

Aletta figured out pretty quickly she didn't like to talk. *Definitely an Indian,* she thought.

They plodded along, sometimes going up and then for long periods heading down. Aletta didn't recognize anything, so she figured this was a completely different trail from the one she'd ascended. Could it have been only the day before? She felt so different, so disconnected somehow from the person who had climbed this mountain such a short time ago. With the experiences of the last twenty-four hours, she knew she could never go back to how she'd been before. It was just like putting out the sign in her yard. Two years ago, she would never have believed she could've done that either. *I've been selling myself damn short for too long,* she thought.

The pain of the blisters on her feet

brought her back from her thoughts. "I need to sit down a spell," she said.

"We're so close," the woman said. "Only fifteen minutes or so."

"Well, if we're gonna keep walkin'," Aletta said, "we gotta start talkin'. I gotta take my mind off these dogs of mine."

"What do you want to talk about?" The woman glanced at Aletta who was walking slightly behind her.

"It was so dark when I first saw you. Don't you use a flashlight?"

The woman turned and smiled. "No real Indian uses a flashlight," she said.

Aletta winced as she stepped on a small rock. It felt like her feet were actually oozing now. "I don't even know your name," she said trying to concentrate on something else. "I'm Aletta, by the way."

"It's nice to meet you, Aletta. I'm Refugia."

Aletta stopped so abruptly, she dropped the prayer stick, and it went clattering down the trail, hitting Refugia on the back of the legs.

Refugia turned, picked up the stick and held it out to Aletta, a slight grin on her face. "Are you all right?" she asked.

Aletta took the stick, but she was thinking so hard, she just nodded.

Refugia turned and began the trek downward again.

"Wait!" Aletta called, stumbling down the trail. "Did you say Refugia?"

"I was named after my grandmother." She seemed to be walking faster and faster.

Tears welled up in Aletta's eyes, but she didn't know why exactly. "Was she an orphan?"

"Yes, she was. I didn't know that until . . . later, though. It was a guarded secret in my family." Refugia spoke over her shoulder, taking Aletta down the trail without stopping to talk.

Aletta hobbled after her. "Slow down. I can't keep up," she said, but Refugia slowed only slightly, if at all. "Was your great-granddad a yard man at the Indian school in Santa Fe?" she asked.

Refugia glanced at her. "That was before I was born."

"But he wasn't your real great-grandfather."

Finally, Refugia stopped and looked at Aletta, who was out of breath, leaning on her knees with her hands. "No, he and my great-grandmother adopted my grandma Refugia," she said.

Aletta stood up straight and looked at Refugia's warm eyes, the tears finally spilling out of her own. "Your real great-grandma is Adelaide Medina, just like she is mine. You and me are related, aren't we?"

Refugia smiled and surprised Aletta by pulling her into a sisterly hug. "I'm so glad you came here," she said.

She released Aletta and looked down the mountain. For the first time, Aletta saw Te-sacoma Pueblo laid out like a toy village in the valley below them.

"Thank you, Jesus," Aletta said excitedly. "Come on, let's go get something to eat. I can't wait for you to meet Senda. I think you're the one they're lookin' for."

Aletta started down the trail, but Refugia didn't move. Aletta turned around, a question on her face.

"I've met Senda and Julian and Maria too." The wind blew Refugia's long hair back, and she looked beautiful as the sun shone on her face. Aletta thought she could see the moisture in her eyes. "Tell them I love them, okay? Especially Maria. She's such a special girl."

Refugia turned and began walking back up the trail away from Aletta and the pueblo.

"Wait! You're supposed to come with me. I don't understand," Aletta called after her, but Refugia didn't turn around, and Aletta knew there was no way she could catch her.

She watched Refugia walk away until she disappeared into the woods, and then reluctantly, Aletta turned downward again and began walking off the mountain alone.

Jimmy drove back to Okay in a kind of hazy fog. He knew he should probably go lie down, but he wanted to see his kids. When he turned onto Elm Street and headed toward Main, he saw a school bus rumbling up the road toward him. Suddenly, Aletta's '57 Chevy screamed around the bus and out into his lane, almost hitting his car before swerving wildly around him. Jimmy put his foot on the brake just in time to allow a white car with two men inside to blow past, closely followed by Joy's brown-and-tan Riviera. The bus driver laid on his horn the entire time.

Jimmy had to let the bus pass before he could pull into a driveway and turn around to join in the chase. When he did, he sped around the school bus. He glanced in his rearview mirror and saw the bus driver gesturing wildly, both hands off the wheel, his face red from screaming.

Jimmy thought he'd seen that wacky girl driving Aletta's car, and when he got close enough, he looked around Joy's car and clearly saw Randy and Ruby looking out the back window of the Chevy, scared and hanging on for dear life.

"That was Daddy!" Ruby yelled. "Did you see him, Randy?" Randy nodded and buried his face in his arm.

Vee sped through a stop sign, turning onto a country road that led out of town, but as soon as she did, she was sorry. There was nothing out here for miles but pastures and crops and farmhouses. The feds or detectives or whoever they were could see her from miles away in this huge pink car. That's when she heard sirens and looked back to see flashing lights from a cop car behind the white car.

"Oh, God," she said, in quiet desperation. She'd gained a little separation, but that wouldn't last long. What was she gonna do now? *Think,* she willed herself. *You've got to think.*

"Hey," she said to the kids, trying to sound casual, "do you guys know anywhere we could hide for just a little bit? Like on TV, how they hide from the bad guys?"

That changed Randy completely. He loved TV, and he loved pretending he was on one of his favorite shows like *Charlie's Angels.* "Hey, I got an idea!" he said, and began pointing frantically. "Turn up here!"

Sissy and Joy saw the Chevy and the white car turn onto County Line Road. As they pulled up to the stop sign, a police car hurtled past in hot pursuit, its sirens blaring and lights flashing. Sissy finally decided to buckle her seatbelt as Joy burned rubber to catch up.

Sissy turned around and looked at her daddy, who was close on their tail. She could barely make out his face because of the glare of the sun on the windshield, but it was definitely him. She didn't know how he'd found them or why he was off work, but for some reason, just knowing he was there made her feel better.

"Your mama's gonna have a tizzy fit to stop the show," Joy said, shaking her head, driving like they do in the movies with the steering wheel moving all the time. "She's gonna string that skinny girl up by her toes and tan her hide, I tell ya, and I'm gonna help. God knows what kinda trouble she's in."

"But she's been so good to us," Sissy said, not very convincingly.

Vee hunched over the steering wheel like an old lady. She was so exhausted and scared, she had to focus extra hard to keep the car on the road when she was going this fast. They raced down the dirt road that Randy had directed her to, and Vee kept the Chevy floored despite the ruts. The enormous V-8 engine was holding its own against the newer cars behind them.

"At the next turn, go left!" Randy yelled.

"Where? Where?" Vee yelled back. "I don't see it!"

"This is Daddy's old place," Ruby said, clutching the top of the front seat.

Randy leaned so far over the front seat, his belly was on top of it. "Behind those trees, there's a road, I promise!"

Just ahead, there was a line of trees along a creek bed, but Vee couldn't see anything behind them. Without a better option, as soon as she passed the trees, she yanked the steering wheel left, and just as Randy said, there was a narrow road.

Ruby flipped around to watch out the back window and saw the white car, the police car, Joy's Riviera, and her daddy's Trans Am speed past on the road they'd just turned off of. "They kept going! They didn't see us!" she cried.

"We can hide behind the barn!" Randy yelled at the top of his lungs, his adrenaline just about to make him explode.

"Hey, hey," Vee said, covering her ear with one hand, slowing the car as she approached the falling-down shack and barn. "Calm down just a little."

Instead of driving behind the barn, she drove right inside its open doors, stopped, and turned off the car.

"Cool," Ruby said.

"What is this place?" Vee asked.

Randy jumped into the front seat and sat on his knees facing her. "It's one of the places our daddy lived when he was a little boy. We can show you the bullet hole in the wall of the little house if you want."

"Yeah," Ruby said. "It's where his brother almost shot his daddy."

"Maybe later." Vee stepped out of the car and almost fell, she was so woozy. "Let's close those doors," she said, holding herself up with the help of the car.

She went to one of the old, rotting doors that was swung open to the outside and yanked on it with all her might. To her surprise, it moved on the first try, and she dragged it closed on screeching hinges. The other one didn't budge so easily, so Randy and Ruby grabbed hold of it with her. They counted one, two, three, and pulled the door out of the dirt and slowly dragged it closed.

Once inside the darkness of the musty old

barn, Randy held Vee around the waist. "It's creepy in here," he said. "Like a haunted house or somethin'."

"Yeah, and it stinks," Ruby complained.

"Oh, it's not that bad, and we won't be here for long," Vee said, trying to sound reassuring. "Maybe just overnight."

Ruby and Randy just stared up at her, their big green eyes bright but clearly worried.

Behind Sissy and Joy, Jimmy was getting more and more concerned. He couldn't get even a glimpse of the Pink Pumpkin anymore, and he wondered if the cops up ahead had lost the trail. The Trans Am was horrible on these bumpy dirt roads, but he furrowed his brow and kept driving, hitting the ceiling of the car with his head more than once.

He told himself he'd known that girl was crazy when he met her, but damned if he'd done anything. He'd been too busy drinking and thinking about himself to do what was right by his kids. So now, here he was, his beautiful children in the hands of some madwoman, clearly on the run from the law, possibly — no, probably — dangerous. He clenched his jaw. *If she laid one hand on those kids to hurt them . . . ,* he thought.

"God," he prayed out loud, the bumps in the road and his emotion making his voice quiver, "I know I've been a shitty dad, but if you save my kids and get them home safe, I'm gonna do better."

Just as he finished, a thought flashed across his mind, and he looked in his rear-view mirror at the receding tree line they'd passed less than a minute before. He slowed down, letting the other cars race ahead, and turned around in a road that led to an oil derrick. He turned onto the dirt drive that went to his boyhood home, pulled his car over, and turned off the engine.

Careful not to slam the car door, he glanced up to see that the barn doors were closed. After approaching the big barn doors, he thought twice about it and crept around to the back of the barn, where a regular sized back door stood open just a crack. He listened intently but heard nothing, so he opened the door as fast and hard as he could, causing a large piece of its termite-infested wood to come off and crumble to the ground.

Light streamed in, catching dust motes like tiny snowflakes in its path. It allowed him to see inside the Chevy. In the back-seat, Vee sat with her head tilted back and her eyes closed, between Randy and Ruby, her arms cradling them underneath her. Jimmy walked to the car, opened the door, and stuck his head inside.

"Hi, Daddy," Randy whispered.

Ruby just waved and gave him a slight grin.

Vee, it seemed, was sound asleep.

CHAPTER
TWENTY-THREE

Aletta sat on a straight-backed chair in Senda's house. It was after three in the afternoon. Unwilling to reveal anything about her journey when she finally hobbled back to Senda's, she had eaten until she was almost sick. She'd called home but no one answered, so she'd left a message, then lay down to sleep, telling Senda to wake her just before Julian and Maria came home from school. Now she sat with the elders staring at her from their postions on and around the couch. Senda rocked slowly in her chair, making the time seem to creep by.

Aletta thought the old Indians looked like they'd be carved on Mount Rushmore if history had been radically different. Their faces, ancient and tribal, the kinds of faces that had been on this earth from the beginning of time, seemed to Aletta like they were cut out of stone, made of something older and more durable than flesh and bone. Yet she also saw tenderness there, and vulnerability and humanity. She hadn't noticed these things before, because she'd feared their disapproval and believed that she was separate from them, an outsider. Now when she looked at these magical old faces, she didn't see disapproval (except for Dominga, whose set jaw and hard eyes remained unchanged). She saw . . . What was it? Hope, possibly.

As they waited, she thought about her kids. She knew that with Vee and Silvia there for the weekend, and now Joy back home next door, they had to be fine, but she couldn't wait to hug and smell and kiss each one of them.

The front door opened, and Aletta started. She'd almost fallen asleep. Maria walked in, followed by Julian, who rushed to Aletta, pulled her up from the chair, and hugged her tightly.

"I wanted to come after you," he said.

Senda cleared her throat before speaking. "I wouldn't let him," she said. "He's always getting into everything, this one."

Aletta smiled, thoroughly enjoying her closeness to Julian. Her tired, aching body felt better as soon as he walked in the room.

He released her from the embrace but

kept holding her hand. "I was so glad when Senda called me at school when you came back."

"I told you I would," Senda said. "You worry too much."

"Yeah, Julian, no need to worry. I only almost died up there, but no big deal," Aletta said, teasing Senda.

"So tender, these young generations," Senda said, teasing back.

Maria watched impatiently, not entering the room any further than the doorway. "Why am I here?" she asked. "This has nothing to do with me."

"Sweetheart," Aletta said to Maria, "come sit by me." She sat down and patted the chair next to her.

Maria rolled her eyes and sat down with a thunk. She looked at her hands, her feet, the wall, anywhere but at the elders or Senda.

"Okay," Aletta said, sitting up straight in her chair like a student about to give a speech. "I'm gonna tell y'all what happened. I can't tell you I got any real clear answers, but I do have some hunches."

Aletta told them about the wedding dream first.

"This is clear to me," Senda said. "It means you belong in both worlds. You are both Indian and white, and you belong to both people."

Aletta laughed a little. "Is that what Dominga thinks?" she asked, and looked at the woman.

Eliseo's eyes twinkled with laughter, and Dominga grunted "We'll see."

"I thought it meant I'd never find the right man or somethin'," Aletta said, forcing herself not to look at Julian, who stood leaning against the wall, his arms crossed on his chest.

Aletta wanted to talk more about the wedding dream, but she knew they were waiting, so she went on. She told them about the elk, and they all nodded with approval.

"The elk is a very strong animal guide," Senda said. "It holds wisdom and knows its own path."

"Oh, good." Aletta nodded like she understood.

She told them about finding the hot spring and how she'd lain in it for hours, unable to move, sweating.

Julian's eyebrows raised as he listened. "That is powerful, Aletta. Many, many Indian people have sweat ceremonies."

Aletta might have grown up in Oklahoma, but she knew almost nothing about Indians. "Really?" she asked.

Eliseo spoke up. "These ceremonies are for purification. They help to cleanse the body and mind so a person can get closer to the Great Spirit."

Julian added, "It is also a ritual of renewal that re-creates birth because the experience is like —"

"Being in the womb," Aletta finished.

Julian smiled. "Yes."

"Well, I tell ya. I feel like a newborn except for these darn feet," she said. "Honestly, I don't know if I'd have made it through the night without finding the spring," she said.

Senda pushed her chair and started rocking. "You had many guides watching over you," she said matter-of-factly.

Aletta looked at Maria before continuing. She was still frowning, but Aletta could tell she was listening.

Aletta went on to tell them about her dream, how Adelaide had given birth to a baby girl at the school, and how the baby had been given to the yard man and his wife.

They all listened with rapt attention. "It was true, then. She was pregnant there," Dominga said, her voice breaking.

"Go on, Aletta," Senda said.

It was the first time she'd used Aletta's name, and for some reason, it felt to Aletta like a show of respect. "Well, this is the part that gets a little confusin' to me," Aletta said. "This hiker, an Indian lady, found me, and helped me down the mountain, or I probly would still be stumbling around somewhere up there. It wasn't until we were almost down that she finally told me her name." Aletta paused, thinking before continuing. "Oh, I forgot to tell y'all something important. The little baby girl that Adelaide had to give up was named Refugia."

Maria turned her head so quickly toward Aletta that Aletta actually flinched.

Julian uncrossed his arms, and his mouth fell open a little. The electricity in the room was palpable.

"What did I say?" Aletta asked.

"Just go on," Julian said.

Aletta continued carefully. "Well, what's strange and where I get really mixed up is that this hiker who found me, her name was Refugia too. She said she was named after her grandmother, who was adopted by a man who worked at the Indian school. She was Adelaide's great-granddaughter too, just like me, but from another father. Can you believe it?"

Maria put her head in her hands and began to cry. Senda and Julian went to her and put their hands on her.

"What is it?" Aletta asked Julian.

"What did this woman look like?" Senda asked.

"She was about my age, I guess," Aletta answered. "Real pretty, with long, straight hair down her back, almond-shaped eyes with these big ole eyelashes. Oh, and she had these big dimples when she smiled."

Maria started crying harder when she heard this.

"She said she knew y'all," Aletta said. "Who was she, Julian?"

With tears in his eyes, he said, "My wife, Maria's mother, was named Refugia, and so was her grandmother. Her great-granddad used to work at the Indian school."

"She came to help you," Senda said.

Aletta felt a tingle run all the way up from her feet to the top of her head. "She told me to tell y'all she loves you." Aletta reached out and put a hand on Maria's shoulder. "She said you especially, Maria. She said you are a special girl."

Maria sobbed and reached out for Aletta. They held each other, and Aletta couldn't help but cry too. "We're family, you and me," she whispered to Maria.

Maria nodded, her head on Aletta's shoulder.

"I think there's something else you should know," Aletta said.

Maria sniffled and raised her head to look Aletta in the eye. "What?" she asked.

"You're supposed to be the next *tcaiya-nyi.*"

CHAPTER
TWENTY-FOUR

Julian, Maria, and Aletta sat in silence in Julian's pickup for the first ten minutes of the hour-long drive to the airport in Albuquerque. Aletta's feelings were all over the place. She still felt awe and disbelief about everything that had happened since she came to New Mexico. She was also absolutely infuriated with Vee. Sissy had told her how the FBI had found Vee in Okay and how the car chase with her children in the car had ended up with Jimmy finding them hiding in an old barn.

Finally, Maria spoke up. "I don't know how to be the *tcaiyanyi*," she said quietly.

"No one does when they start out, sweetheart," Julian said.

"No one knows anything when they're sixteen, hon," Aletta said. "Look at Jesus. He didn't start doin' his thing till he was thirty."

Aletta wished the elders had been more

encouraging after she'd told them Maria was the *tcaiyanyi.* The idea of it had come to Aletta after Refugia had left her on the mountain, but when she found out that Maria was also related to Adelaide and the Medinas, she knew for certain her hunch had been right. The elders, however, were quiet, stoic people and could not be rushed into anything. They hadn't denied her, but they also hadn't embraced her.

"I had a dream last night," Maria said. "Someone died, a woman, and we were performing the burial ceremony so her soul could go back to Shipap."

Aletta glanced at Julian, questioning.

"It's the underworld," he said. "It is where the souls of all Indian people come from."

"Who was the woman you were burying?" Aletta asked.

Maria shook her head a little. "I don't know, but somehow, I knew she needed a burial ceremony, that she had never had one."

"Maybe you were dreaming about Adelaide," Aletta said.

"Maybe that's it," Maria said, her eyes lighting up with understanding. "Her soul has not been delivered. I don't think I can be *tcaiyanyi* as long as Adelaide has not had the ceremony."

"Then you should call for the ceremony," Julian said.

"Can I do that?" Maria asked, incredulous.

"It's what your folks want, Maria. They want you to help them," Aletta said.

Maria didn't speak for a few minutes, then she looked at Aletta. "I believe you, because I know you are a *tcaiyanyi* yourself."

"Ha," Aletta said, shaking her head a little.

Julian put his hand on Aletta's thigh, speaking softly to her. "You can accept this. You are a gifted shaman and medicine woman. The sooner you know this, the more you can serve others. That goes for both of you, actually."

Aletta and Maria looked at each other, then started laughing.

"Maybe we can help each other," Aletta said.

"Oh, I plan on getting your help. You got me into this," Maria said. "And besides, I know you've got the hots for my dad."

Aletta blushed, but Julian squeezed her thigh a little tighter. "Oh, I hope she's right about that one," he said.

Aletta put her hand on his. "I can't tell a lie, but I just wish one thing," she said.

"What?"

"I wish it was just a little more complicated between us."

He laughed, and she burned with a desire to kiss him.

When they got to the airport, Maria stayed in the truck while Julian escorted Aletta inside. He bought a ticket for her, then pulled her to a quiet corner of the terminal. Standing on her tiptoes, she kissed him for at least five minutes before pulling back.

"Well," she said touching her lips lightly, "I'm gonna miss you even more now. I guess we'll just chalk this up to a wild ride in the Wild West."

He smiled that beautiful smile. "Oh, no. You're not blowing me off after just a little smooching."

"What?" she asked, taken aback.

"Don't act so innocent," he teased. "You know you've been using me for my body."

She laughed loudly. "Okay, you caught me," she said, and kissed him again. "So are you saying I get to see you again or something?"

"You can bet on it."

Kissing Julian made Aletta feel giddy as she boarded the airplane for her first-ever flight, but by the time she landed she was almost sick. It wasn't because of the flying. She loved looking out the window at the expanse of earth below. It was because she couldn't stop thinking about Vee.

Betty met her at the gate when her plane got in around six that evening, a huge smile on her face. "How is everything?" Aletta asked.

"Just fine," Betty said. "That cousin of yours is somethin' else, though. We just heard she shot some guy down in Texas in addition to tryin' to rob that bank."

"Oh, my God," Aletta said, and buried her face in her hands.

In the car on the way home, Betty tried to help. "It wasn't your fault for leavin' 'em," she said. "You didn't know."

Aletta groaned.

"I figured out what I'm gonna do with my life," Betty said, changing the subject, but Aletta just looked out the window and gnawed on a fingernail.

Forty minutes later, they pulled up to Aletta's house on Main Street in Okay. There were cars everywhere, like it was a funeral or a party.

"What's all this?" Aletta asked.

"Folks just wanted to help out," Betty said.

Inside the house, Aletta was greeted as if she'd been lost for weeks and had barely survived. It seemed like half of Okay was

515

there, and they were all glad to see her.

"Mama!" her children cried, including Sissy, and ran to her.

Aletta picked Gyp up and hugged them all so tight, Randy finally said, "Mama, you're hurtin' me."

Aletta tried to hold back the tears, but it didn't work. "I'm so sorry for leavin' y'all like that. I had no idea Vee was crazy or would run off. I'm so sorry."

"It's all right, Mama," Ruby said bravely. She and Randy had been quite the heroes since the car chase. "It was kinda fun."

"Yeah," Randy said proudly, chocolate rimming his mouth. "Like on TV."

"I don't know about that," Sissy said.

Aletta hugged Sissy again. "You must be so mad at me," she said.

"A little, but I also can't believe how much work you do every day. Jeez, Mama, you're amazin'."

"Maybe I should leave more often," Aletta said laughing, but as soon as she saw Jimmy round the corner from the dining room, the smile dropped from her face. "Hi, Jimmy," she said, and let Gyp squirm out of her arms to the floor, where he took off running in his diaper.

"Hey, Aletta," Jimmy said, and looked at his shoes. "We're all real glad you're back."

"I thought you'd be bawlin' me out 'bout now," she said.

"Well, I knew that girl was a kook and you had no business trustin' her, but the truth is the kids shoulda been able to stay with me."

Aletta shook her head. "Now, you know that don't work for me with you drinkin'."

"I know, dammit." Jimmy scowled. "That's what I'm tryin' to say, woman, if you'd just listen for one time in your life."

"Oh," Aletta said. "Well, then what?"

"I'm just tryin' to say I know I been a lousy father and all, but when I was chasin' Ruby and Randy in that car, I made a promise I'm gonna keep."

Aletta looked at him skeptically.

"I know, I know. Like they say in AA, a drunk has screwed up so many times that his word don't mean a thing, so he's gotta prove it with actions."

Frank Conway walked over and put his arm around Jimmy's shoulder. "He's tryin' real hard, Aletta," he said.

Aletta was so flustered by the change in Jimmy, she had no idea what to say, so she just mumbled, "That's good," and walked away.

She noticed Sissy talking to Rusty in the kitchen and smiled.

Eugene walked up to her, drinking Kool-Aid out of a paper cup. "Your Chevy got pretty messed up," he said. "She drove it over a thousand miles. I told 'em to bring it on over, so I got it at the shop. I'll get her back to runnin' and lookin' like new."

"Thank you, Eugene," Aletta said. "I'm so glad you're here."

Just then, Joy, Bobette, and Betty walked into the room. "We've waited long enough, girl," Bobette said.

"It's time you told us about what happened with them Indians," Joy said.

The three of them reached out and took her by the arm, herding her into the living room together.

That's when she noticed it. The images flowed in like a dream, one after the other, colorful and clear. She laughed joyfully and let them float away, not focusing on any of them, so that they were forgotten as soon as they disappeared.

Once in the living room, Betty hugged her tight, and an image came through that she couldn't ignore.

"We're so glad you're back," Betty said.

"I think it's gonna be me tellin' *you* that in the future," Aletta said.

The three women looked at one another then back at Aletta.

"I know what you decided to do with your life," Aletta said to Betty. "You're gonna take people on trips all over the world. You're gonna be a tour guide."

Her friends started whooping and cheering.

"The Indians did it!" Joy yelled.

Aletta nodded, but she knew it wasn't the Indians who'd brought back her gift. She'd done that herself.

CHAPTER
TWENTY-FIVE

The prison guard buzzed Aletta into the visiting area, and she sat down on the hard plastic chair that faced a clear Plexiglas wall. The room, with linoleum floors and painted cinder-block walls, was like an oven, and she felt sweat trickling down her back. She was nervous about seeing Vee.

It had taken her three days to even consider speaking to her, and now, a week after Vee had run from the FBI and the police with her children in the car, it was Aletta's last chance to see her cousin. Vee was being extradited to California. The man she'd shot in Texas had lived and was supposed to fully recover the use of his leg.

Aletta waited several long, anxious minutes before Vee walked into the room on the other side of the Plexiglas and sat down. She wore an orange jumpsuit and handcuffs around her wrists. Aletta almost gasped at how bad she looked — thin and frail, her cheeks caved in and gaunt. Dark roots were growing in under her frizzy strawberry blond hair, and her red-rimmed eyes seemed hollow and empty.

Unexpectedly, the monster she had become in Aletta's mind turned into a scared, misguided young woman before Aletta's eyes.

Vee didn't look directly at Aletta. Her gaze kind of roamed. She picked up the red telephone on the wall and slowly put it to her ear.

Aletta hadn't even noticed the phone next to her, but she realized that was how they were supposed to talk, so she picked it up and put it to her ear.

"Hello, Vee," she said coldly.

"Hi, Aletta," Vee croaked, then cleared her throat. "I'm glad you came."

Her voice sounded tinny and distant through the phone. "I know you asked to see me," Aletta said.

Vee nodded. "I did. I wanted to try to explain. I wanted you to know that I was in on that bank thing only because I believed in what we were doing. I did it because I care. . . . You have to know that."

Aletta raised her hand for Vee to stop. "Listen, I know you have very strong beliefs, but all I ever really heard from you is what's

521

wrong and what you're against. Why didn't you try something to help folks instead of bein' an outlaw? It's just pure idiotic nonsense to tell me that you shot someone because you cared."

Vee looked at her directly for the first time. She opened her mouth to speak, but then shut it again and she began to cry. "I'm sorry," she said finally. "I wasn't tryin' to kill that man. I swear it, Aletta," she said, her eyes aflame. "It was self-defense. He was forcing himself on me. And I never, ever would do anything to hurt any of your kids." Her shoulders shook, and she cried hard tears that fell on her jumpsuit.

"You stole my car, my money, and you endangered my kids, and there ain't nothin' worse than that," Aletta scolded.

"But I came back," Vee said weakly, her chin quivering. "I had to see you all again."

Aletta's gaze softened, and she felt the clamp on her heart loosen up a little. "I know you love my kids," she said. "I seen how you are with them, and somehow, you got Sissy to stop actin' like Rusty dumpin' her was the end of her life. The truth is, and I almost hate to admit it, they love you too."

Vee looked up, a smile shining in her eyes. "Do you know the only place I ever felt at home in my whole life was with you and your kids?"

"Here," Aletta said, and took a photograph out of her purse, "I brought you this." She held the picture up so Vee could see it. It was Aletta and her four kids standing in their front yard, smiling and happy.

"Thank you so much," Vee said, gazing at the picture, tears streaking her cheeks. "How did you know I wanted this?"

Aletta grinned. "Because I'm the *tcaiyanyi* of Okay," she said, and then added to herself, "Hey, I think I finally said it right."

"The what?"

"Oh, I'm just kiddin'," Aletta said, and waved her hand. "Some a these folks that work here told me you been askin' and askin' for a picture."

"Can I write to you and the kids?" Vee asked.

"All right, but no revolutionary nothin'," Aletta answered, and pointed a finger at her.

Vee grinned and wiped her nose with the back of her sleeve. "You got it."

Aletta drove home from the prison, excited to get to work. She had three appointments, and for the first time in her life, she was really enjoying using her gift. Since she'd returned from Santa Fe, she'd been doing her readings a little differently. Whenever she didn't know what to tell someone, she got quiet and asked for guidance, and just about every time an answer came through right away. She quit worrying about how folks would react and just followed her gut.

She also wasn't just telling people what she saw when she touched them anymore either. She listened to them now too. Losing her gift for a while had shown her how much healing happened when folks simply felt like they were being heard. And that's what she was — a healer. She was admitting it to herself for the first time, and while stepping into that role felt a little awkward and kind of frightening, she knew it was what Adelaide would have wanted.

The phone was ringing when she walked through her front door. She set her purse down on the bar and reached for the receiver. "Hello."

"Hi, Aletta. It's Julian."

"Julian! Well, howdy!"

Aletta heard Senda in the background. "Give me that phone," she said to Julian, then into the phone she said, "Hello?"

"Senda," Aletta said, "it's so nice to hear from you."

"We've been so busy with the burial ceremony," Senda said. "It takes four days, you know, so we haven't had time to call."

Aletta smiled. Julian must not have told her he'd called her twice already.

Senda continued, "We want you to come and visit us for the feast day in September. You and your family."

In the background, Aletta heard Maria shout, "Please come!"

"Can you make it?" Senda asked. "It's a very important day for our tribe, and we would love for you to be here."

"We wouldn't miss it," Aletta said without hesitation. "After all, y'all are my family too."

■ ■ ■ ■

THE WINGS THAT FLY
US HOME
DAYNA DUNBAR
A READER'S GUIDE

■ ■ ■ ■

A CONVERSATION WITH DAYNA DUNBAR

Interviewer Catherine Rourke is an award-winning journalist from New York City who now lives in Sedona, Arizona.

Catherine Rourke: What inspired you to create a sequel to *The Saints and Sinners of Okay County?*

Dayna Dunbar: My publisher! When I wrote the first story, I didn't anticipate doing a sequel, but when Ballantine wanted more of Aletta, of course I said yes. I'm so glad they did.

CR: Explain how you chose the book's title and its symbolism.

DD: There are many references to birds and feathers in this novel that have more meaning than what is on the surface. So much of this book is about finding home, whether it is Aletta finding another home she never knew she had in New Mexico, or Vee feeling at home for the first time, or Jimmy coming home to himself in his healing process. The birds mean different things throughout, just as there is more than one meaning for home that each of the characters experiences.

CR: How do you invent your plots and characters? Are they autobiographical or based on societal archetypes?

DD: Many of my characters are autobiographical or composites of people I've known, but there are many I create too. Regarding plot, I get an overall idea; then, as I write, the details reveal themselves. I don't think about archetypes or symbolism as I write, but much of what comes through tends to align with universal themes that include these.

CR: You accurately portray the styles, music, décor, and consumer products of the 1970s. Did you conduct extensive research on the cultural icons of that

time or are your details based solely on recollection?

DD: Much of the material about the '70s comes from my memory, but the details and dates I had to research. Just as I began to write *Saints and Sinners,* I was having a very difficult time finding the details I wanted to make the book not only authentic but also fun for the reader who lived during that era. I fretted over this for a few weeks. Then one day, I was in the drugstore, and like a beacon of light, I saw a magazine on the shelf entitled *'70s People.* It was a compilation of the highlights of pop culture of that decade. I practically heard angels singing, and for good reason — it answered all my questions and gave me ideas I wouldn't have had otherwise.

CR: Did you outline the story before you began writing or do you let the plot unfold as you work? Did the story take any unexpected turns as you were writing it?

DD: I outline as much as I can of the plot, but I never know where the whole thing is going. I'll outline a piece, then write that, and then outline some more as it comes through. Many times, the story will take turns I didn't expect, so the outline is just a helpful guide, not a must-do. The characters often lead me in surprising directions. Sometimes a character will show up just as an ancillary character, and then he or she will end up being very important. That happened with Maria in this story.

CR: Your story has an almost timeless quality even though it takes place nearly thirty years ago. Do you think that your characters and settings still exist today – minus the styles and products of the era?

DD: I definitely think so. Aletta really represents a universal experience in that she feels like she doesn't fit in, doesn't know what she's doing, and is doing her best to get by in very difficult circumstances. This story has her growing up in her self-confidence and finding a place where she feels accepted. The place is certainly still there. It's my hometown in Oklahoma!

CR: What challenges, if any, did the evolution of your characters present?

DD: The character that presented the most challenges was Vee. When I began, I knew I wanted to include this political revolutionary who was on the run from the law. Unlike today, the '60s and '70s were filled with revolutionary organizations. As far as this character and her story, however, I wasn't sure where she was going to go. As she spent some time in Okay, it became clear to me that she had basically been homeless her entire life, and this was her first experience of a loving family. In order to make this more evident to the reader, I changed her past a bit during rewrites so that she would have a stronger character arc. My wonderful editor at Ballantine, Deirdre Lanning, helped with this as well.

CR: What can your readers learn from Aletta Honor's challenges? How does she reflect modern women who are still struggling to liberate themselves from traditional female roles?

DD: I think almost every woman faces the challenges Aletta does. Aletta is on a journey of self-discovery, just like every other woman and mother, but she has to squeeze this in while still making a living, changing diapers, and going to kids' activities. It is really only because Jimmy left her and she had to put the sign out to give psychic readings that she begins this journey at all. Otherwise, she was too busy! I'm sure this is deeply familiar to women everywhere, but I do believe that true liberation lies in knowing oneself, so I hope Aletta's story encourages this in other women.

CR: Your prose is woven with the underlying human traits of denial, insecurity, victimization, and codependence. Do you incorporate these into your characters because they are so common?

DD: These traits are a part of everyone I know, even the most successful and secure women and men. Everyone is either working on these issues in their lives or has lived through them in the past. Personally, I believe there is an underlying spiritual issue that each of us has to deal with, and that is the belief that we are separate from our source, from the joy of life within. This creates inherent insecurity, fear, neediness, clinging, bullying, and the rest. Whether or not this deeper spiritual crisis is discussed in a book doesn't really matter, however. What does matter is that these issues, which each of us faces in life in some way, are dealt with authentically through characters that evoke familiarity and kinship in the reader.

CR: Many of the male characters feed off women's energy and display weak behaviors such as alcoholism, chauvinism, rage, and violence. Do you think this reflects the behavior of many men in our society?

DD: No, not the majority of men. I just think that the issues I discussed in the last question play out in the lives of men differently than they do with women. In general, I think men tend to externalize their baggage and that it can come out as anger, competitiveness, and violence. Women tend to internalize their hurt and fear more, and it comes out as neediness, manipulation, emotionalism, and lack of self-esteem. I have to say, however, that I'm not thinking of these things as I write. I just try to be honest with what I observe. I've written about some wonderful men in both books, and I try never to vilify anyone, whether man or woman.

CR: What or who was the inspiration for Vee's character?

DD: When I was growing up, there was a distant member of my family who was very much like Vee. She was involved in radical politics and even hid out from the FBI with us once. My parents only knew this fact later, of course.

CR: What is your purpose as a writer in portraying the feminine experience? How does your work serve today's women?

DD: I always wanted to write something to honor the women I grew up around. These women, including my mother, grandmother, and aunts, as well as all of their friends, seemed to me to keep the world running — but not the world of business, politics, entertainment, and science. Ironically, these seemingly very important worlds were not important to me. What was important back then was love, a warm meal, being given a birthday party, having gifts at Christmas, knowing the bills were paid again this month (barely), or being driven to basketball practice. These were the things women did in my world, and I am grateful beyond measure for it. I hope in honoring these women, I am able to honor all women, many of whom really run the world but rarely get the glory.

CR: What inspired you to weave the Native American component into the story? Did you spend much time in New Mexico or with native peoples? How did you develop such familiarity with the Native American language, culture, and rituals?

DD: I graduated from college in Santa Fe and absolutely fell in love with it. I learned a great deal about the Native American culture while I lived there, particularly from a wonderful woman I was very blessed to meet. Her name is Teresa Pijoan. She is a Native American author, a storyteller of her tribe, and a professor of Native American studies. She helped me significantly with the prayers, rituals, and chants in the book and even gained permission from tribal elders for me to use what is included.

CR: Describe how the creative process works for you as a writer. Do you write every day? How long did it take you to write this book? What serves as your muse or greatest source of creative inspiration?

DD: When I am in the middle of a project, I usually write four or five days a week, and I try to complete at least three pages a day. This book took just over a year to finish, plus the time it has taken for editorial work with my editors at Ballantine. My greatest source of inspiration is my love for people and wonderful stories that honor the heroism in us all. Writing is definitely a spiritual experience for me in that I really just try to get out of the way and let something greater than me do the work.

CR: Are you considering writing another story in this series?

DD: Yes, I have already come up with another story I want to tell about these characters. As long as they keep telling me what to write, I'll keep writing.

QUESTIONS AND TOPICS FOR DISCUSSION

1. How are the themes of home and home-coming played out throughout the novel? What does home mean for each character? How do all of the characters finally come home? What does home mean to you?

2. What does the eagle feather symbolize? Why does Aletta feel she can't conduct a legitimate reading after receiving the feather from Julian? How does she reclaim her gift?

3. Aletta Honor is initially an insecure person. How does she release her past pain to discover her identity? Do you know anyone who has had to let go of their past in order to grow?

4. Aletta lacks the confidence to make it on her own without a man. Does she finally liberate herself? Have women's roles signifi-

cantly changed since Aletta's era?

5. Is Aletta a good single mother? Does she do the right thing leaving her kids with Vee while she goes to Santa Fe?

6. How do the strains of peer pressure and parental divorce affect Sissy's behavior? Do you think the mother-daughter relationship in this story is a typical one?

7. Do you think that Okay, Oklahoma, represents a microcosm of everything that's right or wrong in small-town America? Would you want to live there — then or now?

8. Do you think Jimmy will quit drinking for good? Did you like his character more by the end of the book?

9. Aletta dates Eugene immediately after her marriage disintegrates, even though he "fails to challenge her brain or her soul." What do you think is the key to a compatible partnership?

10. What are the differences and similarities among the men in Aletta's life? Do you think she and Jimmy can repair their mar-

riage? Do you think Aletta and Jimmy's relationship is realistic?

11. Do you think Julian is the right man for Aletta?

12. Do you think Vee is a strong or weak character? Does she help or hinder Sissy? How do the Honors transform Vee? Why do you think she went back to Okay, knowing she would eventually get arrested?

13. What role do Aletta's vivid dreams play in enhancing her journey of self-discovery? Do you believe in the importance of dreams? Can you remember a dream that greatly impacted your life?

14. How does Aletta's family genealogy transform her life? How do Native American women such as Adelaide and Senda link Aletta with her strength and identity?

15. What is the symbolism of Aletta's journey into the mountains? How is she changed upon her return? Have you or would you consider a vision quest for yourself?

16. Near the end of the novel, Aletta declares: "I'm the *tcaiyanyi* of Okay." What

does she mean? Why is it significant that she says this?

ABOUT THE AUTHOR

Dayna Dunbar is a native of Oklahoma and currently lives in Sedona, Arizona, where she is also a screenwriter. This is her second novel.

The employees of Thorndike Press hope you
have enjoyed this Large Print book. All
Thorndike and Wheeler Large Print titles are
designed for easy reading, and all our books
are made to last. Other Thorndike Press Large
Print books are available at your library,
through selected bookstores, or directly from
us.

For information about titles, please call:
(800) 223-1244

or visit our Web site at:

www.gale.com/thorndike
www.gale.com/wheeler

To share your comments, please write:

Publisher
Thorndike Press
295 Kennedy Memorial Drive
Waterville, ME 04901